Hot Flashes

Leila Gaskin

Hot Flashes – a Drakkon novel

ISBN: 978-0615871851

0615871852

Cover design by Tatiana Vila

www.viladesign.net

Dedication

Thank you to the Broads. Without your honesty and tough love, I would have nothing to show for my endless hours hunched over my keyboard.

A special thanks to my parents. My lifelong love affair with the written word wouldn't have happened if not for my childhood and our basement full of wonderful books.

Lastly, to my amazing dog Quizz - I miss you.

Acknowledgements

Stories are not told in a vacuum. To say *Hot Flashes* sprung fully formed and perfect from my brain would be selfish and untrue. I need to thank James River Writers for having an amazing organization that put me in contact with other talented authors. To Kristy, Kristi, Diane, Beth, and Shawna, thank you for the grammar mallet of love. To Kris, the giver of tough love – I promise to find other ways to smile, look, and gesture. To my friends in the blogosphere and outside, you are all amazing. I wouldn't have reached this point without your support. I'm sure I've missed someone, so consider yourselves thanked and loved.

ONE

A stream of fire erupted from the rainy sky, blistering the paint job on Ella Hixson's sedan. The air around her turned red and then transitioned to a scorching orange until combusting into a glaring white. The delicate tissues of her lungs burned. An unvoiced scream remained trapped deep in the remains. Ella cranked the wheel over and over in desperate attempt to avoid the flames. The wheels lost their precarious grip on the damp pavement, causing the car to hydroplane into on-coming traffic. Horns blared and lights flashed as she frantically tried to control the car. Bursts of brilliant colors shot through the sky. The assault stopped abruptly as gravel flew from under the tires. The car shuddered to a stop on the shoulder of the road. Ella gasped for air. She swiped at the clouded windshield with a wad of greasy fast food napkins. When the glass cleared, Ella screamed. Claws, the size of small swords, and iridescent gold wings, the width of a jet plane, dived toward her.

"Oh my God!" She ducked down in her seat and threw her hands over her head. The talons left furrows in the glass and scraped across the roof of her car. Before she could blink again, the air was set aflame. A second blast of fire made the skin on her face and hands crackle.

Air, she needed air. Feeling for the door handle, she yanked on the latch and let her weight push the door wide as she fell onto the wet gravel. Ella let the nominal shelter of the door protect her as she peered up at the stormy sky.

It was empty.

With great care, she pushed herself to her feet. The rain pounded down on her head, flattening her hair and ruining her interview suit. Water poured down her face as she stared upward. As an afterthought, she held her hands out in front of her, not a burn to be seen. She gently patted her face. Her skin was unmarred.

The oncoming traffic buffeted her car with wind. Taking a step back from the door, she started to slide down the sides of the grassy ditch. Her dress shoes had no traction. Grabbing the window frame to steady herself, she looked at the unblemished vehicle. No blistered paint or scratched glass.

It had to be a dragon, didn't it? Ella was unaware of anything that flew the skies that had golden scales, wings, and talons that could eviscerate its prey with a simple swoop from the sky.

Rivulets of moisture slid down her back causing Ella to shiver in the late afternoon rain. She climbed back into the car, her clothing soaking the upholstery, and wondered what had happened. Along the floorboards, she found the wad of napkins she'd used earlier to wipe at the condensation that blocked her view.

Dragons in the sky was a common dream theme for Ella, though she had never hallucinated them while awake, much less been attacked. Her heartbeat started to regain a normal rhythm, allowing her to breathe. She could still feel the searing of her lung. The cool air was a relief. She rested her forehead on the steering wheel as she tried to gather herself, but her eyes welled up with frustrated tears. This was the cherry topping one of the crappiest days of her life. The venomous words her elderly mother had spewed that morning still rang clearly in her mind. And she'd been replaced at her job by the bodaciously bosomed, bottled blond screwing the new owner.

The universe seemed to cut her a break when she scored the interview for the manager position at House Books in the same afternoon she spotted the position. Now she sat, her clothes and shoes a ruined wrinkled mess, shivering.

"You're a screw up like your father." The statement rattled around Ella's brain. Her mother had hurled the words at her like an athlete throwing javelins with unparalleled accuracy. Ella wasn't going to go home without a job. Sending a prayer up to the universe, she turned the key in the ignition. The engine started, heat pouring out of the vents. She had nothing more to lose. She was going to the interview.

Her headlights illuminated the cheery sign welcoming her to Aerie Heights, Maryland, population 7, 624. She lived within the town's boundaries but hadn't done much more there than grocery shopping in years. Working in the suburbs of Washington D.C., she did most of her socializing away from home. Now she seemed to be coming full circle. House Books had been the center of her childhood existence, a place of refuge from her cold and difficult relationship with her mother.

Built in the Gilded Age, House Books was located on the retro-fitted first floor of the mansion built by the affluent Mullins family. Books lined the shelves of the unique floor space, leaving the corners furnished with seating in out of the way nooks to lose oneself comfortably in a story. With stately cornices and imposing columns, the building was rife with rumors of hauntings and magical happenings. The functional and non-functional windows that covered the building had always fascinated Ella. In those simple geometric shapes, she saw worlds without number.

Ella pulled into the large lot, thanking the parking gods when she spotted a space near the large welcoming entrance that had once serviced stately carriages. Clear blue pierced through the moisture-laden storm clouds. Ella hoped it was a herald of good things to come. A horn bleated as she zipped the car into the vacated spot. In the rearview mirror, she saw the losing driver pass by with their hand extended in the universal salute. She ran her hands through her rain-flattened hair in a hopeless effort to bring some semblance of order. Pushing open the door, she slid out of the car, stood, and swiped at the wrinkles in her suit. Their iron grip on the material held strong. After pulling her portfolio and purse from the car, she stepped forward only to stumble over the curb, sending her belongings flying as she tried to break her falls. If 'klutz' were an Olympic event, her landing would have scored a perfect '10'. Blowing on her scraped palms to ease the sting, Ella sat back and surveyed the scattered papers in front of her. The miniscule strip of grass between the curb and the sidewalk saved her knees from obvious injury, but there would be bruises in the morning. Ella suppressed a groan as she regained her feet. Once standing, her hand flew to her neckline to stroke the textured surface of her dragon pendant. She'd never understood why the piece of gold comforted her, but it did. Her best friend had often joked if Ella had been a dragon she'd have a hoard of gold, jewels, and other trinkets just to sit and play with. Ella limped to the bookstore with her shredded dignity gathered tightly around her.

In the middle of the small bookstore foyer, she stopped, dazzled, as a crystalline light enveloped her. Overwhelming joy and acceptance coiled around her heart. The store was her childhood haven filled with wild adventures of the imagination, but brilliant light shows hadn't been a part of that experience. A flicker of movement over the door caught Ella's attention. A tassel, attached to the pommel of a tarnished cavalry sword, swayed gently over the door. Ella closed her eyes, and when she reopened them, the sword had disappeared. Somewhere between the parking lot and the foyer, her sanity had gone on another walkabout. With a quick shake of her head, Ella strode forward over the main threshold of the store. Her eyes squinted reflexively as the glare of fluorescent lights assaulted her. Glancing over her shoulder, the space she'd just walk out of seemed so ordinary with only the evening sun and overhead halogen lights illuminating the sale items and tchotchkes lining the walls.

"Welcome to House Books!" chirped the young woman at the counter. The nametag on her maroon apron said 'Sindie.' "How may I help you?"

She couldn't help it. A smile was an automatic response to the woman's cheerful demeanor. Ella refrained from trying to straighten out the wrinkled suit jacket as she introduced herself, "I'm here to see Ms. …" her mind blanked. Embarrassed by the lapse, she shuffled through her disorganized papers. "I'm here to see Ms. Oakton."

"You're here for the interview?" Sindie grinned and Ella's nervousness.

"Relax, you'll do fine." Sindie pressed a series of buttons on the telephone; after a brief conversation, the friendly woman escorted her through the labyrinth of shelves to a small hallway.

Inside Ella's stomach, a rampaging mob of squirrels was wreaking havoc. Ella concentrated on her breathing to calm herself. The squirrels continued their rioting. Ella and Sindie arrived at an office door. The textured glass window had 'Manager' painted in gilt letters, lending a noir feel to the area.

"Have a seat." Sindie gestured to the ladder back wooden chair sitting to the side of the door and gave the door a brisk rap. "Ms. Oakton will be with you in a minute." She winked as she turned to leave. "Seriously, relax! Ms. Oakton gave up cannibalism a couple of centuries ago."

Eyes wide, Ella stared after the strange woman. A fluttering movement caught her eye. Something long and skinny with a tuft peeked out from under the long tunic, tangling with the apron strings. Ella knew people didn't have tails. After a second look, all she saw was free swinging strings. She stuffed the experience into the 'weird things' box in the back of her brain and firmly shut the lid.

The door opened to reveal a small woman with a tightly wound bun of steel-grey hair adorning top of her head. "Ms. Hixson?"

Despite Ms. Oakton's petite figure, she exuded an aura that demanded respect. At only five foot four inches herself, Ella had to squelch the urge to apologize for her height. "Ms. Oakton, it's a pleasure to meet you."

"We'll see." Ms. Oakton stepped back, signaling for Ella to follow. Ella resisted the urge to fidget as sharp brown eyes took in every element of her less than perfect appearance. Handing her resume to the woman, she waited for the interview to begin. Silence stretched out between them.

Then, an intrusive force filled Ella's mind, picking apart her memories, weighing each moment for its worth. Unable to move, she sat helpless. An indistinct murmuring narrated the entire event. Nothing should have been shuffling, muttering, or moving around in the chaos of her mind. As abruptly the incursion began, it stopped, leaving Ella dazed.

The woman's gaze never left Ella's as the wall clock resolutely ticked each second. Finally, Ms. Oakton glanced at the resume and started the interview. The familiar give and take lacked energy, leaving Ella feeling the distinct bite of failure.

"What would you do if you found a fairy ring?"

Ella blinked. "Excuse me?"

"You heard me," Ms. Oakton snapped.

"A fairy ring. Really?" Ella's shuffled-through mind snapped back into its chaotic glory, and it was un-amused. "I'd avoid it."

“Why?”

“I have too many responsibilities in the here and now to be trapped for any amount of time in the Underhill.” Ella snorted. “Who knows when I’d get back? Time flows differently there. I’d have to be enticed or trapped by a member of the Fae. Seeing as I don’t believe they exist, I don’t think a trip to the Underhill will be an issue.”

The diminutive woman got up from her desk and flung open the office door. “The interview is over. You may leave.”

Ella’s nostrils flared as indignation sparked the tinder of her carefully banked temper. No matter how the universe was spitting on her, she didn’t deserve to be dismissed. She gave the woman a respectful nod of the head. She reigned in her disappointment and anger at the dismissal. Behind her careful façade of calm, she visualized a dragon rending Ms. Oakton limb from limb then flambéing her. Ella stopped at the door to extend her hand. The woman turned her head, staring pointedly at the door.

“It was a pleasure to meet you. I hope we will work together in the future.” With Ella’s pride in tatters, she left the office and flinched as the door slammed behind her. She blinked back tears. She prayed she could make it through the store without meeting the chirpy employee. The universe snickered as she all but mowed Sindie down making her escape.

“Oh!” Dancing an awkward jig, each woman struggled to stay right side up. Ella gasped, “I’m so sorry!”

Sindie steadied them both. “No problem, you didn’t see me.” Her grasp became a reassuring pat. “How did the interview go?”

Ella hated to fail at anything, yet she seemed to have perfected the ability. “I’ll always be a good customer, but I don’t think I’ll be working here any time soon.”

Sindie gave a sympathetic hum. "If it makes you feel any better, you lasted longer than any other candidate we've had."

"Actually, that does." Unable to stop herself, Ella asked. "You wouldn't know why Ms. Oakton would ask me about fairy rings?"

Intrigue flashed across the woman's delicate features. "She asked you about fairy rings?" She glanced over her shoulder toward the manager's office, as she guided Ella toward the front of the bookstore. "I haven't the faintest idea. But out of curiosity, what did you say?"

Ella glanced up at the ceiling as she listened to Sindie's question. The fearsome face of a Celtic inspired dragon caught her attention. She responded, "I told her that I didn't have time to visit the Underhill. I have too many responsibilities to see to."

Sindie stopped them in the middle of an aisle and covered her mouth with both hands. Stifled giggles still escaped. "You didn't!"

"Was that wrong?"

"No, I think you just surprised her. She has some things to think about." Sindie patted her back.

Ella thanked the cheerful woman for her time and kind words. She continued toward the foyer, as she looked around the floor and ceiling for more architectural quirks. The molding pattern drew her attention with the dragon motif. Another dragon peered down from a corbel. Fantastical lights, questions about fairy rings and, now, dragons, the day just kept getting better. As she entered the foyer, the embrace of the light took her breath away with its impact. She stopped in the center of the space as foot traffic flowed around her. Peace, acceptance, and wonder soothed the hurt and anger of the interview experience. Cocooned by light, Ella was unaware of anything but the energy. Dancing arcs of lightning created an otherworldly glow.

With a soft hiss, a hidden wall panel slid open. Silver eyes gleamed in the shadows as a tall, dark man stepped out with a large seal-point Siamese cat in his arms. "You were more than a little intrusive with the candidate." Nathan Mullins stroked the cat between its ears. "She felt you poking around."

"I don't see how she could feel anything in that chaotic mess of a mind." The fountain pen rattled as Ms. Oakton rolled it back and forth on the desk. "Ms. Hixson is too much of an emotional mess to be an asset to the House. If she's not willing to visit the Underhill, then she'll be a poor guardian for the node." The woman's restless fingers stopped moving as she glared at the man before her. "There's something blocked in her mind, a memory or an experience. It felt Drakkon."

"If she were Drakkon, I'd know." Papers scattered as the cat jumped out of his arms onto the desk. "The House has accepted her. We'll unravel the mystery of our Ms. Hixson soon enough."

"This won't end well." Annisa Oakton refused to meet Nathan's silver gaze.

Nathan carefully enunciated his every word. "Whatever is bothering you is acceptable to the House." In a softer chiding tone, he continued. "Annisa, remember how uncertain your predecessor was about a particular Brownie managing the affairs of the House all those years ago?"

"She said she would never go to the Underhill."

"You risked much with the question about fairy rings." Silver eyes narrowed. "We never ask that question until we know the person is ready to learn about the Otherverse."

"I felt it was the right question to ask at the time."

"Be that as it may, she gave the best answer she could for what she knew. 'Who knows when I'd get back?'" Nathan chuckled at Ella's answer. "It showed she has a basic understanding of the tales."

"It won't be enough for what's to come."

"She'll adapt and learn. Her perspective will be different. We need that." Nathan snapped his fingers softly at the cat. "Come, Kaie. Let's go meet our newest comrade in arms."

The Brownie fumed at her desk as the man and cat left the office.

They caught up with their quarry in the foyer. The customer traffic flowed around the woman unaware of the light show. The cat bumped impatiently against Nathan's leg, meowing imperiously.

"Shh!" He hissed at the cat.

A gaggle of teenage girls chattering amongst themselves barreled through the foyer, hands full of bags emblazoned with the House logo, oblivious to the light show. Each one of them seemed to be talking to each other and texting at the same time as only teenagers could do. "OMG!" Bags and bodies tumbled into a messy pile with Ella on the bottom.

"Could you be more in the way?" one of the few who had not landed on the pile said in a voice dripping with contempt.

"OMG! Could you look where you're going?" Ella fired back. Nathan grinned. He watched the woman shove herself clear of the pile.

Like a pack of hyenas scenting blood, the girls closed ranks.

"The proper response is 'Excuse me, are you alright?'" She met the gaze of each girl. "If you can't be polite like I'm sure your mamas taught you, you shouldn't be out in public."

Ella started as a male voice said, "I could charge you rent for loitering in my foyer."

Captivated by molten silver eyes, Ella faced the man who owned the voice. "Wow, are your eyes really that color?" She covered her mouth in horror after the words flew out. The man was the embodiment of tall, dark, and handsome. Gunmetal-gray streaked the hair at his temples, enough to add dignity but not age. The austere black clothing lent an air of mystery to the man. "You have a very nice foyer."

The deep laugh rolled through the lobby. "I'm sure it felt spacious when you were at the bottom of the pile of teenage girls."

Humiliation complete, Ella wished for the earth to open up under her feet and swallow her whole. "You saw that? Great."

"Don't worry. They love to come in as a pack and ask me for books on spell craft." A roguish grin played across his face.

Ella had no response. The bright aura surrounding the man left her squinting. "I'm Nathan Mullins. Welcome to my store."

Ella started as a pulse of electricity passed from Nathan's grip to hers. She watched him closely, but he didn't seem to notice anything.

Fur slid along the back of her calf accompanied by the slide of a damp nose. Startled, she glanced down into the sapphire eyes of a gorgeous Siamese cat. A head butt accompanied by an imperious meow told Ella that she was to pay attention. Ella bent down to stroke the soft head. The cat reared on its hind legs and wrapped its front legs around her arm. In short order, she found herself seated on the floor with her arms full of purring cat.

With a bemused look, Nathan watched the pair become acquainted. "You've made a conquest. Kaie allows very few people to pet her."

Ella worked to extricate herself from the cat. Happy in her current position, Kaie hooked her claws into the material of Ella's suit jacket. Ella rose to her feet with her arms full of purring feline. "It's a pleasure to meet you and your cat. Kaie is an unusual name." Words spilled from her mouth. "It's the Celtic name for combat, isn't it?"

His elegant brow lifted in acknowledgement. "In a pinch, Miss Kaie lives up to her name and more."

Ella couldn't see a way to turn the miserable interview around without the appearance of begging. "I had the pleasure of meeting your store manager, Ms. Oakton. Lovely lady."

With a faint grin, Nathan continued to watch Ella.

Hesitant to tempt the Fates, she put the cat on the floor. "It was a pleasure to meet you and Kaie." The sway of the pommel tassel caught Ella's attention.

"See anything interesting?"

Ella's gaze snapped back to the man. Asking 'Did you know that you have an old cavalry saber hanging over your door that doesn't seem to really exist?' seemed to be inappropriate. "Umm, nothing in particular, the architecture is amazing."

"While you're here, let me give you a tour. There are some interesting structural features I think might intrigue you."

For years, top magazines and newspapers had begged invitations to tour the landmark. Each instance was denied. The more foolhardy, who attempted to sneak past the public spaces, told bizarre tales of never-ending corridors and voices. Ella wasn't one to turn down an opportunity. Touring the facility with Nathan Mullins – priceless. "I'd love to."

As they retraced Ella's steps, the selling floor seemed brighter. Sindie gave a cheery wave and wink as she helped a young mother with two rambunctious toddlers. Kaie brought up the rear of their little procession, adding a cat comment here and there.

Ella felt a sense of déjà vu as they moved through the shelves of books. Passing the office door, her stomach roiled with anxiety. She had no desire to encounter the taciturn manager ever again. A paneled wall seemed to be their destination. Nathan pressed his palm on a spot above Ella's head. A door opened, revealing a set of stairs that lead up into the recesses of the house.

"Ms. Hixson, after you." The cat gave a chuff. "You too, Kaie."

Unease trickled down Ella's spine; the act of walking through the door seemed portentous. Kaie butted her head against her leg, the cat equivalent of 'get moving, I have places to go, silly human!'

"Second star to the left and straight on 'til morning," Ella whispered.

Nathan glanced at Ella. "What was that?"

"Nothing." The moment Ella crossed the threshold, felt a surge of energy pulse through her body. Destiny had clearly crossed her path. Her shoulders squared, she took the directions from the cat and moved forward.

The tip of Kaie's tail swayed in a hypnotic rhythm as they climbed. By her calculations, they should have been well past the roof by now. She tried not to puff. "How many stairs are there?"

"My grandmother had affection for stairs. I'm sure you've heard the odd stories about the house architecture." Nathan gave a little laugh that reminded Ella of an inside joke, the kind she was never a part of. “Most of the stories are true.”

“The gypsy curse?”

“No gypsies, but Grandmother was a superstitious lady who felt the need to confuse and confound the unfriendly, mysterious beings of the universe that might mean to harm her.”

“Mysterious beings?” Ella forgot all about her burning thighs and short breath. “Paranoid much?” Ella realized that her inner censor had slipped up again. “I’m sorry. I’m sure she was a very creative lady,” she added.

The last flight of stairs led straight up to the ceiling and a glistening red door that lay level with the ceiling, at its center a bright brass knob. Ella’s expectations of the bizarre were not disappointed. Nathan pulled out a long gold chain from under his shirt. Upon it was a skeleton key. An intricate Celtic design decorated its bow. Nathan unlocked the door and gave a firm thrust up, allowing Ella and Kaie to precede him into the chamber.

Jewel tones gleamed from the walls, carpet, and furniture. Gold glinted from the shelves that housed books and precious objects that seemed to span millennia. Sinking into the carpet, she resisted the urge to kick off her shoes just to wiggle her toes in the tactile opulence. She knew toe wiggling was not the way to make a good impression. A blissful sigh escaped Ella’s lips at the sumptuous space. Unfaceted rubies, emeralds, and sapphires, from the Indian sub-continent, littered the shelves alongside doubloons. Golden statues from South American sat amongst the clutter. All the glittering objects, scattered throughout the space, splintered her concentration.

“Have a seat.” Nathan gestured to a well-padded chair upholstered in glittering brocade. “Can I get you anything to drink?”

His invitation took a minute to register as it broke through Ella's sensory fugue. As she tried to formulate a coherent response, she obediently sat. "Water would be lovely. Thank you." Her body felt boneless. "This is an amazing room. It's what I would imagine a sophisticated dragon's lair would look like."

Once more, the five-second delay between her brain and mouth had short-circuited.

Nathan turned from the cleverly hidden mini-fridge in the bookshelf, water bottles in his hands, a mysterious expression gracing his face. He placed the bottles on the table between the chairs and sat. Kaie jumped up and settled onto Nathan's lap, arching into his hand as he scratched behind her ears. "What do you know of dragons and their kin?"

Her body tensed as apprehension filled her. The last mythical question had ended her interview. "Do you mean dragon lore from the middle ages or actual existence?"

"Anything you might know."

"Well, I grew up reading Anne McCaffrey's PERN series and had a serious crush on the dragon riders." Ella paused to gather her thoughts before she went on. "When I was a kid, I played a little Dungeons & Dragons but got bored with the entire scoring system. I'd rather create my own stories and worlds, you know?"

Ella felt her muscles tighten and, with the tension, the beginnings of a stress headache. If Nathan wanted her opinion on dragons, she'd give it to him with both barrels.

"I've read the legends of Saint George," she continued. "I always thought that the dragon got a bad rap. Personally, I've always thought Saint George and the Dragon was an allegory about coping with diversity." She focused her gaze directly on Nathan. "Have I seen a dragon? No. Do I think they exist? I have absolutely no idea, but the Universe is a huge place."

Condensation dripped from the forgotten water bottles sitting on the delicate Victorian table between them as Nathan continued to stare at Ella. Her mind counted the seconds, each moment stretching longer than the last.

"That was a lot to say in one breath." He settled back in his chair, reminding Ella of a cat pondering a choice of toys, or a dragon choosing a trinket from its hoard. "So, no personal experience?"

"I didn't know it was a pre-requisite for the tour or the job."

"It's not." Nathan stroked Kaie. "I was just inquiring."

Her façade of calm crumbled. "Look, I came here for a job interview." Ella fought the comfortable grasp of the chair, pushing herself free to perch on the edge. "A normal interview, where the interviewer asks about job experience, goals, and decision making processes." Aggravated, she stood and started to pace. "Instead, Ms. Oakton asks me about fairy rings. Then she gets angry with me because I tell her I wouldn't have time to visit the Underhill." She abruptly stopped in front of Nathan. "And you ask me what do I know about dragons?" The meeting blown, Ella collected her belongings. She knew she'd screwed up royally. "Look, I was hoping that this would be the job for me…"

"You have the job," Nathan interrupted.

"I'm going to have …" The words registered and Ella stopped in the middle of her diatribe. "What?"

"The job is yours. See you tomorrow morning at 10 a.m."

TWO

Conversations ebbed and flowed around Talek Jespreyck as he stared at his lager. A low-beamed ceiling gave the Wyvern an intimate feel; pipe and cigar smoke colored the ceiling. The uncomplicated ambience of the working-class establishment was free of obvious technologies making it easy for the patrons in uniform, civilian waistcoats, and rough jackets to mix together in the common goal of seeking escape from their everyday lives. Rhythmic whooshing of the auto-carriages outside added to the noise level. As people entered and exited the tavern, stray gusts of air ruffled the clothing of those near the door.

A smile flitted across Talek's face as he watched dragons swoop and swirl through the room through the alcohol softened the edges of his awareness. But the smile devolved into a sneer. These people couldn't see what was hidden in plain sight. Drakkon walked among them. Customers yelped as they batted at the air and covered their heads. Drakkon hadn't cavorted in the skies for centuries. Now considered criminals, they teetered on the brink of extinction.

The barkeep slung the damp towel over his shoulder and moved toward Talek. The customer at the end of the bar banged his mug against the wood, diverting the barkeep. With a slight shake of his head, the man pushed a pile of octagonal coins to the barkeep. The coins clanked softly as they slid into the apron pocket.

“What, in the many hells of the Otherverse, do you think you’re doing?” Callem Jespreyck yanked a chair from the neighboring table and sat across from his inebriated brother. Where Talek was lean, Callem’s muscular frame spoke of his years in agriculture.

“Leave me alone.”

“Not going to happen, brother.” Lager sloshed as Callem’s gloved hand moved the tankard away from his brother. He wore gloves to hide his mating mark, a band of gilded flesh woven with copper. The mark started above the knuckle of the middle finger of his left and wove itself into an intricate patter that encircled his wrist in a thick band. His wife, Ane, wore an identical Drakkon mark.

“If you know what’s good for you, you’ll give that back.”

The lager splattered as Callem dumped it on the floor. The barmaid walked toward them. Callem waved her off as he hissed, “You are unshielded, brother.”

Drops of alcohol flew as Talek threw an empty vessel at Callem. “I don’t care!” Talek spat and gestured around the room. “They don’t know what’s happening.”

“No, but you do.” Callem leaned forward. “I don’t know why you’ve turned into a …”

“I’m chasing ghosts. Myths!” Spittle flew out of Talek’s mouth. “I can open the damn portal, but who knows if I can survive the journey.”

Callem glanced surreptitiously around the room while using a napkin to wipe his face. The conversation alone, if heard by the wrong parties, could set the hunters after them.

“Keep your voice down!” Callem hissed.

“I don’t care who’s listening!” He flung himself back against the chair. Its wooden back clattered against the wall.

With a listing occupant, the chair tilted to one side. The world spun as Talek cursed as he slid to the sticky floor.

"That's it. Up you go!" Callem stood up, grabbed his brother by the collar, and grunted as he hauled him to his feet. "Out of all of us, you are the only one who can open the portal and find Mellanei," he whispered. He threw down money on the table then guided his wobbling charge towards the door. No one seemed to be paying attention to the brothers. Their exchange blended in with the dulled roar of the other conversations. Callem staggered under the ever-increasing weight of Talek's body as they left the bar.

Pools of light from the gas street lamps created the illusion of sanctuary against the encroaching night. An auto-carriage with government markings idled at the curb waiting for Callem and Talek. At their approach, the door slid open. Talek landed in a lump on the far side of the compartment. Door secured, Callem tapped on the glass partition.

"Did you have any problems?"

"Finding him wasn't the problem," Callem assured his wife as Talek sang a tuneless song. "He's angry and drunk."

Ane Jespreyck's worried gaze met her husband's eyes in the rearview mirror.

"He'll be fine. Let's get him to the farm." The aggravation in Callem's tone was evident. The auto-carriage pulled smoothly away from the curb, gaining speed as they moved through the streets. Ane flipped a switch on the dashboard and the door locks engaged. The Anakarei constabulary wasn't above appropriating vehicles for their own personal use, locking the doors just made it difficult. As uniformed thugs, the constables never liked to exert themselves. No one was safe after curfew.

With the brothers gone, the taproom settled into its end of night routine. The man from the end of the bar slid off his stool, stretching to work out the kinks in his back. He strode out into the night with a wave to the barkeep.

The circle of light cast by the streetlamp was weak. He leaned against the brick and mortar next to the entrance of a dark alley – waiting. Auto-carriages sped back and forth to make curfew. Taxis slowed at each pass looking for potential customers. The rushing air caused his coat to flap against his legs.

Silent as a ghost, a shadow slid out of the alleyway. The blade laid across the man's throat glinted in the weak light. "Jaczon, you should have more care." The knife pressed deeper, not quite breaking skin.

"Put the knife away," Jaczon Carbehk growled as the blade withdrew. "Now is not the time for games."

"My games have saved your sorry ass."

"Be that as it may, Tmavě Jeden tonight is not the time. It begins." Jaczon stepped to the curb, his shadow following. "Follow them. I want to know they get out of the city without issue or record." Jaczon raised his hand to signal the waiting vehicle. He didn't look back as they merged into the late evening traffic.

The Tmavě Jeden gave a sharp nod and stepped back into the darkness. His chest expanded as he took a deep breath. Industrial fumes and moisture perfumed the air. The bowels of the city were his playground. He stood at the edge of a pool of light with no signs of fear. A group of miscreants stepped to the opposite side of the light, looking for an easy mark. They scattered when they realized who they were targeting. With a barely contained feral snarl, he turned, walking into the dark. He had no time to play.

The Tmavě Jeden did not fear the dark. The dark feared him.

Talek's incessant humming grated on the frayed nerves of the vehicle's occupants. Tensions rose as they approached the western gate. Callem jerked Talek into a sitting position and slapped his brother. The inane tune continued.

"For the sake of the gods," Callem hissed. "Talek, guards ahead."

Getting through the checkpoint was imperative. Callem pinched his brother's arm with a vicious twist. Talek's hiss of pain gave him a small spark of satisfaction. The humming stopped. Momentary focus came back into his gaze as they approached the checkpoint.

Boredom hung from the guard's single word. "Papers."

"Yes, sir." Ane complied.

The rubber of the stamp hit each form precisely. The sentry looked hard at Ane as he handed back the stamped copy.

"You're about to break curfew."

Callem could feel the vibration of Ane's nervous foot tap as she replied, "Yes, sir, we know."

Callem opened the window to his compartment as he assumed his cover as Chief Engineer in Charge of the West District. "The damned pumps went down in the West District again." He rolled his eyes. "If we'd had our way, we'd be safe in our lodgings, not headed for the benighted hinterland. Give me civilization any day."

"No, sir. We can't have the pumps down. The Chancellor wouldn't like that one bit."

The sentry stepped back from the auto-carriage. He snapped them a salute and waved them on. "Good luck."

As the auto-carriage pulled away from the city gate, Talek toppled over. His head landed on Callem's shoulder, and he resumed his humming.

Ane gunned the accelerator, leaving the city behind.

The sentry returned to his office to post record of the passage. The Anakarei believed that good record keeping kept the realm ordered. All transactions were stored in the central archives. The last duty of his shift was to bring his log into Record Central.

The Tmavě Jeden stepped out of the shadows as he watched the sentry finish processing the paperwork. He was mildly irritated at the man's efficiency. Stepping up behind the guard, he gave a soft chuff.

The sentry jumped.

"Who are you?"

"The Chancellor sent me to look at your gate records." The Tmavě Jeden lifted the jacket lapel and revealed his rank insignia.

"Sir!" The sentry snapped a salute. Papers fell off the desk as the sentry turned to grab his gate log. The Tmavě Jeden pulled a finely honed knife from his boot. One slice across the hapless sentry's throat proved its efficacy. He wouldn't be missed until the shift change in the morning. The Tmavě Jeden tucked the sheaf of records in his uniform jacket as he stepped back into the night.

Cold water ripped Talek into consciousness; he glared at the woman holding the empty pitcher. One could not call the Socra old or infirmed. The energy she exuded gave the casual observer the impression she was a woman a third of her years. Her fit figure in farm trousers and a chambray shirt defied the normal feminine convention and her office as Socra. She only wore what she called 'city garb' on her rare trips off the farm.

She led the Drakkon in their fight against the Anakarei and could remember when the Drakkon flew free in the skies. Should someone choose to trifle with her, they did so at their own risk. To him she was simply his Nonne.

"Get up!" She waved the pitcher above his head before slamming it on the nightstand. "Public intoxication, what were you thinking?"

Not giving Talek a chance to respond, the Socra reached over the bed and flung open the curtains. With little regard for his modesty, she took hold of the bed covers and tore them from his prone form. Fortunately, his brother hadn't stripped him bare before he had dumped him onto his childhood bed. Shards of pain ricocheted around his head as the light blinded him and left him whimpering. He knew he had been stupid. Without Callem and Ane, he would have never gotten out of the city.

He risked another censorious volley, "Nonne…"

The Socra ignored him as she marched to the door. With her hand on the door latch, she faced him again. "I said get up! No excuses."

The firm snap of the closing door caused another small explosion in Talek's besieged head. When the lights stopped flashing against his eyelids, he cautiously levered himself up. Caution offered no comfort. He sat in the middle of his childhood bed, with his head cradled like the most delicate piece of porcelain in his hands.

He squinted as he gazed around the room. A series of carvings were etched on the wood casing reminded him of the moments he'd stolen from his studies and chores in order to carve the pinnacle events of Drakkon lore. Talek was surprised the wood hadn't been sanded down. The Anakarei had a no tolerance policy on all things Drakkon.

Talek waited for the world to settle into the correct place before he gained his feet. Too bad, he had only gotten the fat head and not the escape he had been seeking. He carefully dressed and prepared himself for the day. When he finally entered the kitchen, Talek caught the biscuit his brother flung at his head.

"I don't remember you being such a terrible singer," Callem laughed.

Talek fired the biscuit back at his brother before he turned to face the women in the room. "Bright skies to you."

Ane faced her brother-in-law as she swallowed a chuckle. "Talek, you…" She cleared her throat. "You've looked better."

"I've felt better." The Socra's stiff shoulders told him forgiveness would take work. He stood behind the Socra as he waited for her to acknowledge him. She banged the spoon against the pots without restraint. Each concussive beat made Talek to flinch. The aromas wafting from the stove caused his stomach to rebel.

When the Socra turned to face him, she laid a gentle hand against his cheek.

"Are you feeling better?"

He leaned into the tender gesture.

"Yes, ma'am."

The tender hand turned into a sharp slap.

"You risked us all with your foolishness! You let your fear overcome you." She gestured to the kitchen. "Sit. Eat!"

Chastened, Talek sat across from his brother.

Talek took in a deep breath to imprint the aromas of the savory spices, flour, and smoked cooking grease, all the scents that defined home. As the meal ended, Talek and Callem fell into the chores of their youth.

The Socra had Talek stop. "Not today, you have more pressing matters to tend too."

With a brotherly slap on the back, Callem left the kitchen to take care of the barn chores. "Bright skies and kind winds, brother." Ane accompanied Callem out.

Dishes clattered in the background as Talek watched his brother cross the yard. They'd spent their youth working and playing in the yard and the fields beyond. Callem left without letting Talek say goodbye.

The Socra understood the boy she had raised. "Are you ready?"

"Honestly? No." Talek didn't look at the woman who'd raised him. "But no one else can open the portal." He leaned down and kissed the Socra's cheek. "I need to do one more thing."

The Socra stood in the kitchen doorway as he walked away. She watched him cross the yard into the fields beyond. Only then did she let her worry cloud her face. With her left hand pressed to her heart, the Socra whispered. "My fine lad, may the spirits be kind to you."

The sun felt good against Talek's skin. Echoes of childish laughter rose from the mists of memories. The tall grasses tickled his hands as they had his chest during his first transformation and flight. He could still remember the feel of the wind against his Drakkon-self. His body itched with the need to transform, it was imperative he stay human. Eyes were everywhere, waiting to betray. There could be no indulgence.

The sun reached its zenith. Temperatures were well beyond comfortable as he arrived on the lip of the deep crater. At its center, a large obelisk pointed towards the sky. Glyphs gleamed from the distance, enticing Talek to come closer. Radiating from the center of the crater was a series of thirteen concentric circles made of smaller hewn stones, each engraved with the name of those lost in the battle against the Anakarei. A coarse graveled path formed a labyrinth leading to the center.

Talek bowed his head in supplication before he traveled the path before him. The muggy air added weight to the sorrow that permeated the site. Each memorial marker flared as he passed. Seven times Talek circled. The burden on his heart became overwhelming as he approached the middle of the eighth pass and stopped. He sank to his knees between to markers and placed his hands on each. The small monuments incandesced, leaving the world in negative space.

Tears fell as memories of his parents flooded through him. Tender moments, moments of childish pique, lost moments to say 'I love you.' The onslaught of emotions left him sprawled on the ground.

The sweet memories gave way to the final memories, filtered through the eyes of a young boy. He remembered his father's firm grip as they were dragged to safety. Talek glimpsed his mother transforming into her Drakkon-self, fighting the soldiers.

While the battle in the front room raged, his father forced them into a secret hiding place in the back of closet. 'Shh! Not a sound!' A loving brush of his father's hand over their heads, accompanied his last words. Just before the door shut, Talek saw a dark man slip into the room behind his father. The door slammed shut. Terrible sounds filtered through the walls, Talek and Callem clung to each other for solace.

Hours later, the door to the secret room scraped open and someone pulled Talek and Callem out of their exhausted stupor. Light haloed around the figure in the doorway. When Talek's eyes adjusted, he saw a woman who appeared ancient to his young eyes. Talek and Callem stood in the middle of the destroyed space, unaware of the tears trickling down their cheeks, their innocence gone forever.

She straightened their clothes and blotted the tears.

"We have a long way to go tonight." She made a final swipe at rumples on each boy. "You may call me Nonne." She ignored the chaos as she shepherded the two exhausted and frightened boys out the rear entrance of the only home they'd known. Talek's last memory was seeing the front door swaying on a broken hinge.

A soft ephemeral brush of loving hands along his cheek helped ease him back to the present. He treasured the gesture. Rising to his feet, he brushed off his trousers and continued his journey. The ghosts of generations trailed him to the center of the memorial.

Talek circled the center monolith. "Never Forget" was etched deeply in the buff colored granite. His fingers trailed over this stone as he circled, the comforting presence of the Ancestral spirits surrounding him. Grateful for the momentary respite, he rested. He soaked in the peace and strength of his Ancestors, praying it would be enough for the journey to come.

Talek paused at the kitchen door and watched the Socra sipping a cup of tea at the table. He joined her.

The Socra placed the cup in its saucer with great deliberation. She met Talek's gaze.

"Did you find what you were looking for?"

Talek clasped her age worn hand in his own. "Complete answers? No." Meeting her gaze steadfastly, the fear and confusion of the previous night was now tempered with resolve. "I felt them."

"Felt who?"

“My parents.”

The Socra patted his hands with her free hand.

“My dear boy, your parents have been with you all along.” She said to the man she had raised. “You just had to be open to their presence.”

”The Ancestors confuse me.”

“Have I taught you nothing?” The Socra rose, taking her cup and saucer to the sink. “The physical world is just one dimension. You know better.”

The scientific part of his mind warred with the intuitive. He had always straddled worlds, the empirical and the metaphysical. “I felt… loved.”

She came around the table. The Socra laid her hand along his jaw. “So you should. They loved you very much.” Tenderly she brushed her hands down his shoulders. “You have a long journey in front of you today.”

The Socra fussed over Talek, brushing out non-existent wrinkles and flicking off specks of imaginary dust. She might have been the current spiritual leader of the Drakkon-kin, but she was still the only practical mother he had. He stood and embraced his Nonne.

“The salvation of our people rests on your shoulders,” the Socra whispered. Her embrace tightened. “You’ll find more than you ever imagined. Follow your heart, then your head, my boy.” She kissed his cheek and stepped back.

Talek wouldn’t do either one of them the disservice of mentioning their threatening tears. The waiting auto-carriage tapped its horn. With his hand on the door handle, Talek turned for one last look. The sunlight from the kitchen window illuminated the Socra.

“May the skies be bright and the winds be kind!”

Talek felt the parting benediction to his very core. He silently followed it with his own prayer for success as he started back to the city.

Jaczon Carbehk missed the stars.

Gone was the drunkard from the tavern. The crimson uniform changed his entire visage. The reflection in the large picture window showed a man of authority. His holstered side arm lay on the large desk where it was dropped. Golden epaulets of his rank gleamed in the artificial light of the office, and thin black gloves covered his hands. During the day, the view looked over the ragged edges of the cityscape. Night disguised the jagged vista. Nothing broke through the darkness. Not even the stars.

A knock interrupted his reverie. Turning from the window, he barked, “Enter!”

Jaczon’s adjunct stood at the door. His pale face was the only sign of his nervousness.

“The Tmavě Jeden to see you, sir.”

Clad in black, the Tmavě Jeden strode into the room. The adjunct barely had time to step out of the doorway before the heavy door blocked him from the inner office. Daily sweeps keep the room secure, free from breaches. Ambition was a powerful motivator for anyone who wanted to advance in the Anakarei government.

The Tmavě Jeden reached into his uniform jacket and impatiently tossed the gate records on the desk between them. Jaczon would have taking the gesture as disrespect had it come from any other man. Instead, he nodded for his companion to sit.

“If the others hadn’t been with him, he wouldn’t have made it through the checkpoint at all,” the Tmavě Jeden snarled.

Jaczon thumbed through the records and the signed papers. He reached for a match from an ornate black box sitting on the corner of his desk and set fire to the corner of the sheath of papers. The flames quickly consumed the documents.

“Damn it all, Jaczon!” He slammed his hands down on the arms of his chair. “So much is riding on this. How can he be so careless?”

Jaczon coolly met the Tmavě Jeden gaze.

“Talek has always been fortunate to have his brother. They’ve always had each other.” Not letting his gaze slip, he added, “We know from experience that others haven’t been so fortunate.”

The Tmavě Jeden’s gaze slid from the truth of the statement.

“Our roles in this drama were determined long ago.” Jaczon leaned back in his chair. “Talek will do his part. He is cut from different cloth than you and I.”

“He is too green for what is required.”

“No, he holds hope. Something you and I find suspicious. Our world is jaded. Hope is a luxury that we can rarely trust nor afford.”

The Tmavě Jeden remembered a time in his youth when the world was shiny and vibrant. He understood how shadows could quickly destroy all of that. “You’re right,” he added. “More than opening the node, we need allies.”

“Talek’s always had the knack for finding the right person at the right time.”

Both men sat in silence as they contemplated the situation, but the Tmavě Jeden broke the silence.

“There are other issues at hand,” He leaned his head back against the chair in a rare moment of vulnerability.

"Making the node look sabotaged is going to be difficult."

The Tmavě Jeden gave a bleak twist of his lips that normally made people shiver. "Don't worry about that," he reassured Jaczon with a dry chuckle. "I've already worked my way into the data. I left a trail that will end at a very deserving group."

Jaczon didn't need the details. He had no doubt all would be efficiently dealt with. "Ensuring the Chancellor has a bad day will just be a bonus." They sat in silence as they contemplated the interruption in the Chancellor's plans.

"The Chancellor is gathering troops in anticipation of a successful node opening," the Tmavě Jeden said. "He's moving forward on the Otherverse assault, on the supposition that the experiments will be successful."

Jaczon leaned forward, worry creasing his brow.

"I haven't been able to figure out that rationale. Any orders I have been able to intercept have been vague. Some have made reference to a Project Grey."

"Project Grey worries me. I haven't been able to get any intelligence on it." The Tmavě Jeden leaned forward and rubbed his hands along his trousers. "My sources won't reveal anything because they are scared."

"Scared?"

The Tmavě Jeden was at a loss. "Every one of them is terrified."

Jaczon contemplated his options. "A project so secret that there is no information." Swiveling his chair to face the window, he faced the darkness. "That concerns me."

"I'll continue to press my resources." He looked at the back of Jaczon's chair. "I'll walk the shadows. I'll find the answers we need."

Jaczon turned back to face his companion. "You do that. Our priority is to get Talek through the node." He placed both hands in front of him on the desk. "His talent keeps getting stronger each passing day. Exposure to the node just makes it worse."

"Keeping the Hunters off his trail is difficult at best."

Jaczon came around the desk and stood in front of the Tmavě Jeden. He held out his hand in the ancient warrior wrist clasp. "We are Drakkon. We shall not perish!"

The Tmavě Jeden returned Jaczon's grip, fervently echoing the words.

The mournful howl of the city curfew alarm followed Talek into the lobby of his austere apartment building. The familiar beige marble floor gleamed in the dim lobby lighting. City codes demanded public spaces to be clean. Narrow rectangles of light from under neighbors' doors briefly illuminated his shoes as he walked to his apartment. Full of nervous energy, Talek compulsively cleaned and organized the space he'd lived in since embarking on his mission. He missed the glitter of the stars. This place was simply somewhere to lay his head. With nothing left to do, he lay down and attempted to woo sleep.

The unwelcome chimes of his alarm announced morning too soon. He had seen the sky brightening over the high edges of the cityscape. His room wouldn't actually get any sun until just before noon.

He stumbled into the kitchen and started the water boiling for his morning tea. The mundane repetitive tasks comforted him. Talek embraced the bitter kick the strong, dark brew gave him.

Talek started his transformation into an Anakarei scientist. He walked to the closet to select one of the navy uniforms that hung in a precise line. The gold of the shoulder epaulets gave the only clue to the rank he held in the scientific community. His frame grew stiff and straight as he donned each piece of clothing. His face became devoid of emotion as he set his shields in place. He reached down and grabbed a polished pair of boots. The reflective polish hid the hard usage of the footwear.

Talek took a hard look at the mirror and saw a fraud. He hated his job, hated the regime. He had worked hard to get to a position to commit the ultimate betrayal to the Anakarei.

But betrayal was in the eye of the beholder.

Heavy pedestrian traffic filled the sidewalks with a fast-moving mosaic of uniforms, suits, walking gowns, and working women returning from their nightly transactions as he made his way to the transit terminal. He found himself in a sea of people clad in black, maroon, and navy on their way to the secure military complex outside the city limits. The site had once been the trans-universal node that had allowed trade and travel throughout the Otherverse.

Talek fought to keep a calm façade as the transport sped to its destination. The closer in proximity to the node, the greater Talek struggled to keep his shields in place against the latent power. When the maxi-carriage reached the staging depot, streams of uniforms headed to the entrance. Talek struggled to not fidget in the slow line. He'd have time to breathe when he made it through the checkpoints.

A lone shadow stood on a balcony above the embarkation checkpoint and followed Talek's every move. The Tmavě Jeden saw the subtle fluctuations in Talek's personal shields as he struggled with his anxiety.

"Damn it, boy. Get your act together!" the Tmavě Jeden muttered to himself. His hand on his com unit, he saw Talek gathered himself before arousing the first Hunter. The Tmavě

Jeden faded into the shadows as Talek successfully navigated the first checkpoint.

As Talek approached his assigned work area, the node's energy pulled seductively at his senses. He walked down the long, dark corridor to the cramped locker room the scientists used to prepare themselves to work in the secure area. Talek hung his street uniform neatly in the locker as he stripped down to his undergarments then donned the sector's required non-contamination gear.

Last to arrive at the site, Talek rushed to join the other scientists to verify the previous day's test results. A hand gripped his shoulder.

"Today was not the day to be late!" His manager spoke in a low voice as his fingers tightened on Talek's shoulder. "We are being evaluated by one of the Chancellor's men."

"I'm sorry," Talek responded in equally hushed tones. "It won't happen again."

"It better not." The man released his grasp.

A faint smile flashed across his face as he let his control over the node slip. He hadn't lied to the supervisor. He'd never be late again. Huge bolts of electricity flashed through the work area. Sparks flew from overloaded machinery. The containment shield evaporated as the node's energy field expanded. Screams filled the air as the scientists and staff scrambled for the exits.

The siren's call of the node drew Talek towards the vortex. The crystalline facets reflected worlds without number as they spun with dizzying speed. Talek couldn't control where he landed when he stepped through the open portal. He hoped it would be a welcoming world that would help him accomplish his mission.

His world shattered as he crossed the event horizon. Lightning danced across his skin, incinerating his clothing. His molecules dissipated. He couldn't reform as human or Drakkon.

Blinded by the blaze of multi-spectral light, Talek fell into eternity.

THREE

"I got the job!" With her hands fisted, Ella pounded on the steering wheel of the parked car as she screamed with joy. The moment Nathan uttered the fateful words, the stars and planets in Ella's universe aligned for one magnificent moment. The victory warmed her soul and let her push aside the misery of the day.

The rain beating on the roof of her car gave Ella little incentive to run the short distance between the driveway and the front door. She was content to bask in the glow of her success for a few minutes longer. A golden light spilled from the transom over the front door. The warmth belied the cold reception she would meet from her mother, Myrna. The brutal confrontation they'd had in the early hours of the morning was the breaking point in their relationship. Myrna's laundry list of Ella's faults included being the reason why her father left. The little girl that still lived in Ella's forty-something mind saw his desertion as her fault. The grownup part of her knew it was bullshit. It was time to break the cycle, even if it meant kicking Myrna out of the house.

The short run to the door left her shivering and soaked for the second time, her hands shook as she fumbled her key into the lock. The small roof that protected the front stoop offered little protection from the weather. Scrabbling canine toenails and happy barking sounded from the other side of the door. Her Ronan's radar was never wrong about her arrival time. Ella swore the dog had some sort of canine GPS attached to her. As she pushed the door open, a muscular bundle of energy danced around her feet, leaping up to bathe any available skin with lavish kisses. Ella laughed. She knew one day, scientists were going to find that dog slobber was the magical cure-all to the common cold and other ailments. Ella pushed Ronan down, scratching his soft, floppy ears. The dog flopped over for a belly rub, his front legs sticking straight up and his back legs splayed in glorious abandon. He was pure pit bull goofball. When things seemed to be at their worst, Ronan always lifted Ella's spirits.

"Ella! Is that you?" Rubber tires squeaked across the hardwood floors. "Why haven't you answered me?"

Ella ignored the grating voice and concentrated on the dog writhing in ecstasy in front of her. "I just walked in the door, mother." Ronan scrambled to his feet to avoid Myrna's wheelchair, Ella flinched at the sharp edge of the chair's footrest struck her shin.

"Not good enough. You need to let me know the minute you get in the door." Myrna repositioned her chair to ram it forward.

"Who else would have a key to the front door, Mother?" Ella skirted around her mother and moved down the hallway.

"Only the person who had robbed and murdered you!"

"Seriously?" Ella closed her eyes and counted to five; ten seemed too far to go. "As you can see, I am neither murdered, nor have my possessions been removed from my person by force."

"Where have you been?" Myrna threw the words at Ella's retreating form. "I called your office, and they said you had taken the day off."

"You could have called me on my cell."

Tires squeaked as her mother followed her to the kitchen. "What were you doing?"

Ella gathered the ingredients for the evening's meal, her shoulders tensing with each syllable that left her mother's mouth. Small piles of colorful vegetables grew as the flashing knife efficiently cut up the dinner components. The savory scent of chicken browning had Ronan dancing with anticipation around Ella's feet.

"Ella, it's important that I know where you are," Myrna said, changing tact. She turned her chair to a less battle-ready angle. She added a quaver to her voice, "What if something happened to me?"

Ella's grip tightened on the knife handle. Her mother never showed weakness. The break in her voice was simply another gambit to get her way. With great precision, she put the knife down on the cutting board and turned to face her mother. A resentful flush colored her face; Ella was tired of being treated like a recalcitrant adolescent in her own home.

"Mother, I am a responsible adult. One who owns this house and pays her bills on time."

Myrna saw her ploy to gain sympathy had been unsuccessful. Anger burned across Myrna's face. She shed the ill-fitting disguise as she squared her wheelchair up.

Ella grabbed the armrests of the wheelchair as Myrna moved to ram Ella with the footrests, halting the assault. She set the brakes. Chair legs scraped across the floor as she pulled one of the kitchen chairs over to sit in front of her mother. "Things have to change. You need to stop making me feel like a guest in my own home." Ella waited until Myrna met her gaze then started ticking points off on the fingers of her right hand. "You cannot ram me with your wheelchair. You will contribute to the running of this household." Ella gave the wheelchair a sharp jolt. "You will stop kicking my dog!"

Ambivalence warred with duty when it came to her mother. Ella leaned forward as she moved in for the kill. "And one last thing. I want to see proof that you have to be in that blasted wheel chair."

"Well, I never!"

"Exactly, you just decided one day to be in that wheelchair. Ever since then, you've been an unholy terror. I know that when Daddy left, you were angry at the world. You were justified-then." Ella's shoulders sank under the weight of the day's overwhelming events. "You gave up. On life. On me. You just stopped living." Ella sat back in her chair. "I'm tired, Mother, tired of doing everything. I need help."

The harsh glare of truth gave Myrna nowhere to hide. "I gave you every opportunity in your life." She jerked the wheelchair back from Ella. "I worked two jobs while your father wasted his time in his dream world. I'm the one who gave you the drive." Ella stood her ground as her mother shook a finger in her face. "You owe me!"

The old litany of complaints merited an eye roll from Ella. "Mother, I stopped owing you anything a long time ago." Ella took a moment to breathe; despite everything, she loved the cantankerous woman in front of her. She had to let go and move forward – even if it killed one of them. "That Daddy was a lazy, no-good, son-of-a-gun horse is dead and buried." Ella rubbed her aching temples. "You wanted someone devoted to you. The sad truth is? No one would have you."

A flopping, gasping truism landed between the women. Myrna bowed her head.

Ella leaned back in her chair and rubbed her temples to try and relieve the beginnings of a headache.

"I didn't want you to leave me."

Ella barely heard the whispered words. "What did you say?"

Myrna lifted her head and met her daughter's gaze. "I didn't want you to leave me too."

Silence stretched between them. Only the acrid sent of burning chicken caused Ella to move. Ella placed the pan on a cool burner, as she worked to salvage something edible. Ronan laid his head in Myrna's lap. Myrna absently scratched his head, her eyes fixed on her daughter. The parade of her shortcomings in their relationship filled Myrna's eyes with tears.

"You have a funny way of showing you cared. I've lived with you pushing me away every step of the way. I was never 'enough' for you."

"That's not tr…"

"Stop!" Ella held up a hand to deflect one of the biggest lies her mother was about to utter. Myrna sank deeper into her wheelchair. "When I was little, I couldn't do anything right. When I graduated college, you told me 'I owed you' so you moved in, and for the last twenty-five years I have lived with you telling me what a failure I am."

"I may have been strict." Myrna said.

"Mother, strict would have been a walk in the park." Ella looked her mother straight in the eyes. "Did it ever occur to you that you were all I had left too?"

Myrna's gaze slipped away first. Old, destructive behaviors littered the emotional wasteland that stretched between them. Things had to change. "Okay."

"Okay?" Ella paused. "What does that mean?"

"We have new rules to work out." Myrna took a deep breath, she pushed herself upright and out of her wheelchair, "and I apparently have to get over myself."

Rubber squeaked against the floor, Ella looked around to see her mother standing up for the first time in her recent memory.

Myrna swayed on legs that trembled violently due to long-term disuse. "I can't say that it'll be easy, but I'll try to do more around the house. I was getting tired of the stupid chair anyway." Myrna's legs gave out. Her ungainly collapse knocked the wheelchair out from behind her, and she landed on the floor.

Ella rushed to her mother's side and tried to assess the damage done. Ronan danced with agitation as he tried render doggie aid to his fallen humans.

"Ronan sit!" Ella commanded. Ronan's butt hit the ground. He whined his concern quietly.

Myrna had hit her head on the footrest of the wheelchair, with the tile floor adding insult to injury.

"Ooooh! I should have been able to stand." Myrna's head spun from the pain. She opened her eyes to see Ella leaning over her. "Back up! Don't hover over me!" Mortification overrode her pain as she carefully levered herself into a sitting position.

"Am I going to have to call an ambulance?"

"No!" Myrna grimaced as she gently moved her arms and legs. "I'm okay."

Ella rose to her feet to reposition the wheelchair. "Do you need help getting back into the chair?"

Tears leaked down Myrna's cheeks. Her first instinct was to lash out at Ella and Ronan, but she knew she couldn't.

Ella gently helped Myrna up. Wheeling her to the kitchen table, she sat down in a chair next to her mother.

“I’d really like to get you looked at.” The goose egg swelling on Myrna’s forehead had Ella concerned. “You hit your head pretty hard.”

“I’ve got a hard head, nothing that some ibuprofen and a cold compress won’t take care of.”

Ella pulled a compress out of the freezer and brought Myrna a glass of water with some ibuprofen. Her earliest memories of her mother didn’t involve the dour senior citizen sitting before her. She remembered the joyful, uninhibited laughter of her childhood. The dumpling-making, happy woman she knew might never re-emerge, but Ella could help erase the bitterness between them. “I had a job interview today.”

Myrna glanced up at her daughter, surprised. “I didn’t know you’d been looking.”

The corner of Ella’s mouth kicked up. “Neither did I.” She set down the dish she had been scraping clean. “It was a once in a lifetime opportunity, so I felt it was worth the time.”

“What about your current position? Don’t you owe them anything?”

“I don’t owe them a thing.” Resentment dripped from each word. Ella took a deep breath. “Anyway, I got the job. I start tomorrow.”

“What?” Myrna gasped. “What about giving notice? What about being professional?”

“It’s not an issue,” Ella continued stacking dishes in the dishwasher. “Mr. Johnson’s girlfriend will fill my place just fine.”

Myrna stared at Ella’s back. “Excuse me? Mr. Johnson’s girlfriend?”

“Yup,” Ella turned to her mother with a wry expression, "he gave me two weeks’ notice this morning, allowing me the growth opportunity to train his girlfriend." Ella air quoted 'growth opportunity.' "I told him to take his generous offer and shove it." She scowled, "Yes, those were my exact words."

"Well, you might have your father's dreams," Myrna regarded her daughter with pride. "But you have my inner bitch. Good for you."

Laughter bubbled and cleansed the air. Ronan joined the mirth with happy barking.

Ella closed the house up for the night after looking in on Myrna one last time. Ronan trailed faithfully at her heels. The massive emotional swings of the day left her feeling drained yet oddly content. She picked up the box that contained the remnants of her former professional life. The only thing in the box she wanted was the dragon sculpture. A stunning work of a clear quartz point with an intricately carved metallic dragon, of an iridescent material, perched on its tip.

The jewel tones of her bedroom soothed away the rest of the day's stress. She pulled the sculpture out of the box and placed it on a small custom-made pedestal next to her bed. As the piece settled onto its base, it seemed to sigh in contentment. The room held the treasures of her life - trophies from her karate competitions, a case that held her ranking belts of white to the three black belts, diplomas, and certificates. The dragon statuette, given to her by her father when she was a child, represented her dreams and hopes. It completed the room.

A massive wave of exhaustion caught up with Ella. She collapsed on her bed, dreaming of jeweled and metallic colored dragons flying against a periwinkle sky.

The quiet aisles of the bookstore lay dormant as the morning crew worked to prepare for the day ahead.

"Good morning, Annisa," Nathan greeted his store manager. "Any unusual node activity last night?"

Annisa Oakton glared at Nathan. "No, everything was quiet. But that doesn't mean that today won't go terribly wrong."

"I know that I can always count on you to be practical and optimistic." Nathan chose to ignore her hostility; Annisa had a right to be upset. He had superseded her authority by hiring Ella. Nathan waited patiently for her next salvo.

"You didn't see the chaos of her mind," Annisa snapped. "Her life is an emotional human mess. That kind of energy could tip the balance of the node, putting the safety of the House in jeopardy."

"You didn't see the node welcome her," Nathan countered.

Annisa stood by her opinion. "I'm telling you, something is off with her. She's not what she seems."

"Annisa." Nathan placed a warning hand on his manager's shoulder. "None of us are what we seem." He squeezed gently. "You are going to have to be on your best behavior. She's going to be a part of our team."

Ella gave herself a firm pep talk as she walked up to House Books. Kaie sat at the entrance looking out, for all appearances, waiting. The automatic doors slid open, allowing Ella to enter. The cat greeted her with several comments.

Ella felt encapsulated in an exquisite faceted crystal, each surface refracting light in an ever-expanding sphere of multi-colored luminescence. Snatches of lives flowed across each facet for a fraction of a second. The moment she blinked, the scenes changed – some fantastic, some mundane, all making her question her grasp on reality.

"Ah, Kaie let you in. Excellent."

Ella whirled around, her reverie shattered.

"You're still loitering in the lobby." Nathan stood in the entryway to the main selling floor. "Is this going to be a problem?"

"I'm entranced by your amazing lighting system. You'll have to explain it to me. I'd love to learn about it."

"The foyer lights have some unique properties that only a few can truly appreciate. Apparently, you are among them. It can truly be captivating." Nathan waved Ella onto the main store floor. "Come, let's get the day started."

Kaie leaned against Ella's legs, thoroughly inspecting her trousers. Nathan noticed Kaie's interest. "Do you have a cat at home?" he asked.

Ella glanced down at her pant leg, a sprinkling of white dog hair liberally decorating the garment below the knee. She laughed. "No, I have a dog, Ronan." She gestured to the hair. "He goes everywhere with me." Ella leaned down to do her best to brush off the hair. "Kaie must smell him on my clothes."

"A dog? How interesting." Nathan glanced down at the cat. "Kaie has never shown interest in dogs before. I think once things get settled, we'll have to introduce them."

Ella cleared her throat. "While I'm sure Kaie would be more than capable of taking care of herself," Kaie butted her head against Ella as if to say a dog would not be a problem, Ella bent down to scratch Kaie behind her ears, "Ronan really likes cats and is very enthusiastic. I'm not sure how the introduction would go. Did I mention big?"

"I wouldn't worry about Kaie. She'll keep Ronan busy."

Ella hedged; the last thing she needed was to have Ronan overwhelm Kaie, putting her new employment in jeopardy. "Let's take it a step at a time."

"Nathan!" Annisa called from behind the cash register. "The other employees should be arriving anytime. How do you want to run the day?"

Ella wiped her sweaty palms against her trouser legs.

"Ms. Hixson, welcome to House Books," Annisa said.

"Thank you. I'm grateful to be here. Please call me Ella."

"Ms. Hixson, we have a lot to go over." Annisa ignored Ella's extended hand. "Follow m…"

The entire building shuddered as a massive crack of thunder interrupted Annisa's intended instruction. Books flew off the shelves, littering the aisles like fallen leaves.

Knocked off her feet, Ella fell hard to the ground. As she struggled to stand up, another crash of thunder and flare of lightning temporarily blinded her. When her vision started to clear, she found herself alone on the demolished sales floor. She braced herself on the fallen shelving as she struggled through the mess to where Nathan, Ms. Oakton, and Kaie were silhouetted against the tempest.

The hair on Ella's arms stood up straight. An electrical maelstrom, encompassing the entire space of the foyer, threw huge bolts of energy. The hexagonal shape seemed to contain the majority of the damage. A faceted sphere filled the center of the space where a man hung in its center defying of the laws of gravity. The brilliant light prevented Ella from opening her eyes completely, but the suspended man seemed to transform from a man to a golden dragon and back. His body twisted and contorted in the grips of the primal forces that held him.

"Annisa, lock the house down!" Nathan roared. He stepped into the middle of the tempest, laid his hands on the nearest appendage, and heaved. As suddenly as the anomaly occurred, it ended. Ella scrambled backward to avoid the men as they tumbled onto the floor. And the anomaly closed, leaving books and fixtures scattered in its wake. The men's gasping disturbed the eerie silence. Nathan panted from exertion, the other from pain. Heavy shutters blocked the windows, leaving the foyer dim. The man on the floor was naked. Arcs of electricity traveled over his body leaving burns where they danced on his skin. Taking off her jacket, Ella gently draped it over the man in an effort to preserve his modesty.

"Tell me what to do. Do I need to call 9-1-1?" Ella asked.

"No!" Nathan snapped. He made a visible effort to calm down and added more gently, "No, they wouldn't be able to help him. Did Annisa get the house locked down?"

"I'm assuming yes. The shutters are in place over the windows." Ella reached over the man on the floor, putting her hand on Nathan's arm. "Okay, so what are we going to do with this gentleman?"

The hiss and pop of static ceased. Nathan reached over and placed a hand on the man's forehead. Golden eyes snapped open, their exquisite color mesmerizing Ella. A fine scale pattern etched his body in the palest gold, in relief against the angry red of the burn. The man on the floor grabbed Nathan's wrist and started babbling in a fluid, musical language. Nathan responded in kind. Suddenly, the man convulsed. Nathan grabbed him by the shoulders. Ella threw herself across his legs to try to prevent him from hurting himself.

Talek felt the vortex tear him asunder. A hand grasped his leg, pulling him through an opening. He didn't care where he was. He had to get out of the vortex or die. The surroundings were not what he expected. Books lined the walls, with windows above the shelves. A man and woman knelt above him. The woman's blue-green eyes were something he had only seen in his dreams. Talek grabbed the man's wrist, trying to deliver his message. The man thankfully understood him. Then darkness claimed him.

"We have to get him upstairs."

"What was that language? Slavic?" Ella questioned Nathan, as she helped him lift the man. "It sounded familiar."

Nathan stopped. "Familiar? How?"

"I'm not sure." Ella did her best to try to remember. "Maybe in a dream."

Nathan hefted the unconscious man as he directed Ella to open doors. "We need to talk about this."

"Just tell me where you want to go." Books re-shelved themselves by invisible hands as they passed through the aisles to the back of the store. Ella had enough questions buzzing around her head to not pay them any attention.

'One wonderment at a time' was the motto she was clinging to. Right now, she and Nathan had a wounded man - dragon - person - thing that needed care.

Nathan's directions brought them to the door where they had gone for her post interview tête-à-tête. Ella was certain she had seen steep endless stairs there the day before. Today, the door revealed a simple flight of stairs found in any farmhouse. Leading the way, she stepped into a wide corridor lined with doors. Nathan shouldered past her with his burden, the second door on the left opened revealing a large bedroom with a comfortable looking bed. Ella rushed in to pull back the colorful quilt, enabling Nathan to lay the man down.

She left Nathan to make the man comfortable as she searched for a linen closet to locate towels and wash cloths. Ella laid the linens on the chest next to the bed. She collected the pitcher from the basin and went to in search for the bathroom to fill it with warm water. Returning, she filled the basin and handed Nathan a dampened cloth. Their visitor looked like hell. Take care of the emergency first, ask questions later – that was her game plan.

The shrill ring of Ella's cellphone shattered the room's silence. She stepped out of the room to answer the call.

"Hello, Mother." Ella stood just outside the door, aware Nathan could hear the majority of the one-sided conversation.

"Mother, my day just started." Ella paused. "Look, I can't really talk now. Let me call you on my break. I'll have an idea of my schedule and what the benefits will be like." Listening to Myrna for another moment, Ella gave a short laugh. "Yes, I'll find out what the book discount is for family. I'll see you tonight."

Re-entering the room, Ella silenced the cell phone, slipping it in her pocket. "Has he said anything more?"

Nathan didn't bother to pretend he hadn't understood their visitor. "No, though he's in considerable pain. I need you to go down to the sales floor and ask Annisa to come up. She has healing skills."

Ella glowered at looked at Nathan. "When all this is settled, I have a few questions for you."

"You've earned your answers."

Ella headed downstairs. She found the selling floor in pristine order, the store open for business.

"Ms. Hixson!" A familiar voice called Ella.

"Sindie, isn't it?"

"Yep, that's me! Ms. Oakton is on her way upstairs." Sindie linked her arm with Ella.

"Look, I think I should go back up."

"No, they'll be a while." Sindie patted Ella's arm as she moved them to the front of the store. "Let me give you a tour. They'll call you when they're ready for you."

Unsure of how far to push the woman, Ella's eyes widened as she saw the bookshelves restored to their upright positions and the inventory neatly returned to their places. "I'm amazed the store is in such good shape after this morning's events." Ella continued to look around. "How'd you get the floor back into order?"

Sindie gave a tinkling laugh. "We have a talented staff here. Cleanup is a team effort. You could say its magic." She gave another reassuring pat on the arm. "Magic?" The hedging bothered Ella. "Okay. Spill it!"

With her large lavender colored eyes, Sindie blinked innocently. "Spill what?"

"I've seen a dragon who turned into a man, books that have been placed back on shelves without hands, and mysterious lightning storms inside a building." Ella resisted the urge to grab and shake the woman in front of her. Her demand turned into a plea. "Tell me what's going on! Please!"

"Look, I know you're frustrated, but Nathan needs to be the one to explain everything."

"Ms. Hixson!" a voice interrupted. "Nathan needs you upstairs immediately." Ms. Oakton rushed toward them across the sales floor.

Upstairs, chaos ruled; Nathan lay across the thrashing, shimmering form of their guest. Kaie sat at the foot of the bed hissing. Ella dashed across the room to the other side of the bed, grabbing an arm and a leg. She struggled to help keep the man still. His scorching skin made Ella want to pull her hands back, but her touch seemed to sooth the man. A golden web of scales covering his body glowed brightly.

Her touch should not have had any effect on the man. Nathan had called her on a hunch.

"Ella, I need you to trust me."

"Like I haven't already?" Nathan reached across and grasped Ella's head, she stared into his swirling silver eyes. For the first time, she noticed that he had a slit pupil like the man on the bed. Her eyes widened with alarm as she tried to free her head from his grasp. Nathan tightened his hold.

"Učit se!" Nathan commanded.

Visions of places she had never been filled the crevices of Ella's mind. She screamed with the weight of the knowledge and language forced into her mind. Nathan let go, and she collapsed like a rag doll at the foot of the bed.

Her 'self' struggled to maintain its dominate place in her psyche as she tried to catalogue and comprehend the new information. Ella flinched from the helping hand Nathan extended. She rose to her feet and faced him. A burning flush swept through her body. She struggled to form a coherent thought. "Trust you?" Ella spat. "What the hell did you do to me?"

"What was necessary so you could help," Nathan replied without remorse.

"You violated my mind!"

Nathan waved off Ella's histrionics.

"I gave you the knowledge needed to help me care for our guest and deal with matters of the House." Looking at the man on the bed, he added, "Your training time table has been accelerated."

Ella was enraged at being dismissed. "I don't care! You went into my mind uninvited! That constitutes violation!" Ella jumped to her feet, her body tense and ready to strike at something or someone. "What, you were going to go over inter-dimensional vortexes next week? I don't care what you're trying to justify!"

Nathan lost his patience. "I need you to think beyond yourself! You said you'd heard his language before. Where?"

The question was more of a statement.

Ella's eyes narrowed at Nathan's tone. "I told you, in a dream."

The scene from the foyer crashed into Ella's memory; this time she understood the language with perfect clarity.

"Where am I?" Gasped the man. "Do you know Mellanei?"

Nathan stiffened as the man grasped his arm. "I know her. She is no longer here."

"No! I must find her! Warn her!" The man arched in agony.

"Warn her about what?" Nathan held the man still as Ella covered him. In an effort to keep the man conscious, Nathan gave him a hard shake. "Tell me!"

His golden eyes cracked open as Talek regained his senses. He watched the man and woman arguing violently above him. Unfortunately, his pain started to overcome his ability to remain quiescent.

Already pushed beyond the limits of her temper, Ella exploded. "You, you…training? Accelerated? I applied for a manager position in a frickin' bookstore, not an inter-dimensional way station! I've been accepting up until you messed with my head." She was speechless as she pushed herself back into a standing position from the bed, forgetting about the visitor

Talek started to fidget; Ella shot a soothing command in his language-, 'Být v Klidu." Talek calmed as his pain eased. Ella was oblivious to what she had done. "What exactly are you? What is this place?"

FOUR

A shimmery, glow engulfed Ella's body as smoke wisped from the corner of her mouth. "Well, this is a surprise." Nathan delved into Ella's mind where chaos reigned. He held her still as she fought against the intrusion. Energy sparked throughout the room. A mental obstruction blocked his probe. Nathan held Ella steady as she fought. As he breached the barrier, Nathan flew across the room, crashing through the wall into the hallway.

Pain exploded through Ella's head. Memories of places she'd never been and people of whom she had no recollection swarmed through her mind. The room mirrored the mental tumult as furniture flew. The eye of the storm centered on Ella and the visitor.

Nathan stared at the unconscious Drakkon sprawled across the guest room floor with disbelief. The stunning transformation left Nathan with more questions than answers. The scales of her blue-green form rippled in an opalescent sheen with each breath. Groaning as he struggled to his feet, Nathan surveyed the destruction as Annisa hurried down the hall.

"What happened?"

"It would seem we have a bit of a Drakkon problem." Unsteady on his feet, Nathan picked his way through the debris of shredded clothes and bedroom furniture. He gestured to Annisa to see.

Annisa stood in the doorway amazed at the wreckage she saw. Ella took most of the floor space in the room, leaving only the bed, occupied by the newcomer, undisturbed.

"Oh, my god."

"This is our own Ms. Ella Hixson." Nathan waved at the supine form. "It would seem what bothered you during Ella's interview had merit." Nathan crouched down near Ella's head. "This puts a new wrinkle in the grand scheme of things." He tilted his head as he regarded his new employee. "She doesn't know or didn't know she was Drakkon. I forced a mind-lock open."

"She had a mind-lock?" Annisa's brows drew together as she contemplated the scene in front of her. "This is not good. The locks are used to protect not only the person, but the people around them."

"I know." Nathan settled into a lotus position by Ella's head. "While she is unconscious, I'm going to have to go in and find out more."

"Before you do that, I'm going to make sure the floor is shielded."

Nathan shook his head at his thoughtlessness. "You're right, I should have thought of that."

"Nathan, between our visitor and Ms. Hixson's surprise, you're allowed a mistake once in a while. Before I go back down, at least let me heal you."

"I don't think we have the time, Annisa." Nathan gave her a grateful glance. "I need to find out as much as possible before she wakes up – for all our sakes."

A muffled yowl caught their attention. The sound came from between the bed and the prone dragon.

"Kaie!"

Kaie wiggled her way out from under the bed, and then stalked toward the door with a disgruntled meow. Annisa followed the cat. "Take care of things up here. I'll keep things under control downstairs."

Nathan gave a cursory glance at the bed. "You're awake." He didn't move from Ella's side. "Can you tell me your name?"

"Talek." He nodded to the unconscious Drakkon at his side. "Who is she?"

"This is Ms. Ella Hixson, who is our current conundrum." Nathan stood and approached the bedside. "Why did you come through the node? You said you had a warning."

Talek struggled to sit-up. "I seek Mellanei. Do you know where she is?"

Nathan placed a hand on Talek's arm. "You're in no shape to get up. Mellanei is not on this world. We'll talk more about this later." His attention focused on Ella. "Rest, we will talk as soon as I solve this mystery." Nathan focused on Ella.

Talek looked at the supine Drakkon. "How is it possible that a Drakkon is here?"

"That's just it. Very few have ever visited our world or stayed. This particular Drakkon was unaware of her heritage. It was sealed behind a mind-lock."

"A mind-lock? Your people know how to do such things?"

"No. We don't. Very few Other-kin have come through the node with that particular knowledge. Only the High Socri can perform such rites." Nathan resettled himself by Ella's head in a comfortable cross-legged position. "This is very worrisome. While she is unconscious, I'm going to see what information I can find."

Talek protested as he once more tried to move off the bed. "No! She should be awake when she tells you the information. This is wrong."

Nathan made a frustrated sound. "Events have forced my hand. I don't have time to be particularly nice." He took a deep breath, "I don't know if she knows how to regain her human form." Nathan sent Talek a steely look that settled the man back down on the bed. "Your presence means that things have gone from bad to worse on Drakkonon. The plan was to drain the node when Mellanei passed through."

Talek fell silent as Nathan leaned forward, placing his hands on the dragon's delicate arched eye ridges. He uttered the ancient chant and slipped from his mortal form into the ether of the mind.

Pandemonium reigned in the landscape. Lightning crashed and thunder rolled as new memories emerged in a violent mental lahar. The emergent memories seemed to be more historical than personal, which left Nathan puzzled. Ella may not have been born on Drakkonon, but she carried the Drakkon generational secrets. The why's and how's were somewhere in the chaos. Nathan searched for Ella through the clamor and mayhem that was her mindscape. As an observer, the experience overwhelmed Nathan. He couldn't imagine the effect it had on Ella. He climbed through the shattered points of view, until he finally located a traumatized Ella cowering on a ledge above a raging flow. She stared blankly at the anarchy. Gently, he reached out to her. "Ella."

She flinched at his voice and huddled tighter to herself. Nathan inched closer. "Ella, I can help you."

Ella moved away, edging perilously close to the crumbly edge of the ledge. He eased back. Tears streaked through the dust on her cheeks. Her eyes looked hollow. Each second the torrent of information eroded the stability of the ledge. Facing her, taking care to not move closer, Nathan started to give her instructions.

"You are the floodgate that controls all the currents."

Ella gave no response.

"Separate the familiar from the unfamiliar. Create two pools."

Her brow furrowing, Ella's gaze gained focus as it shifted on the torrent below. The ledge crumbled another several inches. Its dirt crumbled into the turbulent chasm below.

Large blocks appeared forming a chute at the opening of the cascade of data. Ella started dividing off the plains of her mind, keeping it all accessible. Nathan watched her direct the flow. He knew she had no experience in this type of exercise, yet she handled the task with the skill of a seasoned Socra. The more she accomplished, the more stable the ledge they sat on became.

The torrent slowed to a trickle. Ella witnessed the flooded plains of her mind. Bits of her life bobbed like so much flotsam in the currents and eddies that flowed below them.

Ella turned to Nathan. "I am not happy with you."

"I imagine you aren't. Let me help you.'

She gestured to the mess of information contained in various pools in front of her. "What is all this?"

"That I can't tell you. I'll help you sift through it all to find your answers."

Ella pursed her lips as she regarded Nathan with mild suspicion. "Fine, but I want complete honesty from you. None of this inscrutability crap."

"Agreed." Nathan held out his hand for Ella to grasp. "Can I help you find your way out now?"

Ella wobbled as she allowed Nathan to pull her to her feet. "I need to give you some very specific instructions." Nathan continued to hold Ella steady.

Ella felt a wisp of premonition dance across her soul. "Why?"

"You are a Drakkon. You have to change back into human form."

Laughter erupted from Ella.

"A what?"

"A Drakkon," Nathan stated. "With everything you've seen today, is being a Drakkon so far out of the realm of reason?"

Ella stared across the transitioning mindscape. The information swirled into the designated spaces of her own creation,

"Tell me how to change back into human form."

"I need you to look into my eyes."

In the swirling silver depths of Nathan's eyes, images began to form. Her gaze sharpened. The images focused into dragons swirling in complicated patterns. Mesmerized, Ella found herself whirling along. Her world shifted and reshaped until she found her human self.

Blinking, Ella found herself sitting on the floor of the guest room. Broken furniture lay scattered around the room. The man-sized hole next to the door frame puzzled Ella. The sharp edges of debris dug into Ella's prone form.

Ella screamed and dove for one of the blankets on the bed. "I'm naked! Why am I naked?" Ella covered herself as she glared at both men in the room.

Nathan approached Ella with the care of a bomb squad approaching live ordinance.

"Ella, what do you remember?"

"You! You were in my head!" Ella sputtered, "Dragons, I was a dragon."

"Technically, you are a Drakkon…"

A rumbling commotion interrupted Nathan. Ella heard the distinctive business growl of her Ronan. Standing, Ella hitched the blanket securely around herself. Her ability to stay upright was debatable. She brushed aside Nathan's help and headed for the door. Before she got there, Ronan burst through with Ms. Oakton making a last futile grab for his collar. Kaie hung on her skirt like a furry pendulum.

Ronan sighted his mistress and made a beeline. The dog stood in front of his owner growling protectively at everyone in the room. Ella sank to her knees. "Ronan, how did you get here?" She didn't expect the dog to answer, but after everything that happened today, who knew?

Annisa ranted. "This is not a zoo or a kennel! That creature cannot be here! This is a place of business."

Nathan raised an eyebrow. "I take it this is your Ronan?"

Ella nodded. Kaie came over. Reaching up, she gently touched her nose to Ronan's in a feline greeting. Ronan, exhibiting the best behavior Ella had ever seen, bent down and gently nuzzled the cat with his large square head. Animal salutations completed, Ronan returned to guard mode. Kaie took up sentry position next to him.

Nathan watched the reunion. "Annisa, how did Ronan get in the store?"

Annisa flung her arm in the direction of the smug cat. "Kaie let that creature in." Her glare encompassed the room.

"The dog frightened customers as he ran through the store. Kaie aided and abetted."

Ella rewarded Ronan with a good head rub. "Aren't you the loyal protector?"

"I wouldn't let him up the stairs. That's when she," Annisa sent a fuming look at the cat, "joined in the disturbance and brought down the shield." Kaie cleaned her paws, unimpressed with the accusations. "People could have been hurt. Worse, they could have asked questions."

"Annisa, you need to make nice with Ronan." Nathan tried to sooth his angry manager. "I have a feeling we are going to be seeing a lot of him."

Ella swiped at her cheeks surprised to find them wet with tears. Her hindbrain caught up with the overwhelming events, and she buried her face in the soft fur of Ronan's neck. The day had been too much. Ronan, sensing her turmoil, gave her a comforting lap with his tongue. Violent tremors started to rack her frame. The impact of everything came crashing down – inter-dimensional nodes, magical houses, dragons. Oh, and lo and behold, she was a dragon herself. Was she trapped in a Technicolor nightmare? Reaching up, she gave herself a good vicious pinch on the underside of her arm.

"What is wrong with you?" Annisa said.

"Just making sure I wasn't still asleep."

Annisa released Ella's hands, looking her straight in the eye. "No. You're not losing your mind. Your perception of the universe has just been greatly expanded."

Ronan nosed his head back into Ella's hand. "More than expanded, it's exploded. I'm just trying to wrap my mind around it all." She looked at everyone miserably, "I don't know if I can."

Talek understood Ella’s turmoil at the new parameters of the world as she understood it. He cleared his throat. “We have greater problems at hand.”

Everyone in the room, including the animals, turned to look at their forgotten guest. Nathan and Ella understood him. Annisa, who spoke most of the Fae languages, didn’t speak Drakkon.

“You are correct,” Nathan responded. “There are greater problems at hand. Let us parlay.” He turned to Annisa. “We need clothes for Ella and our guest. Can you procure the needed items?”

“The House will provide all that is needed.” Annisa glanced around the room with a pinched look on her face. “Just keep all creatures upstairs. We can’t afford any incidents with customers.”

Ella hitched the blanket up again. She was grateful to be getting clothing of any kind.

“Nathan, you and I have things to discuss.” She glanced at the man she hadn’t been properly introduced to, “I’m sorry, I don’t know your name,” She reached out her free hand to shake as she introduced herself to Talek. “I’m Ella.”

“I'm Talek.”

Ella squeezed his hand as she greeted him, “Nice to meet you, Talek.” The moment Ella grasped his hand, shimmers of electrical current eddied up his arm and through his body. Talek snatched his hand back as if he’d been shocked. Ella didn’t notice Talek’s withdrawal and turned to Nathan. “You ‘gave’ me Drakkon speech. Can you give Talek our language?” She gestured around her, “when in Rome and all that.”

“You’re right, that would make life easier.” Nathan looked at Talek, who was following the exchange with a look of confusion on his face. “As I gave Ella the Drakkon tongue, I can give you our tongue. I believe it will make things less complicated." Talek nodded his consent. Nathan sat on the side of the bed, placing his thumbs along Talek's brow line with his fingers resting along Talek's temples.

Ella watched the process with detached curiosity, finding it much less dramatic than her experience. She was going to have to have a talk with Nathan about execution and delivery.

Annisa stood at the doorway with a neatly folded pile of clothing,

"Ms. Hixson… Ella." Annisa took a deep breath, "we're going to be working closely together, please call me Annisa. We've survived this event, so I think we can rid ourselves of any ceremony between us."

Ella recognized the concession. "I'm sorry about Ronan. He's always been protective. He really is a good dog." She gestured to the dog and cat seated next to each other comfortably observing everything around them. "He and Kaie seem to be friends already."

Annisa extricated her hand from Ella's grasp. "The morning has been overwhelming. Your dog and I will come to terms." She gestured toward a door. "Get dressed now." With great care, she moved through the debris and placed clothes for Talek on the end of the bed.

The blanket trailed after Ella like the train of a royal robe as she entered a well-appointed bathroom. She leaned against the door as it closed and looked at herself in the mirror over the sink.

Despite the traumatic events of the last several hours, Ella glowed with unexpected youth and vitality. Ella couldn't see 'ma'am' ever being uttered again in the grocery checkout line. The changes were subtle: her eyes a deeper blue-green, a barely visible gossamer web of iridescent scales on her skin replacing the freckles that once sprinkled across her nose.

Gone was the frizzy, mousy hair. Her hair had that salon vibrancy she'd always wanted.

Ella's finger touched the bridge of her nose, with a start she realized her glasses were missing. Crisp and clear, her vision had changed with the rest of her. She leaned forward to examine her appearance. Gasping she saw her slit pupils dilated in surprise. Colors took on saturation reminiscent of the old colored films. With a little snort, Ella whispered, "Looks like I'm going to need glasses after all." The enhanced eye color and strange pupils were going to be hard to explain.

Her mind swam with memories and knowledge of a world she didn't understand. Her own innate smarts had received a boost, giving her full use of her faculties.

She changed into the clothes Annisa provided. The sumptuous silk of the jewel toned blouse and the super-fine wool trousers that glided against her skin. Ella had never been able to afford such luxurious fabric; she couldn't help but run her hands up and down the textiles.

Ella opened the bathroom door. She peered into the hallway before she emerged into the corridor. Nathan cleared his throat, causing her to jump. He stood next to the door facing the hole in the bedroom wall.

"Is Talek okay?"

"He's getting dressed." Nathan stood up straight, "When he's finished, we'll go down to the office. I've asked Kaie to keep Ronan up here. They seem to be getting along."

"Ronan has always loved cats. Cats haven't always returned the feeling. I'm glad Kaie is being good." Ella realized that Nathan had spoken about Kaie as if she were a person. "Is there something I need to know about Kaie?"

"I'd say 'all in good time', but the time is here." When Talek appeared, Nathan gestured for them to follow him.

"Talek, tell us the news of Drakkonon."

With the language still settling in his mind, Talek began slowly to speak.

"Two hundred cycles ago, a Drakkon named Mellanei helped close the Node in our world to prevent the Anakarei from breaking through to the Other Worlds. Their plan was to rule the Otherverse or destroy it."

Ella held up her hand in confusion. "Help me out. What exactly is the Otherverse? The concepts are in my head, but it's not sorted yet."

"You said you read science fiction?"

"All my life."

"Then you're acquainted with the theory of multiverse?"

"Multiple universes that exist in parallel time and space? They don't interact but run concurrent to each other." Nathan looked impressed with her explanation. Ella said tapped her forehead. "I told you, lots of information both useful and useless in my mind."

"Essentially, the Otherverse falls in one dimension, but connects all the worlds."

"How many world are we talking about, and do these connection break through to other dimensions?" Ella's inner geek wanted to know.

Nathan continued, "The universe is crisscrossed by ley-lines of meta-physical power. Where they connect are nodes. Nodes allow travel between worlds." He gave Ella a pointed look. "Once in a great while there is an inter-dimensional breach." With a wave of Nathan's hand, a four dimensional diagram appeared in the middle of the office space. To Ella it looked like a game of battleship on steroids, each quadrant filled with points of light and connecting lines. She restrained herself from shouting 'you sank my battleship.' Nathan continued, “Most Nodes have no impact on the Otherverse and are known as minor Nodes. However, every Other World has at least one Major Node that can traverse dimensions. The House sits on a Major Node.”

Ella looked at Talek to confirm her guess, as she inched closer to the image in the room. “You came through a Major Node?” Talek nodded. “When I was standing in the foyer, I felt like I was in a faceted crystal. Each facet had a scene from another world.”

“Only a few people or creatures can feel, see, or even manipulate the Nodes. You are one of the few.”

Ella shook her head. “I was in and out of this store as a child, and the Node never had the effect on me that it had yesterday. Why?”

“That could have been because of the mind-lock you had in place.” Nathan mused out loud.

“Wasn’t still in place yesterday? What changed?”

“Drakkon powers often do not manifest until puberty or early adulthood,” Talek interjected. “The node would not have manifested itself to an immature talent.”

Everyone looked at Talek. Annisa looked at Ella with her sharp brown gaze. “That would make sense.”

“I can see why you’re particular about who works here.” Ella gave the room a jaundiced look. “Why didn’t I manifest during my teens or early adulthood?”

“It has to be the mind-lock,” Nathan nodded to confirm Annisa’s supposition. “It was a powerful block to her Drakkon heritage.”

“It must have inhibited her Drakkon physiology.” Nathan studied Ella. “Your father must have been a powerful Drakkon.”

"I don't know what my father was; he disappeared when I was little." Memories bubbled up from newly released memories. She squelched them down; she wasn't ready to deal with them – yet.

Annisa reached over to pat Ella's arm. "You have no idea how special you are." Ella looked at the woman in disbelief. "I've been here a hundred years, and no one has been able to wrap their minds around the eccentricities of the House the way you have."

"Boy, I feel so special."

Talek interrupted the joke he didn't understand. "Mellanei was the last through the Major Node on Drakkonon before it was drained. The Anakarei have found a way to power it back up. The Drakkon are one of the three races who can open and manipulate the nodal network. On Drakkonon, the ability has become rare. The lineage of the high Socra were known to be able to consistently keep the Node functional for off-world trade. The last of this line went through the Node and was never heard from again. Now the Anakarei government hunts for anyone with a hint of sensitive talent to bring the node back to full power. Those they capture have been burned through and left as husks who hunt their own. The Anakarei have amassed an army and are almost ready to launch their assault." Talek looked at everyone in the room. "None of the Other Worlds have any idea or are prepared to handle such an attack."

"How do you know so many details?"

"When we learned that the Node had started to regain strength, we knew that we had to have someone on the inside who could manipulate the Node and its energies." He regarded Nathan and Ella with wariness. "I'm one of the few remaining Sensitive's that hadn't been captured and conscripted into the services of the Anakarei."

Nathan asked. “How did you manage that?”

“The Socra trained me, helping me shield myself from the purges.”

Talek’s words triggered memories that scrolled across Ella’s mind in an immersive, full sensory historical film. The conversation that flowed around her faded as the kinesthetic experience left Ella focused on the unfolding history of her heritage.

“My grandmother was afraid this day would come.” Nathan started pacing the small space. “This is why she is not here. She went to travel the Otherverse and warn those who would listen.”

“Your grandmother was Mellanei?” Talek confirmed.

Nathan nodded as he continued, “She’s been gone the last hundred years. We last heard from her seventy-five years ago.”

The mention of Mellanei pulled Ella out of her immersion. “A hundred years ago, seventy-five years ago?” she interrupted. “Exactly how old are you?”

“I’ll be one hundred on my next birthday. We all age very well.” Nathan said with a grin.

FIVE

Pens and other items clattered across Jaczon's desk as an explosion rocked the complex. The wail of sirens filled the air as he stepped toward the outer office.

His adjunct rushed through the door.

"They're evacuating the complex."

"What happened?" Jaczon played ignorant. "Do we know the damage?"

"No, sir."

Directing the adjunct to sweep the floor for stragglers, Jaczon entered a seldom-used maintenance closet by his office. He let the dark embrace him for a moment and then waved his hand in the vicinity of the light pull. The exposed filament of the bulb lit the small room in a harsh glare. He rubbed his nose to stifle a sneeze from the strong scent of cleaning chemicals. A maintenance smock hung on the back of the door; he pulled it on over his uniform. Jaczon patted the pockets. The Tmavě Jeden often left communications there. Jaczon pulled out an envelope. Printed neatly on the front were two words: 'Project Grey.'

"Crazck!" The Tmavě Jeden had been successful in finding the elusive information. He slipped the packet into a secure pocket in his uniform before he buttoned up the other garment. The bulk of the smock would hide the bulge. Jaczon pressed a tile block over the utility sink, revealing a familiar narrow passageway that opened into an alcove in the lobby, allowing him to merge with the evacuating personnel heading for the city. Conversation and speculation swirled around him as he pondered the situation. He ignored the crowd as he focused on the situation. The Chancellor had a way to open the portal. The explosion wouldn't be enough to contain the man's ambition. Jaczon shed his command persona and faded into the evacuating crowd.

The rich smell of hops and the drone of conversation embraced Jaczon as he entered the Wyvern. The woman slinging drinks and insults behind the bar glanced at the door the moment it opened. She gave him a nod, allowing him to pass through to the backrooms. Pans clattered as he passed the kitchen to reach the staircase at the back of the building. Filtered noise followed him up the stairs. The sound ceased the moment the door closed behind him. His ears popped with the pressure change. Designed for absolute privacy, the sparsely furnished room provided what he lacked at the complex – security. As one of the few remaining sanctuaries in the city for the Drakkon and believers, the Wyvern served well in its capacity as keeper of confidences. The kin could gather, hidden in plain sight as the non-kin patrons sought to escape from their lives and duties.

Jaczon shrugged out of the oversized smock and flung it onto the nearest chair. Pulling off his gloves, he dropped them on the table. The intricate copper and gold mating mark wove around his left wrist ending in a band around the base of the middle finger revealed his greatest secret: he was Drakkon.

Unbuttoning his uniform, he slipped the packet out of the inner pocket and laid it on the table. Releasing the flap of the small pouch attached to his belt, Jaczon pulled out a pair of transparent rubber gloves. The chair scraped against the floor as he settled into place at the table. Jaczon examined the plain manila envelope. With his hands protected, he peeled open the flap and pulled out a sheave of papers. Whisper thin, the paper would melt into dust with a simple exhalation. Jaczon held evidence that damned Anakarei in a series of confidential communications. The Chancellor had a Sensitive powerful enough to manipulate Node energy. The Drakkon had done everything possible to protect the Sensitives left among them. The Chancellor's tool had to be a lost Sensitive. Jaczon sent a prayer for mercy.

Jaczon read the last memo and laid it on the table. He swore virulently and creatively. Even though Talek had skewed the test results, there was enough true data that the Chancellor was going to be able to open the Node. A knock on the door startled him. Stepping around the table, he peered through the peephole. The Tmavě Jeden mouthed, "Open the door!"

The door made a popping sound as it opened, the pressure in the room changing slightly as the seal was broken. Jaczon stood back as the Tmavě Jeden strode into the room. "We've got problems."

"Yes, we do." Jaczon gestured to the memos on the table. "Project Grey is a mirror project to Talek's. What did you have to do to get the information?"

The Tmavě Jeden stared Jaczon dead in the eye. "Do you want to know?"

"I think I need to know this time. We're going to have to run interference."

"The collateral damage wasn't too bad." The Tmavě Jeden nodded. "There will be people who might lose their jobs for losing confidential files and memos, but no one can put me in the vicinity." The Tmavě Jeden gave Jaczon a grim expression. "No bodies this time."

"Bodies will be the least of our worries." Jaczon pinched the bridge of his nose. "They've got a Sensitive. After all the readings from Talek's experiments, they'll be able to extrapolate and manipulate the Node. We have no way to warn him."

"I'll use my sources to warn the Drakkon in the city." The Tmavě Jeden closed his eyes in an effort to formulate a plan. "They've already felt the Node open once. Twice, they'll give themselves away."

Jaczon traced the pattern on his left hand. "I need you…"

"You don't have to ask. I stopped here on my way out of the city. I'll shift out of sentry range, I'll make better time." The Tmavě Jeden held out his hand in solidarity. "The Socra will be sad that you aren't the bearer of news. Your absence at the farm has been too long."

"We both have our roles, no matter how difficult." Jaczon gripped the Tmavě Jeden's hand hard, "Tell her…"

"Another thing you don't have to ask." He gestured to the papers. "Do I need to take these with me?"

Jaczon had seen all he needed to, committing to memory names, dates, and information. "Yes, she'll want to see for herself."

The Tmavě Jeden placed the information in a pouch that hung around his neck by a lanyard. When he shifted, it would accommodate his transformation. His onyx colored eyes met Jaczon's gold.

"May the wind be swift and the skies bright in your journey."

"Fly high, fly swift, my son." Jaczon gave the traditional reply, the unvoiced emotions weighting each word.

The door closed firmly behind the Tmavě Jeden.

The sun melted into the horizon when the Tmavě Jeden arrived at the edge of the patrolled land outside of the city. The distant lights of the city glowed along the horizon, obscuring the rise of the moons. He stripped himself bare and stuffed the trappings of his humanity in a specially constructed pack. Dark lightning glittered in the moments as he shifted between man and Drakkon. He leapt into the shadowy sky, embracing his Drakkon-self with joy.

The speeding wind caressed his obsidian scales, bathing him in ecstasy. By the time he reached the farmlands, the lover moon had joined its intended above the horizon, pursuing their nightly courtship. Their light danced across his body as he soared through the sky. The freedom an intoxicating elixir.

The rapturous flight felt cut short by the lights of the Socra's farmhouse. Flight was a freedom he seldom enjoyed. He landed with the grace of a feather and donned the accouterments of his human self, his Drakkon-self shimmering under the surface. With soft footsteps, he walked across the compound yard. The familiar sounds of birds shifting in their house and cows lowing in their pens gave him a small sense of comfort. The only resistance he encountered was the pet wolf Callem had tamed as a pup. Hackles raised, teeth bared, it stood braced to attack when the kitchen door opened.

"I see Callem has yet to teach the beastie any manners," the Tmavě Jeden said to the woman silhouetted by the light spilling out from the room behind her.

The Socra hissed a command to the wolf. The beast relaxed his stance, allowing the Tmavě Jeden to pass by with a warning snarl.

"If you came round more often, he'd recognize you. You'd not have to go through this every time."

"If I came around more often, our people would be mind-stripped and drooling." The Tmavě Jeden brushed a kiss on the Socra's cheek as he stepped into the kitchen.

The Socra didn't bother with a rebuttal. "Did Talek pass through?"

"As far as we know." He faced the woman who'd given him life and purpose. "But we have larger problems. The Chancellor has a Sensitive who can open the Node."

The Socra fell against the doorframe. The Tmavě Jeden moved toward her to assist, but she waved aside his help and closed her eyes, concentrating on metering her breathing.

"I don't know who he could have from the old days." She straightened up and made her way to the kitchen table. The Tmavě Jeden leapt forward to pull out a chair for her to sit. She sat and placed her hands on the table, a fine tremor betrayed her fear. "No one I know could have survived the wipe."

She met the obsidian gaze across from her. "Could it have been someone the hunters found?"

"No."

"Are you sure?"

"I'd have known if any of my hunters had captured a strong Sensitive. If powerful enough, I'd have killed them or smuggled them out of the city to you."

The Socra reached across the table with her copper and gold inscrolled palm facing up. "I'm sorry. Your duty is not in question. I'm worried. Forgive an old woman."

The Tmavě Jeden gently patted the hand that held his. His sins committed for the benefit of his people weighed on him heavily. The comfort offered weakened the barriers he couldn't afford to have breached. He tenderly disengaged their hands.

"I am what I am because of you and Jaczon." The Socra flinched. He shook his head. "Shadows exist. Someone has to walk in them. I can. I know that when I choose to step out into the light, I'll be able to."

The Socra brushed the hair back from her son's forehead. "The light will always welcome you." Then stroked his cheek. "The effect of the Node is going to be a shock to the Kin in the city. We'll have to find a way to evacuate them."

"I know. Jaczon is working on the plan. You and the Jespreyck's won't be able to stay here."

The Socra gazed around the kitchen, soaking in the memories.

"This place has been a good place to raise my boys." Her gaze fell softly on the man across from her. "All of them."

The Tmavě Jeden smiled fondly at the woman in front of him. "A wise woman taught a young boy, a place is just a place. Memories stay with us-always."

"Ever my smart son." She embraced the Tmavě Jeden. "Fly high and safe."

The Tmavě Jeden relished the embrace. Memories of a more innocent time in his life caused his eyes to burn with the unfamiliar sensation of tears.

"We'll send who we can to the gathering place. I have to keep the hunters busy chasing ghosts."

"We'll be ready. Send them as soon as you can."

"Bright skies, mother."

The Socra echoed her son's farewell as he disappeared into the night. She sent prayers for his safe journey back to the city.

Callem stepped out of the shadowed hallway that entered the kitchen. "Did Talek make it through the node?"

The Socra jumped. "Callem, I didn't think you'd be up."

"Certain energies disturb the animals." Callem stood next the woman who'd raised him. "I knew he would not come out to the farm unless it was important."

The Socra seemed to collapse in on herself, showing her age for the first time in Callem's memory. "As far as anyone knows, Talek was successful." Worries creased her brow. "But the Chancellor has a Sensitive that can manipulate node energy."

"Crazck!" Years of habit had Callem apologizing to the Socra for his profanity.

"This time, my boy, I'm in complete agreement." The Socra sighed heavily. "It's time to evacuate. Jaczon will send out as many city-folk as possible before they close the gates."

"I'll wake Ane up."

"No, let her sleep." The Socra extinguished the lights in the kitchen leaving only faint squares of moonlight falling through the windowpanes. "One of us should get a decent night sleep."

Callem's footsteps faded as he strode down the hallway. With a heavy sigh, the Socra sat in the dark waiting for the dawn.

Dawn glimmered on the horizon as the Tmavě Jeden entered the city. The streets were full of the normal pedestrian traffic. Familiar faces were scattered through the exiting crowd. He knew that Jaczon had been busy distributing exit papers to all the Drakkon he could. The shifters had to evacuate, no matter the age. The fluctuating Node energy was hard on those hiding their dual nature.

The Tmavě Jeden made his way to the Wyvern, using his key on the front door. The main room of the taproom was quiet. The usual chaotic energy was dormant, waiting for the first customer of the day. He slipped past the bar to the back as he headed to his rooms above the bar.

"Petroj."

The Tmavě Jeden stiffened at the use of his name. Very few people knew it, much less used it. Turning, he saw the tavern owner's wife, Katja, and gave her a swift bow.

"Bright morning, mistress."

"Is it true? The Drakkon are evacuating?"

"Aye, the Node is active again." This woman, her husband, and their two children were his family away from home. He had done what he could to protect them.

Her hands clutched her apron, her eyes filling with tears. "The children have to go."

"I didn't think anyone shifted in your family." The Tmavě Jeden saw agony in her eyes and understood. "The twins just reached puberty. They became Drakkon?" She nodded wildly as tears ran silently down her flushed cheeks. "Keep them out of school and indoors. I'll get them out somehow."

"I didn't know what to do." Katja began to tremble. "It all happened so suddenly."

He gave her a stern shake. "Keep about your normal day. You have too many customers who would turn you in."

Katja did her best to contain her emotions as she nodded. "Gram will keep the boys indoors."

"It'll be a rough couple of weeks until they get stable." He knew he would get no rest this day. "I'll be back to you as soon as I can."

A series of convoluted maintenance tunnels brought the Tmavě Jeden to the section of the complex he worked. Taking precious time, he checked on his charges. Alcoves lined the wall, with the exception of the few on patrol, each held a masked, black-clad hunter in sleep mode. With his flying gear hidden in the tunnels, he changed into a clean uniform. The matte black material let him blend in with the perpetual shadows of the complex. He used the shadows to his advantage as he made his way to Jaczon's office.

When he arrived at the reception area, the adjunct rose from his desk, standing in front of the door.

"The Colonel isn't in. He is in a meeting."

"That's fine. I'll wait for him in the office." The Tmavě Jeden arched an eyebrow at the adjunct's reticence.

"I'm sorry, sir. I can't let you."

He gave the adjunct a look that would curdle a lesser man. "Fine." He sat down in front of the man. "I'll wait with you." He relaxed into a chair directly across from the desk. Eyes narrowed, he watched the frenetic, repetitive movements of the man whose usually calm demeanor made him a valuable asset in Jaczon's office. Flushed cheeks and feverish eyes gave away the man's involuntary change of loyalty. He was under the influence of the Chancellor's drug of choice - praxitrol.

Jaczon strode into the antechamber, dumping a pile of notes on the adjunct's desk. He stopped at the sight of the Tmavě Jeden.

"Why are you here?"

"I requested the files from your office days ago."

He gestured for the Tmavě Jeden to follow him. "I have the information you need."

Jaczon grimaced as the door closed. The adjunct had been free of the corrupting influence of praxitrol when he'd left for the morning meetings. His office was no longer a secure environment.

The Tmavě Jeden quickly wrote down, "4 passes out of the city."

Reading the note, Jaczon shook his head. "Here are the files." He scratched out a reply, "no more."

"2 new Drakkon." The Tmavě Jeden underscored the next word. "Puberty."

"Czazck!" he whispered. "I'll have the paperwork by sundown."

The Tmavě Jeden nodded as he left the office. The adjunct's eyes tracked him to the door where he paused and sent the man a chilling smile.

He slammed the door as he entered the barracks. Tendrils of dark lightning crackled around him giving him an eerie glow. The hunters not out on the sweep all stood in their respective alcoves waiting for activation, dormant until the next hunt. Clothed in body armor, face shields distorted their features making their eyes dilated and soulless.

At the back of the great room, a door opened. The three hunters sent out earlier on a sweep came in on a 'V' formation. The front hunter veered to the Tmavě Jeden, while the other two went directly to their alcoves.

The Tmavě Jeden hated this part. He picked up a cable with a plug at its end and moved to the back of the hunter. At the base of the skull was a plug with seven pins. Aligning the cable in his hand, he completed the connection. The hunter jerked in her seat, emitting a small squeal. The Tmavě Jeden had no way to prevent the pain.

A monitor on the table flickered to life, and the digital recorder to the side started downloading the hunt. The sole purpose was to find any Drakkon or node-sensitive citizen, apprehend the individual or individuals, and then bring them to the Complex for processing. The Tmavě Jeden forced himself to watch every hunt, his penance for his dark deeds.

This particular one had little to offer. He unplugged the hunter, sending her back to her alcove to recharge and rest. Pressing the appropriate buttons on the recorder, he sent the hunt to the central archives.

A sharp staccato bang sounded through the barracks. Very few people ventured into his part of the complex. The Tmavě Jeden opened the door to reveal a group of fifteen armed men. The leader's hand hung in the air mid-strike.

"You have been summoned to The Chancellor's office."

The Tmavě Jeden stared at the group and tilted his head as if examining a repugnant curiosity. Despite the advantage of numbers, the group shifted nervously under the scrutiny of the Chancellor's most feared weapon. "I understand the summons part. Is there a doubt I would comply?"

"We were sent to ensure your compliance."

"Gentlemen, I would never refuse an invitation from our illustrious Chancellor." The Tmavě Jeden stepped through the human barrier and strode down the corridor. He called over his shoulder. "After all, I am his loyal Tmavě Jeden."

With the men trailing after him, he reached the research zone. The node pulsed in the middle of the workspace. The light from the event horizon cast multi-layered shadows against the walls. The equipment had been damaged, the walls scorched. A large pit cleared the middle of the room.

A man of unremarkable features paced around the perimeter of the room.

"There you are!"

As he approached the Chancellor, the Tmavě Jeden kept the sneer that threatened his features leashed. Energy danced across his nerve endings, threatening to unmask his deepest secret. He summoned every bit of control he could as he faced the man whose secret he knew. He glanced at the men who flanked him.

"Your request seemed urgent."

"Nonsense!" The gleam in the Chancellor's eyes belied the jocularity of his tone. "I wanted to know how the hunters were doing. Any new acquisitions to report?"

The Tmavě Jeden replied with blank features. "No sir, the hunters have brought back nothing."

The Chancellor snapped his fingers, and a soldier brought a chair to him.

"I'm disappointed."

"Disappointed, sir?"

"We need new blood in the hunter ranks." As he sat, the Chancellor began to slap his gloves lightly against his thigh. "The current ones have grown weak and feeble. Find new, and dispose of the Old Ones."

"Sir..." A blow from behind forced the Tmavě Jeden to his knees and a firm grip kept him immobile.

"Don't!" The Chancellor shed his relaxed pose. The power he hid oozed through his jovial façade. "I know there are Drakkon in this city." He surged to his feet and started to pace, the gloves continuing to snap against his thigh. "I feel their malformed presence."

The Chancellor turned sharply and swung at the Tmavě Jeden's face, striking him across the cheek. The blade sewn into the seam of the leather gloves sliced his face. A predator pretending to be prey, The Tmavě Jeden's obsidian eyes never left the Chancellor's face. He watched the Chancellor carefully during his rant and watched the man's eyes shimmer in a prelude to a change.

With a carefully controlled shake of his shoulders, the Tmavě Jeden freed himself from the soldier's grip and rose to his feet. He let the Chancellor see the pending threat flash in his gaze for a brief moment, then lied with conviction. "My hunters have missed nothing. After all, they are the very thing you hate – Drakkon stripped of their essence." He wiped the blood oozing from his face with his thumb and licked it clean with a feral grin. "The city is clean. Just the way you like it."

The Chancellor's gaze narrowed. "You are lying. My skin crawls from their presence. I want the vermin exterminated and expunged from this world." He stalked away from the Tmavě Jeden, "The Node opened briefly today, and we lost one of the scientists." The Chancellor turned back to the Tmavě Jeden. "I don't think he was a scientist at all. He was a Drakkon."

The Tmavě Jeden raised his eyebrow.

"I thought your screening methods for employment made sure you had none of that filthy element contaminating your work."

Veins throbbed in the Chancellor's forehead. He knew he had already over played his hand. "I had a Drakkon working on a top-secret project here in the complex!" The Chancellor stomped his booted foot. "Here!"

"You have my hunters combing the city night and day for any Drakkon," the Tmavě Jeden coolly stated. "I don't have the resources to search a place where you have supposedly screened for the unwanted." The Chancellor returned to stand in front of the Tmavě Jeden. "I want you to re-arrange the hunter schedule to have the complex swept weekly."

The Tmavě Jeden inclined his head, indicating his agreement. "I'll need access to the entire complex."

"Fine." The Chancellor carelessly waved his hand. "All sections are yours to inspect. One of my guardsmen will escort you."

"Of course," The Tmavě Jeden bowed. "If that will be all, I must see to the new orders." He turned to leave.

"One more thing." The Chancellor gestured toward the pulsating Node. "The Drakkon scientist will be hunted down and destroyed when I reopen the node."

The Tmavě Jeden faced the Chancellor again, playing ignorant. "You can now open the Node?"

"I have my own pet Sensitive, a remnant from the old days." Four guards brought a cloaked figure to him. The Chancellor threw back the hood of the cloak, revealing a gaunt dead-eyed man.

The Tmavě Jeden controlled his flinch, the lost Hereditary High Priest of the Drakkon, Ethias Hixson, stood before him. He'd been one of the last to escape through the node before it was closed. The man shouldn't have been in their world. "You say this man can control the Node?"

"Control it and give me access to the Otherverse."

The Tmavě Jeden stared at the shell of Ethias Hixson, searching for any spark of the man he had been. The vacant eyes were devoid of animation. The Chancellor's gloating rubbed the Tmavě Jeden's soul raw. "Gain access to the Otherverse? For what purpose?"

"Get me my chattel."

"I will do what I can."

The Chancellor turned to survey the pulsing light of the Node. "Do it," he snarled. "We will begin tomorrow."

Not giving the Chancellor an opportunity to pull him back, the Tmavě Jeden left the area. The empty eyes of Ethias

Hixson strengthened his resolve to keep the Chancellor's plans from finding fruition.

Eluding his escorts in the labyrinth of tunnels under the complex, the Tmavě Jeden returned to the barracks to account for all the hunters. He would have to find a way to get them out of the city.

He slipped into the shielded room at the Wyvern. He sat, closed his eyes, and slipped into a meditative trance as he waited for Jaczon to arrive at the normal rendezvous time.

The air changed as the tight seal of the door broke when it opened. The Tmavě Jeden's eyes opened as Jaczon entered. He sat across the table from him after he closed the door.

"I got the family passes out of the city."

The Tmavě Jeden's hands, lying flat on the table in front of him, tensed then relaxed. "Good." He watched Jaczon carefully. "Do you know what happened to Ethias Hixson?"

"Ethias Hixson?" Jaczon tilted his head in puzzlement. "I haven't heard that name in years. He got out with the first wave of evacuees before the node closed."

"Are you sure?"

"Yes, I saw him through the node myself," Jaczon said unequivocally. "He took with him the most sacred relics of our kind in order to hide them from the Chancellor."

"Project Grey is real. The Chancellor spent an hour gloating in my presence then demanding that my hunters find more Drakkon to feed his project."

"What does this have to do with Ethias?"

"He is the pet Sensitive the Chancellor is using to control the Node. The man is nothing but a husk." The Tmavě Jeden watched Jaczon pale. "They are planning on launching an assault as soon as possible."

"We've got to stop this…"

"No!" The Tmavě Jeden interrupted. "We evacuate every Drakkon we can and abandon the city for the sanctuary."

"Our positions will have been exposed." Jaczon stopped. "With Ethias as the Sensitive, we've already been compromised."

The Tmavě Jeden nodded. "We can assume no less. I have to see to my hunters."

"What will you do with them?"

"If I can get them out of the city, I will." The alternative was left unspoken. The Tmavě Jeden was already formulating plans.

"They are transmitters for the Chancellor." Jaczon stated the obvious.

"No, they're not."

The Tmavě Jeden's expression unnerved Jaczon, "What have you done?"

"I know the secret to the Chancellor's unholy brew, Praxitrol. The hunters are loyal to me." He sneered as he leaned back in the chair. "I marked every loyal member of the Chancellor's Council and their families as Drakkon. The hunters will be busy tonight."

"This will be a bloodbath. What about Errol and his family?" Jaczon sat back shaking his head.

"I've contacted Pacol. He takes care of his own."

The two men made plans to finish the evacuations for that night. Time was limited. Fortunately, the actual number of Drakkon in the city was far fewer than in the past. Jaczon had transport waiting beyond the city limits for the refugees.

Before the Tmavě Jeden left, he stopped by the taproom and pulled aside Andros, the owner.

"Take only what you can carry. Your boys need you more than this city."

With shaking hands, Andros took the papers handed to him. They clasped forearms. "We'll leave tonight."

The Tmavě Jeden entered his barracks for the last time. All the hunters were accounted for and in their alcoves. One by one, he packed them into their sensory deprivation compartments. Safely ensconced on a vehicle headed for the Sanctuary, the hunters would be safe under Jaczon's watch. The Tmavě Jeden's sole purpose was to disrupt the day's activities.

When he opened the door that lead to the complex, he found armed guards standing at attention. Expecting no less, he strode past them to the Chancellor's offices. He presented himself to the adjunct in the reception area, standing at attention. The door opened in short order.

The Tmavě Jeden entered the Chancellor's office ready to start the most important game of his life.

"Tell me, dark one, if you were to find a traitor in you midst, what would you do?"

The Tmavě Jeden didn't hesitate. "I'd kill him."

SIX

"Who is Mellanei specifically?" Ella didn't care if Nathan or Talek answered the question, but she felt she needed more information. "What did she do?"

"Before she escaped through the portal," Talek explained, "she was one of the last Socra's who could accurately manipulate node energy. Compared to the lineage of the High Socra, it was nominal but enough to get her through to escape the Anakarei."

"You said the node had been nulled," Ella continued. "What caused the node to fail?"

"The last remaining Socri choked the node into dormancy." Talek rubbed the back of his neck in an effort to release some of his tension. "Chosen to warn the otherverse, Mellanei passed through the node, and the others overloaded the vortex."

Ella asked Nathan, "The nodes can be shorted out?"

"That would be an apt description. Picture the energy expended for Talek's journey here and multiply it by a thousand-fold." Nathan got up from his seat and went to lean against the office door. The light from the hallway created an aura around him. "Each node is a convergence of power that can create or destroy. Controlled, people of all races can travel throughout the otherverse."

Talek walked over to the image of the Otherversal network of energy lines still shimmering in the middle of the room. Waving his hand, Drakkonon filled the space.

"Our Node was particularly strong. Even the non-sensitive could see the energies. The lights danced in the skies." Talek smiled briefly at the memory. It faded swiftly under the weight of the rest. He sat on the corner of the desk with his arms held tight across his chest.

"After the explosion that wiped out the entire complex and destroyed the Node, the area was abandoned for the next hundred years. The devastation was both physical and meta-physical." Talek stared at the image in the center of the room, "Eventually, the Node energy fell back into familiar ley lines and began to pool back into the Node."

Fear filled Ella's gaze as she added what she knew. "The Anakarei built a complex around the site in order to monitor the dormant Node. They hunted down everyone they thought was involved with the revolt and executed them and their families. Whole bloodlines where lost."

Talek was shocked. "How do you know this?"

"Not all the memories in my head are old." Ella blinked as she tried to control the information. "I feel a connection – a data feed." Old and new information swirled around her head like the bits of white in a snow globe. "Not all major Nodes were destroyed. Drakkonon has one other Node on the other side of the world that was forgotten by time and history."

"That is just myth." Talek stopped his pacing in front of Ella. "A pretty tale told children to give them hope for a better future."

Ella stood up and stood in front of Talek. "You only know that Drakkon came in gold, silver, and bronze, but at one time we flew the skies of Drakkonon in all colors of precious jewels and metals." She smiled up at Talek. "Am I not proof enough?"

"My grandmother never spoke of Drakkon history."

"When Drakkonon traded freely throughout the otherverse, colonies of Drakkon's were established off world." Ella searched through the information in her head. "When Mellanei went through the node, her intention must have been to establish contact and warn them."

"The Anakarei became aware that the Node was reviving and started running scientific experiments on it." Talek's voice filled with tension as he recounted recent history. "The faithful were aware of the Node's reawakening, so we made plans. By the time the Anakarei had built their complex, they had started sweeping the population for anyone with any modicum of Sensitivity. People would disappear in the middle of the night, never to be heard of again."

"Nobody did anything about this?" Ella asked.

"Nothing could be done. Protesters were killed." Talek stated. "My brother got a permit to work in agriculture outside the city where the acting Socra lives and I worked in the city that had grown up around the Node site. My abilities were heavily shielded and undetectable." Talek picked up the pen from the desk and fidgeted with the cap. "I finally obtained a position on the Node research team. I used my nature to activate and manipulate the Node to my own ends, making the research team think that their science had successfully found a way to manipulate the Node."

Nathan nodded his approval at Talek. "You distorted all their data."

Talek met Nathan's direct gaze. "Yes, unless they have a Sensitive who is as powerful as I am, they won't be able to open the Node."

“Are you sure they don’t have another Sensitive?” Ella asked.

“I can’t be positive, but I’m nearly certain.”

Ella’s gut clenched in anxiety. “Talek, what if they were using you? What if they knew what you were?”

“There was no way for them to know.” He put the pen back down on the desk. “I was shielded. The hunters wouldn’t have been able to detect me.”

“Nothing is infallible.” Ella said in a gentle voice.

“We’d know if there were other Sensitives.” Alarm swept over Talek’s face. “We knew the surviving families and hid them.”

Nathan continued, “The Otherverse has a way of compensating for lost resources. If the normal balance was artificially disrupted, more Sensitives could have come into existence, starting new bloodlines.”

Talek paled. “I don’t know…”

The jangle of a dog collar announced the arrival of Ronan and Kaie. Kaie wound herself around Nathan’s legs before she placed herself on the empty corner of Annisa’s desk. Ronan found Ella’s side with a moist nose in her hand. Ella reached down to scratch his ears. Kaie held Ella’s necklace dangling from her mouth. Ella held out her hand, Kaie gave up her prize.

Talek fell to his knees when he saw the pendant. “You hold the pendant of a High Socra of Drakkon. How?” he stuttered.

Ella held the pendant her father had given her as a child. “It’s one of the few things I have of my father’s.” Rubbing it between her fingers, the fine detail work of the scales caught on her fingertips. “He deserted us when I was a child,” she continued. Her hand closed tightly around the pendant, its edges cutting painfully into her palm. “He said that this was the only piece of his family he had and that everything depended on him keeping it safe. That was the day he disappeared.”

The wall clocked chimed five times. By Ella’s estimation, a year should have passed not a mere eight hours since the beginning of this odyssey.

“Look, we have a lot to figure out, but I have responsibilities at home.” The potential drama waiting made Ella queasy. “I have to get Ronan home and figure out more about my father’s family.”

Nathan wanted to continue their conversation, but he could see the exhaustion weighing on everyone in the room. “Ella, you’re right. We need to rest.”

Talek started to protest.

“I’m locking down the node. There shouldn’t be any surprises,” Nathan reassured Talek. “You’ll be safe. We are all exhausted, and we need to regroup.”

Ella gave an inelegant snort. “Yesterday I was wondering why the universe was crapping all over me. Today, I find out that we are a merry band of saviors working to save the Otherverse and defeat the bad guys. My only question is…”

Nathan quirked an eyebrow.

“Does your health insurance cover all this?”

With her dog sitting confidently in the passenger seat of her Camry, Ella allowed the car ride to relax her. Ronan’s company always helped her relax. When she parked the car in the driveway, she pulled out the Italian takeout bag from the back seat. Ronan’s tail beat a happy rhythm against the upholstery. His attention focused on the take out bag, he gave a hopeful whine.

"Nope buddy, no Italian for you."

Ella counted getting the dog and the food into the house without mishap as a success. She waited for her mother to make her normal appearance.

Nothing.

No demands for details on her day, no accusations for being an inconsiderate daughter – just nothing. As she checked the house, Ella's heart raced with anxiety. The living room was empty, as was the family room. Slowly, she approached the closed door of the master bedroom and turned the handle with trepidation. She opened the door slowly to find her mother sitting in the dark.

"Mother?" Ella didn't want to startle her, "are you alright?"

"Oh, is it that time already?" Myrna reached up and wiped her hands across her face. Her voice muffled. "I didn't hear you come in."

Myrna rarely showed any emotion other than irritation and anger towards the world. The hallway light illuminated the room as Ella approached the wheelchair and knelt. "Mother-Mom, what's wrong?"

"Ella, I know that I'm always complaining about that dog." Tears welled up in Myrna's eyes and trickled down her cheek. "But I don't really mean it."

Ronan chose that moment to trot into the room. Myrna gasped.

"You stupid, stupid dog! Where have you been?" She slid from the chair and to the floor and hugged the dog.

"I let him out into the back yard late this morning, like I always do, and he disappeared." Myrna's words muffled as she clung to Ronan. "I looked everywhere, called for him, but

I couldn't find him." Her voice cracked with relief as she asked, "I didn't know how to tell you. Where was he?"

"Today was a really strange day. I was upstairs working on something, and Ronan came up the House stairs with Nathan's cat like he owned the place." Ella explained as she sat on the floor next to her mother. "That was this afternoon. I kept him corralled up there while I finished and then came home."

Myrna got back into her chair and shook her finger at Ronan. "You are in trouble!" Ronan made his patented pathetic face.

Ella got to her feet. "I'm sorry that Ronan worried you today. I'll figure out how he got out and see how I can fix it."

"I know he's just a dumb dog, but I like the company." Ella stepped back to let Myrna wheel herself out of the room. "I smell Italian."

"I stopped by PJ's for dinner." She unpacked the bag, putting dinner on the table with Ronan dancing at her feet, attending to her every move.

Myrna rolled into the kitchen and carefully got up to set the table. Ella was surprised and pleased at the gesture.

Dinnerware clinked as they ate in silence while Ella figured out a way to talk to her mother about her father. The topic had been taboo for so long. She didn't want to disrupt the fragile truce between them. Her hand reached up and stroked the pendant on her shirt.

Myrna noticed Ella's hand stroking the dragon necklace she always wore. She had always hated the damn thing. It was one of the few things of her father, and Myrna couldn't bring herself to forbid Ella from wearing it. There was something different about Ella. Last night she'd been frazzled and worn. Tonight, she exuded strength and vibrancy from within she'd never had before. Myrna didn't know what to make of it.

"You said that your day was crazy. Is that good for a first day?"

"The job is more than I expected, much, much more." She tore apart her garlic bread. "It has a lot of components that I need to learn, but it'll never be boring. I'm going to learn a lot about myself."

Myrna sensed there was more. "You've always done well in a challenge." She watched her daughter fiddle with the necklace. "Like that dragon you're always wearing, you are tough and flexible."

Blue-green eyes met worn blue ones.

"Mother," Ella reconsidered her address of her mother. It was time to work on bettering things. "Mom, I need to ask you some things about Daddy."

Myrna stiffened in her chair. Ronan got up sensing the tension in the air and laid his head in Myrna's lap. "Why?" she snapped before her new resolve could assert itself. "He left us and never looked back." Myrna's knuckles were white as they clenched in her lap.

"Mother…"

"Sorry." Myrna exhaled in order to release her anger. She knew things had to change. Being bitchy wasn't going to improve the situation. "I've been so mad at him for so long." She pushed her plate back on the table and stroked Ronan's head. "I loved your father so much. He was magic."

Ella leaned forward. "Mom, I remember before he left, we were happy." The memories that rose to the surface of her memories left her longing for the days long gone. "It was magic. I need to know more about him and his family."

Myrna chewed on her lower lip. "Why?" Fear laced her voice. "Have you heard from him?"

"No," Ella reassured her mother. "That's not it. But I may have run into someone who knew of him."

"He always said he was an orphan, with no family." Myrna squinted at the table in an effort to remember anything. "He always carried with him a book that he said carried his family legacy. That was the only secret he ever kept from me. He made me promise never to look at it."

"Book?" A frisson of excitement danced across Ella's senses. "Do you know what happened to it?"

"I put it in the box with everything else when he left. I kept my word. When I knew he wasn't coming back, I didn't want it."

"Mom, this is important. Where is that box?" Ella was frightened that Myrna may have destroyed her father's things in anger. "What did you do with the box and book?"

Myrna knew that she had to be honest. "It's in the storage unit on Sky Drive." She gazed directly at her daughter. "As angry as I was… am, but I couldn't destroy his legacy."

"When were you ever going to give it to me?"

"Until recently? When I died." Myrna gave a hoarse laugh, "I'm finding that change is good for the soul. Painful, but good."

Ella had no idea what was in the box, much less if it was important. "Let's go together in the morning and get the box. Okay?"

Myrna knew that this was a concession on Ella's part. "I'd like that. What about your job? Don't you have to be in the store in the morning?"

"I have the late shift tomorrow." Ella wasn't ready to tell her mother everything about the store and what she'd learned about her father. "I'll have time to go by the storage unit in the morning."

Together they cleaned up the kitchen and had a quiet evening. Bidding her mother good night, Ella headed up to her room. Ronan followed her up the stairs as he did every night, settling himself on the foot of her bed.

She always had a lot floating around in her mind, but the sea of her memories, mixed with the new knowledge, boiled in a terrible storm. Meditating wasn't helping.

Ella focused on her memories of her father, particularly that last day. She might not be able to achieve peace, but at least she'd be able to direct her subconscious to the information she needed. She sank into a twitchy sleep.

"Ella!" called her father. "Let's go get some ice cream."

Ella came running as fast as her ten-year old legs would take her. Going anywhere with her daddy was always an adventure. "Coming, Daddy!"

"Ethias, don't you spoil her dinner or yours," Myrna called. "I'm making chicken and dumplings."

Ella jumped up and down in her favorite flowered sneakers. She couldn't believe it, "Chicken and dumplings, Daddy! We must have been really good today."

"You are always good, my little dragon." He ruffled her hair. "And your mother knows it."

Ethias asked Myrna. "Do you want me to bring you your usual?"

A soft smile answered Ethias. "Why don't you surprise me today? You and Ella pick. Just don't eat too much."

He reached over and stroked Myrna's cheek. "A surprise it is." He leaned over his bouncing daughter and kissed her.

The doorbell rang.

With a puzzled look on his face, he went to answer the door. "I'll see who it is." Ethias placed a hand on his impatient daughter's head. "Ella, we'll leave in just a minute." He left Myrna and Ella in the kitchen.

"Where's Daddy?" Ella hands patted the dough in the flour.

"He'll be back in a couple of minutes, sweetheart." She glanced down the hallway at the front door. "I can't wait to see what ice cream you pick for me."

Ella giggled as her mother swiped a flour covered finger down her cheek. "We'll pick you the best."

Her mother laughed. "I know you will." She untied the apron and laid it on the back of a kitchen chair. "We need ten more dumplings for tonight; do you think you can make them?"

"You bet, Mommy." She watched her mother walk down the hall, then went back to the business of creating the perfect dumpling. She made all ten and neither of her parents had returned. Mimicking her mother, she took off her flour-covered apron and laid it on the chair. Ella went into the living room and peered out the bay window onto the front porch.

Deep in a conversation, they didn't see Ella's face pressed against the window. Ella could barely hear them. He looked funny, his face pale and hands shaking. Her mother sat next to him with her arm around his shoulders.

"Ethias, I know something is wrong," she pleaded. "Talk to me."

"I can't." He cupped her mother's face and rested his forehead against hers. "The less you, know the better." He kissed her mother. "Let's get the dumplings finished." They stood up.

Ella scampered back to the kitchen.

"Mommy, I finished the dumplings." Ella looked at her daddy. "Are we ready to go?"

Ethias twirled his wife into the kitchen, surprising a laugh out of Myrna. “Yes, we are - my dragon.” He helped wipe off the smudges of flour and held out his hand. “Shall we?”

Ella giggled and said as regally as she could, “We shall!” Myrna laughed as she waved them on.

Father and daughter walked together into the sunshine. Ethias told Ella fantastical stories of dragons and worlds of wonder.

Ella loved her father’s stories.

“Daddy, you tell the best stories.”

“Ella, my little dragon, what would you say if I told you the stories were real, and dragons did exist, and there were worlds without number beyond our Earth?”

Ella’s face scrunched up in concentration. She walked hand in hand with her father for a little while. “I’d say that the Universe was an amazing place.”

Ethias laughed at his daughter’s words. Ethias scooped Ella up and he swung her around and around. Ella shrieked in laughter. “You say the wisest things, daughter of mine.” He snuggled her close to his heart and held her.

Ella returned the embrace. She loved to cuddle with her father. He always made her feel safe. But then she felt sleepy. Her eyes drooped while her mind filled with the most amazing things and then scary things. Ella started to struggle in her father’s arms.

He kept a firm grip on his daughter as he finished what he had to do. Ella was the keeper of knowledge and lore, by birthright and now desperation.

He worried that she was so young, but he had no choice. The stress he was putting on her young mind was immense. Finishing his task, he carefully placed all the new knowledge behind a mind lock. The legacy and curse he left his daughter was the knowledge of his people. He locked it tight in her mind in a vault that couldn't be breached without the correct knowledge and authority.

Ella woke up in her father's arms as they approached the ice cream place. It was crowded and noisy. By the time they got to the front of the line, she didn't remember much about the walk to the stand or the dreams of dragons flying in periwinkle skies.

They walked home together with ice cream dripping and silly stories floating between the two of them. They grinned as they arrived home to the mouth-watering fragrance of chicken and dumplings. Dessert should always come before dinner.

Ella shifted restlessly in her bed. She didn't want that dream to end – the day of endless sunshine, melting ice cream, and laughter. The reoccurring dream was a mixture of her memories from the point of view of a child and adult. Now her father's memories were included.

Ella had a moment of perfect clarity; she knew what had happened to her father. A Drakkon had found her father that last perfect day. They had warned him of an assassin. He had left to protect his family.

Tears flowed down her cheeks, the knowledge cold comfort. She would have given anything to have more time with her father and her smiling mother. Ronan moved to her side, trying to comfort his mistress the best way he could. She embraced him, grateful for his warmth. Finally, the dark tide of exhaustion claimed her and dragged her under into the dreamless depths of slumber.

The sharp bounce of paws landing on her sternum forced Ella to curl into a reflexive ball. Ella knew that the pink tongue of doom was seconds behind Ronan throwing himself on her. She gave a heartfelt groan as she opened her gummy eyes and saw sunlight shining through the curtains. She risked glancing at the bedside clock and saw it was nine in the morning. She never slept that late. No wonder Ronan took it upon himself to wake her up.

“Okay, okay.” Ella swung her feet off the bed and onto the floor. Her mind was fuzzy from the dreams and memories. Ella ran downstairs to let Ronan do his doggy duty. Exhaustion slowed down her normally speedy morning routine. She grabbed her satchel from the bedroom closet and switched out the contents of her purse into the bag. As an afterthought, she grabbed her dragon statue, wrapped it up in a soft cloth, and put it in the bag.

Ella saw that her mother was sitting motionless at the sliding glass door that led to the back yard. Ronan sat patiently on the other side of the door. Ella let Ronan back in and feed him breakfast. “Mom?” she approached the wheelchair, “Are you ready to go?”

“I can’t do this,” Myrna said. “I can’t open up all those memories again.”

Ella closed her eyes. “Mother, I need to see what Daddy left behind.” She crouched beside the wheelchair. The unforgiving lines of Myrna’s face told Ella her night had been just as difficult. “I know that this is hard, but I would like to see what is in the storage unit.”

Myrna pushed the wheelchair violently away, the arm of the chair caught Ella in the shoulder knocking her off balance. Ella barely saved herself from sprawling on the floor.

“You demand to see the remaining earthly possessions of the man who deserted us. Left us to starve!” The wheelchair whirled again, the footrest connected with Ella’s leg causing her to gasp in pain. “He left us without ever looking back!”

Ella clutched her leg knowing the bruise was going to be a spectacular specimen. She saw any headway she had made in the last couple of days in her relationship with her mother drain away in her mother's pity party. She knew that Myrna had years of unresolved anger, but she'd had enough. "Look, I know that you are angry. I get that! He walked away from me too!" She grabbed the wheelchair to prevent any more injuries. "But here's a thought: what if he had no choice?"

Myrna snorted. "Your father was a self…"

"Selfish, son of a gun, two-faced coward. Blah, blah, blah!" She moved away from her mother. "Get another tune. I need to see what is in the storage unit. You either give me the address and key, or I'll figure out another way."

"You can't get into it without me." Myrna's white-knuckle grip on the armrests of her chair broadcasted her fear and anger. "It's my property! You try, I'll have you arrested!"

"You have me arrested, and I'll have you declared incompetent!"

Myrna moved her chair forward to ram her daughter.

"Don't you dare! I'm sick of you using that damned contraption as a weapon when we both know that you don't need it."

The chair stopped inches from Ella's shins.

"You need to look at this situation with different eyes." She grabbed a kitchen chair to sit herself at Myrna's level. "Ask yourself the question, what if Daddy was forced to leave to protect us?"

"He would have told me! He would have told me something." Myrna snapped.

Ella persisted, "You said yourself that Daddy never talked about his family or where he was from. That in the beginning, the mystery was part of his charm."

Myrna's face started to lose some of the hard edges of anger and smooth out to thoughtfulness. "Why are you suddenly so interested in your father's things?" She leaned forward in her chair. "Why now?"

Ella knew she couldn't tell her mother everything. 'Hello, Mom, Daddy was a dragon. Hey, so am I!' She didn't think Myrna was up to that kind of revelation. "Someone recently approached me asking about him. It got me thinking."

"Who approached you?" Myrna demanded. "Someone we know?"

"No," Ella hedged. Myrna was not ready for any bit of the truth. "Neither one of know him. I just need to find the truth."

"The day your father disappeared, a stranger came to the door." Desperation glittered in Myrna's gaze. "I should have destroyed his belongings."

Ella kept a tight grip on her temper. "I think that I can find answers to why Daddy disappeared, but I need you to trust me."

Myrna once more stared out the window. Ella waited patiently.

The doorbell sounded, sending Ronan into a frenzy of barking. Both women started at the sound, looking at her mother, "I'll get it." Ella was grateful for the fortuitous interruption.

"Surprise!" Sindie chirped. "I'm sorry to bug you, but Nathan asked me to swing by your house on my way into work and give you this." She held out a large envelope.

"Great." Ella had no idea what Sindie was talking about. "Would you like to come in for a minute?"

Ronan struggled to sit. His tail beat a furious rhythm, making it impossible. He recognized Sindie from the day before. Apparently, they were old friends.

"Hey, Ronan!" Sindie knelt down and scratched his head. Ronan gave his patented growly purr. "You've got the best dog. Yesterday, when he walked into the store looking for you, he was very polite."

"According to Annisa, he terrorized the customers."

Sindie looped her arm around Ronan's neck. "No, Kaie opened the door for him. He had the goofiest grin and charmed everyone with his wiggly butt."

Ella grinned at her dog. "He definitely is a charmer."

The sound of wheels on the hardwood interrupted them.

"Ella, who is it?"

Ella introduced her mother to Sindie.

"It's a pleasure to meet you, Mrs. Hixson." Sindie stood up and gently grasped Myrna's hand. "You have a delightful daughter."

Myrna viewed Sindie with suspicion. She didn't like strangers coming to the house. "Thank you."

Sindie turned back to Ella. "I'll see you at the store."

"Tell Nathan I need to run a few errands this morning, and I'll be in for the late afternoon shift."

Sindie nodded and waved as she left the house.

Ella turned to her mother. "Mom, I really need to see the stuff in the storage unit. You don't have to go with me. But I have to look through it."

Myrna turned her wheelchair toward her room. "I haven't been in the unit for years." She returned with the key and an apology. "I can't remember where I put the box, but everything fit in a box. The rest of unit is old furniture and stuff."

"Mom..." Ella cleared her throat and knelt in front of Myrna's wheelchair, "thank you. I'll only take what I need, and I'll let you know what it is."

Myrna waved her daughter on as she watched Ella leave the house. Ronan sat by her chair. "I'm afraid, my boy." Myrna stroked his head absently. "I'm afraid she'll be disappointed. I'm afraid she'll find something." She sent the dog into doggy bliss as she scratched behind his ears. "Mostly I'm afraid she'll leave me."

Ella pulled up to Castle Storage at the end of Main Street. The crumbling façade had seen better days. The narrow, shadowed alleyways between the rows of storage units had always creeped Ella out.

Myrna hadn't been to the unit in years. Ella brought bolt cutters and a new lock with her. She counted the units as she drove down the alley. The entire time she felt like she was counting down the minutes to something momentous. For all she knew the box held nothing of significance, but better to be prepared than not.

On Unit 313, the first three hung upside down and swung lightly in the morning breeze. She got out of her car and paused as she worked the key into the weathered lock, struggling to turn it. The years had taken their toll on the padlock. Ella only hoped that the contents of the unit hadn't suffered similarly.

Frustrated, she went back to her car and got the bolt cutter. With an efficient snap, the lock clattered to the ground. The rolling door clattered on its upward journey, and Ella flicked the switch next to the door track. A single, hanging bulb cast jagged shadows as it illuminated the space. Ella expected to see the unit stuffed full of her childhood and her mother's life. Instead, it was surprisingly sparse. Boxes neatly lined the walls with the sides labeled. Furniture was stacked in the middle of the unit. On a table in the front sat the summation of a man's life in a medium sized box marked 'Ethias Hixson.'

Ella used her car keys to slice though the yellowed packing tape. The box held a motley collection of a man's life. Photographs of Ella as a laughing child held in her father's arms. A man and a younger version of her mother in scenes around her childhood home. The photos of her parents cradling an infant had her wiping her cheeks free of tears. A picture of Ella with her face covered in chocolate frosting had her laughing. A dog-eared copy of 'Zen and the Art of Motorcycle Repair' caused Ella to chuckle. A dragon studying the book tickled her fancy. At the bottom of the box sat a large velvet pouch. Age creased the material, the nap worn. She gently picked the pouch up, a frisson of excitement dancing down her spine. The shape revealed a weighty sphere.

Under the pouch was a large hand-bound leather book. Jewels formed deceptively simple patterns around the edge of the cover. A large buckle, in the shape of a dragon, held the book closed. Lifting it carefully, Ella set it with the velvet pouch. Her newly awakened Drakkon sensitivities assured her that the stones and precious metals that embellished the book were real. Her mother would have assumed the adornments were paste.

Ella put everything but the book and the sphere back in the box. She wanted to take it all back to the house, but she had promised Myrna she would only look and take what was pertinent to her search. She closed the box, leaving it where she found it, and closed the storage unit back up with regret.

Driving out of the complex, Ella glanced at the velvet pouch and book sitting on the passenger seat. Energy tickled her senses, causing her to shiver. Exploring the significance of the items was not something she was willing to do in the middle of Castle Storage. With her luck, a portal would open, and she didn't have the skills to handle the chaos.

Intuitively, Ella drove to the bookstore. She parked, taking the time to stuff the pouch in her purse, and clasped the book to her chest. Her life had changed so much in forty-eight hours, leaving her feeling off-kilter and skewed. As she entered the bookstore foyer, the comforting glow of the node enveloped her. Ella took her moment to bask then muttered to herself, "Moment over." She made a beeline for the back of the store, waving at Sindie.

The stairs led Ella to the guest level, the ruined wall repaired. Ella marveled at the efficiency of the House as she headed for a room with an open door farther down the hallway. She needed to be alone when she examined her finds.

A large, cushy chair sat in the corner of the room. Ella sat down and started examining the items from the storage unit. A strange, rhythmic squeaking distracted Ella. Opening the door, she found Kaie batting her paws against the wood, demanding entrance. With a regal meow, the cat stalked over to the bed, jumped up and settled next to Ella's purse.

"Okay then." Ella looked at the cat. "You're obviously here to help me."

She placed the dragon statue on the table by the chair. Ella laid the rest of the items on the small wooden table in front her. The aged velvet was silky to the touch, and the opening of the pouch closed by a complicated knot. Kaie batted at the tassels impatiently. Ella didn't want to cut the binding.

"Patience, cat!"

Kaie reached over and delicately sank her teeth into Ella's forearm.

She jerked her arm away and looked for blood, "Hey! That was uncalled for, I said patience!"

Ella met Kaie gaze directly as she tapped the cat on the nose. "You don't bite me, and I won't swat you!"

Kaie broke the eye contact and averted her gaze.

Her memories told her she had some of the most valuable artifacts to the Drakkon laying in front of her. The names of each item rose to the forefront allowing her to name each one – the Sphere of Drakkon and the Writ of Drakkon.

Before Ella could focus on the objects in front of her, the building shook. The node was active again.

Annisa threw open the door to Nathan's office, interrupting the conversation between Nathan and Talek. The loud claxon filled the space.

"We've got a problem." Ruddy cheeks and disheveled hair were out of place on her.

"How long has the alarm been sounding?" Nathan pulled her to his chair and pushed her onto the seat. "Shortly after Ella came into the store and went upstairs." Anissa tried to brush her hair into place, but her hands were trembling. "The store has been evacuated. Sindie told everyone that the store was running a systems check on its alarm system. After the last customer was evacuated, the node started going berserk."

Nathan didn't wait for anyone to follow him as he raced down the stairs.

Ella grabbed the large leather satchel that lay on her bed. When she'd been reading the Writ, it hadn't been there. The House's ability to change floor plans and, seemly, anticipate needs made Ella nervous. Without thinking, Ella slid the book and her purse into the bag and ran for the sales floor. The Node vibrations shook the building violently. Ella could only imagine what the downstairs looked like.

Chaos reigned as Ella rushed out on to sales floor. Books flew as shelves toppled like dominoes. Lightning flashed violently, leaving negative space in the after light. She navigated for the foyer where the node discharged huge amounts of energy.

When Anissa noticed Ella, she yelled over the din. "Something is trying to force the node open. Nathan isn't sure if the lock will hold."

Ella's eyes watered furiously with the bright flashing light. Searching by feel, Ella fished through the satchel for her sunglasses. The polarized lenses allowed her to see the pulsating energy patterns. Nathan and Talek stood on either side of the node, acting as grounding posts for the saber that hung over the outside door. Ella could see the saber drawing energy from the ley lines, in an effort to contain the tumult.

The energy pattern seemed to be a flexible net that seemed to concentrate where the force was the strongest. The strategy was only effective if the shield could contain the assaults. Ella could see the shielding web begin to fray. The Node was fixed only on one facet- Drakkonon.

A staging area, filled with a well-organized force, filled the facet. Slinging her bag off her shoulder, she handed it to Anissa and entered the fray. "Guard this."

"Ella! Stand back!" Nathan shouted.

Ella simply raised her hands, adding her strength to theirs. All the instructions were in her head, she just had to apply them. She went with her instincts.

"The node pulls from the ley grid, right?" she shouted at Nathan.

Nathan squinted through the bright light and nodded at Ella.

"We've got to shut this down!" Ella shouted back to Nathan. She muttered to herself, "Right now." She spread her feet shoulder width apart, centered herself, reached down and grabbed the ley energy. Ella screamed as the energy engulfed her.

Time faltered. Eternity stretched out before her, as she struggled to lock the gateway. The ley energy pulsed through her. The building shook from the power strikes around the node. A clinical detachment separated Ella from the drama, allowing her to work. She saw the other side of the conduit clearly, the fine details of the scene exposed. A cloaked figure stood at the forefront of the armed forces mirroring her stance. He was the key to closing the node.

Ella sent a pulse of power through the vortex, scattering the forces on the other side. The fierce gust pushed the cloak askew, revealing a gaunt figure. The face struck a familiar chord in Ella. She didn't have time to ponder the brief thought, as the energy flared wildly on both sides. A final push tested the limits of the House defenses. She screamed, or so she thought. Ella couldn't tell in the cacophony.

The ley energy pouring into her flooded her with molten heat, causing her body to start the transformation process into her Drakkon-self stopping mid-process. Energy filled the room and beyond. Ella fought to control the primal surge. She reinforced the failing shield, before she directed her attention to the army on the other side of the conduit. Intoxicated with the unlimited power at her disposal, Ella sent another violent pulse through the vortex. Soldiers and equipment scattered like leaves. The cloaked figure was carried away in the surge. A dark, savage part of her wanted to follow the energy and finish the job, stomping the invaders, making sure that they would never make such an arrogant gesture again. She spent critical moments rebuilding the centuries old ward on the saber as the last and easiest task. Ella didn't have time to examine all the sensory input. She was on overload. Her nerve endings were on fire. Stopping the flow of energies and returning them to their original pattern was harder.

Time resumed its normal flow as Ella tried to manage the power surging through her. She shrieked with pain and bliss. Then she knew nothing.

SEVEN

Ella surfaced through layers of murky pain. Opening her eyes, she found herself surrounded by a circle of faces – Drakkon, Brownie, and one cat. Ella closed her eyes again, and then opened them. "Nope, you all are still there," she rasped.

A wet nose touched her cheek as Kaie rubbed her head against Ella. Ella realized that she was feeling more fur than she should have and looked down at herself and saw assorted jackets covering her nudity.

"Naked again? Really?" She brought up her hands to cover the fierce blush that turned her face puce. "Why are my clothes always disappearing?"

Loaded with a pile of clothing, Annisa shooed the men away and got Sindie to help preserve Ella's modesty as she got dressed. The process was slow. Her entire body felt like she had been beaten by a thousand, spiked mallets. Dressed, Ella felt less exposed but not better.

"What did I miss?" She asked as she limped into the manager's office.

Talek vacated the chair he was sitting in and moved to lean against the wall. He was staring at Ella intently. "The Anakarei were ready to make their move. I thought we'd have more time."

"We saw organized troops; the vortex has always pummeled the travelers." Nathan asked Talek. "How did they expect to move troops and not suffer losses?"

Talek's direct stare made Ella shift uncomfortably in her seat. "What?" She demanded.

Talek ignored Nathan's question.

"How did you direct that blast through the portal?"

"I don't really know." Ella leaned forward with her elbows on her knees and her chin cradled in her hands. "All that information unlocked in my brain helped. I just let go and let my instincts take over." Ella studied the grain of the hardwood floor. "I didn't think I had anything to lose."

Absently tapping a pencil against her chin, Annisa joined the discussion. "The Drakkon might not have been able to focus that kind of energy but the higher Fae of legend were known to send blasts of ley energy through to various Underhill kingdoms when at war. The effects were devastating." Annisa frowned. "An accord was reached with all the High Fae to ban the attack."

Nathan leaned forward, watching Ella intently as he realized where Annisa was going with her history lesson. He started to get agitated.

Annisa's revelations made Ella think. "Based on what I've been told and the information unlocked in my mind, ley energy is a constant throughout the Otherverse." The room nodded in agreement. "When we were fighting to strengthen the node shield, I had the idea to ground myself and tap into the ley grid to get the boost we needed."

"Are you insane?" Nathan abruptly crossed over to Ella and pulled her up from her chair. Ella gagged at the abrupt movement.

Talek intervened. "Nathan, release Ella." Energy crackled around him as he let his own power peek through his calm façade. "Now." Ella sank gratefully back in her seat. "The extra boost of energy came from you. I'm impressed."

Everyone started talking at once. Nathan cut through it all. "Ella, no one…" He caught himself. "Very few people can tap directly into the ley energy. It's the equivalent of grabbing a 50,000 volt electrical cable."

With a wry twist of her mouth, Ella agreed. "Yes, it was a rather energizing experience. But there's more." Everyone looked at her expectantly. "While Nathan and Talek were stabilizing the shield, time did something really weird for me."

"Weird?" Nathan demanded, "Explain."

"Well, I know when I jumped in to help, everything was absolutely insane." Nobody in the room disagreed with Ella's assessment. "The minute that I tapped into the ley power, time slowed down around me, I was able to…" Ella paused, struggling to find the words, "I could analyze everything, find the solution, and fix the problem. I had all the time in the world."

"The moment you joined us, the shield gained power, and the node shut down." Talek worked through his thoughts aloud. "I glimpsed the Anakarei troops gathered. Since I'm from Drakkonon, I'm attuned to node activity involving them."

"Are you sure they don't have another Sensitive?" Ella asked.

"I can't be positive, but I'm nearly certain."

"You glimpsed the staging area. I saw more because time was slower for me." Ella took a deep breath. "I saw a cloaked figure in a large containment-type field. The figure was amorphous, shimmery."

Panic passed over Talek's face. "That's impossible. All the Sensitives have always been accounted for."

A worm of worry wiggled deep in Ella's mind. "Look, I know that you did your best to protect those who were Sensitive, but you saw what was on the staging area." Ella gestured between them all. "They have someone or something."

"We stopped them for the moment," Nathan stated. "But we need to be prepared."

"You started to change and the node collapsed. Then you regained your human shape and passed out." The entire company in the office was staring at Ella making her even more uncomfortable. Talek snorted. "You have no idea who you are."

"I'm Ella Hixson."

"No, I mean your true nature." Talek shook his head. "Only the high priests and priestess' of times long past could handle the energy you did. Yet you are a mere infant."

"Watch who you're calling an infant!" Ella glared at Talek as she rubbed the itching band around her left wrist. The burning irritation reminded her of the summer she'd strung chili peppers without gloves.

"Our people live to be three hundred years old or older." Not backing down, he continued, "You are an infant."

"Talek, you never call a woman a child." Nathan refereed. "Ella, your ability to manipulate the node and handle ley energy is extraordinary."

Ella shook her head. "I'm still me – just Ella Hixson." She tilted her head back and stared at the ceiling. "I've spent my whole life just being ordinary. Deep down, at the edge of every dream, I thought, I hoped, I was something special." She gave a self-deprecating sigh. "If anyone one outside this room knew how 'special' I was, I'd be a resident in a psych ward.

Annisa gave disgusted snort. "I have always found it curious the human need to box, label, and quantify everything in their experience. The shelves of the bookstore are lined with books that tell people how to be special, yet like everyone else." She shook her head. "Humans squander their own magic."

"What magic?" Bitterness tinged Ella's demand. "We're killing the world with our excesses." She looked at the diminutive creature of magic in front of her. "As far as I know we have 'wanna be's' but no actual magic."

"That is what I mean! Humanity is supremely unaware of the magic that saturates them." Annisa made a disgusted noise. "Imagination, audacity, and diligence are what make humans amazing. Yet, they seek to conform."

"Magic does exist amongst the humans, but it generally goes untapped." Nathan agreed with Annisa. "But you, Ella, are half human, half Drakkon." Kaie leapt up into his lap. "Creation in any form is magic, and humans are one of the few species in all the Otherverse that processes their magic completely subconsciously. Only a few become aware, and they stand out in history."

Ella gave Nathan a dubious look. "So you're telling me Da Vinci, Rembrandt, Einstein, or Wright all tapped into their 'magic' and that's what set them apart from the rest of us."

"That's just to name a few." Nathan confirmed.

"Your mother must have been very adept at controlling magic." Annisa shrugged at Ella's gasp of denial. "Whether she knew it or not. That's part of what's making you so powerful."

"No, my mother…" The conversation from the previous evening flashed through Ella's mind. "My mother said something about how the world was magical when she and my father were together. Could he have brought out her magical abilities?"

"Yes, if your father was a high priest, everything was magnified around him." Annisa gave Ella a kind smile. "Life would have indeed been magical."

"I have to assume that my father didn't come through this node, right?"

Nathan went over to a set of shelves behind the desk and pulled a globe off the shelf. Spinning it around, he stopped it abruptly at Thailand, leaving a long finger there. He then turned the globe around to England, placing another finger there. "He must have come through trade routes managed by the Fae." He turned the globe to show Peru.

"You mean Angkor Watt, Machu Pichu, and Stonehenge are all nodes?" Ella rubbed her temple, "All three locations are known for strange phenomenon. Daddy never mentioned visiting any of those locations."

"You were a child," Nathan asked quietly. "Why would he?"

"You're right." Ella slumped in her chair. "I have so many emotions and thoughts mixed up between the adult me and the child me." She straightened up. "I'll get it sorted. You said Fae trade routes?"

"Each site equipped with a very special security force." Nathan frowned. "Ours is the most active node on the planet. All guardians are supposed to alert the others to all activity."

Annisa stood up. "I'll contact my sources about node activity. If Ella's father came through one of them, we should have known."

"If he came through, that means others from Drakkonon may through the trade routes from another world." Talek stared at the globe as he remarked. "They'll be looking for a direct connection to Earth. This node will provide one."

Ella struggled to wrap her brain around all of this. She had a sphere, a book, and an apparent destiny she knew nothing about. Oh, and she could do things that no one in generations could do. "Okay look, I'm overwhelmed. I don't know what to do or think about all of this."

"We need to deal with the current situation. The Anakarei are ready to move. They've found a way to stabilize the vortex." Talek broke the silence. "You just delayed the inevitable."

"What is the level of technology there?" Warfare may not be her forte, but it was the next logical question. "I doubt we have to worry about anyone shifting into dragons. Are we talking Dungeons and Dragons or ray guns?" She clarified what she had seen before she had blasted the area clear. "I saw armed, organized troops. The weapons didn't necessarily look up to par with anything with our military, but definitely rifles."

The references confused. Talek

"It's a good thing we have a bookstore at our disposal. Talek, I think you and I need to take a look through the history section and see what looks familiar in the armament area." Nathan headed for the door with Talek, but then added, "Ella, I suggest you start reading the Drakkon Book of Writ."

"What about the store?"

"The store is back in order." Annisa smirked, "the staff is very good at dealing with the unexpected."

"You'll introduce me?" Ella asked. "I never expected you to survive a day with us. I'm glad I was wrong," the short woman said. "You'll meet the rest of us in time, but we have other matters more pressing."

After thanking Annisa for her support and help, Ella returned to the guest room. Her gut told her she needed to become educated – fast.

Settled in the comfortable chair next to the bed, Ella concentrated on the knot. She turned it over and looked at it closely. As a kid, she was the one who could always unknot delicate necklace chains, skeins of yarn, and shoelaces. Ella allowed her eyes to un-focus. The loops and twists glowed, revealing the path to its release.

Ella's hands worked the path and loosened the intricate knot. The top of the pouch opened to reveal a clear sphere. Ella gently touched clear material, a shaft of energy snapped between her fingers and the globe. Mesmerizing jewel tones began to swirl in the sphere, as a palpable wave of emotional energy radiated from the orb. The pulse rattled the furniture in the room and beyond. Ella could only hope that the shields of the house would block any impact the energy might have.

With hesitant hands, Ella removed the sphere from the fabric. She set it gently on the bed, carefully secured against rolling off. Ella found a folded piece of paper at the bottom of the pouch. The paper's edges remained curled skyward, cradling the impression of the sphere. She carefully pulled the paper out from the pouch.

Her father's handwriting filled the page. Ella eyes burned with tears. Kaie got up from her observation post and leapt into her lap. The cat's presence steadied her nerves. She sought to clear her vision before she started to read the letter. Her different perspective on the events of her childhood gave the letter new meaning.

'Ella, my dearest little dragon,' the old endearment sent the tears rolling down Ella's cheeks. She could hear her father's voice saying the words. 'If you are reading this letter, I have not returned. I didn't leave you or your mother willingly. I left to protect you both. You are heir to one of the oldest families of power in the Otherverse. You are the last High Socra of our people.

'With this letter is the Sphere of Drakkonon. Its purpose is to unify our people in times of turmoil. The Writ is a complete history including the holy writings of Drakkon. Each High Socra adds the accomplishments and failures of their tenure while maintaining the laws we live by. I smuggled them from my home world so that they might be kept safe. Whatever you do, do not let them fall into the hands of the enemy.

'I love you. – your father.'

Overwhelmed by her discoveries, Ella cradled her head. Paws balanced themselves on her knees, and she looked up into Kaie's blue eyes. "What? No cat comments?"

Kaie leaned up and touched her nose to Ella's. "Thank you for your support." She cuddled the cat to her chest. "This dragon business is overwhelming, and to tell the truth, I don't know if I can do it."

Sharp rapping on the door interrupted Ella's musings.

"Ella, are you in there?" called Talek.

Ella let Kaie go, and the cat made her way on to the bed, "Come in!"

Talek pushed the door opened slowly. "Did you feel…" He came to a halt in the doorway when he saw the objects on the bed.

Ella turned toward to see what had stopped him in mid-sentence. "What's wrong?"

With great reverence, Talek slowly approached the bed. He reached out to touch the Sphere and the book and stopped himself. "They are real." His voice choked as he dropped to his knees by the bed.

“Talek, you have to help me. Please explain to me what is going on.” Kaie leapt off the bed and left the room.

“We thought these were lost to history, lost forever.” Never taking his eyes off the items on the bed, Talek took a deep breath. “The Sphere of Drakkon was said to be able to keep peace among all dragon-kin. Held in the inner chambers of the lost Temple of Drakkonon, it united all. If you look at the Sphere, you can see all the colors of the dragon-kin. Only the High Socra’ could hold or control its influence. At our cultural zenith, the Drakkon lived in a society of amazing discovery, art, and philosophy.”

“No wonder you had a mind-lock.” Nathan observed from the doorway. “You are the last of the High Socra, priceless to our people.”

Ella jumped at Nathan’s voice. “My father put the mind-lock in place, and you unlocked it!” She whirled to face Nathan. “I know, as guardian of this Node, you needed to know, but I’m not ready for any of this!”

Talek stepped to Ella’s side. “Ella.” He laid his hand on her shoulder. “No one is ready. We do what is necessary.”

Ella went back to the bed and placed the Sphere back into its pouch, turning back to Nathan, “do we have a safe place for this? Somehow, Castle Storage won’t be sufficient anymore.”

Nathan laughed. “That’s where it was?”

“Yes, my mother packed up all my father’s things and put it away where she wouldn’t be reminded of him.” Ella shook her head. “If all this hadn’t of happened, I wouldn’t have found it until she died.”

“The universe has a way of working things out. You’re true nature would have revealed itself.” Nathan gestured for them all to follow him and led them to a doorway at the end of the hall.

Ella gathered up the book and sphere, following the men to the doorway she knew hadn't been there when she came in.

"Okay, Nathan, you have to tell me the truth about the house. Does it have a real floor plan, or does it grow floors and rooms as it needs them?"

"What do you think?"

Ella found herself back in the office where Nathan had told her she had gotten the job as store manager. The room still had the same sensory impact on her. This time she slipped off her shoes and wiggled her toes in the lush pile of the carpet.

Nathan went over to the bookshelves and pulled a series of books in a combination revealing a safe. "This is one of the most shielded places on the planet. The Sphere will be safe here. Go ahead and place it in." Nathan was careful not to touch the Sphere himself.

"Both you and Talek won't touch the Sphere. Why?"

Nathan and Talek looked at each other.

"Only the guardians selected by the High Socra can handle or use the Sphere," Talek answered.

"Well, as the Temple is currently inaccessible, and I am the last High Socra, I'm telling you that you both are going to be helping with the Sphere!"

"Ella, I don't think it's that simple." Nathan said.

"Why? You are a Node Guardian, aren't you?" Nathan fidgeted, as Ella looked at both of them. "And you, you have been a keeper of knowledge and tradition on Drakkonon?"

The men both nodded. "Then it's settled. I name you both guardians. Too serve and protect."

Nathan looked at Talek. "Talek, can she do that? Can she just decree this?"

Talek shrugged. “The Sphere has been lost with the Temple for so long – I have no idea.” He looked at Ella. “I suggest you consult the Book of Writ and see what it says.”

“I’m telling you, what I say goes.”

The Sphere’s incandescent glow revealed the fine pattern of scales on Ella’s exposed skin. Nathan and Talek both shimmered in the light, their scales glimmering. The orb emitted an enchanting hum that sent chills coursing across everyone in the room.

The intoxicating effect alarmed Ella. “If that’s the effect it had on us, I can imagine what it could do to an entire population.” She walked away from the safe. Ella could still feel the swirl of the orb in her mind as she looked at the men. “I’m not taking the Sphere out of the safe until I understand it more.”

Nathan nodded his agreement. “The moment the Sphere left its dormant state, I was drawn to the room. I knew exactly where it was and what had happened.”

Talek confirmed with a nod.

Worried, Ella paced a short circuit around Nathan’s desk. “This is not good. The Sphere was dormant.” She scrubbed her hands over her face. “The moment I touched it, I felt a shockwave radiate from it. Then the colors started to swirl. If you both were drawn to it, who or what else will be drawn to it next?”

Nathan looked at Talek.

“Do you think that the awaking was felt beyond this world?”

Nodding his head, Talek affirmed their fear. “Without a doubt. I think every Drakkon in the Otherverse felt its awakening.”

Ella tilted her head toward Nathan. "How secure is the Node at the moment?"

They all knew that Nathan had locked down the node using his considerable shielding powers, but he wasn't the only being in the Otherverse to be able to manipulate nodes and shields.

"As secure as I can make it." Nathan ran his hands through his dark hair. "I've got a locking mechanism my grandfather put in place over the entrance of the foyer."

"The saber that is there and not?" Ella said.

Talek felt lost again. "Saber? How does this lock the Node?"

Nathan explained to Talek, "My grandfather, Carter Mullins, was one of the few humans on this world who could manipulate and use node energy. This particular Node had a tendency to wander the globe before it settled here."

"An unstable node?" Talek started pacing, "Nodes should be locked into the global energy ley grid."

"I agree, but my grandfather concluded that something had caused a significant drain on the ley grid…" Nathan did a quick calculation in his head. "Roughly one hundred seventy-five years ago. The node network shifted then."

"How many major nodes are here on this world?" Talek asked as he walked over to Nathan's desk to get paper and pen. "Where are they located?"

"In Carter's day, before the shift, seven major nodes existed. Only five were accessible by land. After the shift, only four existed, with three on land."

Ella broke into the men's discussion.

"What caused the drain on the ley line network?" She still didn't understand nodes or ley lines, but she could wrap her mind around the fact that something had caused a significant change. “Why did the nodes diminish in numbers?” A fact from an earlier conversation niggled in her brain. “Didn’t you all say that most of the Otherworlds have one major node and maybe a couple of minor nodes?”

When Talek and Nathan both nodded, Ella continued, “Then why does this world have so many major nodes?”

Talek quickly sketched out a grid on a piece of paper that looked like an algebraic lesson. Ella hated algebra.

“Normally, nodes represent fixed spaces in quadrants in known portions of the Otherverse,” he said, pointing to his drawing. “Earth is a Nexus, allowing travel to greater portions of the Otherverse.” Ella was already overwhelmed; add algebraic equations to send her over the edge into a full-blown headache. “If Earth is a Nexus, any of the major nodes could theoretically provide access to anywhere in the Otherverse.”

Annisa interrupted the conversation. “Ella, have you called your mother since all this happened this afternoon?”

Ella glanced at the clock on the wall and was shocked to see they were well into evening. “You’re right, I need to give her a call and at least get dinner delivered.” She looked at Annisa. “I swear to you that this place is a time-warp. Time never seems to be normal here.”

“You’ll get used to it. Why don’t we go out and pick up dinner for everyone? We’ll drop dinner off for your mother.” As she headed back to her office, Annisa called over her shoulder. “I’d like to meet your mother.”

Ella stopped in her tracks. Having her mother meet anyone she worked with was worrisome. Their relationship was still tender.

Annisa reassured Ella. “I think she’ll enjoy the company.”

While they were out, Ella took the time to check her messages. A bright cheerful voice greeted her on one of the messages, 'Hey, girlfriend. This is now an official game of phone tag and you are it! Call me when you get a break. Just for your information, I get the friend book discount for helping you find the job! Ciao bella!' Bethany's voice chirped out of the cellphone speaker.

"Your friend helped you find this job?" Annisa inquired.

Ella explained Bethany's part in finding the Help Wanted ad in the paper. "The Universe seems to have had a plan along." Parked in the driveway, Ella turned to Annisa. "There's something you're not telling me."

"I know many things, but in this case you are correct." Annisa unbuckled her seatbelt. "Your father protected all your knowledge and your true-self. I'm wondering if he might have done the same thing to your mother."

Ella sank back into the driver's seat. The fact that her mother might be a mage of sorts was just starting to register. Annisa's posit of her father protecting her mother in the same way was unsettling.

"This messes with my entire relationship with my mother."

"Let's get your mother's meal into her." Getting out of the car, Annisa continued, "All will be as it is supposed to be."

Ella joined Annisa on the front walk. Light spilled out from the front door, leaving Myrna in silhouette. Ronan's happy barking soothed her apprehension.

"Into the fray!" Ella muttered under her breath.

Myrna stared intently at the small woman.

"Forgive me," Myrna finally said, "but you look remarkably like a woman I knew a long time ago."

Annisa smiled as she pulled a chair next to Myrna's wheelchair. "It has been far too long, my friend." Annisa patted Myrna's hand. "I didn't realize that Ella was your daughter until today."

Stunned, Myrna stared at Annisa. "How?" Her voice cracked. Clearing her throat she started again. "How can you be the same after all these years? How can you be the same person?"

"Well, I have many things to tell you." Annisa looked at Ella preparing dinner for Myrna. "Ella, why don't you take dinner back to the store. Your mother and I have some catching up to do."

Ella felt as shell-shocked as her mother. Unanswered questions were piling up. She bent down to scratch Ronan, admonishing him to be a good boy. "Call me on the cell if you need anything." Ella kissed her mother on the cheek.

Ronan sat by Myrna as Annisa walked Ella to the door. "Everything will be fine. I'll take good care of your mother."

Ella glanced back at her mother with trepidation. "You really knew my mother after my father left?"

"I did." Annisa returned to Myrna's side. "I do believe your father attempted to protect your mother in much the same way he did you. I won't unlock anything, but I will do my best to center her."

Back at the bookstore, Ella's heart and mind bowed under the weight of the day's revelations. She carried in the sandwiches into the kitchen area. Ella left Nathan in charge of explaining Otherworld cuisine to Talek. Kaie joined her as she headed up the stairs hoping they would lead to the familiar guest wing. The homey feel of the rooms was soothing, and with today's events, she needed all the comfort she could get.

The room she'd claimed earlier was now furnished with a large overstuffed chair with an ottoman. Ella chalked it up to the idiosyncratic happenings of the House. She slipped off her shoes, settling into the chair. Kaie jumped up on the side table next to the chair to observe and witness the proceedings.

Ella wasn't sure what to expect – a chorus of angels, flying monkeys, dragon scales? The book's clasp refused to unlatch. Running her finger around the clasp, a sharp edge under the buckle drew blood.

"Ouch!" She sucked on the offended digit to keep the blood from contaminating the manuscript. A flash of power filled the room, unlocking the fastener. Ella cautiously opened the cover, it had more heft than she expected. A pocket, fitted precisely to the inside cover, caught Ella's interest. She lifted the flap and revealed a large lens of transparent material with ornate brackets attached to the long edges. The material magnified everything, revealing the fine interlocking scale pattern on her skin. Under the magnification, the material of her pants look like burlap. A furry head pushed her hand away. A large blue eye appeared, the slit pupil enormous. Ella laughed.

"So, Kaie, how do I look from that angle?"

Kaie gave a regal meow. Carefully setting the lens on the ottoman, Ella slipped her hand into the pocket to verify she hadn't missed anything. At the bottom of the pocket was a lanyard of sorts with two sturdy clips that fit the brackets.

Not wanting to miss anything, the cat jumped up on the arm of the chair to watch the discovery process.

Ella turned the first page.

Without the lens, the writing appeared to be an army of microscopic ants running amok on the page. Miniscule dots broken up by tiny illustrations, the pages saturated with detail. The magnification lens now made sense.

Gently setting the book aside, Ella attached the lanyard. The heavy lens sat approximately three inches below her collarbone. Her neck took some of the weight of the magnifier off her chest making her grateful for the chair she sat in. Her eyes took a few moments to adjust. With the lens, she could see the exquisite detail of each page. Engrossed in the history of the Drakkon, she was unaware Kaie sat guard as the new High Socra of Drakkonon was educated.

Myrna stared at the woman who had helped her hold her sanity together during the first year of her husband's disappearance. Annisa had remained the same, while Myrna had withered and become bitter. Resentment roiled in Myrna's stomach as she watched Annisa put the finishing touches on their meal. Ronan laid his head in Myrna's lap.

"Why are you here? Why now?"

"Time might have passed, but I have always been your friend." Annisa brought the plates to the table. "When we took our walks, what I did and who I worked for was not important. You needed to vent your anger."

Myrna grimaced, remembering the rage she felt during those days. It was all she could do to get Ella on the school bus in the morning.

"When you disappeared, I had no one to talk to. You deserted me." Myrna met Annisa's gaze. "You were one more disappointment."

"There is a time and season for everything," she continued, unfazed by Myrna's anger. "We have a lot to catch up on. First, let's eat."

For the first time in years, Myrna felt interested in things outside her own reality. Between bites of dinner, they discovered their friendship. Annisa's appearance cemented the regimen of change in Myrna's heart.

"You have a remarkable daughter," Annisa remarked as she cleared the table after they finished their meal. "She is much more than I thought she could be."

"More than you thought she could be? What's that supposed to mean?"

"When I interviewed her, I have to admit, I didn't think she was up to the special requirements of House Books." Annisa explained. "The manager position has certain requirements that must be met, and I didn't believe Ella's experience would suffice."

"Ella said that she had met someone who knew her father." Myrna watched the other woman carefully, waiting to pounce. "Were you there?"

Annisa parried. "I'm not aware that she met anyone who knew your husband."

"She wanted to know if he had left anything behind when he left." Myrna pushed away from the table, settling herself back in her wheelchair. Ronan followed the women. "She's never been particularly interested before. I…" Myrna faltered. "I don't want her to be disappointed." Closing her eyes, Myrna whispered, "I don't want to be disappointed."

"I don't believe that you or your daughter has anything to be disappointed about. It is only natural for a daughter to be interested in her parents."

"Ella asked me if it would change everything I felt if I knew Ethias left to protect us both." Ensconced on the overstuffed living room chair, Myrna met Annisa's gaze. Her eyes filled with tears. "I've spent so much time hating him for deserting us…" She slammed her hands on the arms of her chair. "What could he have been protecting us from?"

Ronan jumped to his feet and started to bark menacingly at the front of the house. His hackles stood straight up, gone was the lovable, goofy pit bull. Myrna looked at Annisa with fear in her eyes. "Something's wrong, Ronan never makes this kind of fuss. I'm going to call the police."

The lights flickered as Annisa grabbed the phone and dialed the store. "Answer! Answer!" she muttered.

"House Books…"

"Sindie, tell Nathan, there is trouble at El…" the line went dead.

Annisa uttered the foulest Fae curse word she knew then worked as fast as she could to erect a protective shield around Ella's house. Myrna's universe was about to be expanded.

"Myrna, stay in the living room with Ronan," Annisa yelled. "Ronan, guard your grandma!"

Ronan's barking grew more ferocious as he faced the front of the house. Annisa knew that she couldn't effectively shield the entire house for a long period of time. Trusting the dog's instinct, she focused the energy barrier to the front of the house. Annisa prayed to every deity she knew on Earth and in the Otherverse for the speedy arrival of the cavalry.

Sindie found Nathan and Talek seated in a far corner of the sales floor surrounded by books and papers. "Nathan!" She skidded to a stop in front of them. "Annisa said there was trouble but the line went dead. I think she started to say Ella's house."

Nathan looked up. "Annisa's at Ella's house?"

"Ella's back, but I think Annisa stayed behind with her mother."

Nathan knew that Annisa wouldn't have called without a reason. Getting up, he ordered Sindie to find Ella. "Talek, come with me!" The men ran through the shelves, dodging seating areas, as they headed for the front door.

"Ella!" Sindie yelled as she ran up the stairs. "Ella! Where are you?"

A nip on her ear pulled Ella from her immersion in the Writ. The sharp teeth were enough to hurt, but not enough to draw blood. "Curse you, cat!" Ella hissed, unconscious of the smoke wisping from her nose. "What did I say about …"

"Ella!"

Ella heard Sindie. "I'm in here!"

Sindie burst into the room. "There's trouble at your house."

"What?" Ella's heart began to race. "Is my mother okay? What happened?"

Sindie repeated all she knew, which was very little. "Talek and Nathan just left. Nathan sent me to find you and tell you."

Sindie urged Ella out of the room and down the stairs. "I'll close the store for the evening. We'll be fine."

Ella took Sindie at her word and ran to her car after setting additional warding around the store that drew directly from the ley line. Sending a prayer above, she raced home, terrified of what she might find.

Annisa stood in the middle of the living room. Her hands held in a defensive position in front of her, all of her concentration was dedicated to the defense of the woman behind her.

The house shook. Myrna's fear-filled scream echoed through the room. Ronan stood ready at her side. He shifted with Annisa as she faced a threat that Myrna couldn't see or address. Forces battered the house. Pictures flew off the walls. The sofas and coffee table slid across the floor with the ease of a skater in an ice rink.

Annisa visualized the outside of the house with her inner eye. All she could see of their enemy was a dark and murky energy signature. As long as she kept up with its attempts to gain entry, they would be okay. But her energies were flagging.

Muttering in her own language, she prayed and promised anything to any deity listening.

Ronan turned away from Annisa, placing himself in front of Myrna. Annisa didn't notice the man behind her. Ronan howled as he launched himself at the intruder. His compact, muscular body knocked the man back from the women.

Annisa's shields sparked and sizzled with each external attack. The noise overpowered everyone in the room. When the assault from the front of the house ceased, Annisa fell forward on her hands and knees. She didn't have the luxury of catching her breath as she scrambled to her feet returning to her old friend. In the living room, Annisa's heart stopped in horror. Huddled against the fireplace, Myrna brandished a poker and ash shovel. Ronan lay bleeding and torn on the floor. Before him was a human form Drakkon with bronze eyes.

Talek burst in the back door, Nathan in the front. But Annisa didn't have time to let out a sigh of relief. The Drakkon stood between all three of them wild eyed. Looking for an escape, he started to shift. Hands raised, Annisa, Talek, and Nathan threw bolts of energy at the intruder, rendering him senseless. Annisa collapsed, her energy spent. Nathan raced to her.

"No, see to the dog." Annisa mustered what little strength she had left and crawled over to Myrna, still tightly clutching the poker and shovel.

"What are you?"

Annisa's voice and body shook with exhaustion. "That, my friend, is a tale of great length." The slamming of a car door interrupted her.

Ella skidded to a halt and stared at the tableau of destruction in her living room. Her mother and Annisa leaned against each other. Myrna looked exhausted, scared, but otherwise okay. An unknown man lay unconscious amongst the destroyed furniture. Talek secured curtain ties around his ankles. Nathan was crouched by Ronan, who whimpered softly.

"Ronan!" Ella screamed. Nathan desperately tried to staunch the bleeding. Not knowing how to comfort her beloved companion, she knelt gently by his head, laying a gentle hand between his ears scratching gently. Ronan lapped at her knee.

"Do something!" Ella sobbed.

Nathan pulled Annisa forward, "Do whatever it takes. He still lives."

Annisa knew that the dog's wounds were mortal and that healing them would upset the balance of magic. "It is against the rules." She reminded Nathan.

Nathan looked at the badly wounded dog. "Screw the rules."

Annisa knelt by Ronan's body. She placed her hands over the worst of the wounds. Then her hands started to glow. Ronan's breathing eased. His whimpering lessened. Ella felt the energy being expended by the smaller woman to heal the dog. She didn't care about the how; she just wanted her dog better and not to hurt.

"Ronan is the hero you always said he was." Myrna leaned against the wall by the fireplace as she struggled to find the words of comfort. "That man attacked us, and Ronan leapt at him. He protected me."

Ella curled herself around her faithful friend, cuddling him close. She stroked his head, muttering comforting nonsense words, as Annisa worked.

When Annisa finished with Ronan, she looked across at Nathan. "What happened to the other one?"

"He's dead. He wasn't expecting an attack from the rear." Talek let his primitive side of his Drakkon nature slip past his civil façade. "We'll need to dispose of the carcass."

"Carcass? What carcass." Myrna valiantly tried to calm herself and not be her normal self. "Somebody had better give me some answers. The house! Who's going to fix this mess?"

"Mrs. Hixson, you are most definitely entitled to answers," Nathan stood in front of Myrna and offered a hand of assistance. "It's not safe to stay here. Let Annisa help you. I have a safe place for you, and I'll get the house put to rights. No one will ever know that anything happened here tonight." With great care he pulled her to her feet and guided her to Annisa.

Talek manhandled the Drakkon to his feet. Nathan crouched in front of Ella and gently raised her chin so that their gazes met. "Ella?" Her eyes slid away back to the dog in her lap. Her mental and physical exhaustion beat down on her. Nathan bent closer, forcing her to meet his gaze. "Ella, come on. Let me help you."

She refused to give up Ronan's limp body but did allow Nathan to help her to her feet with her precious burden.

"We'll bring him with us and get him comfortable," He added with a tired attempt at a grin. "Kaie will enjoy watching over him."

Myrna placed a hand on Ella's back in support as Ella carried the weak but healing dog out of the wreckage. The space didn't resemble their home anymore. Ella felt lost and angry, irrationally angry, at everything. . Standing at the doorway, she didn't know if she could ever live here again.

"Let's go, Ella. Annisa is taking us somewhere safe." Myrna said. Looking at the prisoner in Talek's possession,

Ella knew nothing was safe. It never would be again. She wished that she never been awakened.

EIGHT

Power swept through the staging area scattering troops and artillery like toys. The Tmavě Jeden flew on the blast, landing in a crumpled heap at the base of the vast structure wall. While he was airborne, every instinct screamed to take Drakkon form to escape. He straightened out his body as pain radiated throughout his battered form. A pile of fabric now to his right had a foot poking out from a fold. The fabric was the heavy material of a thick cloak; the Tmavě Jeden pushed back the hood. The ravaged face of Ethias Hixson stared back at him, gaunt with sunken eyes.

He pulled the hood back over Ethias's face. Screams of pain hung in the air. The mobile tried to help the immobile. The node now floated in an enormous crater that took the majority of the space. Broken pipes vented gaseous compounds, while others gushed liquids. Before the world had exploded, he had glimpsed a woman on the other side wielding the unfathomable power. The Chancellor's visions of Otherverse domination had just suffered a serious setback. The Tmavě Jeden could hardly feel pity for the situation. He hoped that he had a chance to thank the woman someday.

Alone, buried deep in the shadows, he evaluated Ethias's condition. The damage was minimal, a separated shoulder and a broken leg. Getting to the barracks undetected would be the challenge. Just having Ethias in his possession was a risk, but leaving him in the Chancellor's tender care put Drakkon and the Otherverse at risk. Hefting the unconscious man up and over his shoulder, the Tmavě Jeden took the long way to the barracks with lights strobbing behind him as.

A corpsman with a stretcher rushed by, stopping at the sight of the Tmavě Jeden with his burden.

"Sir! Let me help you!" he offered putting the stretcher down.

The Tmavě Jeden firmly refused the offer.

"He looks like he could use a stretcher."

"I'm almost to the infirmary. Your help is needed at the node." He urged the corporal on his way, "Go!"

The corpsman was reluctant to leave the Tmavě Jeden with his burden. "If you're sure, sir."

"There are many more critically wounded. You are needed there." With his free hand, he gave the young man a not so gentle push. The Tmavě Jeden waited until the corpsman was out of sight before continuing to the barracks. Juggling his burden carefully, he swept the main table free of any items and carefully laid the man on the table. The Tmavě Jeden knew he had to keep his senses obfuscated until he could disconnect him from the Chancellor's influence.

He rummaged through his medical supplies and worked on splinting Ethias's leg and immobilizing his shoulder. After stabilizing the immediate medical issues, he ruthlessly bound the ears and eyes of his charge. He had to ensure that the Chancellor couldn't track his pet past the barracks.

In the Hunter alcoves stood cocoons, heavily padded sensory deprivation modules that would guarantee Ethias's safe passage to the Sanctuary. The Tmavě Jeden pulled one free, wrestling it into position next to the table.

Sirens sounded through the complex, but the Tmavě Jeden worked steadily. He gently placed Ethias in the cocoon with needed supplies that would ensure his health. Securing the lid to the module, he dragged it to the outside door of the barracks. A transport was always on standby for his use, a common looking cargo truck that would pass unremarked on in the streets.

With the siren shrieking at his back, the Tmavě Jeden gunned the transport as guardsmen flooded the barracks. The Chancellor seemed to be aware of his dual loyalties after all.

The transport careened through the alleyways and husks of buildings that still housed the poorest of the poor. Braking in front of a building that seemed to be deserted, but if one looked closely, the structure was fortified. Armed men swarmed out of the building. The Tmavě Jeden had arrived at the compound of Pacol Brakel. The usury was no friend of the Anakarei. His organization made the Chancellor's people look unorganized and ineffective. As much as he wanted to, the Chancellor had never been able to get a spy into the operation.

"You!" The Tmavě Jeden gestured to the first man to appear. "Help me." He leapt on the bed. "Here, grab this end." He pushed Ethias's module into the hands of the men. "Gently!" he shouted.

The men were familiar with the Tmavě Jeden. One was already in the cab of the transport.

"Drive it into a ditch. Destroy it. Just get rid of it." He looked the man in the eye. "Don't let anyone you know or like keep it. It'll bring them nothing but trouble."

The man's face lit up with an unholy glee. The Tmavě Jeden felt pity for the enemy about to befall a series of unfortunate events.

Pacol met the Tmavě Jeden at the door to the compound. "What trouble have you brought to my doorstep?"

The Tmavě Jeden smirked. "Nothing you can't handle, my friend."

"Trouble at the complex tonight, sirens sounding, troops running around." Pacol assessed the dangerous man in front of him. "You wouldn't have anything to do with that?"

"This time I can say I'm entirely free of fault." The Tmavě Jeden gave a humorless laugh as he walked to his precious cargo. "…this time." He laid a hand on the container. "I need to get through to the old tunnels tonight."

Pacol stepped forward with a gleam of avarice in his eye. "What have you stolen?"

"Nothing you can sell." The Tmavě Jeden squelched the covetous look in Pacol's eyes. "I just tendered my permanent resignation from the Chancellor's employ. He'll have a hard time moving forward with his plans."

"Just for the opportunity to stick it to the Chancellor, I'll help you." The scar on Pacol's cheek gleamed in the foyer's light. His demeanor grew more serious. "I heard that Drakkon have been evacuated."

"We've gotten as many out as we can." He laid a hand on his cargo. "The Chancellor's ability to manipulate the node has been severely diminished."

"What happened?" Pacol needed all the information he could get. "Last I heard from my informants in the complex, he was able to open the node only to have his arse kicked."

The Chancellor's plans were rejected with extreme prejudice from the other side." The Tmavě Jeden remembered the blow of energy wave that scattered the gathered troops like leaves. "We don't know who it was, but they were powerful."

"Can you tell me more?"

"I have no more to tell you," The Tmavě Jeden rubbed at the ache in his shoulder. "I'll send information when I can."

"All right." Pacol nodded, the man in front of him had always dealt fairly with him. "Last question, did you get all the Drakkon out of the city?"

"We got the ones we know of out."

Pacol's eyes swirled gold revealing his true nature before reverting to a light brown. "I won't run. I felt the Node energy spike. I'm shielded." Pacol turned to his second in command and started barking orders. "We'll look for those who couldn't get out and take care of them."

"We're gathering at the Sanctuary. I can …"

"No!" Pacol stopped the Tmavě Jeden. "The Socra and I came to an understanding a long time ago. She knows I'll protect those under my care."

"Get your cargo safely there." Pacol grasped the Tmavě Jeden's arm in solidarity. "You'll always have safe harbor here."

Hidden in a camouflaged compartment of a transport, he spent the time plotting his next course of action. The journey to the tunnel entrance was dangerous and slow. He was grateful his charge was oblivious to the ordeal.

At the edge of the Wild, the Tmavě Jeden carefully laid out his harness. He draped the long lengths carefully over the ground and then stripped.

The air around him shimmered. Bits of the heavens mixed with the conversion energy. The Tmavě Jeden's body shifted into his elegant, obsidian Drakkon self. His wings unfurled behind him. He stretched the muscles, warming up to work out any kinks. His twitching tail was the only indication of anxiousness. The evening breeze fluttered the fringe that swept up either side of his head, framing his eyes.

Carefully, he settled the harness in to place. His clawed hands worked the buckles. Once the harness was comfortable, the Tmavě Jeden worked at securing the tethers to the container.

The cargo cradled and secured against his chest, he freed himself from gravity. Air rushed against his face. His Drakkon senses sang at the caress. His strong wings brought him higher into the moonless night sky. Stars reflected off his obsidian scales. From below, he was just a swift shadow crossing the sky.

With every beat of his wings, the Tmavě Jeden shed the façade of the Chancellor's tool and allowed his true self emerge. Despite his heavy burden, he reveled in the air that caressed his scales.

Petroj Carbehk was reborn.

Alexi and Natov Smyzac bickered amongst themselves. Jaczon had fantasies of muzzles and straightjackets. He understood they missed their parents, but he hadn't dealt with boys this young in years.

Jaczon's nerves tingled with unfamiliar anxiety over the quiescent hunters under Callem's care. Risking the Sanctuary was unacceptable. Jaczon pondered the situation as they waited for evacuation stragglers before he and his charges continued on.

The soft whoosh of an air carriage reached his ears. Grabbing the battling twins, he shoved them behind a rocky outcropping. "Don't make a sound!" he hissed. Two sets of large bronze eyes blinked at him.

Jaczon stood in the shadows as he waited to see whom the air carriage held. The vehicle stopped nearby. A man helped an exhausted looking woman out of the vehicle. Both looked ready to collapse. Jaczon stepped out of the shadow ready to make his presence known when two bullets of energy shot past him.

"Mama!"

"Papa!"

Both boys shouted at the same time. Their voices held all their fears and relief bundled together. The woman gasped as she held one of the boys. The man fell to his knees holding the other in a tight embrace. Jaczon couldn't find it in his heart to reprimand the boys, but he knew they had to be on their way.

Andros recovered first. Looking around he finally recognized Jaczon. "Praise the heavens you had the boys. Katja and I were worried sick."

Jaczon stepped forward, clasping Andros's hand firmly. "I'd forgotten the questions boys could ask." He grew serious. "Were you able to leave without any problems?"

"We were the last to get out of the city." Katja answered. "The sentries closed the checkpoint behind us." She shook from the stress of the journey. "We kept going, heading the opposite of where the directions told us to go."

"We didn't want to bring anyone with us," Andros continued. "I don't believe we were followed. We drove all night without lights."

"Did you hear from…"

Andros interrupted Jaczon, "The last thing we heard from the Tmavě Jeden was when he gave us the papers and told us where to meet you. We didn't know you'd have the boys."

Jaczon started walking to the boulders that were large enough to hide the transport. He pulled a small box out of pack he wore on his back and called to the boys. "I need you to take your parents over to the air transport. I'll be with you in a few minutes."

Loaded down with their possessions, Katja and Andros let their sons lead them to the secondary transport.

Jaczon walked around the air transport the couple had driven, putting small discs around it at even intervals. They could not leave it out in the middle of the wasteland deserted as a beacon to the Anakarei. The extra vehicle would be nice to have, but it would make their passage easier to track. Setting a fuse, he walked away with a steady pace. He was confident in the timing of the detonator.

A backdraft was the only announcement of the bloom of soundless fire behind him. Jaczon knew that nothing would be left of the vehicle. A brutal twelve hours later over rough terrain and with fractious adolescents, they reached the rendezvous point. No one was there.

Andros radiated concern. "Where is everyone?"

"I don't know." Jaczon motioned for the others to join them.

"Crazck!" Jaczon muttered under his breath. Signs of a recent evacuation were evident. Jaczon looked around frantically for a sign from the Socra – nothing. The fine layer of loose soil was rife with scuff marks left by feet and parcels. Running toward the end of the canyon, Jaczon let loose a sigh as he saw a small stack of rocks shape, they'd moved on through the cave system that led to the other side of the mounting range. Just because you could not see the enemy, did not mean they were not present.

Katja looked worried.

"Petroj? Is he coming then?"

"Yes, while I was en route with the boys, I received a signal from him that he wasn't going to stay in the city." At the expected stares, Jaczon shook his head. "I don't know what that means." He led them to a hollowed out divot in the canyon wall concealed by some boulders. He had Katja settle the boys there, while he motioned for Andros to follow him. "Let's get your things unloaded."

Grateful for something to do, the men worked together unloading all the supplies. A strong whump-whump-whump of wings echoed along the canyon. The sound was distorted by the acoustics of the high walls, but recognizable as the wing beat of a Drakkon. Jaczon prayed hard for the arrival to be his son. He pointed Andros back to his family and crouched behind the stripped down vehicle. Sweat trickled down his face as they waited.

The sound stopped. It was replaced by the sound of an object being dragged along the sandy bottom of the canyon. Hopeful, Jaczon left the vague security of the transport. He crept toward the sound as he hugged rough stone of the canyon wall. Jaczon readied himself as he waited at a bend that concealed the newcomer.

The Chancellor kicked his way through the broken equipment and limp bodies. His rage caused his form to shimmer ever so slightly. His plans lay in ruin at his feet. Oblivious to the cries of pain around him, he searched for the Key to the node.

“Sir!” A lieutenant ran up to the Chancellor’s side.

“Report,” the Chancellor snarled as he continued his search.

The lieutenant did his best to keep up with the man’s pace.

“We won’t be able to regroup for several days, sir.”

The Chancellor turned on the hapless lieutenant.

“Unacceptable. I want the troops ready to go forward immediately!” He took a moment to evaluate. “Put the word out to the Council. I want them ready for a vote in an hour.”

“But, sir! We don’t even have accurate numbers of the injured.” The lieutenant changed his tact at the fire in the Chancellor’s eyes. “I’ll try and convene the Council.”

“I did not say try. I said convene the Council.” The Chancellor sneered at the man and gestured at the men upright and fallen. “If they can walk, they can be deployed. I want every available body ready.” He stalked off continuing his search for the Key.

When the Node opened, he had seen a woman on the other side of the vortex holding the Node stable. Then she decimated his forces. This creature’s power was unacceptable.

Nothing. He found nothing. Picking up a twisted rifle, the Chancellor flung it aside. A sharp cry coincided with the clatter of the landing. He simply didn’t care.

A colonel arrived at his side.

“Well, have you found it?” The Chancellor snarled. “Our plans are useless without it.”

The colonel knew his answer could mean his death or demotion. “There is no sign of the creature, sir.” He stood his ground in the face of the Chancellor’s sizzling anger. “We’ve searched everywhere. Only one person had anything remotely close to a description.”

“What do you mean?”

“A medic came across two men in the back passage ways. One was cloaked, the other out of uniform. They seemed to be heading for the infirmary.” At the lack of reaction, the colonel gained more confidence in his news. The Chancellor did not strike out at him. “His offer of assistance was refused,” he continued.

“What do you mean out of uniform?” The Chancellor had a suspicion forming.

“The man, clad in black, was carrying the cloaked figure.”

The Chancellor grasped the colonel’s arm and dragged him behind as he headed for the back entrance.

"Ready a squad and meet me at the Hunter barracks immediately."

"Sir?"

"Don't question me. Do it or die."

The man took off grabbing any mobile and armed soldier he could get his hands on. The troops pounded down the corridor to the Hunter's barracks. A battering ram slammed the door open to nothingness. Nothing stirred. The Chancellor upended the table in the middle of the room, scattering serving ware and papers.

"Where are they?" he roared.

No one dared answer the enraged man – no one could.

Every soldier in the room turned with exact precision a messenger ran down the corridor to the door. Skidding to a stop, the boy who hadn't earned stripes past corporal, blanched at the sight of the armament facing him.

The Chancellor shoved his way to the door.

"What do you want?"

The hapless corporal stood at attention as he delivered his message.

"Sir, the Council cannot convene."

"What!"

"They've all been imprisoned in the Drakkon kennels with their families." The corporal trembled. "They were rousted late last night. Orders came down that no one was to disturb you."

A vein throbbed in the Chancellor's temple. His face infused with deep color. The men surrounding him all stood perfectly still. No one was willing to provoke the predator in their midst.

The Chancellor grabbed the front of the corporal's uniform. He shook the boy, tossing him into the gathered ranks.

"Find me the Tmavě Jeden. Find me that traitorous sack of crazck!" The men in the barrack stood frozen. Two supported the dazed corporal. At the collective lack of reaction the Chancellor bellowed, "Go!"

As the rush of men flowed past, the Chancellor grabbed the colonel, who had gathered the troops, by the back of the collar. He leaned close to the man's ear, hissing, "Free my council members and their families by the time I get to my chambers."

The threat hung in the air.

An obsidian Drakkon crawled along the slot canyon floor dragging a long narrow box awkwardly behind it. Its wings were scraped raw by the sides of the narrow chasm. The Drakkon collapsed as it cleared the bend. Jaczon recognized the Drakkon form of his son.

"Petroj!" he called as he ran toward the supine creature. Andros and Katja broke cover at Jaczon's cry.

The air around the Drakkon shimmered as he regained human form. Petroj's skin was translucent in his exhaustion. Katja unbuttoned her cloak, throwing it over Petroj's nude form laying supine in the tangle of harness straps. Jaczon worked to free him from the jumble. He took care as he bundled the harness. They would need it for the rest of the journey.

"Katja." Jaczon put a hand on her shoulder. "I need you to get something for Petroj to eat. He'll be ravenous when he wakes."

She ran back to where the boys waited by the supplies. Andros looked at Jaczon.

“Who did he bring out of the city?”

Jaczon stared at the box.

“Someone who will cost us much if he wakes up.”

He walked over to the container. After a quick perusal, it appeared intact. Jaczon grabbed the harness leads and started creating hand holds that the adults would be able to handle. Andros watched impassively.

Petroj groaned as he sat up. “By the Bright Sky, I’m never flying cargo again.” He took stock of his surroundings; his father was making the module travel worthy. Katja came to his side with some travel rations.

“Thank you, mistress.”

Katja nodded her head and went back to her sons.

The canyon spun around Petroj’s head as he struggled to sit up. He didn’t even have the strength for that. His muffled curse drew the attention of Andros and Jaczon.

Jaczon rushed to his son’s side. “Stay seated, you fool!” He placed a restraining hand on Petroj’s shoulder. “No need to move until we are ready to clear out.” He shoved the uneaten food in his son’s hands. “You know better than anyone the price we pay when we over extend ourselves. Eat!”

Seeing Jaczon in a parental role was a hard shift for Petroj. The part of son was uncomfortable. He fought the impulse to snap at his father but forced the food down his throat.

As he sat eating, two small forms bracketed him. He knew the imps well. The fact that his father had been their escort was a source of great amusement to him. From his left, came the first question.

“What was it like to fly?”

From the right, “Will we be able to fly at the Sanctuary?”

"Why are you a black Drakkon? Mum says Drakkons are the metal colors."

Petroj let the questions flow until they ran out of steam. His body felt better as he finished the last of the food. The canyon walls had stopped spinning. He looked at the boys on either side of him.

"Did you ask Jaczon all these questions?"

The most talkative, Natov grimaced.

"He told us to be quiet..." The brothers passed a look between them. "A lot."

The first grin in years stretched Petroj's face. He raised his voice so it carried.

"Well, boys, you'll have to forgive the old man." Petroj's eyes met Jaczon's across the space. "He hasn't been around anyone your age in a long time. You'll be good for him."

Jaczon made a subtle offensive gesture in his son's direction. He refused to let Petroj see the pride shine in his eyes. Andros and Jaczon finished removing anything useful from the vehicle before placing the charges that would destroy it. Their shadows danced along the walls of the canyon as the vehicle burned. Jaczon secured the crate and supplies.

"Alright, old man." Petroj rose to his feet, wobbling just a little. "We've got to move."

Katja and Andros exchanged glances. She asked Petroj, "Where are we supposed to go?"

Jaczon led his rag-tag group to an out-cropping of rocks the boys hadn't climbed. Sharp edged, the shadows hid a space behind the back edge. No matter the time of day, the light that filtered down from above never revealed an opening to the cave. The shadowed entrance was wide enough to force the crate through, narrow enough to only accommodate one person through at a time.

As the Chancellor strode into the Governance chambers, the council's disheveled, malodorous presence offended his nose. They stank of urine, rotten food, and feces. The moment he entered, the council members surged toward him, voicing their complaints. The Chancellor cut through the cacophony with one look.

"You are all here by my grace only." He surveyed the group with utter disdain. "Your inconvenience is of no import to me."

The group took their seats as fear superseded their collective anger. Their lives and comforts were a gift of the Chancellor's whim.

"Now you have firsthand knowledge of how I contain the Drakkon problem. Be grateful a taste is all you received." The Chancellor took his accustomed seat at the head of the assembly. "The key was stolen from me by someone I trusted," he continued, peeling his gloves off one finger at a time. "It makes me wonder who I can trust."

No one spoke. A whiff of sedition was a death sentence.

"My Key is far from the city. I can do nothing about it." His eyes narrowed, a wicked smirk played across his lips. "You, my dear gentlemen, are going to start earning your positions."

The Chancellor began to outline a plan for city governance that left no citizen unaccounted for, no matter their allegiance. The city was the Chancellor's. He did not take defeat or disrespect well. When he snapped his fingers, the side door to the chamber opened. Hollow-eyed men entered the room balancing trays with crystal goblets on them. Each goblet was filled with a blue viscous liquid.

One of the council member's faces broke showing revulsion at the praxitrol filled goblets. The Chancellor refused to accept another betrayal. He smiled as the mind-altering drug was distributed, then the council members stared in collective horror as The Chancellor pounced on the man who had showed his revulsion.

He grabbed the man's jaw with one hand and a goblet with the other.

"Erol, how brave of you to volunteer to partake of my elixir."

He poured the liquid down the man's open mouth. The Chancellor held Erol's mouth closed as he waited until the man swallowed or choked. The Chancellor raised an eyebrow at the others. A soldier stood behind each man, ensuring compliance. The men each swallowed the contents. One by one, the men became vacant vessels awaiting the Chancellor's whim.

Only the Chancellor knew under the effects of the drug, their very souls were trapped – aware of everything, unable to fight or flee. In his estimation, praxitrol was the perfect weapon. He got obedient servants with the side benefit of torture.

"Well, my new hunters. You will behave as yourselves, implementing my plan immediately. No traitors left. No exception." He proceeded to instruct his new hunters on their collective duties.

The men all rose to their feet. Their right fists slammed against their chests and extended in a flat-handed salute. The men turned in unison, leaving the room. The Chancellor stayed behind pondering the current situation. He still needed to get the Node open. He wanted that miserable female creature that defeated his forces with no apparent effort. To do that, he needed a key.

The Chancellor threw the empty wine glass across the empty room. He turned and seated himself on the large chair at the head of the room. He knew that many of the council members referred to it as his throne behind his back. The only win in the current situation had been several weeks prior. He had gotten his key to open the node briefly to the place it had hidden so successfully for all those years, a side benefit was the exposure and capture of Drakkon in the city. A team of three assassins was sent through to ascertain the situation on the other side. Only they knew who the key was. 'It took a Drakkon to catch one.' The Chancellor gave a sinister twist of his lips at the stray thoughts. He had a few Drakkon who'd been willing to betray their kind.

When he obtained his Key, that wretched female would pay a heavy price for ruining his plans. Wouldn't it be ironic if he could make her his next Key? With the creature's power, the Otherverse could be his.

The Chancellor's eyes gleamed fevered brightness at the thought.

The song of the awakened Sphere of Drakkonon pulsed, the Chancellor cried out and fell to his knees, any thought of Otherverse domination pushed from his mind.

His Drakkon-being sung.

Rejoiced.

Wept.

Bereft in the aftermath, the Chancellor's anger surged through the negative space. The Sphere had been touched by a bloodline High Socra. The Chancellor erupted, roaring his anger. He had destroyed the bloodline himself. Only his pet lived.

"Gods be-damned! I'll not have that filth regain power in this world or the Otherverse. Ever!" His voice resounded in the empty chamber. He picked up the heavy chair he had sat in and hurled it. Its shattered pieces only added fuel to his anger.

"It was supposed to be me to rule this world and all the others. All I needed were the lost tools. The Key was nothing. I would have made the Sphere and the ancestors bow to my will." The Chancellor struggled to compose himself. He stalked down the empty corridor to a guarded elevator.

The guards turned their backs as the Chancellor entered the combination to the lift. The door closed behind him before the guards could turn back to face him. He trusted no one.

The elevator doors opened to reveal a cavernous opulently appointed room. Despite the Chancellor's actions, the room reenergized him. Rich in texture and color, the room revealed he Chancellor's secret – he was Drakkon.

A roughly hewn stool sat in the corner of room. Objects of his youth scattered in the space, some in pristine condition and others worn and damaged. He had no need for this detritus. The only purpose of the objects was to torment his Key; after all, keeping family close was a core Drakkon teaching. The Chancellor kept the only surviving member of his family close. Ethias Hixson, his younger brother, had been favored by the Ancestors-gods damn him. Receiving the Chancellor's rightful inheritance. But the Key had nothing left. The Chancellor had seen to it.

Ethias had whelped. The existence of a child, an heir, was unacceptable. If he couldn't have his brother, he would find the child and make her his Key.

The Chancellor trailed his fingers over the long worktable covered in beakers and bottles filled with blue liquid. He smiled. Ethias wouldn't be able to survive long.

Andros and Petroj destroyed the auto-carriage in the canyon. The rest of the party carried what they could. As they readied themselves to move the module, Jaczon pulled Petroj aside.

"Callem was supposed to await our arrival."

Petroj looked high at the surrounding edge of the canyon.

"I don't sense any troop movement. I didn't see anything during my flight." He looked at his father. "He had the hunters?"

"Plus a large company of evacuees." Jaczon shook his head. "He must have felt the group was too large already. The evacuees would have had no idea what the pods were. As long as no one got curious, their camouflage would keep them safe. But I'm worried." He rubbed his gloved hands. "Unless the Socra gave him the rest of the directions…" He shook his head in frustration. "That would be just like her to ignore protocol."

"Don't look at me. You married the woman."

Jaczon gave his son a jaundiced look. "Yes, and you inherited your mother's uncanny knack for trouble."

Petroj snorted as he slapped his father on the back. "I know that we're going to be heavily burdened, but we have to make sure that this module makes the Sanctuary."

The imp standing next to his mother piped up. "Why?"

"Alexi! Hush!" Katja looked apologetically at those around her.

"No, it's alright," Petroj reassured the boy and his mother. "We carry with us a long lost piece of our history." He placed a reverent hand on top of the container. "He has been abused and sorely tormented. But in the end, I believe that he can help us defeat the Chancellor and the Anakarei."

Alexi's brother Natov asked. "Are we going to help?"

Jaczon joined in. "Yes, we all are." He stood at the end of the module with the straps laid over his shoulders. "You and your brother are going to be light bearers for us." He looked at Katja. "You'll help guide the boys."

Andros stood at the front of the module.

“I’ll take the first leg of the journey. Petroj, you still need to regain your strength back after that flight.”

Petroj felt a very unfamiliar feeling bubble up from his gut. After a few moments, he realized it was pride and gratitude. He had spent so much time walking in the underbelly of society. To have people do things for the right reason was a source of amazement to him.

As the group stood ready to embark, the rapturous power swept over them. The adults reveled; the boys shimmered in transition. Jaczon and Petroj each grabbed one of the pubescent Drakkon, shifting would be dangerous to their development. They each used their own experience to stabilize the boys as the parents stood helpless in a mix of rapture and worry.

The pulse stopped as soon as it started. “Was that…?” Petroj asked his father.

Tears ran down his father’s cheeks. It was all he could do just to nod. Jaczon struggled to compose himself.

“The Sphere…” He cleared his throat again. “The Sphere of Drakkonon is not lost after all.”

“By all that’s Holy,” Petroj ruffled the tousled heads in front of him. “You both are witnessing the Time of Strife and Miracles.”

“We need to leave. All Drakkon would have felt it.” Jaczon pushed. “We need to get to safety.”

“All right, let’s go.” Petroj checked the packs on the boys and Katja. Their loads were heavy but manageable. Andros, Jaczon, and he would shoulder the rest.

Andros and Jaczon lifted the cocoon.

NINE

Nathan and Talek pushed fallen supports from the stoop overhang out of the way so that the exhausted party could exit the damaged home. Ella lagged behind the rest as she struggled under the weight of her injured dog. Great gouges were torn out of the earth front yard. Twenty year old trees were broken at the base of their trunks, the remains tossed across the space like pick-up sticks. The remains of the large dead bronze creature lay amongst the debris. Siding was ripped from the front of the house and windows broken. Ella concentrated on each breath Ronan took, thanking God for each one.

Myrna opened the back door of the Camry, allowing Ella to maneuver Ronan onto the back seat. Not saying a word, Myrna went around to the other side of the car and settled herself next to the dog. Creating an iridescent shield over the dead Drakkon, Nathan called lightning to incinerate the body. Bolt after bolt pounded the ground inside the protective barrier. The light show was surreal without the sound. All Ella could think was that she was grateful that she lived in a rural area. The resulting light show would definitely have drawn unwanted attention. The sounds of a fight brought Ella's attention to Talek and their unwanted guest. The man struggled against his restraints. Ella wasn't sure why he wasn't able to shift into dragon form but frankly didn't care at the moment.

Ella waited until Nathan and Talek had their captive confined in their vehicle, then headed to the safety of the

House. A comforting nimbus of light surrounded the store as she pulled into the parking lot. She pulled the car as close to the front door as possible. She didn't want to jar Ronan any more than was necessary.

Sindie and Kaie flew out the front door.

"You're back!" Sindie skidded to a stop by the passenger side of Ella car. She saw Ronan, "Oh no! Is he…" The question hung between them.

"The dog is badly hurt. I have much to do," Annisa answered her unfinished question.

Kaie leapt up into the car and climbed into the back seat. She gently touched her nose to Ronan's, gently butting her head against his. She looked at the people surrounding them and gave imperious cat instructions. Annisa opened the back passenger door.

"Yes, Kaie, we have to get him indoors." She picked the cat up and placed her on the sidewalk.

Ronan whimpered softly as Ella gently lifted Ronan from the car. He was still in considerable pain from his wounds. Kaie lead the way into and through the store, up the stairs to the guest rooms. A very large dog bed was waiting to receive Ronan in Ella's room. She sent out a mental thank you to the House. The response was warm and soothing.

"I'll take a look at his wounds again," said Annisa as she knelt by Ronan's side. "Just to make sure I haven't missed anything vital. Why don't you get your mother settled in a room," she suggested with a gentle nudge. "I'm sure the House has a room set up for her."

"The House has a room set up for me?" Myrna asked. "What does that mean?"

Ella weaved back and forth on her feet. She wanted to stay at Ronan's side, yet understood she had nothing to offer in the way of help. Myrna leaned heavily against her daughter as her own exhaustion began to manifest.

“Thank you, Annisa,” Ella responded. She placed her arm around her mother’s shoulders. “Mom, this is a truly amazing place. I’ll show you what Annisa means.”

When they left the room, Ella saw an open door two doors down from hers. She supported her mother’s limping form. “You’ll stay here tonight.”

“This is a beautiful room.” The antique poster bed was draped with a beautiful basket-weave patterned quilt in Myrna’s favorite colors of burgundy, blue, and green. Delicately carved bedside tables flanked the bed. Fatigue weighed heavily as she tried to take in all the details. “I can’t believe that the store has guest rooms just waiting for people.”

“This building is a completely unique place, Mom.” Ella marveled at the room. The soft tones in blue and mauve soothed and comforted. She could feel her mother relax. “You’ll be safe here.”

A bed had never looked so welcoming in Myrna’s eyes. The fluffy comforter matched the room’s colors. At that moment, Myrna felt every one of her sixty-eight years as the exhaustion pushed her to seek the comfort of the bed.

“I’m not even sure what happened tonight. I felt so helpless.”

“You didn’t look helpless.” A shadow of a smile flitted across Ella’s face. The memory of Myrna clutching the fireplace tools caused her to smile. “You looked like you had everything under control.” She knelt in front of her mother to remove her shoes. “I don’t have all the answers, but this has to do with Daddy.”

"Ethias?" Myrna struggled not to let her habitual anger get in the way of the situation. "He's been gone for thirty-six years. How can he have anything to do with tonight?"

Originally, Ella had never intended on telling her mother anything about the bookstore, her Drakkon heritage, or anything Other-related. Myrna had never been anything other than firmly planted in her own reality. If you couldn't touch it, see it, or have an explanation for it, it simply wasn't. Ella took a deep breath then exhaled.

"Mom, you said that your time with Daddy was magical. What did you mean by that?"

Myrna did her best to put aside the anger of the past three decades to revisit the memories of a time that were pure and innocent.

"When we met, something clicked between us, and we became inseparable." Myrna reached out and cupped her daughter's cheek. "Then you came along and your father was over the moon. You… you were just another part of the magic."

Ella sat transfixed. She had never heard her mother describe her relationship with her father in such a positive way.

"Our lives were filled with a light and laughter," her mother continued. "We had enough for our needs with a little extra. Your father was handy with mechanical things. He always said, 'You have to have a little magic to make the machines sing.'" Myrna's face lost the glow of happy recollections; her hand fell away from Ella's face. "Then everything changed that summer's day. The sun and magic went away." Myrna turned her head away to hide the tears. "He left us."

Ella rose from her knees and to embrace her mother. "Oh, Mama." She laid her head on Myrna's shoulder. "The sun and magic went away for both of us that day."

Myrna returned the embrace and wept.

A soft knock interrupted the women. Turning, Ella saw Annisa standing at the threshold. Before she could state the fear that jumped to the front of her mind, Annisa quickly said, "Ronan's settled and sleeping." Relief flashed over Ella's face. "We'd better get downstairs and see if Nathan and Talek have arrived."

Ella turned to her mother. "Do you want to rest or come downstairs?"

Myrna was still processing everything. "I'm going to stay here." She felt the day weighing on her. "I'm not sure if I'm up for any more revelations tonight. I'll keep an ear open for Ronan."

Ella gave her mother's shoulder a thankful squeeze and followed Annisa downstairs. She felt jittery from pushing past her exhaustion. They arrived on the selling floor just as Talek and Nathan wrestled their 'guest' in the front doors. She moved forward.

"Annisa, does the House have someplace to hold a prisoner?" Ella had no idea what to expect. They turned back to the office. Ella saw a door, the same color as the wall, to the right of the Manager Office. Annisa grabbed the handle and opened the entry revealing a set of descending stairs.

The man cursed as he struggled in Talek's and Nathan's grip. Ella couldn't help herself. As they passed by, she reached out and slapped the man on the back of the head. "Shut up!" She hissed in Drakkon. "You have limited value to us. You should be more concerned about staying alive."

Annisa looked at Ella with admiration. “Ms. Hixson, you have unplumbed depths to you.” They followed the men down the stairs.

After the men shoved him in, the prisoner fell to his knees in the cramped cell. The door clanged shut behind him. The only part of the cramped enclosure that didn’t have exposed bars was the floor, a roughhewn base of planks.

Annisa stood by a switch on the far wall. Nathan gave her a nod. The prisoner had been attempting to shake the bars of the cage to loosen them, to no avail. At the flip of the switch, a howl of pain filled the space. No one felt any particular sympathy for the prisoner.

Ella circled the structure as she evaluated the captive. The man hissed at her, calling her names as she circled him. She continued to watch him and smile –not a pleasant, nice to meet you, how are you smile. “So you’ve called me every unpleasant name you can think of, insulted my parentage, and called into question my sexual preferences.” Ella paused. “Anything else?”

“You are nothing, you Drakkon scum.” The man spat. “I will take pleasure in your death.”

“Nice. I’m sure your mother raised you better.” Ella gave him a pitying look. “Seeing as you are the one in a cage, you might want to reevaluate your whole ‘death to me’ stand. Let’s get down to business. Who are you?”

“I am your end.”

“Blah, Blah, Blah.” Ella waved her hands dismissively at him. “You’ll have to come up with something more original. Your comrade is dead and ash.” Bronze eyes met blue-green as she made eye contact. She decided to try what Nathan had done to her. She concentrated on the man in front of her and evaluated her options on how to conduct herself next. Ella sorted through the man’s secrets, such as they were. He was a mere foot soldier, trapped by a substance that took away his will. She filed that away for further examination. He was Drakkon like them, yet he had betrayed his heritage partly by uninformed choice and partly from the drug that influenced his every move. Nathan had killed his companion. His handler was still at large.

With a smile that was far from pleasant, Ella started. “You aren’t the one we really want, Becr. How does it feel to be worthless to us?”

Becr’s eyes grew wide at the use of his name but quickly narrowed in defiance. Spittle landed at Ella’s feet. She didn’t flinch. “I won’t tell you anything.”

Ella clicked her tongue in admonishment, correcting Becr. “No, the correct answer is you can’t tell us anything.” She circled the cell again. “I’ve been inside your head. What a waste. You felt the call of the Sphere, and you felt revulsion, instead of joy. What have they done to you?”

“I resisted your Drakkon-craft! I won’t be seduced by the animal in me!” Becr screamed at Ella. She turned to Talek. “Is that what the Anakarei are teaching our brethren?” Ella asked.

“There are those who want to conform to what they consider ‘normal,’ eschewing their heritage.” While Becr spat obscenities and vitriol, Talek looked at Nathan and Ella, “Drakkonon is a world without balance.”

Annisa joined everyone by the stairs.

“The cell will hold him for as long as we need.”

Ella glanced at the prisoner.

“We’ll probably have to feed him at some point.”

“Tomorrow will be soon enough,” Annisa she shepherded them up the stairs.

"You didn't see what node they used to gain entry to your world, did you?" Talek asked.

As they ascended the stairs, Ella thought about what she had seen in Becr's mind.

"I caught images," she said slowly. "I'm going to have to think about it. The journey wasn't easy for them."

This time, the stairs brought them to the guest room floor.

Ella shook her head. "You know, this is like living in an M. C. Escher drawing. You never know where you are going to end up."

"The House knows we are all exhausted." Annisa patted Ella's hand. "Basically, this is its way of telling us to get some rest."

Ella glanced at her watch was shocked to see it was well past midnight. "Nothing good ever happens after midnight," she murmured. Her hand shook with exhaustion as she opened the door to her mother's room. "I never expected it to be true."

She peered in to the room, but her mother was nowhere to be seen. Her stomach clenched in fear. Taking a deep breath, she turned toward her room. She quietly opened the door and saw her mother wrapped in a blanket sitting in a comfortable chair next to Ronan's bed. Kaie lay awake in her position next to Ronan. Ella gently shook her mother awake. "Mom," she whispered. "Come on, let's get you to bed."

Myrna offered little resistance as her daughter led her down the hall to her room. As Ella tucked the covers around her shoulders, Myrna asked in a voice raspy from sleep, "Is everything under control?"

Ella stroked her mother's hair. "As much as I can make it."

"Okay." Myrna let sleep take her away.

Ella wished it would be that simple for her as she returned to her room. Instead of going to bed, she sank to the floor by Ronan. She took comfort in the steady rise and fall of his chest as she spent time stroking his head.

A warm rough tongue woke Ella up from a fitful sleep. Warm brown eyes met hers as she opened hers. "Hey buddy, how are you feeling?" Ronan's tail thumped against the dog bed. She took it as a good sign and gave him another scritch before leaving to find breakfast for him. As she opened the door, Kaie entered the room.

"Good morning to you, cat!"

Kaie returned the greeting. At least Ella hoped it was a greeting. Cat wasn't one of her languages. She settled herself by the injured dog, proceeding to groom him. Ella shook her head as she left the room. When the cat got tired, she'd move. Priorities were food and water for the dog, caffeine for herself, and then figure out the rest.

Ella's mind was still fuzzy from exhaustion. Visions of her version of coffee danced through her head. If the universe were benevolent, in any fashion at all, she would find what she needed in the kitchen. If not, the outcome was not worth contemplating.

As she headed toward the stairs, hoping she would end up near some sort of kitchen facilities, Annisa appeared carrying bowls of food and water.

"You're up! Good." Annisa lifted the tray in her hands. "I've brought food for Ronan and Kaie."

"I was just going to try and find something for him." She reached out to help Annisa with her burdens. "Kaie is already keeping Ronan company."

Annisa turned her body to block Ella's efforts. "I'll take care of Ronan. You go on downstairs. There is a kitchen at the back of the store floor. You'll find breakfast there."

Ella gave the woman a grateful look before she headed down the stairs. The enticing scent of brewing coffee guided her through the selling floor. Without customers, the empty area was cavernous. People really added life to the area. Ella ran her fingers across the spines of the books of the shelves. The feel of books, as always, was comforting.

Something needed to be normal.

When Ella stepped into the eating area, she realized their guest was most likely starving. Time to show Becr that the Drakkon weren't the bogeymen. She grabbed her mug of coffee from the already brewed pot, the dark and heavenly brew was just as she liked it. Rummaging around the kitchen, she put together a quick breakfast of bagels and fruit on a tray and headed downstairs with the selections.

Softly descending the stairs, Ella saw Becr curled into a ball in the center of the cell with his face buried in his arms. The lights of the basement were harsh fluorescents. Ella realized they should have turned off the lights last night. She cleared her throat. There was no movement in the cubicle, but she wasn't about to open the door and check on him. She had seen too many movies to know that was a bad idea.

Ella set the tray on the floor and pulled a small table from across the room to the side of the cell, and then found a stool to sit next to it. She placed the breakfast items on it and waited. The tension in Becr's shoulders told her he was awake and aware of her. An imaginary clock ticked off the seconds in her head, causing her to fidget on the stool.

"Look, I know you're awake." Becr's form twitched. "We need to talk."

Minutes passed. Ella waited. Finally, Becr uncurled into a sitting position. His face covered in bruises that were just starting to shine in all their glory. With one eye swollen nearly shut, the other glazed with exhaustion, he looked at Ella. The night had not been a comfortable one.

Ella met his gaze, her tolerance for his actions extremely limited, yet she felt he needed to be shown some respect. She gestured to the food on the table. "If I open the door, are you going to be difficult?"

Becr eyed the food with avarice.

"I need nothing from you!"

"Once more, that is the incorrect answer." Ella chided him, her intentions to show him a kinder gentler Drakkon fraying, "You need me more than you know." She watched Becr. "Here's the deal, you're going to sit still while I give you some food and water. So that you see, I will eat from the same plate that I take your food. It is untainted, as is the water." She divvied up the bagels and fruit on the plates and cautiously opened the cell door after turning off the electrical current. "I need you to move to the far side of the cell." He made no move. "NOW!" Becr's one good eye narrowed, but he complied. She reached in, placing the plate of food with a large plastic glass of water on the edge of the platform. Before he could move back to the center of the cell, she asked one thing, "Whether you are hungry or not, I would ask that you not throw the food or water."

Becr's hunger won out against his need to rebel. With trembling hands, he retrieved the food and water. Ella went back to her table after locking the cell door. She didn't re-engage the circuits for the electricity. Becr saw this as a possible opportunity to escape. He needed the fuel, so he ate.

Ella sat down and watched Becr eat in a slow and methodical fashion. She bit into a slice of apple, pondering the situation.

"I need you to listen to me." Becr's chewing paused for a moment, then resumed. "I am not your enemy, yet your actions have surely put you in the category of mine." Ella rubbed her forehead. "I don't want to have to be anyone's enemy, but you crossed a line. You threatened my mother, destroyed my home, and hurt my dog." She stepped to the door of the cell, crouching down so she could make eye contact. "I don't believe that you fully understood the scope or consequences of your actions. You only have one piece of the puzzle."

"You cannot be allowed to spread your ways." Becr said.

"What ways would that be?" Ella asked. "Explain this to me."

"The Drakkon-craft cannot be allowed to corrupt my people."

"Drakkon-craft. You've said this twice. What is this?"

Becr couldn't believe the woman of power who had settled into a more comfortable position before him was so ignorant. "You should know. You beckoned all Drakkon with the call."

Ella nodded in realization. "When the Sphere awoke." Ella's hands unconsciously clenched. "I didn't know what would happen when I touched it."

"The Sphere of Drakkonon was supposed to have been destroyed with all those who held the heritage to awaken it."

Ella regarded the man in the cage. She knew that he truly believed what he was saying despite the presence of the drug in his system. At a young age the man had turned his back on the Drakkon. The knowledge in her head spoke of the few Blood-kin traitors through the ages. This one was particularly pathetic. Becr had gotten nothing but servitude out of his betrayal.

Ella continued to observe the man.

"Tell me, Becr. Do you have any family?"

The change of tact confused Becr. He remained silent.

Driven to her feet, Ella started pacing. "I have family, a mother. Our relationship is dysfunctional, but in the end we're family." She stopped in front of Becr, staring at the man. "I've seen your mind, as small as it is." She paused as she heard footsteps on the stairs. "You've never known kindness. Even as a servant to this 'Chancellor' who uses you as fodder in his war for otherversal domination."

Talek stood at Ella's side listening to her conversation with the prisoner.

"Even with your original choice, you can still change the outcome."

Startled, Talek looked at Ella. Becr just looked confused.

Becr stared at Ella as pain fogged his mind. Every bone and muscle ached. She confused him. She should be hurting him, punishing him. She should be shutting him in the dark. Instead she brought him food, talked to him-treated him as a person, not an animal.

She radiated the energy of the Drakkon. Yet, she was more. No Drakkon had ever treated him with any modicum of respect. He stared at Ella. "Drakkon-craft seduces the Drakkon into thinking they are better than the other people." Picking up the bagel from the plate, Becr ripped a piece from it. "Drakkon ruled the world and enslaved the people and other Drakkon. There was a war."

Ella looked at Talek for confirmation of Becr's story. In a low voice, Talek confirmed this was the Chancellor's revisionist history.

Talek crouched down in front of the cell at Becr's level. When Becr scrambled back from him, Talek held his hands in front of him in a non-threatening way.

"Becr, how long have you been in the Chancellor's employ?"

Becr thought about his response. The praxitrol only allowed him to say certain things. He was due for another dose in the next few days. "It doesn't matter."

Talek looked at Ella. "It matters. I can't imagine the Chancellor would send any Drakkon under his influence without a handler."

"From what I saw in his mind, he's been under the Chancellor's influence since he was a young boy."

Becr started to squirm. Talek walked over to the wall and re-engaged the circuit, electrifying the cell walls. "The cell is made of a material that inhibits transformation. Add electricity to the mix, and he won't be able to break out." Talek looked at Becr with profound pity. "I'm sorry, your withdrawal will be miserable. We'll do everything we can to help you survive. We really will."

"What do you mean, we'll help him survive?" Ella demanded.

Talek pulled Ella to the stairs. "He is the victim of long term exposure to a drug called praxitrol," he explained in hushed tones. "It causes the victim to imprint on a person. In our world, it is the Chancellor. He controls every aspect of the drug." The more he explained, the grimmer his face became. "The person then becomes psychically linked to The Chancellor, an unwitting spy."

Alarmed Ella glanced at Becr. "Now?"

"Most likely to his handler. I don't know if the link will send between worlds." He guided Ella up the stairs. "I can guarantee we'll have one more incursion. The handler will want his instrument back."

“Instrument?” Ella said. “These people aren’t viewed as human?”

Talek’s answer was simple and concise. “No.”

Ella confronted Talek. “He made one poor decision. He’s paid for it his entire life, no freedom, betrayal and enslavement at every turn.” She looked Talek directly in the eyes, the stairs allowed the feat. “Can you say that every choice you’ve made has been pristine?”

Talek was the first to break the gaze. He knew the point she was making.

“No one has ever come back from the effects of praxitrol.”

“How do you know?” Ella demanded. “Do your people have scientists that have studied it?”

The door to the stairwell opened before Talek could reply. Annisa stood in the guest quarter hallway. The changing stairway still freaked Ella out.

“Nathan wants you both upstairs in his den,” Annisa announced. “How is our guest?”

“Trouble,” Talek replied before Ella could say anything.

Ella shot Talek a dirty look.

“Conflicted. Non-cooperative but confined.”

Annisa waited for the pair to pass by her.

“Is it going to be worth it to keep him alive?”

Ella stopped in her tracks, turning to face the diminutive woman.

“Every life is important, no matter how lost. I’ve seen a flicker beneath all the loss, all the fear, all the betrayal. Isn’t that enough to fight for?”

Annisa met the taller woman’s gaze without flinching.

"You'll do." And then she walked away.

Ella turned to Talek.

"That woman really confuses me."

Talek tugged Ella down the corridor.

"Your world confuses me."

The tension from the staircase had dissolved.

Once more Ella found herself in the elegance sensory feast of Nathan's den. She took a second to revel. Having acknowledged her Drakkon-self seemed to have lessened the opiate effect of the room on her senses.

Nathan gestured them both over to a bank of monitors that sat in a well-insulated, ornate cabinet. The screens showed different aspects of the selling floor, currently devoid of customers. Only Sindie and Annisa roamed the space.

"What are we looking at?" Ella finally asked Nathan.

"Just wait for it." His intent gaze never wavered from the monitors. He seemed to track something Ella couldn't pick up. Suddenly, Talek tensed next to her. Nathan's finger stabbed at the lower left screen. "There!"

Ella's gaze caught a shadow blur across the screen. She had no idea what she was looking for, but judging by the looks on Nathan and Talek's faces, it wasn't good. Impatient, Ella cleared her throat. "Hello? I saw a blur." She nudged Nathan, "What are we looking at?"

Nathan shook his shoulder free of her hand, "The creature's handler has come to reclaim his instrument."

Ella leaned closer to the monitors trying to see more than just the store, Sindie, and Annisa. On the upper right hand screen, Kaie strolled onto the viewing screen, pausing for a moment to look at the camera with a deliberate wink. "Aren't you going to warn them?"

"Shh!"

Ella turned to go to the selling floor to help the women. Nathan's hand shot out, grabbing her arm in a firm, implacable grip.

"Let me go! They need help!" Ella writhed to release herself from his grip.

Nathan finally turned around. "Ella, what have you learned about the House over the last several days?" He returned his gaze to the screens. "Annisa, Sindie, and Kaie know exactly what is happening. Just watch."

Ella stopped pulling away from Nathan's grasp. Talek had been listening to the entire exchange as he watched the progress of the intruder in the store.

"There!" Talek's finger stabbed at the screen.

Annisa and Sindie had cornered a man in the space around the information desk. Kaie was on the counter behind the man ready to begin her assault. In a flash, the cat's claws were tearing the man's face to ribbons. While the man's hands were occupied trying to free himself from the feline's attack, Annisa threw Sindie a small bundle. With the sudden appearance of large functional wings, Sindie rose above the fray with a shimmery net in her hands. The net dropped and Kaie leapt into Annisa's arms. The man toppled as the net engulfed him.

Sindie dropped gracefully back to the floor, her wings folding themselves back to wherever they'd been hiding. With a warrior's grin, Sindie signaled success at the camera. Kaie leapt down from Annisa's arms, stalking by the struggling man. Adding insult to injury, the cat squatted and urinated on him.

Myrna woke rested and ready to find answers. She peered into Ella's room, where Ronan's familiar snoring told her he was in a deep sleep, and then closed the door quietly to seek the others. The events of the previous night had left her exhausted. With a derisive smile on her face, Myrna realized she was changing. Instead of choosing to be a recluse, she was seeking company. The door at the end of the hallway was open, the stairs leading down. Griping the banister, she slowly descended. Her legs were still wobbly from disuse but getting stronger. Her years of inactivity weighed heavy on her. Lost in her thoughts, she finally noticed that she seemed to be descending more stairs than necessary to get to the first floor. The final flight down opened into a large basement with a barred cell in the middle of the floor.

A man sat in the middle of the cell. He shook convulsively, his arms wrapped around his middle in an unsuccessful attempt to maintain control. Myrna recognized the man from the previous night, and froze on the stairs. His evident distress was at contrast with the fearsome attacker of her memory. Myrna stepped into the basement.

Becr heard the steps descending and didn't look up. What was the point? He was dead. He had failed. He was an outcast from his own kind, a spy for their enemy. He waited for their judgment. The steps shuffled closer. On some level, Becr knew that he was suffering from the withdrawal effects of praxitrol.

Acknowledging his visitor, Becr looked up. He saw an old woman, with an unsteady step, making her way toward him. His eyes widened as he recognized her from the previous night. He straightened his posture, not in defiance, but in respect. He had been under compulsion to attack the night before. He hadn't wanted to hurt her or the noisy wolfish creature. This world confused him. He understood more of the language than he could speak.

"I see they have you unrestrained." Myrna stopped in front of the cell door. "Have you had anything to eat this morning?"

Becr nodded.

"Good." Myrna asked the question that had nagged at her. "Why? Why did you attack my home?"

Becr looked Myrna in the eye. "I'm sorry.

Myrna stared in the eyes of the man who would have killed her. All she saw was a lost man, a man as lost as she was in this new world unfolding before her. She acknowledged his apology with a nod, before she went back up the stairs.

Ella found her mother emerging from the basement stairs. "Mother! What were you doing down there?"

Myrna recognized concern, irritation, and fear in her daughter's tone. "I thought the stairs would take me to the store floor." She shrugged. "Instead they took me to the basement."

Ella gently guided her toward the first floor kitchen. "Let's get something to eat. Then we'll talk."

Talek and Nathan rose from their seats in an old world courtly gesture as Myrna entered the room. She could not fault the men on their manners.

"Mrs. Hixson," Nathan greeted her as he pulled out a chair for her. "Did you rest well?"

"Well enough," Myrna replied. "Why does a bookstore have a prison cell in the basement?"

Nathan looked startled at the question.

Ella jumped in. "The House took Mother to the basement instead of the first floor. She met our guest."

"Ah." Nathan contemplated the older woman before him. Like her daughter, she was proving to be of sterner material than he had anticipated. "How is our guest this morning?"

"I don't think he is doing particularly well," Myrna said. "He's shaking and afraid."

"Given the events of last night, he should be afraid." Talek joined the conversation. "He is a foot soldier in a very nasty war."

Myrna looked at Talek. "Who are you?"

Ella quickly made introductions.

"What kind of name is Talek?" Myrna asked.

"Mother…"

"Ella," Talek interrupted and turned to face Myrna. Bowing, Talek introduced himself. "I am Talek Jesperek. I am Drakkon, here to carry a message to a lost Priestess as a warning."

Myrna blinked and blinked again.

"A what?" She asked in the politest tone she possibly could.

"Drakkon, Mom." Ella could see and hear the gears in her mother's head starting to crank. "A shape-shifting species from another world known as Drakkonon." She waited two heartbeats. "Daddy was one."

Annisa entered the kitchen still high from the victory of the fight. The tension was palpable as she heard Ella tell her mother that her husband had been an Other-kind.

"Nathan, the intruder is secured away from our guest. Sindie is taking first watch."

Nathan nodded and turned his attention back to the unfolding drama.

"Mrs. Hixson, you've been exposed to much in the last twenty-four hours," he added. "I'm sure that you are feeling…"

"You have no idea what I'm feeling or experiencing." Myrna sent a fulminating glare that singed everyone in the room. "Do not presume to think for me." In the not so distant past, she would have snapped and snarled at everyone. But today was a different day. Myrna speared her daughter with a look. "Ella, tell me true. Is what these men say real?" A nimbus of energy crackled as it gathered around the old woman.

"Mother?"

"Word-craft?" Annisa asked.

Talek stared at both women. Drakkon did not possess this gift.

Myrna felt the shockwave of power emanate from her words, encircling her daughter. The power wasn't violent or ill-intended. She had none of those feelings toward her daughter. She just wanted to know the truth.

Ella let the energy wash over her, before it shimmered into nothing. The experience was curious. "Yes, all that they say is true." Ella tilted her head as she observed her mother. "The Universe is a bit more complex than you and I ever expected."

Energy still humming through Myrna's body, she shook her hands out in front of her to dispel the feeling. "Mrs. Hixson," Nathan respectfully addressed Myrna. "Tell us about your family."

"Nothing special, we're normal." The experience left her dazed. She had no recollection of anything similar happening to her – ever.

"Um, Mom." Ella cleared her throat. "You cast a spell."

"I'm not a witch." Myrna exclaimed and then looked thoughtful.

Ella picked up her mother's hand. "No one is saying that you are. You gathered energy about you then attempted to compel me into telling you a truthful answer. That's not normal."

Nathan tried again. "Where does your family originally come from?"

"The last couple of generations have been scattered around the country." Myrna gave a shrug. "Granny Fischer always said she had a bit of the witch in her from Salem, but not really. Her people came from the Balkans in Europe."

Ella and Nathan stared at each other. Annisa stepped forward. "Myrna, I need to look inside your head."

Myrna stared at the woman who had helped her through the disappearance of her husband suspiciously. "You have to look inside my head? What exactly does that mean?"

Ella raised an eyebrow at Annisa. "I trust you'll be less intrusive than you were with me?"

Annisa gave Ella a small but mean smile. "You made me itchy." She leveled a steady gaze at Ella. "You turned out okay." Annisa turned her attention back to Myrna. "Just relax, you shouldn't feel a thing."

Ella stepped away from Annisa and her mother and moved over to Nathan and Talek. "What is Annisa looking for?"

"She had mentioned that she had found a memory lock, like the one we found in you, in your mother's mind."

Ella's eyes widened. The implications were huge. Her father had been a busy man. Just how far had he gone to protect them?

"With her calling of power, Annisa feels that she might be able to safely disable the lock and help your mother figure things out..." Nathan stared straight ahead. "Less traumatically," he finished.

Ella rolled her eyes as she resisted the urge to kick Nathan. "Gentlemen, we've got problems. This Chancellor raised the stakes last night."

"What are you thinking, Ella?"

Ella gave a mirthless laugh.

"Nathan, this world isn't ready to accept Other-kin or magic. We can barely tolerate differences amongst ourselves."

Nathan nodded in agreement.

"What I've seen of your world, you seem to have plenty of defenses," Talek interjected. He had been reading history books.

"We have no defenses against Power or magic. Inter-dimensional travel and any threats are going to be problematic." Ella looked to Nathan. "You said that the other nodes were guarded by Other-kin. Is there a way to contact them?"

Nathan saw where Ella was going. "The fact that nothing out of the ordinary has been reported is troublesome. I'll contact them again."

"You have regular node activity on your world?" Talek asked.

Nathan responded absently, his mind was going through possibilities. "The greater races travel through this world on a regular basis. After the Anakarei came to power, the presence of the Drakkon in the Otherverse became rather limited."

"I didn't recognize any landmarks around the node Becr came through." Ella thought about the nodes Nathan had pointed out earlier. "I should have at least recognized something."

“They would have travelled through the main node on Drakkonon.” Nathan said, “They’d just have to land on a world with an established trade route able to access Earth.”

Ella sorted through all the Node related information in her head.

She started, “Nathan, you said there were a number of major nodes here on Earth?” When Nathan confirmed, she continued, “That makes Earth one of the major nexus points in the Otherverse.” Ella realized what this meant. . “We can’t have any more Drakkon attacks here. If the Chancellor wants a fight, we’ll have to take it to him.”

Both men looked at Ella as if she had lost her mind.

TEN

An electric energy swept through the Sanctuary. Joy overcame the Socra. For an instant, the world around her stopped as she reveled in the moment.

"Nonne!" Callem came running towards her. "What…"

The Socra waved her hand to stave off the questions.

"Gather everyone downstairs in the meeting room of the Sanctuary. I will explain then."

Callem ran from the room shouting. The Socra shook her head at the noise.

"Gather, boy!" She stretched to work out the kinks the fast-paced journey and the labor of cleaning out the dust of decades had left in her old body. "Not shout!"

She looked down at herself, dust and grime streaking her sturdy brown skirt. The once cream colored apron was now dingy grey. The slovenliness of her appearance offended her sensibilities. She pulled the scarf from her grey streaked hair, stuffing it into the skirt's pocket.

The Socra felt the contentment of the Sanctuary. It welcomed the hustle and bustle of the newly gathered inhabitants. The walls danced with shadows of current and past occupants. The entire structure hummed with energy. She ran her fingers along the wall of the hallway as she moved down the corridor. The Sanctuary had responded joyfully to the awakening of the Sphere.

"Socra!"

"What was that…?" Questions pounded her from all sides the moment she entered the great meeting room. Intricately carved latticework graced every other wall, creating an open feeling to the octagonal space. At the pulpit, she raised her hands to silence all the questions and demands that echoed through the room. All eyes avidly turned their gaze to the front.

"My brothers and sisters, we have journeyed." Callem and Ane came forward to stand on either side of her. "Today…" The Socra's emotions rose to overwhelm her. "Today, our lives change. The Sphere of Drakkonon, thought lost to time, has been awakened."

Shouts of joy erupted from the crowd. The learnings of the Holy Script foretold of the restoration of the Sphere.

"Where is the Sphere?" a voice from the crowd asked.

"I do not know. Yet it is confirmation not all of our precious bloodlines have been lost. The blood of the High Socra continues for only those of this line can awaken the Sphere." The spirits of the Ancestors buoyed the Socra's spirit, filling her with jubilation. "The Time of Strife and Miracles is upon us. Our lost will be gathered. We will be tested. New allies and new enemies will walk among us." She paused as she looked over the gathered Drakkon. Faces were filled with fear and jubilation as the throng felt the presence of the ancestors. Shouts of elation filled the room as the fear subsided leaving only joy. She raised her hands and the crowd subsided. "Our kind will be strengthened with our friends and neighbors who struggle with the oppression of the regime. We cannot forsake them in their hour of need." Her countenance grew brighter. "We are Drakkon! We help all in need, Drakkon or not!"

A roar erupted from the room. Every soul who stood, sat, or knelt felt the rapture and swore their support. Tears fell freely from the Socra's eyes. She knew that she would not bear the mantle of leadership alone any longer. A small selfish part of her was tired; it looked forward to the respite.

The Socra claimed their attention once more by raising her hands, palms up. "Brothers and Sisters we have much to do in preparation. Let us not tarry. For some of us, this will not be our final stop. The Sanctuary has waited a long time to be of service again. Let us bring her to readiness in preparation for the next step in our journey."

The crowd broke apart in small groups, families or friends, all talking about the revelations. The last cleared the wide doorway before the Socra sagged, succumbing to her exhaustion. Callem caught the woman who ranked second in his heart.

"Callem hush!" Ane soothed. She recognized the signs of exhaustion that plagued the Socra. "She hasn't rested fully since we evacuated. Bring her to the quarters she chose. They are prepared."

The Socra murmured, but Ane sternly rebuffed the protest.

"Nonne, you are not a fledgling."

The Socra gave the impertinent girl a glare then sighed. "You'll make a fine Socra one day."

Ane brushed the springy gray hair from the finely lined forehead. "I can only hope." She glanced at her husband. "Let's get her to her room."

When she settled the Socra into her chambers, Ane changed her into a nightgown. She draped a cool cloth across her eyes and gently ordered the older woman to sleep.

Jaczon was grateful that the twins were ahead with their father scouting out a place to camp for the night. By his estimation, they were a day's journey from the Sanctuary. If he had to listen to the twin's ask one more time any variation of 'Are we there yet?' to any of the adults, he was going to possibly have to deprive their parents of the joy of raising them. He saw Petroj watching him with a sly grin on his face.

"What?" Jaczon snarled.

"Are we there yet?" Petroj danced away from Jaczon's flying fist laughing.

"While I love your mother, I could always replace you," Jaczon threatened.

Petroj knew the threat was empty. "You could, but Mother wouldn't let you live long enough."

Katja watched the interplay between the men. They were so different from the men she had known in the city. In many ways, it was more comforting to see the relationship. She had been aware of the friendship, but now knowing they were father and son explained many things.

"Gentlemen, my sons are all driving us demented with their questions. Just do what I do."

Both men focused their gaze on Katja. "I simply picture us getting safely to the Sanctuary and letting them loose on the unsuspecting inhabitants there," Katja answered with the serenity of an experienced mother.

Both men chuckled as the miscreants in question returned with their harried looking father.

The end of the following day brought the exhausted party to the Sanctuary boundary. Alexi and Natov looked at the edifice with wonder and reached out to touch the iridescent shimmering air.

"No!" cried Katja. She had no idea what the shimmering meant, but she was willing to ere on the side of caution.

Jaczon smiled as he reassured her. “They can touch it.” He remembered the first time he had ever touched the Veil. “All will be well.”

The family reached out tentatively, smiles of pure pleasure graced their faces as the Veil flowed over their hands and caressed their bodies, rejuvenating them. Motioning for the family to continue on, Jaczon knew that their presence had been recognized and announced. Jaczon reached out to partake in the ritual of welcoming to the Sanctuary.

Only after they’d become accustom to the feeling did they realize that Petroj stayed on the other side of the Veil with the module. Sorrow filled Petroj’s face. Jaczon wasn’t surprised at his son’s reticence. The Sanctuary was a place for the pure in heart. Those with souls unfettered. Both men felt the burden of actions perpetrated to protect the Drakkon.

Jaczon passed through the Veil. He stood in front of his son on the other side. “Come, we must …”

“I can’t go in there,” Petroj interrupted his father. His voice rang with the conviction of the damned.

His nape prickled as Jaczon stared at his son. He knew that his wife stood near them. The mate bond vibrated with the powerful chanted prayers his wife offered up on behalf of their son.

Tears tracked down the tormented face of the man once known as the Tmavě Jeden – the Terror of The Chancellor, the Betrayer of the Drakkon. His carefree childhood played across Petroj’s mind. All that changed the last time he stepped inside the Sanctuary’s walls. He’d been asked to protect his people by walking amongst the enemy.

Gripped in the paralysis of his fear, Petroj didn’t see the most innocent come forward. Alexi and Natov each grasped a hand and pulled him forth toward the Veil. With the support of the Ancestors, their gentle grasp was implacable. Together, they stepped through.

Petroj was embraced by the Veil and the Sanctuary. His soul exulted in the joyful reunion.

Moments, hours, eternities later, Petroj opened his eyes; the first thing he saw was clouds painted on a ceiling. A loving hand brushed a cool cloth across his brow. He turned his head and saw his mother.

"Shh!" The Socra admonished him. "Silly boy, how could you think that the Sanctuary wouldn't let you return?" She stroked his brow gently. "After all, you drew your strength and resolve from here." The Socra watched the confusion play across Petroj's face. "You were never alone," she continued. "At such a young age, your belief was so strong. I knew your path would be difficult. I just didn't know how." She lovingly cupped his face. "Can you forgive your Socra for asking such a sacrifice and your mother for letting you?"

Petroj reached up, his hands resting on top of hers – the same hands, though older more worn.

"Mother, it was never a matter of you letting me. I knew what would happen if no one stepped forward."

"My sweet boy, that is what makes you exceptional."

"The module!" Petroj's dull mind was catching up to the events of the past. "Where is it?"

"I recognized the cocoon as one used that housed the hunters. It is safe in a shielded room." She anticipated her son's next question. "Jaczon explained the one you carried needed to be kept separate. The hunters are safe as well."

Petroj relaxed a little as he let the energy of the Sanctuary seep into his battered soul.

Pacol glanced at his second-in-command, Davist Bencak, swearing, "Damn it all! We don't have time to deal with all these extra patrols."

"What did you expect when the Chancellor's plan went to crazck?" Davist muttered. They crouched in the shadows of an alley six blocks from the Wyvern. Their goal was to get to the tavern and open it for business. Having it mysteriously close wouldn't do anyone any good. "For that matter, why did you think I'd become a good barkeep?"

"Your shining personality has always won the peoples trust." Pacol smacked his longtime friend on the back of the head. "You'll do fine. Just don't poison anyone important."

The deep of the night helped conceal their journey. Only the most criminally minded were on the streets. Most knew Pacol by sight, the rest by reputation. Davist pasted on a less than inspiring smile as he faced the leader of the crime world.

The Wyvern had always been a neutral place for all the citizens of Annak who were looking to unwind after a long work shift. Pacol had no problem keeping the establishment open, he knew why the family had left and respected it. For a man of no particular faith, Pacol believed in the oddest things. His most important belief was to take care of one's own. Pacol and his team would keep this business afloat and out of Anakarei hands, gathering information as they gathered empty cups and cutlery.

The dawn mist settled down from the tops of the buildings, flooding the streets with a sea of grey. Streetlights glowed in the sea of mist that sought to envelop the lower levels of the city. Vapor clung to the front of the Wyvern, as if attempting to seep into the sealed door. Pacol pulled out a large ring of keys and sorted through it until he found the one he wanted.

The lock resisted the invasion of an unfamiliar key. Pacol paid no attention to its reticence. They pushed open the door and entered, the second door pulling slightly toward them with the seal being broken from the outside. Quickly locking the door behind them, they entered the empty tavern.

Davist had been in the Wyvern plenty of times as a patron. The energy had been lively. Now, it was dormant. Chairs were up on the bar and tables, waiting for their day to start. Pacol was behind the bar checking out the supplies when the door to the upstairs opened up. Brandishing a bat, an old woman stood in the doorway.

"By all the winds that blow, Pacol," she spat. "Boy, don't go sneaking about in places you don't belong."

Pacol bowed respectfully to the woman. "Mistress Smyzac, you know that sneaking is what I do best."

Mistress Smyzac lowered her bat and entered the taproom. "What brings you night dwellers here?"

"With Katja and Andros out of the city, we can't let the Wyvern close." Pacol pulled out a chair for the woman. "People need a gathering place that is safe." He watched relief flash across the woman's face. "Why didn't you leave the city with your family?"

"I'm too old. I'd have only slowed them down," Mistress Smyzac stated.

Pacol had to respect the woman's grasp of the situation. He gestured to Davist. "This is my second, Davist." Davist sketched a courtly bow. "He'll be running the Wyvern in Andros' absence. Your family won't have to worry about their home when they return."

Mistress Smyzac reached up and patted Pacol's cheek. "You are a good boy." She looked at them both. "You both are." She motioned Davist to the counter. "I'll help you in the kitchen. I know what the regulars want."

"Alright, Mistress." Davist looked at Pacol. "We'll get through this."

"What about the Chancellor and his men?"

"Jaczon Carbehk always used this place as a way of gleaning information from loose tongues." She gave an unsettling cackle. "You can count on the staff to keep their ears open."

Pacol's head nodded as he reformulated his original plans. Being able to keep up with workings of the Anakarei would keep so many trapped in the city safe. He left Davist with some last minute instructions and in the capable hands of Mistress Smyzac.

The Chancellor sat in front of the weekly grand council session. The praxitrol controlled council members were simply boring. He missed the miasma of fear that always shrouded the council room. Most had already given in to the inevitable, but one in particular struggled against the compulsion. His movements were precisely as directed, but the bead of sweat trickling down the side of his face gave away his mental struggle.

Time for a little entertainment, the Chancellor thought.

"Erol," The Chancellor called. "Come here."

With jerky movements that were reminiscent of a stringed puppet, the council member moved toward the front of the chamber. The Chancellor smiled at the man standing silently before him.

The rest of the men stared blankly at each other across the council table, an audience of blank canvases. The survival part of their brains was still present enough to instill a modicum of fear.

The perfume of terror was sweet to The Chancellor. Erol's pupils were dilated with terror "Erol, I want you to face your fellow councilmen."

The man stiffly rotated until he stood facing the large room.

The Chancellor rose from his seat and unsheathed the blade he always carried on his belt. "You and your house are built on lies. I don't like traitors." He circled the motionless man and shouted. "Do you think I wouldn't know about your filthy proclivities toward the Drakkon?"

Spittle landed in Erol's face. Locked in his mind, Erol screamed for his body to move. He shook his mental arms and legs and ran as far as he could in his mind, only to go nowhere. A tear trickled down his cheek.

"Oh look, the Drakkon-scum has a feeling." The Chancellor tilted his head in evaluation at the man before him. "We can't have that. Raise your arm, palm up."

Erol's arm rose haltingly.

"Faster."

The arm snapped up with the hand extended palm up. The Chancellor had a reptilian smirk on his face, as he placed the pommel of the blade in the man's hand.

"Take the blade."

Erol saw scenes of his family, laughing and smiling, play across his mind. He and his wife had wanted to change the system, to help the Drakkon regain their place in society, to give their children an opportunity to be proud of their heritage. He remembered the last words he and his twin brother had: "Working for that scumbag will only bring ruin down your family. See if I'll be there to pick up the pieces."

"Slice your throat." The cold calculated command resonated through the room.

Erol's physical body gurgled quietly while his spirit screamed.

Pacol's hand had just reached the entry door of the Wyvern when his brother's death scream swept through the psyche plain shared by all Drakkon. The pain drove him to his knees. Tears flowed as he mourned his brother.

"Pacol!" Davist ran to his fallen friend.

Pacol grabbed the shirt collar of his second. "Get two trucks over to Councilman Erol's house. I'll meet them there!"

Davist didn't ask questions. He grabbed the telecom behind the counter and made the call. Mistress Smyzac bustled toward the back rooms. "Come, we must prepare."

"Mistress Smyzac, I don't think that you need to be involved with this."

She held the door open to the upper levels that housed the family quarters. "Boy, I'm already involved. Councilman Erol was well known to all the Drakkon."

"What happened to Councilman Erol?" Davist knew that Erol was Pacol's brother.

"The Chancellor killed Erol."

"Crazck!"

"Watch your tongue!" With a reproving cuff, Mistress Smyzac led Davist up the stairs. "We have to get the rooms ready for the family and their loyal retainers."

"What rooms?" The old woman with more energy and knowledge had expertly flipped the tables. Davist ceded authority to Mistress Smyzac.

Armed cargo transports roared up to the front and back entrances of the elegant mansion. Pacol didn't bother with ringing the front bell. Using his booted foot, he kicked the massive front door in, his strength augmented by fear and his Drakkon nature. The scene was what he expected, a puppet of the Chancellor threatening his brother's family.

"You traitorous piece of crazck!" Pacol snarled. "Did you not think that I wouldn't come looking for my family?"

Erol's widow's voice was tense as she looked at her brother-in-law with relief. "As usual, you wait until the last minute," Jenne said.

"The delay keeps things exciting, darling." Crashes from the back of the house told him that his team was taking care of the praxitrol-controlled staff there. "Give me the guns." Pacol gaze fell upon each of the men threatening his family. Their deaths would not be easy. "Whether you live or die is unimportant to me, but I suppose the Chancellor will want a report."

Jenne held a child under each arm. Her oldest boy lay slumped across her feet, blood trickling from his temple. Her chin held high, Jenne gave the man who'd run her household no quarter. Distain dripped from her voice.

"Kill the scum, Pacol. I have no use for him anymore."

Pacol had always liked his brother's mate.

The majordomo's head turned awkwardly toward Pacol. His body followed.

"You will turn your traitorous self in."

The gun hand pointed at Pacol's forehead. All attention was off the family.

"Really? Why would I do that?" Pacol sneered. "As usual, the Chancellor can't even do his own dirty work. What a coward."

A panel behind the settee the family sat on slid open. Jenne turned the children's faces to her bosom. The simultaneous three shots deafened the remaining inhabitants of the room. The boy at her feet started to stir.

Pacol didn't give anyone a minute to process. He grabbed the boy. Each man from the passage grabbed a child and helped Jenne to her feet.

Jenne stopped Pacol. "Did you get Karlie?"

"She's in the transport waiting for her mother." Pacol shifted the awakening boy in his arms for a better grip. "Let's get a move on."

The cargo transports roared away from the mansion. There was no point in secrecy. Instead of heading to his normal headquarters, the party ditched the transports near an Anakarei loyalist and took to the sewers.

Erol's youngest, Bellith, tripped, falling face first in the tunnel muck. She started wailing. Pacol plucked his filthy niece up from the sewer. She sobbed into his neck as he patted her back.

"We are almost to safety. I promise." The rest of the children gave small grunts of disbelief. "Two more corners and we'll be there."

Davist stood by the well concealed entrance at the back of the Wyvern's storeroom. Bawdy, raucous laughter floated above the steady flow of the taproom conversation behind the closed kitchen door.

BANG!

Davist jumped from the tunnel-side noise on the door. He pulled the access open to reveal the filthy group before him.

"Gods! Man, did you have to walk all the way in the sewers?"

In no mood for back talk, Pacol led the exhausted group into the brightly lit room.

Mistress Smyzac bustled into the room.

"You're here! Good, good!" She placed the tray on a box and got a good whiff of the group. "You poor souls, follow me." She took the youngster out of Pacol's arms. Another door opened with the quick press of a ceramic tile, revealing a set of stairs leading up. "Come on, everyone. Just a little more and you'll be able to rest."

Pacol stayed behind with Davist. The man's eyes watered at the foul odor wafting off of his friend.

"Look, don't take this the wrong way, but you need to get clean before the stink starts to chase away customers."

Pacol tried to get past his grief as he dealt with the mundane issues of survival. "The house was completely compromised. We'll have to carefully check out the base."

Davist stared at Pacol in horror; the staff knew location of their headquarters. "Did you even get over there?"

"No, I had to get the family out."

Davist understood Pacol's priorities, but he was ready to do some reconnaissance.

"I'll go and check out the situation. The Drakkon would have felt what you felt and evacuated who they could." He pushed Pacol toward the door where everyone had disappeared. "Go, get cleaned up. I'll report back."

"Don't do anything stupid," Pacol muttered. "Don't get caught."

"You know me. 'Stupid' is my middle name!"

"I mean it! I don't have time to rescue your sorry hide."

Davist laughed on his way out the sewer door. "You'll miss me if you don't!"

Pacol shook his head. He knew that Davist would get the information they needed. The Wyvern would be a good temporary place to set up, but they needed to find another facility as soon as they could.

Mistress Smyzac met him at the top of the stairs. Shoving a towel in his hands, she ordered him to strip before he went any farther. Pacol wasn't a particularly modest man, but the old woman's forthright manner was a bit disconcerting.

"Come on now, young man." she leered, "You don't have anything that I haven't seen raising my boy and grandsons."

Pacol wrapped the towel around his waist. He was completely naked for the first time in years. The light in the passage way revealed his Drakkon heritage. The exposure of the fine bronze lines that covered his body made Pacol uncomfortable.

He stepped into the steamy bathing room. He only hoped that the hot water would last until he felt clean and his heart stopped beating in time with his many regrets.

Petroj felt peaceful for the first time in years, free from the weight of his role as the Tmavě Jeden. The door to his chamber opened revealing his mother.

"Good, you're awake." The Socra entered the room with a bundle of clean colorful clothes, not a scrap of familiar, comfortable black. "You've had some very worried young men keeping vigil." She chuckled. "I believe you are their hero."

Petroj tried to hide the unusual rise of color that stained his cheeks. He was the feared Tmavě Jeden; he didn't blush. The clatter of feet heralded his admirers.

"Petroj!"

"You're awake!" Both voices spoke over each other.

Petroj raised his voice over their jubilation, “I am better. Rested.” He looked at their excited faces. “Tell me, have you been exploring?”

Petroj let their excited voices wash over him as his mother left the room smiling. A few minutes later, their own mother came into the room clapping her hands to gain the twins attention. “Boys, what did I tell you?”

Neither boy showed remorse.

“You could check on him, but you weren’t to bother him.” She gave Petroj a harried look as she shooed the boys out of the room. “How are you feeling?” she asked before she followed.

“Better. I feel sore but overall better.”

Katja glanced over her shoulder. “The Sanctuary is amazing.”

“That it is.” Petroj smiled at Katja’s enthusiasm. “I haven’t been here since I was a young boy. Go ahead, I’ll be out shortly.”

Petroj could feel the healing energy of the Sanctuary filling his body and soul. Putting his hand on the wall behind the pallet he laid on, he sent a mental thank you.

After dressing, Petroj sought out his mother and father. Most people didn’t look twice at him. Without his standard uniform of black, he was just another man. He found his mother in a small room that glowed with power. With normal sight, the room was ordinary. He switched to his Drakkon senses. He could see the ebb and flow of the node-like power that filled the room. Petroj could sense no actual Node present.

He kissed his mother’s cheek before he sat down. “The Sanctuary is bigger than I remember it.”

“This place has always met the current need.” The Socra replied as she patted the cushion at her side. “Your father should be here in a moment." They sat in a comfortable silence.

Jaczon's entrance in the room let some of the noise from the corridor enter the chamber. He settled on a pillow across from his son. This was the first time in years the family had sat in the same room together. Each one savored the moment.

Petroj broke the hush. "Do we think everyone who evacuated made it?"

"I've organized patrols to follow the roads to meet any stragglers." The Socra rubbed her hand against her skirt. "The later the straggler, the greater risk of Anakarei spies."

Jaczon placed his ungloved hand on his wife's marked hand. He had no means to reassure her as they had one of the greatest liabilities in stasis in the Sanctuary. "The Sanctuary defenses will help us figure out who has been compromised. We will watch for telling behaviors."

The Sanctuary peace was shattered the instant Petroj felt the death scream on the psychic plain. He saw his father's flinch. They looked at each other. Petroj knew that his peace at the Sanctuary was going to be short lived.

"Erol," the Socra gasped. Neither man had to confirm her utterance.

Petroj started to rise "I have to return! There are people that have to be protected."

Jaczon grabbed his son's arm, preventing him from rising to his feet. "Pacol will take care of his family and the rest. We have to take care of things here first."

The Socra looked into her son's eyes with regret. "Yes, you'll need to go back but not now."

Petroj knew his parents were right. "We have to talk about the hunters and the one Jaczon and I brought with us."

“I understand why you were reluctant to leave the hunters, but they are a true liability to us.”

Petroj gave a smile that turned the Socra’s blood cold. “Mother, I’ve been running a counter game to the Chancellor for quite some time.”

“What do you mean?” Jaczon demanded.

“You both knew that I was chosen for the role of The Tmavě Jeden for many reasons. The main one was to be smarter and more duplicitous than the Chancellor.” Petroj settled back into his Tmavě Jeden role. “The hunters are under the influence of praxitrol but not under his control.”

Jaczon narrowed his eyes. “How can that be?” Praxitrol was the Chancellor’s own tortuous invention with no known counter.

“The years I played the role of the Chancellor’s puppet, I was privy to secrets that even he was unaware of.” The sinister sneer was at odds with his new found peace. “I found the secret of the formula.”

His parents stared at their son with a mixture of horror and wonder. The paranoia of the Chancellor was legendary. This was not a conversation to be overheard. Jaczon leaned forward. “You can break the hold?”

“The influence of the praxitrol is permanent,” Petroj said with regret. “But I can change the focus of the bond. The hunters all are loyal to me. Every last one of them.”

“Oh my Gods of the Sky! That is why they had to come to the Sanctuary,” the Socra marveled. “Why the Sanctuary allowed them entry.”

“I couldn’t leave them behind. If The Chancellor found out, any advantage we might have in the future would be gone.”

Jaczon stared at the floor between them stroking his chin. "How difficult was the process?"

"Difficult enough," Petroj stalled as he ran his hands over his hair. "I'm worried about our special problem. He's dosed heavily and should stay sensory deprived as long as he is in his module."

"Can you do the same for him?" The Socra's voice was filled with hope tinged with sadness.

Petroj closed his eyes, "I don't know."

"Surely…"

"Father, Ethias has been under the control of this drug far longer than anyone." Petroj was filled with an uncomfortable need to get up and run. He'd never run from a problem, he faced them and defeated any obstacle thrown at him. "I could try to shift the drug's focus, but I doubt he'd survive the process."

Jaczon shook his head in frustration. "I do not understand what brought him back."

"Not even Mellanei knew where he went when he stepped through the Node," she murmured. "He needed to keep our heritage safe"

Petroj put a reassuring hand on his mother's shoulder. "I can try to change the attachment, but it'll have to be in a completely shielded room."

ELEVEN

Ella absently listened to Nathan and Talek argue against going to Drakkonon. The plan felt right. In her head, history and knowledge unspooled across the screen. She had always had the talent to boil data down to the essential task. She had the knowledge for safe Node manipulation. It was her genetic heritage. Now her human half just needed to catch up with the understanding. Ella didn't have time to stand whimpering in a corner over the turn of events.

She brought the men's discussion to a halt.

"We have no other choice. I know how to manipulate any Node to go where I want." Ella looked directly at Talek. "Without the power burn you experienced. That is the gift of my family." Myrna's anguished cry interrupted any arguments from the men. Ella ran to her mother. "Anissa, I thought you said this would be gentle!" Talek placed a gentle hand on Ella's shoulder as Nathan assisted Annisa. Myrna writhed in the chair.

"Do something!"

"Ella," Talek ran his hands soothingly along her arms. "Let them work."

Myrna arched backward, her mouth still open after her initial cry of shock. Her mind was wide open for the first time in decades. Emotions, good and bad, overwhelmed her. Tears streamed down her face as the muffling filter on her life ripped open her new reality.

"Mother!"

"Ella." She grabbed her daughter's face in her hands. "Oh God! What happened to my life?"

She understood her mother's distress. Ella gently grasped her mother's wrists. "Both our lives, Mom, both our lives."

"I can't decide whether to hate the man or be grateful." Myrna's face started returning to her normal color. "I understand the need to protect…."

Ella glanced at the group surrounding them, "I think he had a really good reason. But, I don't think he meant to leave us permanently."

"How do you know that?" Myrna demanded.

"He locked my mind too. Daddy meant to return to instruct me. All the knowledge in my head would then have a reference point – stories and histories to illustrate the teachings. Instead, circumstances ripped the wall down, and I became aware." Ella pinned Nathan with a pointed look. "Of everything – about Daddy and my heritage."

"Let me revisit the earlier question about my family. Part of the block was about my heritage." Myrna focused on Annisa. "You weren't just drawn to me as a friend were you?"

"That was a beneficial by-product." Annisa watched Myrna with a worried frown.

"Your kind is drawn to Power like moths to a flame." Myrna regarded the Brownie suspiciously. "What were your original intentions?"

Annisa knew that Myrna's temper was still formidable, even in her enlightened state. "Brownies live to serve the Light. We are attracted to Power. We want to help powerful families. I felt your anger and pain. I knew that the only way to help you all those years ago was to be your friend."

"Was it real?"

"Absolutely." Anissa placed a hand on Myrna's. "The friendship grew because you were unaware of my Brownie nature. I was under no compulsion to do more than listen. You treated me as a friend."

Myrna frowned as she asked the question that had been bothering her since they had renewed their acquaintance. "Why did you disappear?"

"You'd reached a place where I could no longer help you. I knew that you'd start asking questions about me," Annisa answered. "Despite the compulsion your husband put on you, I would be compelled to answer your questions truthfully. You weren't ready for any of those answers."

"I don't think I'm ready for any of the answers now." Myrna collapsed against the back of her chair.

"Mom…"

"What is wrong with the three of you?" Myrna demanded, "Why are you glowering at my daughter?"

Nathan jumped in before Ella could say anything. "Your daughter is rash and impulsive." Ella's outraged gasp filled the room. "She wants to leap into a situation without knowing all the ramifications of her actions."

"Actually, that's not entirely true." Talek countered. "Her point is not without merit. She holds the accumulated knowledge of the ancestors."

Nathan stared at the Drakkon in disbelief.

"I'm trying to make sure that no one gets killed. Going off half-cocked…"

"I didn't say we'd be going off half-cocked," Ella interrupted. "I said that we needed to take the fight to the Chancellor. Earth is not prepared to deal with the Otherverse."

Annisa joined the argument.

"Nathan, she has a point. Human beings, while having an innate ability to use Power, have an incredibly fragile grasp on their perception of the Universe." She glanced at Ella and Myrna. "Present company excluded."

Myrna demanded an explanation from her daughter, "What are they talking about? Who is this Chancellor?"

"Okay, Mom. Get ready for history according to the Otherverse." Ella centered herself finding the knowledge in her mind. She began the story from the beginning in a Reader's Digest fashion. Nathan and Talek both added information as necessary.

A demanding meow followed by a not so delicate setting of teeth on Ella's calf, interrupted the telling. Ella blinked as she looked at the clock on the kitchen and realized that it was well past noon. Kaie twined herself around every available leg then headed for the stairs that led up this time.

Ella realized that there were mundane tasks to attend too.

"Mom, let's take a break."

With glassy eyes, Myrna surveyed the group in front of her.

"I need to process all of this." She got to her feet, "I think you all are insane, but I'm starting to understand why."

Talek stepped forward to support Myrna, who didn't reject the help.

"If everyone will get settled upstairs, I'm going to have lunch brought in," Annisa announced. "We all have things to attend to before we make any major plans. Talek, after you've brought Myrna upstairs, would you come back down and help me with our guests?"

Talek's stomach clenched. He really didn't want to face the incarcerated men. He knew that they were both under the influence of praxitrol; he had no idea how to combat the drug.

"I know that Ethias was trying to protect us," Myrna said when they reached the stairs, "but don't count us out. If Ella says she can do something, she can." She met Nathan's silver eyes. "My daughter is capable of knowing her mind and abilities."

Talek looked at the older woman at his side. "You have much faith in your daughter."

"She is my daughter. Stubborn to the bone and twice as hard headed," Myrna said. "If my husband left information about his people inside her and kept it locked up, she'll be able to process it." Myrna gave a small smile. "When she was little, he called her his 'little dragon.'"

Ronan padded carefully into Myrna's room, she was in awe that the animal could move at all. His recovery was nothing short of miraculous. Ronan groaned as he settled himself on the dog bed that lay at the foot of her bed.

"You had no idea of your husband's nature?" Talek pulled another guest chair close to Myrna.

She watched the man, who was apparently a dragon, beside her.

"I knew he was special. A dreamer, who could make me dream with him." She smiled at the liberated memories. "I loved that man. I would have done anything to protect him. He knew that."

Talek crouched at her side as he clasped her hand. "Mistress Hixson, I believe he knew that. That is why he protected you and Ella in the manner he did."

Myrna stared into the golden eyes. Ethias's had been the same blue-green of her daughter's.

"How could this have protected us? Our lives were changed irrevocably."

Talek thought about his home and the power of the Anakarei.

"Where I come from, Drakkonon, the regime that governs is ruthless. They seek to enslave or destroy all Drakkon."

"Why?"

"On Drakkonon, we are the only kind that can control the Nodes. This ability allowed open trade to the rest of the Otherverse." The memories caused Talek to clench his jaw in distress. "Many have perished in the quest of the Anakarei to obtain this power. My parents included."

"What do these Anakarei want with the Otherverse?"

"Domination and subjugation. The regime has decimated the resources of our world. Without Drakkon who can manipulate the node, we have no Otherworld trade. My job was to find a way to open the Node." Talek shrugged. "I worked my way into the top science team so that I could travel to the Otherverse to find Nathan's grandmother and warn her of the impending invasion."

Myrna sat thinking about everything Talek was saying. "What about this drug that the young man in the basement is on? What can be done about that?"

"There is no cure for the addiction." Talek shook his head. "No one knows the origin of the drug, but the effects are devastating."

"I can't stand the thought of him suffering. If you go to Drakkonon, will you bring him with you?"

"We can't, he is a live transmitter for The Chancellor. Here at least he has his freedom and a modicum of his essence back. If he returns, he will be a liability." Talek hid the sad truth of Becr's situation from Myrna. Without a regular dosing of the praxitrol, Becr's life would no longer be an issue. He tucked the covers around Myrna. The older woman reminded him of his Nonne. "I must return downstairs. Can I get you anything to make you comfortable?"

Myrna waved him off with a thoughtful look on her face. She didn't believe in absolutes, or at least her old self hadn't.

Myrna listened to the soft, whuffling snore of the dog. So much had happened this morning alone. She had to reacquaint herself with who she was.

Crabby, selfish Myrna needed to meet the Myrna of the past and reconcile. Memories of her past, her familial history, and her current life all battled it out for dominance. Her last thought before she slipped into an uneasy trance was "Will I be happy-me, cranky-me, or more?"

Talek rejoined the others in the kitchen. "Has anyone checked on Becr?"

"I just got back from the basement," Annisa responded. "The boy is in bad shape. If he were a rampant alcoholic, I'd say he was suffering from the DT's."

"Are you sure there is nothing we can do about the praxitrol?" Ella asked Talek. "Surely there is a way to detox the man?"

"No, we have never been able to find out the drug's origin. Only the Chancellor knows." Talek looked at Nathan. "The only way I know how to get a sample would be to find out where Becr and his handler were staying."

Anissa gave a nasty grin.

“Leave that to Sindie, she still wants a piece of that miserable cur.” Annisa snarled. “He must have taken his own dose prior to coming. He hasn’t exhibited any of the withdrawal symptoms as of yet.”

“What exactly is Sindie?” Ella had to ask. “And why does she have a tail?”

Nathan gave chuckle. “I thought you’d be asking about the wings, before you asked about her tail.”

Ella thought back to the day they met less than a week ago. “When I interviewed, I thought I saw the tail twitching out with her apron strings. With everything happening that day, I thought I was hallucinating.”

Annisa laughed. “No, you weren’t hallucinating. Sindie is one of the Other-kin that work here. She is of Faery, specifically a pixie.”

“Aren’t pixies supposed to be small?”

“Only in children’s movies, my dear.” Annisa patted Ella’s knee.

Ella tried to get back on track. “Okay, so we let Sindie do the questioning. Do you think she can get the information out of the man?”

“Without a doubt.”

“Let’s get it done.” Ella glanced at Talek. “I think if we can get a sample, maybe we can figure out something your people haven’t.”

Talek could only look at Ella helplessly. He had no answer for her misplaced optimism.

For the first time in years, Myrna felt rejuvenated. She understood she was part of a powerful bloodline of hereditary witches, earth guardians. Ethias had been aware of her heritage. Much like her husband, she had had access to a vast knowledge of archetypal knowledge for Ella when she came of age. Ethias' meddling had changed those plans.

The sound of a thumping tail brought her attention to Ronan. Myrna slipped out of the chair, kneeling down to scratch his ears. "So, my boy, you are feeling better?"

The enthusiastic lapping tongue answered her question. He rolled over to his side to offer his belly for a scratch. As Myrna obliged the dog, the door to the room pushed open to reveal Kaie. The cat came in, touched noses with Ronan, and then rubbed herself against Myrna.

"So, cat, what do you have to say about all of this?" Myrna really didn't expect any response.

The cat settled herself next to the dog. Her blue gaze locked with Myrna's hazel. "There is much to do and little time to accomplish."

Myrna fell backward on her bottom. The end of the bed prevented her from sprawling inelegantly on the floor. "Excuse me?"

"You are a woman of Power. From a family of Power. I do not know why my speaking to you is such a surprise." Kaie raised her paw and inspected her claws. "Your ancestors would have at least offered me a bowl of cream."

Ronan reached over, giving Kaie an affectionate swipe of this tongue.

"Look dog, I don't need to know that the cat has your seal of approval. That much is obvious." Myrna was still trying to process everything. Her daughter had inherited her husband's Drakkon traits and probably some of her family's as well. While everything was settling, her mind kept circling back to the young Drakkon in the basement. He was so ill. The others were so sure there was nothing could be done. Myrna wasn't. "Okay, cat. I know that you are well cared for, so you'll get no cream from me. I'm not ready to serve tea and crumpets to a cat – yet. But since you are going to be my familiar, maybe you can help me with our little problem in the basement."

"Familiar is such an antiquated term, you can call me your …mentor."

Myrna fixed the cat with a gimlet stare. "You are a cat. I will call you cat."

Kaie leaned into Ronan's side, her tail twitching. "You refer to the Drakkon who is incarcerated in the basement."

"Yes, he's as much a victim of a poison that controls him as the apparent circumstances. He deserves our mercy." Myrna was fairly confident the cat was more in the know that she let on. By nature, cats were notoriously stingy with information.

Kaie purred her satisfaction at Myrna's answer. "They are currently trying to obtain another dose for the boy. His life depends on it."

"Nothing was said about the boy's life."

Kaie rose to her feet and strolled toward the door, "The 'boy' is a pawn. In his world, he is expendable."

Myrna followed Kaie as they left the room. The click of toenails let them know that Ronan was right behind them.

Ella began to have second thoughts about getting the information from the other prisoner. "Is Becr in any condition to tell us anything?"

Annisa laid her hand on Ella's shoulder. "He's in bad shape. If he survives the detox, there may be nothing left to save."

Ella rose to her feet. "Maybe we don't have to stoop to their level."

Talek stood in front of Ella. "Ella, both of them would have killed your mother without a second thought."

"Maybe, but if I'm supposed to be this High Socra, aren't I supposed to be above thuggery? Aren't I supposed to change things, including this?"

Talek let Ella pass. "You're right. If mercy and kindness can't be extended in the direst of circumstances, then…"

Covered in blankets, his body quaked. Ella recognized the shimmering energy enveloping him as a transformation unable to be completed. She was horrified at the damage being inflicted on the man. The praxitrol prevented him resting, keeping his body in a state of rigor as it broke down in his system. Ella rushed into the cell with the sick man, placing her hands on either side of Becr's head. Her first objective was to stabilize his form to his human shape. Her merge gave her the shock of her life. She had seen his memories, but seeing his life pattern was another thing. His very essence looked like rotted cellulose, full of holes with scabby edges, rough and uneven. She didn't know if anyone or anything could ever come back from something so deleterious.

The connection severed abruptly. Ella blinked myopically up at the faces of Talek and her mother. Her right hand still rested on Becr's head. Her left hand brushed against her cheek and came away wet with tears she couldn't remember shedding.

Talek's hands rested on her temples, just as hers had rested on Becr's. He was humming deep in his chest. She could feel the vibration from the crown of her head to the soles of her feet. Her mind came back into focus, and she realized three things. Becr was awake, staring at the ceiling. She could feel the floor boards of the cell on her skin. Talek's eyes were open.

In Drakkon form, Ella might have been a beautiful blue-green, but embarrassment left her ruddy and mottled. Talek's eyes never left her gaze. He saw her come into awareness of her situation. His humming softened to a sigh and stopped.

Myrna gasped at the scene in front of her. Becr and Ella were crammed in the confines of the cell. Ella's head rested in Talek's lap, while the rest of her body was exposed to the room. Snatching a blanket from a pile by the stairs, Myrna hurried over to cover her daughter.

Ella refused to acknowledge her nudity. On the scale of embarrassing events, this would be the one thing that would pop into her mind at two in the morning, ruining a good night's sleep.

"Okay, what happened this time?"

Talek reached down, taking her left hand, clasping it gently between his.

"You tried to help Becr."

Ella's eyes fell on Talek's hand, the beginnings of a patterned tattoo wrapped from the knuckle of his middle finger, forming a Mehdi-like pattern on the back of his hand to circle his wrist. A random thought floated across Ella's mind that she should have noticed the marking before now. "How'd I break free?"

"You convulsed and screamed," Myrna said, her worried tone conveyed her fright. "I had reached the cell just as you had your fit."

Talek continued to gently stroke the back of Ella's hand.

"You tried to shift, but the cell prevented you..."

Ella clutched the blanket as she struggled to sit up. Talek moved in behind her to support her.

"When I was in his mind… so much damage. I can't describe it."

Still holding Ella's left hand, Talek drew her closer to lie against his chest.

"I saw a glimpse of the damage before I severed the connection." Talek knew how much Myrna wanted to save Becr. "I don't see any way for him to recover."

Myrna looked at the situation. "I think we need to take all of you out of this cell. The boy is not a danger to anyone." She looked around the basement. "He is so sick; I think the House should be able to help contain him upstairs in the guest area."

"Mom, I agree. Becr is too sick to hurt anyone." Although she appreciated Talek's warmth, she also knew she needed to get up and find some clothes. But her traitorous brain sent the signal to nestle back more against Talek. He was not opposed to the action, tightening his arms around her. "I'm going to have to get up and get dressed."

Myrna eyed her daughter. She quirked an eyebrow and suppressed a smile. "You both stay down here with Becr. You'll know what to do with him if he gets worse. I'll go upstairs and get you your clothes."

Ella could feel a blush riding her cheeks, flowing down her body to the tips of her toes. Talek chose to be a gentleman.

"We'll wait."

Myrna left the three as she ascended the stairs. Nathan met her at the top.

"Myrna?" He looked her over for signs of stress. "Are you alright?"

"I'm fine, Ella needs clothes." Myrna gestured toward the basement.

"Oh?"

“She tried to assess exactly how much damage the drug had done to Becr. The cell prevented her from transforming, but not before her current clothes disintegrated. We’re moving Becr upstairs.” Myrna gave Nathan a reproving look. “The boy is too sick to harm anyone. The basement is not the place to keep him. I have all the confidence in the world that the House will be able to help contain our guest.”

“We were able to obtain a sample of the praxitrol,” Nathan said before Myrna could continue on with her task.

The old woman paused.

“How are we going to analyze it?” Myrna asked.

“I think that you’ll be able to analyze part of it.”

Myrna’s view of the universe might have been expanded over the past twenty-four hours, but not enough for her to be sweet. “I’m a portable lab? What do you mean - you think I’ll be able to analyze it?”

“You’ll figure it out.” Nathan moved down the stairs to help the others.

“Just because I’m a witch,” muttering direly in Nathan’s directions, “on more levels than you know, this doesn’t mean I can divine what’s in that devil’s brew.”

Annisa met Myrna at the top of the stairs. Myrna didn’t like being pressured. She barely understood her new memories. How was she supposed to do what was asked of her? She glared at Annisa, “I don’t like your boss.”

Annisa gave an inelegant snort. “He grows on you.”

“He’s working off assumptions that I can help figure out what is in that brew.” Myrna complained as they entered Ella’s room. She found a set of clothes laid out neatly on the bed. Distracted, she knew that her daughter had no clothes at the House. For that matter neither did she. “How does this place do this?”

"Do what?"

Annoyed, Myrna glared, "Don't play games with me, the clothes, and a room that suited me to a 't'. How does this House fulfill these needs?"

Gathering up the clothes, Annisa reached over to the chest of drawers and pulled out simple sweatpants and t-shirt for Becr. "The House is a bit of an enigma. Its primary purpose seems to be to fulfill the needs of the Node Guardians and protect the surrounding community from rogue Node activity." They walked to the door that led to the hallway. "The House takes its guardianship seriously." She patted the doorframe affectionately. "But it also has a sense of humor."

Annisa spoke about the House as if it were a sentient being; the concept unnerved Myrna,

"Staircases that never seem to go to the same place twice?"

"Exactly!" Annisa reached back and grabbed Myrna's hand. "Come now, with everything you've seen, how can this be any less real?"

Myrna looked at the woman who was more than she ever expected and shook her head in surrender.

"Come on, my Universe has expanded exponentially, but not enough to let my daughter stay unclothed in the company of men." As they left the room, she softly patted the doorframe in thanks, just to be safe. She received a soft jolt of positive power back that energized her. Myrna started to question Annisa. "What do you know about this Talek?"

As Annisa started laughing, Myrna couldn't help but join in. Things might be serious, but they certainly were lively at the same time.

Talek and Nathan settled Becr in a guest room. While neither trusted the man, neither wished him to suffer. Before they could close the door, Kaie imperiously demanded entry. Nathan looked at the cat. In typical cat fashion, Kaie chose not to illuminate them as to why she chose to keep Becr company. Leaving the door ajar, Nathan glanced back and saw Kaie settling on the pillow next to the Drakkon

The men joined Ella, Myrna, Annisa, and Sindie on the sales floor where several large tables had been pushed together to form a large conference area. A small box sat toward the center of the tables. "Becr is settled in his room. Kaie is watching over him." Nathan announced to the group.

Myrna rolled her eyes. "I hope she isn't as chatty with him as she was with me! The boy will never get any rest."

Nathan had just pulled out his chair to sit down. It clattered as it dropped from his hands. "Chatty? Kaie?"

"Kaie doesn't talk!" Annisa proclaimed at the same time.

"She sure has plenty to say to me." As Myrna looked at everyone, she started to get a little nervous. "Apparently, she's taking it upon herself to train me."

Ella laughed aloud. She couldn't stop herself. Talking cats, dragons, brownies, pixies, magical houses, other worlds, and a villain who wanted to wreak havoc in the Otherverse, she was afraid to ask if there was more. Everyone looked at her. "I feel like I'm living in a Chinese proverb with each new revelation. I'm excited yet terrified to see what's next."

Talek just looked confused. Annisa took pity on him. "The proverb goes along the lines of 'May you live in interesting times.'"

Talek smiled, "Ah, we have a very similar proverb on Drakkonon. Some things are truly universal."

Myrna's attention bounced between the conversation at the table and her conversation she had with the cat. She turned to Nathan. "You're right. Kaie seems to think that we can analyze the elements of the praxitrol. I just hadn't a clue about what she was talking about."

"Talek, you'd said you'd been…" Ella corrected herself. "You are a scientist on your world."

Talek thought about what he could contribute. "I can most likely separate and identify substances that seem to be common between our worlds." He massaged his left hand. The appendage had started itching, the pattern more pronounced. "So maybe your world can identify the element we couldn't."

Ella shivered at the memories of Becr's mind. "I can only hope, because I think that this knowledge will make the difference when we cross back into your world."

Without warning, Kaie jumped up on the table, projecting into Myrna's head. "Tell your daughter she is correct, identifying the elements of the substance will provide a distinct advantage as they go to Drakkonon. Tell the Drakkon man to come with us." Kaie jumped off the table, heading out the room.

Myrna collected the small box that contained the praxitrol as she passed along the message. She assumed Kaie meant Talek. Myrna grasped Talek's arm, pulling him with her.

Annisa looked at Nathan. "Did you know Kaie could speak?"

"No, she's bossy enough without actually giving orders." Nathan shuddered with apprehension. "But it does answer some questions and pose several more." Myrna followed Kaie to another doorway she hadn't noticed before. Kaie paused impatiently in front of the door eyed Myrna. "Well?"

"Well? What?"

The cat gave a hiss and impatiently batted at Myrna's leg. "I do not have hands, human!"

"Hey!" Myrna reached down, picking Kaie up by the scruff of her neck. She brought her up to eye level. "Patience, cat. No, hissing, spitting, or swiping."

Talek watched the exchange with a raised eyebrow. "Is everything in order?"

Myrna put the cat down then reached over to open the door. "Everything is fine, just establishing a working relationship, the cat and I."

Talek waited until both had preceded them into the room before he entered. The sight that greeted him was comforting. Two large worktables were covered with scientific equipment he recognized. He also recognized materials that were of use in the metaphysical sciences. Blowing out a breath through his teeth, he moved down one side of a table, his fingers trailing over the surface.

"Are you all right?" Myrna asked.

He shook himself out of his introspection. "I'm fine. I find it amazing so many things are similar yet not."

"Maybe, that's because people, whether they turn into dragons or not, are still the same."

He faced the mother of one of the most powerful Drakkon known in generations. "You are a wise woman, Mistress Hixson."

"Please call me Myrna."

"Myrna, you honor me with the privilege of your name." He bowed respectfully. "Thank you."

Myrna smiled a little as they pushed on. "Okay then, let's see what we have." Knowledge swamped her. She knew the process for analysis. Chemistry and alchemy were ancestral skills.

Time passed in a strange paradox of swiftness and incomprehensible slowness. Talek and Myrna found themselves in a working companionship, identifying the common elements that were otherversal was the easy part. Three unknown substances left them confounded.

"Talek, these last three components look organic." Myrna peered through the microscope. Things that looked like red blood cells seemed to be suspended in the solution. The cells ebbed and flowed through the sample. "They are three separate elements but are bound together." She waved him over. "Have you ever seen anything like this?"

"We've never been able to break the praxitrol down this far before." Talek looked into the adjustable oculars of the microscope. "It seems to destabilize…" he suddenly fell silent.

Myrna placed her hand on Talek's shoulder. "Talek, what's wrong?" She grabbed his shoulder, giving him a hard shake. "If you don't tell me, I can't help you."

"This is impossible." His tone filled with horror as he peered back into the microscope. "Praxitrol is derived of Drakkon blood."

Nathan walked into the workroom at that moment. "What?" He and Myrna demanded in unison.

"The unknown element is transformed Drakkon blood." Talek's face was ashen as he shook his head in disbelief. "I don't understand…" He pulled a stool out from the workbench and sat.

"Boys, help an old woman out. I don't understand. What does the blood have to do with anything?"

Talek headed for the door. He didn't want to talk about this obscenity more than once. "We'll need to tell Ella as well." Talek didn't wait to see if Nathan or Myrna followed him.

Baffled, Myrna turned to Nathan. “Do you know what all this meant?”

Nathan watched Talek all but run from the room. A less than gentle bump against his leg reminded him that Kaie still with them.

“Well, cat? Any words of wisdom to add?”

Kaie looked directly at Myrna. “Go! Talek needs you both. This is important.”

“I get this is important.” Myrna snapped. “What I don’t understand is why!”

“I only know all this is important. I don’t know details.” Kaie hissed as she spoke with Myrna.

As Myrna headed for the door, she asked Nathan. “We need to meet up with Talek. I don’t suppose you heard any of that?”

“No, I take it she only knows we have to follow Talek, but no details.”

Myrna stopped short. “How…”

“It’s the way of the cat. Inscrutable.”

Myrna continued through the open door, barely blinking when she found herself on the guest level. “Your house is spooky.”

“This time I’ll agree.” He looked around nervously. “I’ve never seen it this active before. I only had stories from my grandfather.”

They walked down the hall to the only open door. Myrna recognized it as the room that Ella had been using. Raised voices floated out of the doorway.

"… I don't care what you say! I know there is something that can be done to reverse his condition!" Ella's voice rose with conviction.

Talek explained patiently. "Praxitrol is made with transformed Drakkon blood. Once transformed, the blood creates a mindless servant to the one whose blood is used. Their very being erased, leaving them a husk. A body to be used at the bidding of the binder."

"How can you be so sure?" Ella demanded. "You're making an assumption based on a first pass analysis."

When they stepped into the room, Myrna and Nathan found the pair nose to nose. Ronan watched the confrontation curled up on his dog bed with his ears flat against his blocky head; the strife in the room was making him uneasy. Kaie was grooming him in an effort to put him at ease. How the cat had beaten them to the room was another mystery of the House.

"The Memories do not hold a cure for the misery that is his abomination." Talek clenched his hands at his side, as he took a step back. "Don't you think I want a miracle?"

Kaie left her ministrations, leaping up on the table where the Drakkon Book of Writ lay. She sat next to the book and batted it with her paw, her tail swishing back and forth rapidly. "Tell your daughter to look in here."

Myrna was learning to pay attention to the cat. "Ella, what is that book?"

"It is…"

Talek interrupted Ella. "This is one of the sacred Drakkon relics thought lost to time. It contains all the history of the Drakkon." He looked at the tome with reverence. "From the beginning of our kind."

Ella gave Talek a fulminating look. "This is what was in the box of Dad's stuff." She picked it up. "The history it contains is amazing. Reading it is a kinesthetic experience. It goes along with all the memories locked up in my mind."

"You are the hereditary repository of the Drakkon memories," Talek confirmed. "You wouldn't be able to have opened the book or read it if you weren't."

Ella weighed the book gently in her hands. "It covers more than a spiritual history, Talek. It covers the good and the bad. It truly is a comprehensive record of our people." She settled herself on the edge of the armchair in the room. "The knowledge in this book is dangerous. I'm sure it contains a fix to the praxitrol problem." With great care, she ran her hands over the cover. "I just have to find it."

"No! The Socri would have known," Talek yelled.

Ella understood Talek's fear; the fact that this abomination was most likely documented was horrifying to her as well. "Talek, you told me that my bloodline was charged with guarding the entire knowledge of the Drakkon." Ella stared him down. "Why? What makes me and my ancestors so special?"

The question broke through Talek's anxiety. "The holy script tells us that your bloodline is bound to the continuation of our kind, guardians of knowledge and blood."

Ella looked at Nathan for help clarifying her answer. "Where did this holy script come from? Does anyone know?"

"Mellanei spoke of the Script as a simplified version of the Writ. A 'Dummies' version if you will." Nathan explained.

"Great, 'Drakkon for Dummies.'" Ella was trying not to be blasphemous, the image of the yellow and black book coalesced in her mind. She contained her need to laugh. "The Script would contain the guidelines by which to live, the 'shalt-nots' and other useful historical information for being Drakkon." She looked to Nathan for confirmation. "Is that it in a nutshell?"

Talek nodded his head.

“Yes, major historical events have all been documented in the Script as well.”

“But the Writ is everything unvarnished. The good, bad, and ugly.” Ella verbalized her train of thought. “The Writ has all the decisions, including all the mistakes. If my bloodline was set to be the Guardians, a major check and balance system would have been set in place to make sure we never used any of that knowledge inappropriately.”

Talek interrupted, “The Supreme Council of Drakkon was the check and balance to the High Socra,” Talek continued. “This council hasn’t existed in centuries. It died out when the other colors of the Drakkon became legend.” He looked at Ella. “You are the only gem colored Drakkon I’ve ever seen.”

Ella interrupted, “What colors are the most common on Drakkonon?”

Nathan stepped into the conversation. “Metallic - bronze, gold, silver, and copper are the most common.”

“Rumors exist of the rare obsidian as well.” Talek added.

“What happened to the other colors?” The room violently swooped around Ella as waves of memories crashed violently through her head. She took a moment to gather herself and retreated into her headspace to try reclaiming control of the maelstrom of information. She collapsed against the chair unconscious.

TWELVE

Myrna looked her daughter's prone form.

"What happened?"

Talek knelt by her side, holding her left hand. A very faint outline was starting to emerge on Ella's hand. The intricate pattern started around her middle finger and ended wrapped around the wrist. Talek met Nathan's gaze and shook his head. He wasn't ready to talk about the marking with anyone but Ella.

"Your daughter holds all the archetypal knowledge of the Drakkon," Talek explained. "As she asks questions, her mind tries to provide the answers she seeks."

Nathan picked up the narrative. "The problem is the amount of information she has in her head is overwhelming. She's trying to control it. She's looking for a small needle in a vast field of other small needles."

Ella's body occasionally twitched but she didn't wake up.

Nathan met Talek's gaze. "I'm going to have to go in and help her."

"Not alone." Talek said.

Myrna felt out of her depths again. "Going in where? Not alone?" Frustrated, her tone had sharpened. "What are you both talking about? What is wrong with Ella?" Ronan pushed his head into Myrna's lap. In an effort to gain some sort of control, Myrna stroked Ronan's soft ears.

Talek reached over to comfort Myrna. "Your daughter is wrestling with her vast knowledge in an effort to find out what she can about the effects of the Drakkon blood." He was blunt. "She's been immersed too long in the memories. We have to help her."

Each man knelt on one side of Ella's chair. Talek on the left, Nathan on the right, each clasped a hand. They reached up and placed their free hands gently above her temple along the ridge of her eyebrow. Talek and Nathan each took deep breaths, centering themselves, and then merged their consciousness with Ella's.

They found themselves in a violent tempest. Ella wasn't a terrified figure on a ledge this time. With her arms stretched out wide, she was a conductor directing a symphony of chaos.

"Ella!" Nathan yelled with all he had to get her attention. She gave no indication that she heard him. Nathan gestured to Talek. They had to reach her side. Driving winds buffeted them. Talek held Nathan back for a moment. He crouched close to the ground where the battering seemed to be the least and transformed to his Drakkon self. The sheer mass of this form allowed him to move through the storm of information. Nathan followed suit.

Ella stood in the eye, trying to control the flow of information. Waves crashed at her feet; winds tangled her hair; she was rapidly losing strength. She knew that she had to gain control or lose everything. But what that really meant, she had no idea. Her intuitive alarms were sounding; she had learned never to ignore them.

The iron clasp of clawed Drakkon hands on either shoulder startled her. Talek and Nathan, each presence helped ground her in the chaos, bracketed her. Nathan's calm voice entered her mind. "Use our combined strength to organize all this knowledge."

Talek's voice bolstered Ella even more. "Once you have it organized the way you need, you'll be able to access it."

She drew on their added power and went back to controlling the squall. Little by little, the fury faded. Finally, the last of the manic clouds wisped away leaving a changed landscape. Ella could see the memories of her life linked and collated with the ancestral memories of her Drakkon and Power heritage. From her elevated view, it resembled a series of Fibonacci spirals, elegant and organized.

Her mental legs gave out. She collapsed on her bottom, flanked by two Drakkon who shimmered back into their human form.

"Well, that was fun." She said as she brushed her hair behind her ears. She leaned back against Talek surveying vista. "So you guys think I'm going to be able access all this information?"

Talek looked out on the landscape with awe. "I don't understand how you managed to organize the volume of information."

"It'll take time," Nathan added. "You've done something no human or Drakkon has been documented to do. You've reorganized your thoughts like you would a closet." The heir of House Books laughed as he slung an arm around Ella's shoulder. "You'll do."

Ella laughed. "I guess we'd better get back."

"Your mother will be beyond worried by now," Talek said. "Can you return?"

Ella looked around her. "Yes, I know how to do it now." She embraced them both. "Thank you for helping me."

"Ella Hixson, don't you dare leave me!" Myrna's frantic voice was the first thing she heard when she woke up. "I mean it. I won't be responsible for your dog!"

She focused on the face of her frantic mother. A demanding nose slipped under her hand seeking reassurance.

"Mom." Her voice was weak. Clearing her throat, she tried again, "Mom, I'm okay. And you'd totally take care of Ronan. I know you would."

"Fat lot you know!" Myrna snapped. "You don't look 'okay.' What the hell happened?"

Nathan knew the ordeal had cost Ella in terms of strength. He sought to calm Myrna down. "Your daughter is a very unique individual."

Myrna's eyes narrowed.

"She holds two powerful birthrights, Drakkon and your Earth Power heritage. Both potent in their own right, together they are something the Otherverse may have never seen before." Nathan attempted to sooth Myrna's fear. "Your daughter just might be the end to this conflict with the Chancellor."

"Mom, Nathan's right." Ella bared her teeth, unaware of the wisp of smoke that steamed from her nose. "He'll never see me coming." She scratched Ronan's ears, the reflexive motion comforting as she thought. "I can solve the praxitrol problem."

"I hope so. The Chancellor has used it as an indefensible weapon amongst our people for far too long." Talek moved forward. "To be able to reclaim the lost would be an advantage beyond measure."

"What I say here in this room is sacred knowledge not to be abused or used." Ella met the eyes of every person in the room. "Praxitrol is not the original incarnation of this abomination. During a very dark period of Drakkon history, terrible things occurred for the sake of power. The crafting of absolute power was one of them. In the blood of a transformed Drakkon of certain bloodlines, specifically of the Socri, is an element that commands the mind of any species." Ella felt her strength returning and she sat up straight. "One of my specific bloodline found a way to break the hold and abolished the practice."

"Your bloodline was thought to be lost," Talek murmured. "Lost with the Sacred Temple of Drakkonon and the relics that I see before me."

"No, not lost." Ella looked at Talek with a glint in her eye. "Just hidden away for safe keeping. The other jeweled Drakkon went out into the Otherverse – each group with a strong Socra – to establish bastions of Drakkon should our home fail." Ella looked at Nathan. "Your grandmother got a little distracted here on Earth."

"My grandfather wouldn't call establishing the House a distraction, more a necessity for today," Nathan said. "She left to continue her mission as soon as things were settled."

Overwhelmed by the history lesson, yet grateful that Ella seemed to be feeling better, Myrna interrupted. "All this history tells us the where and the why." She saw Talek's protective stance over her daughter. "Do we have a why and how to help out Becr?"

"Yes," Ella said thoughtfully. "Yes we do. I only hope it won't kill him. Let's get to work."

With a practice that belied their new working relationship, Myrna, Talek and Ella worked in tandem. First, they had to develop an organic compound that would heal the physical damage. While Myrna and Talek worked on that, Ella ran to her room to retrieve her statuette.

"What are you doing with that?" Myrna demanded as Ella placed it on the workstation.

Ella grinned. "This is the key to negating the Drakkon blood essence."

Talek looked confused. “I don’t understand. What is it?”

“This is the lost Statue of Drakkon.” Ella ran her hands over the piece.

“This isn’t listed in the Holy Script.”

“Exactly. The piece is so powerful; it was kept out of the Script and only mentioned in the Writ.” Ella explained. “Only my bloodline can harness the transformative power.”

“Your father gave that to you as a child!” Myrna gasped. “Was he insane?”

Ella laughed. “No, I think he was planning on being around when I came into my heritage.” She sent her mother a look of sorrow. “We both know how that worked out.”

Myrna and Talek mixed the organic compound with the praxitrol sample. The initial results were nothing but sludge-like mixture. Ella took the statue in both hands. Holding it over the bowl, she concentrated on the energies locked inside the stone.

Everyone in the room watched as the statue glowed. Ella pulled energy from a ley line and the statue incandesced, leaving everyone blinking furiously to clear their vision.

The bowl now contained a liquid that sparkled, almost alive.

Talek took a sample to the microscope, “Praise the winds, the praxitrol is neutralized. I think we can administer this to Becr.”

Ella entered the room first. Becr lay on the bed shaking, his body barely holding his human form. Praying it wasn’t too late, Ella softly walked forward.

“Becr,” she whispered. The form on the bed gave no indication he had heard her. Ella tried louder. Still nothing.

Kneeling by the side of his bed, she placed a hand on his shoulder.

Becr screamed and writhed in agony. Talek and Nathan ran through the door to help Ella restrain the man. Becr appeared to have no target. His actions seemed centered in pure suffering.

"Hold him down!" Ella yelled.

Turning her attention back to the patient, she uttered the word to 'Calm' in Drakkon, "Učit se!" Becr's convulsions only worsened. "Crap!" she muttered. "I don't want to force this down his throat."

"Ella!" Talek shouted over the din. "Do what you have to do!"

Ella grabbed Becr's jaw in a grip born of determination, forcing his jaw open and pouring the emulsion into his mouth. She held his mouth closed, pinching his nose closed so Becr would swallow. She prayed to the otherverse with all her might that what they'd done would work.

She released his jaw and sat back to watch their patient. Within minutes, his convulsions lessened. He still looked like hell but less transparent.

Myrna walked into the crowded room.

"Kaie says to let him rest. She'll keep an eye on him." She looked down at the man. "It's up to God if he makes it or not." Everyone filed out of the room as Myrna tucked the blankets around Becr. "Mom," Ella paused. "We can only pray, and we will."

"I know." Myrna wiped a tear from her cheek. "It's stupid of me to care so much. The boy tried to kill me."

"This is what sets us apart from the people who controlled Becr – our desire to care for and help." Ella put her arm around her mother's waist as they walked out of the room.

"What we are doing today will save more than we can possibly know."

Talek waited for them in the hallway. He heard Ella's last comment. "You will save hundreds of innocents that are trapped by The Chancellor's poison." He looked at the partially closed door. "I only hope we'll be able to help them reclaim their essences."

Myrna gave Talek a sad smile. "There's always a price." She sighed, leaning heavily against Ella. "We can only make their lives the best we can. I think I need to lie down. Talek escorted mother and daughter down the hall to Myrna's room. Talek waited as Ella saw her mother comfortably settled. When Ella stepped back into the hallway, he opened his arms, and she walked into them. She didn't realize the tears were running down her cheeks until the cotton of his shirt dampened under her cheek. He gently stroked her back in comfort.

"How can I do all this?" Ella murmured. "I'm so overwhelmed."

"Shh. We'll get through this." Talek stroked his back. "You're not alone."

Nathan joined them in the hallway. "No, you are not alone. You've done more for that man than anyone has in his life. You could have walked away."

Ella's whispered into Talek's chest. "No, I couldn't."

Myrna voice joined them.

"She's right. It's not how we are. We don't walk away from those in need." Myrna leaned against the doorjamb, "I'm too jumpy to nap. I might as well be useful."

Talek's voice rumbled under Ella's cheek. "And that is what makes Ella unique among Socri. She doesn't say 'there is no solution.' She finds one." He gave her one more comforting squeeze and gently loosened his hold. "Let's get go down to the kitchen to wait. We can plan out our strategy."

The silence was broken by the soft clink and scrape of silverware against plates. No one wanted to start the conversation. Ella sighed as she took the lead. "I was able to figure out the Node used by Becr and his group. His memories were choppy blurry. The praxitrol has made a hash of his memory. They came out of the Stonehenge node."

Ella raised her hands for silence as the room erupted with questions. "I'm to understand that that particular Node is still active to a certain extent, so their arrival wouldn't have been questioned too closely. Their journey was a true walkabout in the Otherverse."

Nathan was not amused. "Are you saying we are going to have to leave through Stonehenge?"

"Yes. Not because we are going to repeat their journey. I'm positive I can get us to Drakkonon without a problem." Ella paused with consternation. "But we can't use this Node. After our last encounter, it seems to be locked on the Chancellor's."

Talek swore softly.

"I think the House's safeguards can continue to keep the Node locked down from this end." Nathan said. "As long…"

"As long as they can't regroup or find another Drakkon capable of opening the gate." Talek completed the sentence.

"I strengthened the wards created by your grandfather. They will be drawing their strength directly from the ley lines." Ella reassured the room. "That saber should be able to withstand just about anything."

Annisa walked into the room with what appeared to be ticker tape trailing behind her. She read the information on the tape intently. Ella didn't think ticker tape existed outside of movies.

"According to Alaric, the Stonehenge Guardian, the party we're looking for came through six months ago. They made quite a mess too." Annisa didn't look up as she stopped at the table. "They stepped out in front of a bunch of tourists. The energy fragged their digital cameras and camcorders."

Ella eyed the fluttering streamers. "Ticker tape, really?"

Annisa didn't rise to the bait. "By the time they'd taken care of the tourists, Becr and his people were gone."

"Didn't they think this was news to share?" Nathan growled.

"Nathan, you know as well as I do that the Old One's have a different set of priorities." Annisa set down the mess of tape on the table. "We're lucky they responded to our inquiry. You didn't think I was collecting antiques, did you?"

Ella stared at the mess on the table and piped up. "We're going to have to use the Stonehenge node." She looked at Annisa, "Are these Old Ones going to give us any trouble?"

"Ella, you can't know for certain how to manipulate the Nodes, much less get to Drakkonon." Annisa said. "You've grown strong in your knowledge, but if you don't know what you're doing, you'll die. It wouldn't be fair to your mother to lose another person she loves."

Ella understood the fear. She was getting ready to go to a world where she had only second hand knowledge. Faith was playing a huge role in her decisions.

"Annisa, I have to at least try. Will these Old Ones give us any trouble if we approach them to use the Node?"

Annisa looked at Ella. The woman she'd interviewed and dismissed didn't exist anymore. "I'll go with you to help with introductions with the old one. Who will be going to Drakkonon with you?"

Without hesitation Ella responded, "Nathan and Talek. We'll keep the group small. I've named them guardians. They need to accompany me to be recognized."

"Recognize us?" Nathan asked. "Ella, where are we going? I know that we can't just show up in the center of The Chancellor's seat of power. Where did you have in mind?"

Ella gave them an inscrutable smile. "We're going to go straight to the lost temple."

Everyone but Myrna erupted in a cacophony of protest. She looked at her daughter under the din of protest. "You can do this? Get there safely to this lost temple no one has seen or visited for generations? Thought lost to time?"

"Knowledge of the temple was removed from the memories of the Drakkon for safe keeping." Ella shared her memories. "Daddy knew where it was all the time. He even visited it once with his brother." Tears welled up as sorrow overcame Ella "That ended in a tragedy so great." She felt tears she didn't know were still falling drip on her arms. "Jealousy over took the brother. He sought power. He coveted his brother's inheritance. When rejected by the ancestral spirits, he sought to destroy all things Drakkon, denying his own Drakkon heritage."

"The Chancellor – you are talking about the Chancellor?" Talek interjected.

Ella was afraid to meet Talek's gaze. So much had developed between them. The marks on their hands signified a future. "Yes," she whispered.

Talek reached over to lift Ella's chin. "That would explain so much about his rise to power. Ella, your father has nothing to do with the choices of his brother."

Relief flooded Ella. "I was worried about …"

"If we could pick our families, the worlds would supposedly be perfect," Nathan said. "Look, you have no way to control the Chancellor's choices or actions. Neither did your father. We now have a way to mitigate the damage he has inflicted on our people."

"I think that your choices are solid," Myrna cut in. "I will stay here and watch over Becr. I'm too old to go traipsing between worlds." Myrna rose, crossing to her daughter. She embraced Ella. "I'm going to miss you, but you have responsibilities that need to be addressed." She tightened the embrace to savor the moment. It had been so long since they'd partaken in this simple act. "Don't forget to come home."

"You can't get rid of me, Mom." Ella embraced Myrna, perhaps a little too tightly. "We have a lot to do yet. Together."

Annisa clapped her hands.

"Okay, enough with all this emotion."

The distraction brought them back to the logistics of putting the plans in place. An envelope appeared on the corner of the table, Talek's name scripted on the front. Everyone watched him open it to discover a set of identification papers: birth certificate, driver's license, and passport.

Myrna looked at Annisa, voicing Ella's feelings exactly, "This place is really starting to freak me out." She looked about the room, in an effort to not offend the structure, she said. "I'd like you to explain how this place works." Myrna waved her hand toward Talek's ID, "Especially stuff like that."

"When I get back, we'll have a long talk over tea. I promise."

Myrna gave Annisa a stern look. "I'm holding you to that."

Talek stumbled off the airplane in Heathrow. "Drakkon flight is more civilized than your method of air travel."

Nathan clapped Talek on the back. "It's all what you're accustomed to, my friend."

"I'd rather fly naturally than in a metal tube. I don't think Drakkon or man was ever meant to go as high as we did."

"Boys," Ella interrupted the ribbing. "We need to get to the rental car agency." She smiled sweetly as she looked at Nathan. "You get to drive." The long flight had made Ella tired and cranky. She never could sleep on flights; the droning of the engines drove her crazy.

Nathan realized he shouldn't have bragged about his previous trips to England and his driving experiences. "I'll be sure to get one with a GPS. We'll want to get a solid night sleep before we find Alaric."

They drove directly to the small town of Amesbury and immediately checked-in to their aptly named bed and breakfast-The Stones. Everyone but Annisa crashed in an effort to be coherent for their meeting with the Old Ones that night.

Ella woke up knowing that announcing plans to the universe was always a bad idea. She had overshot her planned naptime by two hours. Vivid dreams of flying against violent whirlwinds contributed to her nap hangover. A good therapist would tell her she had a 'Don Quixote' complex, tilting at windmills she couldn't possibly understand. She'd always felt that Don Quixote had always understood more than the world had ever given him credit for. She stumbled into the shoebox bathroom where she splashed cold water on her face in an effort to regain some mental sharpness. Coffee, she needed strong, black, sludge-like coffee before she could even address the situation at hand.

With her satchel slung across her chest, she headed to the front desk on a mission to find a coffee house. Armed with directions, Ella headed out into the small town. When she arrived at the coffee shop, she was surprised to see Annisa engaged in an intense conversation with a man who looked like Mr. Hooper from Sesame Street. Mr. Hooper had never had looked like a sourpuss. Ella wasn't sure what was happening but she didn't like the way Annisa sat with her head bowed and hands clasped tightly in her lap as the man harangued her.

Ella's need for coffee drove her to the counter, where the barista balked at Ella's instructions. A large tip smoothed the way. She took a moment to savor the first sip before she engaged in her next battle. Her synapses started firing with the influx of caffeine. With her to-go cup in hand, Ella approached Annisa and the stranger. Now that she was caffeinated, Ella realized this must be the Old One, Alaric. With the nasty manner he was treating Annisa, she wished that he didn't look like her beloved Mr. Hooper.

"Is this a private conversation? Or may anyone join?" Ella didn't give anyone a chance to rebuff her intrusion as she set her coffee down and grabbed a seat. She looked at Annisa. "Introduce me to your friend."

The man curled his lip in distain.

"You Americans think you can waltz in any place and do whatever you want."

Ella looked at the man, whose resemblance to her beloved character was fading with every word that came out of his mouth.

"We Americans haven't 'waltzed' into anywhere. I saw my dear friend Annisa seated at this table and asked to join you." She held out her hand. "Hi, I'm Ella."

"I know who you are, daughter of Ethias."

"That's nice, but I was raised that introductions were polite before warfare began."

"Ella, be quiet," Annisa hissed.

"Annisa, it is clear to me that this person has no respect for you. I demand that he extends the courtesy."

The man waved his hand negligently at Annisa. "She is nothing but a Brownie, born to serve. Not to negotiate with one such as me."

Annisa made to leave the table. Ella put her hand on her arm. "Well, aren't you an arrogant piece of work. 'One such as I,' 'Born to serve.' I guess this is where I'm proud to be an American." Ella leaned forward, her eyes swirling. "Annisa is a valuable member of my team. Her task was to make contact with 'one such as you.'" The Old One sat back, stunned by her lack of fear. "You see, we were going to be polite and let you know that we'd be using the Node tonight."

"No."

"No, what?" Ella demanded. "No, I can't use the Node? No, tonight is inconvenient? Why don't you clarify for me?"

The Old One gathered his arrogance about him like a tattered cloak. "No, you may not use the Node."

Ella gave the Old One a mean smile, one that should have had him rethinking his response. "Let's review. I walk in here and find you being inhospitable to my associate. And you are telling me you will deny me access to a Node that you already let a Drakkon assassin team through."

The Old One stiffened. She wasn't feeling particularly charitable as she pressed her advantage.

"What did you think they were doing? Being tourists? You screwed up in your stewardship and tried to cover it up."

The Old One stayed silent as he chewed on the information Ella threw at him. He raised a hand to reach inside his suit jacket.

"Don't make me nervous, old man."

With his facing pruning in distaste, the Old One kept one hand on the table and pulled an envelope out of his inside breast pocket. He slid it across the table. Ella's eyes widened as she recognized the writing, she'd reread the letter her father had left her with the Sphere and Writ more times than she could count. The script was her father's.

"Thirty odd years ago, Ethias Hixson came to this place to meet with me." The Old One's demeanor thawed. "He was frantic to escape this world. I met him at the sacred circle, when the moon was high and full, not a bloody tourist in sight."

"My father left through this Node?"

"He apologized for the rude manner in which he commandeered the Node saying he had no choice. That for my protection I couldn't know where he went." The Old One smoothed out the paper napkin in front of him. "He told me that one day his daughter might try and follow him through the Node and that if I had any compassion, I would give her this letter."

Ella looked at the letter. Slowly, she reached for it. Her hands shook. Annisa reached out to place a comforting hand on her shoulder. With careful fingers, Ella folded back the flap, pulling out the single sheet of paper.

'My dearest little dragon,

I have so little time, not enough to prepare you. If you are reading this, you are preparing to step through the Node into a world that wants you dead.

You are the last of our line. Preserving our bloodline is more important than finding me or fixing the mess that is our home world.

You've always been smarter than you ever could know. I need you to live so that my sacrifice can be worthwhile.

I'm afraid if you go to our home world, we'll meet again, and one of us will die.

I love you. I love you and your mother with all my heart. All that I have done, I have done to protect you both.

Your loving Father,

Ethias, High Socra of Drakkonon'

Ella handed the letter to Annisa. She looked at the Old One.

"Did you know the contents of the letter?" she demanded.

He shook his head. "I was honor bound by his wishes to deny you access to the Node." He raised his hand to stop Ella's attack. "But a promise made thirty years ago cannot take into account the circumstances of today."

The Old One looked at Annisa directly. "My view of your kind is tainted. I see Ms. Hixson values you as a friend and a mentor. I will do my best to assist you."

Stunned, Annisa took the hand of apology extended to her. She bowed her head. "Your courtesy is appreciated."

"Here, none of that." He gave a wave and looked at Ella. "As reminded by someone younger and wiser than I, we live in a new and different world." Annisa raised her eyes to the Old One. "You both may call me Alaric."

Ella took the hand Alaric extended with a more hospitable smile.

"I'm sorry I cannot give you more information."

"We won't be following his path." Ella gazed out of the café window. "I have a more specific destination in mind. It's time for the Drakkon to come home or at least have the choice."

Alaric's eyes grew wide.

"The Time of Strife and Miracles!"

"Excuse me?" The reference caught Ella off guard.

"The time was foretold when the Drakkon would be able to gather home. Or, at least be able to travel freely through the Otherverse, like they once did during their Golden Age. This time is referred to as the Time of Strife and Miracles."

"Why those words specifically?"

"While mighty miracles might occur, great tests of faith must precede them, causing times of great strife." He pushed his chair back and rose to his feet. "I'll meet you and your party at the north gate of the Stonehenge complex at eleven p.m. Pack well." With that, he strode out of the coffee house. Ella's gaze followed him into the sunshine where he shimmered into nothing.

Ella took a swig of her coffee, making a face. Luke warm, the brew was plain nasty.

She blew out a long breath and looked at Annisa.

"So, mission accomplished?"

"You are an incredibly fortunate young woman," Annisa marveled.

"What's the worst he could have done to me?" Ella asked. "We were going to use the node regardless of his answer."

"Ella, he's an Old One. He could have turned you into stone."

Nonplussed, Ella stared at Annisa. "Okay, so I have no sense of self-preservation." She laughed weakly as they walked out of the coffee house. "Annisa, will you make sure Mom gets that letter? She needs to see it."

"Are you sure?"

Ella stared at the letter held in the Brownie's hand. "She needs to know that she was… is loved. We both know that Daddy left for a good reason, but she needs to see the letter."

"I'll see that she cares for it during your absence."

"Thanks." They walked back to the bed and breakfast. "Let's go find the others."

The afternoon light was bright. The differences between the small village and her hometown fascinated Ella. Both had a presence that spoke of history. She soaked in the ambience as they strolled back to the bed and breakfast.

Ella flinched as a hand clamped around her arm the second she and Annisa entered the foyer.

"Where have you been?" Nathan hissed in her ear.

"Release the girl, Nathan. She was with me," Annisa calmly said. "We've been arranging your passage through the Node."

Nathan made no effort to let go of Ella's arm. She could tell he was upset. Wiggling her arm to try to free herself, she found herself marched into the dining room.

"Nathan, if you don't let go of me right now…"

"You just disappeared!" Ella overbalanced as Nathan let go abruptly. "We are in a strange place, and you disappeared!"

Talek pulled out a chair for Ella and gestured for her to have a seat.

“We were worried.”

“I slept longer than I thought I would and went looking for coffee.” Ella looked at her companions with the caution reserved for live ordinance. “I found Annisa at the coffee shop having a conversation with Alaric, the Guardian of the Stonehenge Node.”

Nathan slapped his hand on the table. “Annisa’s job was to make contact with the Fae. You don’t just talk to the Old Ones. There are protocols.”

Ella gave Annisa a glance that spoke volumes. “Well, I’m not a rock. He found me charming. Apparently, I am of rare courage.”

Nathan exploded. “What?”

Annisa took over.

“The Guardian found our Ella unique. He’ll be meeting us at the North gate of the Stonehenge grounds at eleven p.m. tonight. We need to get some shopping done.”

Talek looked at Ella with a smile. She squirmed in her seat, refusing to meet his eyes,

“What are you looking at?”

“A rare courage, indeed. You just ran over him, didn’t you?” Talek’s grin grew wider.

Ella refused to answer the question and concentrated on ordering more coffee.

Nathan looked at the pair with annoyance.

“I don’t know why you are so calm about this, Talek. She’s your mate.”

Talek objected, "You do not want to broach this particular topic."

"We all know what the marks on your hands mean," Nathan started. "She just can't go off without protection."

"I know what the marks mean." Nathan's highhanded manners were getting on Ella's nerves. Ella looked down at the beautiful markings. Her heart beat fluttered and she felt tingly, feelings she was not opposed to. Something about Talek had captured her attention from the beginning. "I'll wrap my mind around the entire significance of that after we get the task at hand done."

Talek moved between his mate and Nathan. "You need to attend to your own business." He met Nathan's gaze with a stony look. "Unless you can't."

Nathan sat back down. "You have a stake in all this."

"Yes, I do," Talek said. "Everything in its own time."

Annisa looked at the two men with exasperation. "Are you both quite finished?"

"I don't like dealing with the Old Ones," Nathan declared, glancing at Annisa. "They make me itchy."

"Nathan…" Annisa started.

"I carry my grandfather's prejudice with me. I'm working on it." He stared at his hands on the table. "The thing is with the regular Fae, we've always known we were in the fight together. The Old Ones have always picked and chosen their battles."

"I take it the results were not always to the benefit of everyone?" Ella drew her own conclusion.

"My role and oath as a node guardian has always been for the greater good, not for when it was convenient or good for the moment."

"Nathan," Annisa placed her hand on her employer's arm. "You humans and human-blends are a conundrum to all the Fae. You see none of the old rivalries or power struggles." She looked around the table with the gaze of wisdom. "That is one of the things that make you some of the most powerful beings in the Otherverse. To be feared and held in awe. Some of the Old Ones are beginning to see this and change. Others will always play their games." She admonished, "Don't become as stultified as they are."

The group arrived at the monolithic site in the middle of the night. The stars studded the black velvet of the night sky. Ella wondered when she would see her own sky again. The headlights were unnecessary due to the brightness of the full moon. She shivered in anticipation of the cold outside the car and the events that were to come. She couldn't say that butterflies were fluttering through her stomach; it was more like squirrels on a rampage. Talek reached over and took her hand. His calm presence calmed the riot.

A beam of moonlight brightened as Alaric stepped out of it in front of them.

Nathan looked impressed. "Neat trick," he muttered to Talek.

Alaric laughed aloud. "Neat trick indeed, grandson of Carter Mullins." The Old One threw wide his arms. "Welcome to the Node that I have long held Guardianship. Come, a brisk walk will warm you up."

They grabbed their gear from the boot of the car and followed Alaric over the field. The old Fae was dressed as an English gentleman enjoying a stroll on a summer evening. In contrast, they were bundled in warm coats. Alaric's presence lifted the night around their party so they could see as clearly as high noon.

Ella interrupted Alaric's guide to Stonehenge patter. "How can we see clearly in the middle of the night? And can others see us?"

Alaric gave a booming laugh.

"I'll be mysterious and say it is the magic of Faery. I know you'll want more, but we don't have time for that kind of discussion." He stepped forward. "We are completely shielded from the patrols that keep Stonehenge safe from the nutters."

The hair on the back of Ella's neck stood up straight as they approach the outer circle of the monument. The ley energy shimmered throughout the site. She stopped at the first circle to acclimate to the energies of the area. The energy had a distinctly different flavor from the node in Maryland. Ella opened her senses.

"Ella! Come on now, wake up!"

Ella felt her face being gently tapped. "I'm awake. What happened?"

Talek was crouching in front of her. "You tell us. One moment you're standing, next you are passed out on the ground."

"No, not passed out." Ella searched for the right words. "I was syncing. Yes, that's the word. I was syncing with the ley line energies."

Alaric appeared in the line of her vision. "Are you out of your wee little mind? You could have been lost!"

"No, I was swimming. Tasting. Coming back." Ella pushed herself to her feet. "If I'm going to open the gate to the Temple, I needed to know the energies here. That way I can come back if necessary."

"You, miss, are reckless." Alaric snarled.

Sparking with energy, Ella stayed calm. “Determined, Alaric, determined.” She gave the Old One a winsome smile. “When all this is done, I’m coming back for a formal history lesson.”

His eyes widened with apprehension. “I can’t decide if that is a threat or not.”

Ella laughed, “I’ll let you decide.” The laughter faded. “Your hospitality and stewardship of my father’s trust is greatly appreciated.”

“You gave this old Fae something to think about.” Alaric turned to Nathan. “I recognize your appointed guardian,” he said, gesturing to Annisa, “is more than capable of defending your Node. The structure you call the House has kept the Fae puzzled for more than a hundred years. If Mistress Oakton calls for help, we will be there to lend any assistance.”

Annisa and Nathan gaped at the offer of assistance. Nathan took the proffered hand. “We will be honored to accept your offer, sir.”

Alaric handed Annisa a charm strung on a necklace. “I don’t have to tell you how to work one of these.”

“No, sir, you don’t.” Annisa fingered the charm in appreciation.

Ella gave Alaric a smile as she turned to Annisa, but before she could say anything, Annisa stopped her and reassured Ella she’d keep her mother and dog safe.

“Thank you.” Ella gave the woman a hard hug. “Do what you can to keep Becr alive. When we get to a stable place, we’ll try and send a confirmation of our arrival.”

Nathan made his own farewells to his longtime friend. Talek hung back hoping he’d see his nonne, Callem and Ane when they returned. He missed his family. Alaric waved his hand allowing the Node to flare to life. Lights flashed with eye-watering brightness.

Ella centered herself to the ley energies that ran into the site. Her hands held in a catcher position in front of her body, she tapped into the ley lines. Those energies joyfully leapt in response to her request. Using the memories of her ancestors, Ella visualized the Node room of the Lost Temple of Drakkonon.

Ella extended her hands to the farthest point she could reach, and a tunnel opened in the vortex. At the other end of the vortex was a room bathed in the glow of daylight. The energies were exhilarating. "We have to go now!" She yelled above the crackling din.

Talek grabbed the bags at Ella's feet. Nathan grabbed the rest. They both sprinted through the tunnel. Talek marveled at the differences between his experiences in Node travel.

Once they were through, Ella glanced back to acknowledge the ones left behind. Alaric and Annisa raised their hands in farewell. With her hand still extended, she walked through the tunnel.

HOT FLASHES

THIRTEEN

Electric energy danced over every square inch of Ella as she stepped through the stable vortex. Her skin tingled with the power of the node. She glanced back before the gate collapsed. The moonshine illuminated the megaliths of Stonehenge in silver and shadows. She tucked the memory away in her head, hoping that she had a chance to see it again.

Beside her, Talek stood slack-jawed in the middle of an enormous chamber. Graceful columns held up a glass dome. The marble floors glistened in the sunlight. The walls beyond the columns depicted elaborate life scenes of verdant landscapes, thriving metropolises, and Drakkon in mosaics created with gold, silver, and bronze, enhanced by a wild assortment of gemstones that ran full spectrum of reds, blues, and greens. Ella felt as though she were in a full sensory kaleidoscope. Her entire being felt the energies from the wealth surrounding her.

Ella, Talek, and Nathan basked in the peaceful energy of the vast room. Ella closed her eyes in an attempt to ground herself with the energy lines that fed the Node. The energy emanated from the entire structure. They stood in a vast pool of power.

When she opened her eyes, Ella gasped. The room was no longer empty. Her ancestors surrounded her, imparting their memories and experiences. Like a super computer, all the information was going into long-term memory with meta-tags for easy retrieval.

Ella laughed as she reveled in the love. The Drakkon pendant that hung at her throat swayed from the transparent fingers caressing it. The only spirit missing was her father. Ella's mind and heart was full. The ancestors pressed close to her giving her final memories for her journey ahead.

Ella saw that Nathan and Talek were both experiencing a similar welcome.

"And you both wondered if I could declare you my guardians?" Ella stated, "I don't think that's a problem. Do you?"

The ancestors flowed back from the living in the Temple. Ella's left hand burned with an infuriating itch. She saw the outline had solidified into an intricate pattern of teal with golden accents woven through. The appearance of the ornate mark and the significance were not lost on her. Ella flexed her hand, staring at the every nuance of the pattern. The beauty was something to behold. She could feel the weight of Talek's stare on her.

"Were you ever going to tell me? Ask me? Court me?" Ella asked softly.

Talek stepped directly in front of her and took the marked hand with his own. The two hands matched and were unspeakably beautiful together.

"Even with the marks, I really didn't know if I was worthy of you. And you still have a choice in all this."

Her head still bowed, Ella closed her eyes and allowed a small loving smile to play over her face. She raised her swirling blue-green eyes to look directly into Talek's gold.

"Haven't you figured it out? It has never been an issue of worth. You are a good man. And the right man for me." She placed a soft kiss on Talek's lips. She gave his hand a squeeze and stepped away. Talek stared at her stunned.

Ella felt empowered with the knowledge of what they needed to do.

"Okay boys, time to head out."

"What?" Talek was still processing her acceptance of their mating. He could feel the ancestors rejoicing. He could also feel them telling him to catch up and declare himself.

"You didn't think that we'd be staying here, did you?" Ella ran across the chamber, pushing open enormous folding glass doors, with stained glass patterns that reflected the rest of the room. Air rushed and a large, stone terrace, overlooking an enormous plain, was revealed. The space could easily accommodate their Drakkon forms. The Temple was positioned on top of a mesa with limited ground access.

"I hope they have clothes where we are going."

"Ella, where are we going?" Nathan stood on the edge processing the input from the new environment. The sky on Earth was an ever changing study in midnight blue to pale blue-gray. The periwinkle sky was something from the tales his grandmother, Mellanei, would tell him as a child. He never dreamed he'd stand under this sky.

"We're going to the Sanctuary and from there to the city to have a talk with a certain Chancellor. At least that's the basic plan."

Both men stared at her. Ella now seemed larger than life as she embraced her role as High Socra. There was no doubt in their minds as they saw her embraced by the ancestors.

Talek approached Ella. "We have no idea what waits for us at the Sanctuary. How are we going to get there?"

Ella shimmered before them, her clothes falling to the ground. Before their eyes, she became a beautiful blue-green Drakkon, a color that hadn't graced the open skies of Drakkonon for years.

"We fly!" With a joyful mental shout and a melodious bugle, she launched herself from the patio on her virgin flight.

A torrent of wind rushed past the men as they watched in horror as Ella dove off the edge secure in the knowledge of flight that had been imparted to her by the ancestors. Her Drakkon body arced in graceful loops – once, twice, three times. Holding their breath, they heard her wings snap open. She shot up in the sky a streak of iridescent teal. The spirits surrounding them teased them, ruffling their hair, tugging at their clothes. Beckoning them to come and play.

Nathan stared after Ella.

"If we had any doubts about her flying…"

Talek snorted.

"I never had any doubts. I don't know if we'll get her out of the sky." He gestured to their supplies. "Come on. Someone's got to be practical." While Ella cavorted in the sky, he quickly fashioned two harnesses that would hold their gear.

The men shifted and then launched themselves with powerful beats of their wings into the periwinkle sky, silver and gold chasing a jewel.

The air of this different world caressed Ella's scales and she bugled in joy as she twirled and swirled with those who had been before. A symphony in flight, fantastic patterns of transparent color wove complicated patterns in the sky over the Temple. A blue-green spirit broke away from the spectacle in the sky and led them toward the Sanctuary. As they approached a boundary, the ancestors flowed back to the temple, leaving the three living Drakkon to continue on their own.

Annisa walked back into the familiar foyer of the House. The comforting feel of the structure soothed her travel weary nerves. So much to prepare for, the possibilities were endless. Kaie meowed interrupting Annisa's ruminations. Looking down at the cat, she grinned at the familiar.

"Still only talking to Myrna, I see." The cat butted against her. "I'm moving. Be patient." She moved toward the office, surveying the area as she went. Sindie had reopened the store. Customers milled among the book stacks. Myrna was behind the information desk. Her pinched look, born of anger and loss, had lifted leaving the woman looking years younger.

"Annisa!" The joy in Myrna's voice let Annisa know that things were stable. "I'm so glad you are back." The older woman stepped out from behind the information desk. She took Annisa's bag and walked toward the back of the store with her.

"How did everything go? Did the departure go as planned?" she finally asked when they arrived at the manager office.

Pulling the desk chair around to the front of her desk, Annisa sat down and pulled the letter out of the bag. "Ella asked me to give this too you."

Myrna wasn't sure what to expect as she took the other seat. The envelope was yellowed around the edges.

"This was given in trust in the event Ella was to ever come into her inheritance without the guidance of her father." "Ella specifically wanted me to make sure that you read this."

Myrna opened the letter with shaking hands and her eyes filled with tears as she saw the familiar handwriting. Old hurts healed as she read the contents. After she finished, she raised her eyes to the woman in front of her. "Ella went despite the warning?"

"The Old One believed that Ethias didn't take into account that circumstances would demand her journey and that your daughter would have two champions with her." Annisa leaned forward, taking Myrna's hand. "I agreed with his assessment. Alone, Ella should have stayed. With Talek and Nathan, she will be able to face whatever is on the other side."

Myrna bowed her head as she absorbed impact of the letter. "He sounded like he would be her enemy."

"We don't know what happened to Ethias after he left here." Annisa leaned back in her chair. "Your daughter is unique. She surprised a being that was so old he has seen mankind at its most primitive." She gave Myrna the bravest smile she could muster. "I'll put it this way, the power of prayer never goes amiss. We'll pray for all of them." Annisa guided her to the stairs. "Tell me about Becr"

"That young man is very lucky." Myrna allowed the change of subject. They reached the top of the stairs where Ronan greeted them with an enthusiastic wiggle. "Becr is slowing regaining his facilities. Kaie's been keeping him company and he's responding to her presence."

Annisa gave a weary sigh. "Good."

The Chancellor sat alone in his chambers as he contemplated his next step. His Key was gone, stolen by his trusted Tmavě Jeden. He snarled as he threw the drink he had clutched in his hand across the room. The breaking glass didn't register any level of satisfaction; the sound just underlined his growing frustration with his failure.

Energy poured across the metaphysical plain. The Chancellor's mouth opened in a soundless scream of rage. He scrambled across the chamber to a hidden panel. He grabbed for the glowing jewel hidden there. The heat emanating from the crystal seared his flesh. This was his only way to find out where the node incursion was.

The Chancellor's mind filled with the ornate grandeur of a room he had only been to as a child. The node in the Holy Temple of Drakkonon was active anew. Only one chosen by the Ancestors could open a vortex into that Node. He watched a woman and two men step unscathed from the vortex. One of them was his missing scientist. He roared.

"You'll be dead soon, your traitorous piece of crazck!"

His hand was losing strength due to the immense pain, but the Chancellor couldn't yet let go. He had to find out more about the intruders.

Who was this woman? Centering his attention, his inner eye zoomed in on her. He lost focus for a moment when he recognized her as the one who had shut down the Node. He committed the woman's features to his memory. Something about her triggered a memory.

The pain had become excruciating. The scent of scorched flesh reached his nose. He peeled back his burning fingers with his empty hand, letting the artifact drop carelessly on the stone tiled floor where it bounced with a terrible clatter. The Chancellor was disappointed it didn't shatter. Then again, the Stone of Clarity had survived war, division, and theft. The Stone itself was benign, completely influenced by the wielder. The Chancellor ripped a tapestry from the wall. He picked up the stone from the floor, tossing it back in its hidden safe. Tearing the fabric into strips, he bandaged his burnt hand.

He activated the com unit on the wall and demanded his adjunct call an immediate session of the Council within the hour. He might not be able to gain access to the Temple, but he knew he could strike a blow at the Drakkon gathered at the Sanctuary.

He strode toward the lift and jabbed the call button. Anger and hatred rippled off the Chancellor like the stench of decay. The lift attendant carefully kept his attention on the controls, not daring to draw attention to himself for fear of any repercussive consequences.

Betrayal surrounded him. The ancestors had chosen his worthless younger brother over him, denying him his birthright. His skin crawled as the thing he despised struggled to free itself. He couldn't reveal himself to be what he hated the most.

His brother must have bred while he was off world. The thought weakened his already taxed control. That meant that female was his niece. Now his brother's reappearance on Drakkonon all those years ago made sense. He had been protecting his off-spring. The Chancellor affixed an ill-fitting expression of calm on his face. Excitement shimmered along his spine as he prepared to assault one of the last sacred bastions of Drakkonon. Mania-tinged laughter erupted from him.

Wind caressed Ella's Drakkon form, ruffling the frills over her eye ridges. The sensation was thrilling, leaning toward the ticklish. All the senses were bordering on overload. With gold and silver figures on either side of her, Ella started paying attention to the landscape below. She had been expecting the verdant landscapes of the murals of the temple; instead, the view was brittle and thirsty.

"Talek, where's the green? I thought your world would be more…"

"Drakkonon hasn't been the lush world of our ancestors for several generations. When the Anakarei came to power, things became unbalanced."

The dry brutal landscape below her broke her heart.

"What will I find when we get to the Sanctuary?"

Talek sent a mental shrug.

"I don't know. From what Nonne describes it to be, I think you'll find it to be much like the House."

"Who's Nonne?" The respect and affection that colored Talek's voice made Ella curious.

"She is my adoptive mother and the acting head Socra."

Nathan laughed. "You never got away with anything as a child, did you?"

"You have no idea."

"Acting Socra? What does that mean?" Ella was still digesting the hierarchies of the Drakkon society and priesthood.

Nathan filled in the blanks. "With your bloodline hidden away, there were other families who served as Socri. I think you could look at them as the parish priests. With all the persecution, they also became the keepers of the words and wisdom, very much respected. The ancestors blessed a few to guide and shepherd the many."

Ella let the explanation settle in her head. "Your Nonne must be a remarkable woman. I can't wait to meet her."

"I can't wait for you to meet her. You both share common traits," Talek replied.

The trio flew toward the Sanctuary. The terrain below them varied from desert to gullies flowing into sweeping mesas surrounded by large plains. The desert colors of ocher, maize, umber, sienna, and faded greens spoke of the desiccation of the region. They reminded Ella of a trip she had taken with her parents to the Grand Canyon. Ella's sharp eyes caught movement of animal life scurrying for cover as they passed over the ground. She had no way to identify the animals and filed the question away for when they reached their destination.

Talek surged ahead, diving for the deep canyon floor. The direction change broke Ella out of her reverie. Out of instinct, she and Nathan followed. Talek flew through a series of canyons. Ella paid close attention to the path, terrified to extend her wings fully. The walls of the canyons progressively narrowed. Finally, Talek landed with a graceful hop and skip, Nathan right behind him.

For Ella, grace didn't apply. She had a quick glimpse of what Talek and Nathan had done to prepare to land. She extended her front and back legs.

"Ella! Don't!" Talek yelled. "Bend your knees. BEND YOUR KNEES!" The warning came seconds too late.

Ella's feet hit the ground, her Drakkon body's natural instinct was to absorb the energy and rebound into the sky. Not prepared for that particular body response, she panicked. Her body was askew in the sky. This time when it hit the ground, her legs were splayed. She performed the most spectacular belly flop on the canyon floor in the presence of her mate and friend. Her body skidded for a length and a half as she tried to retract her wings and curl into a ball to minimize the damage.

The men had transformed into their human form as soon as they saw the impending doomed landing. Grabbing their packs, they sprinted for the fallen Drakkon. Once her body stopped its ill-fated landing, Ella no longer moved.

"Ella!" Talek slid to a stop by her head. He cradled her head and carefully placed his hands over her eye ridges under the frills. "Come on, sweet one. Open those beautiful eyes. I really need to see them."

Her head lifted slightly.

"I'm not so good at the landing."

Talek gave a gravelly laugh as his head touched hers. "No, you're not. We'll work on it. The next time we'll be where the landing area isn't so hard."

"Yes, please." She gave a heartfelt mental groan and opened her eyes, only to snap them shut again. "I know this is my thing, but did you guys bring the bags? You both need clothes."

The men started laughing as they unzipped their packs.

Ella gathered herself focusing beyond the pain and embarrassment of what had to be the worst landing in the history of Drakkonon. Reaching for her human form, Ella tried not to think about her own nudity. Her body ached from the transformation and the road rash from the unfortunate landing. Grateful there was no actual blood, she reached for the bundle of clothes Talek had left in reach. She could hear them as they walked to stand on the other side of the bend in the canyon. She clutched the clothes to her chest and patted her neck to make sure the chain was still there. The necklace had shrunk back to human size, the pendant hanging comfortably above the hollow of her breasts. She smiled as she dressed herself and limped to her companions.

"The Sanctuary isn't that far from here." Talek assured them both. "How are you feeling? Anything broken?" Talek conducted a visual inventory.

"My pride is possibly shattered beyond redemption after that amazingly graceful landing."

Nathan snorted.

"That was a stunning score of 10 in my book."

Ella shot him a glare.

"Considering I had no instructions, the first flight went pretty well." She looked around at the canyon, marveling at the towering walls. "What's the plan? Where do we go from here?"

Nathan started coiling the rope to sling across his body. Ella reached down to pick up the pack she had forgotten at the

Temple in the euphoria of her first flight. She nodded her thanks to the men.

"We'll have to walk the rest of the way to the Sanctuary. When I went through the node, I know that plans were in place for the Drakkon to gather there."

Ella shivered as a whisper of foreboding dampened the jubilation of the first flight. "Guys, we need to get there as soon as we can."

The men stopped, looking at her for an explanation. She shrugged. "I don't know. Something is wrong, I don't know if it's happened or about to. We just need to get to the Sanctuary."

Talek took the lead, heading toward their destination as fast as their exhausted bodies would let them.

Pacol stood facing his angry sister-in-law.

"I want that man killed. Killed the way he killed my husband!" Jenne shouted at him. Her usual restrained countenance was unruly in her grief. Her children sat in the corner, wide-eyed and pale.

He knew he couldn't attempt to soothe the rage of the grieving woman and tried a different tact.

"Yes," Pacol agreed. "You deserve justice for the loss of your husband. You and Erol sacrificed much to try and make a difference for the Drakkon, only to have it stolen by that soulless piece of crazck." Despite their grief, the children giggled at their Uncle Pacol's swearing.

Jenne looked at her dead husband's brother. The harrowing journey through the sewers and being held hostage by supposedly trusted family retainers shredded her societal mask. Mistress Smyzac entered into the room at that moment, stepping between the two. She motioned to the children. "It's time for dinner." The old woman gave the two adults in the room a reproving look. "Let the grown-ups continue their discussion in private."

Jenne watched the spry old woman depart with her children. "How is it I feel chastised?"

Pacol drew Jenne to the bed and sat her down. He pulled a chair over to sit in front of her. "You aren't going to be the one exacting revenge, Jenne. You have the children to take care of." When Jenne turned her head away to hide the tears in her eyes, Pacol reached out to gently grasp her chin. "I loved my brother too. We aren't the only ones working to bring an end to the scum's reign. We have to be smart."

"I don't know what to do." Jenne's voice was choked with tears. "I just don't know…" The tears started flowing.

Pacol sat on the bed beside her and pulled his sister-in-law into his arms. He rocked her gently through the storm of her grief. "You don't have to know. You just have to survive so that your children know the man their father was." He pulled on the dormant seed of faith he thought long buried. "He is with the Ancestors, finding a way to guide and protect you and the children." Warmth filled his heart he had never felt before.

"Pacol, you never believed that."

"Funny how things change." He could hear his brother's laughter in his mind. "Davist should be back with a recon report. We'll know of the state of the Complex soon enough. Then we can make plans." He held his hand out after he got to his feet.

Jenne allowed Pacol to assist her to her feet. She wiped away her tears with the back of her other hand. "Let's go see what the children are eating for dinner."

Their footsteps echoing off the canyon walls kept time with the clock ticking down in Ella's head. Each step increased her sense of foreboding.

“Talek, how much longer before we reach the Sanctuary?”

Talek glanced back. He heard the worry in Ella’s voice.

“At least a couple more hours."

Ella wanted to weep. The euphoria of her first flight had long since worn off. The aches and pains of her ill-fated landing made themselves known with each step, and her lack of sleep was catching up with her.

“We’ve got to go faster.”

Nathan sensed her agitation. “What’s so urgent? What are you feeling?”

“I can’t explain. I just know the sooner we get there, the better. Something is going to happen.” Frustrated by her lack of information, Ella stepped up her pace. “We just need to move faster.”

Talek glanced back at Nathan. “Okay, we’ll go as fast as we can.”

The stupid rhymes and songs Ella had used to keep her walking rhythm were losing their effectiveness. Her exhaustion left her dazed as she stumbled along the canyon floor. Ella squinted at the bright sunshine as they left the high walls of the ravine. She couldn’t tell how much time had passed and couldn’t find the wherewithal to truly care. She just had to move and keep moving.

Ella ran into Talek, jarring her back into her senses. As she stepped around Talek and Nathan, she saw the sheer face of a mesa rising from the ground. They could go no farther due to an iridescent barrier.

“We’ve arrived.” Relief colored Talek’s voice. “They’ll know we’re here. We should see someone anytime now.”

Ella shrugged off her pack, letting it drop with a thud.

“If we are going to wait for an escort, I’m going to sit down.” She collapsed into a boneless heap.

Nathan understood Ella’s desire to stop moving. “Don’t get too comfortable. I don’t think we’ll have to wait too long.”

“I really don’t care. I just want to stop moving for a while.” Nobody could disagree with her assessment. Idly Ella looked at the bubble shimmering in front of her. She raised her hand extending her finger to poke the surface.

“Don’t!” Talek warned her

“Hmm,” Was Ella’s only response as she continued to observe the iridescence, it reminded her of the Sphere. With her finger just above the surface, she noticed that a small bump seemed to follow her finger.

The playful interaction felt inviting, not threatening. She ignored everyone around her and allowed her finger to touch the surface. Tendrils braided themselves around her finger. Ella watched the material flow up her arm. She watched the phenomenon with a detached fascination. She felt no pain, no threat. A blessed welcome filled her soul and replaced the spent energy.

Nathan watched in horror as the field that protected the Sanctuary swaddled Ella. Talek held Nathan back. “Don’t. We can’t do anything.” They watched the bubble envelop her. “Let it do what it needs to do. Nothing bad seems to be happening.”

Jaczon and his wife arrived at the edge of the Sanctuary protection unnoticed by the group. He recognized Talek. The remaining members of the party had him on edge. The barrier’s reaction to the woman worried him.

The Socra gasped at the reaction of the Sanctuary’s barrier. It embraced this woman, fully welcoming her. Then she saw the pendant that hung around Ella’s neck.

“Oh my gods,” she gasped. “She’s of the lost blood. Look at her.”

Jaczon looked at his wife in puzzlement. “Lost blood?”

“She is of Ethias’ blood. I can guarantee it. Look at her."

Jaczon couldn’t deny the physical similarities to the man he had known.

“Well then. That would explain why the barrier is treating her like a fledgling instead of an enemy.”

The Socra cleared her throat.

“Talek!”

Talek looked startled to see the woman who’d raised him on the other side of the barrier. “Nonne!”

“Step through, Talek. Bring your friend, and be welcomed.”

Talek stepped through the barrier with his belongings. Nathan followed closely behind. Both men felt a joyful rush of energy, followed by a rejuvenation of the spirit and body that soothed their weariness. Talek stepped into his Nonne’s arms. Her embrace was comfortable.

“My sweet boy,” the Socra murmured in his ear. “You’ve done well.” She pushed him away, just enough to look at him. Her eyes widened with delighted surprise as she noticed Talek’s left hand. “Tell me about your friends.”

Talek stepped back and got a good look at the man beside the Socra. He choked. He recognized him from the Anakarei ministry. The man was one of the most powerful generals he knew. Eyes wide, his gaze shifted between the two. Jaczon stepped into the conversation.

“Boy, how do you think you got so far embedded in the science division?”

“Jaczon, stop it,” the Socra scolded her husband. “Talek, this is my husband. He paved the way for you to play your part and helped protect you when you were in the city.”

Talek’s mind reeled. The many opportunities that had fortuitously been presented him in his infiltration of the Complex made sense now.

Nathan stepped forward to introduce himself. Talek looked like he had a lot to digest. “Hello, I’m Nathaniel Mullins. I’m Mellanei’s grandson.”

“Mellanei got through the vortex?” Jaczon asked. “We never knew for sure.”

The Socra anxiously asked. “Have you had any recent word of her?”

“Not for a couple of decades,” Nathan said. “The last time she contacted us, she was organizing the lost colonies, readying them for the day we could gather as a people again.”

“That’s good.” The Socra nodded as she acknowledged the news of Mellanei. “Very good.” She looked at the girl still encased in the barrier. “Who is the young lady?”

Talek broke through his own revelations, “That would be Ella. I’m going to let her explain her circumstances, Nonne.”

She pierced her foster son with a knowing gaze. The Socra heard the tone of affection in Talek’s voice. She placed a hand on his arm as they watched Ella commune. “I know what she is. She’s what has been lost to us all these generations.”

Ella’s exhaustion sloughed away as the barrier engulfed her. The energy danced along her nerve endings. A warm presence existed in the energy, one similar to the House on Earth. A download of the Sanctuary’s current information, inhabitants and situation joined the accumulated information in her mind. Twenty-five odd anomalies registered in the Sanctuary inventory. Something about the patterns was familiar. She was too overwhelmed with the new information to figure it out.

An assault, the Chancellor was planning an assault on the Sanctuary. Ella struggled to break free of the fugue to warn the others, but the entity hadn't finished. The new information flooding her mind assured her the Sanctuary could handle the onslaught, but they had to prepare the inhabitants. Ella synchronized herself to the energies of this physical location, much like she had on Earth at Stonehenge.

The energy gently expanded, leaving her on the Sanctuary side of the barrier. Ella blinked as she found herself the center of attention. "Wow, this is really awkward." She grimaced as she muttered, "At least I'm not naked." Ella rose to her feet, noticing the aches and pains seemed to have been healed. Ella sent a mental thank you to the Sanctuary.

"Hello. I'm Ella Hixson. Sorry to be a bearer of bad news, but the Chancellor is planning an attack that will most likely happen sooner rather than later. Any other niceties will have to wait until we make sure this place is secure."

"Attack?" Jaczon demanded. "You just arrived. How do you know?"

Ella didn't have time to take offense at the man's angry tone.

"Your Chancellor is not what he advertises himself to be. He's Drakkon. I, apparently, can track all things Drakkon."

Nathan and Talek sent Ella startled glances as she amended her words. "The Drakkon plane of psychic energy has been sending out warnings since I got here. I've just gotten myself tuned in." She looked at Jaczon. "He's coming. We've got to get the Sanctuary prepared to protect, more importantly defend."

The acting Socra introduced herself as she placed a restraining hand upon her husband's arm.

"You're Talek's Nonne." Ella paused and smiled at the woman who'd helped shape the man who'd become so important to her in such a short period of time. She held out her hands. "It is an honor to meet you."

The Socra's eyes fell on Ella's marked hand, her eyes widening.

"I'm grateful for your presence here."

"I'm going to need your insight and wisdom. I have so much to learn about this place and the people." As Ella looked around, the earth was tired and filled with scrub and the occasional reptile scurrying around looking for food. "I only know what the Ancestral memories tell me and it isn't going to be enough."

The Socra looked at the woman before her. She saw the matching mate markings on Ella's hand. "Please call me Tennei." She gestured to her husband. "That is my mate, Jaczon. Protecting the Drakkon from the Chancellor is his priority."

Ella nodded her understanding.

As the party entered the Sanctuary, the feeling of urgency dogged Ella's every step. Jaczon led them all through the great ornate outer doors. Ella ran her fingers over the geometric patterns that were similar to what she'd seen at the temple. She only wished she could take the time to study them in depth. The party moved through various passageways, passing Drakkon large and small.

Ella stopped, feeling a strong pull as they passed a side passage. "What's down there?"

Jaczon was still not convinced of Ella's credentials. "Nothing to concern you."

Ella walked up to Jaczon, standing toe to toe. She tilted her head up and studied the man in front of her. The weight of responsibility was evident to her and Ella respected that. "Look, I know you don't know me. You do not trust me. You have no reason to." She pointed down the passage. "I really need to know what or who is down there."

Petroj rounded the corner at a dead run. The only thing that saved him from flattening his mother was Talek and Nathan grabbing the running man, forcing him to stop.

"We've got a problem," he panted. "Our special cargo has broken out of its stasis."

"What!" Jaczon roared at Ella. "It's your fault."

Petroj recognized the scientist who went through the node.

"Who are these people?" His attention zeroed in on Ella. If he wasn't mistaken, it was the woman from the other side of the vortex The Chancellor had tried to stabilize. "Who are you?"

"I'm Ella Hixson." She looked Petroj directly in the eyes. "Take me to this problem. I need to be there. Everything else can wait."

"Wait?" Jaczon yelled at Ella's retreating back. "You tell me the Chancellor is coming. Now you tell me it can wait?" He started after her. "Get back here!"

Jaczon make a grab for the pack slung over Ella's shoulder. Nathan and Talek blocked the older man. "Don't even try it." Nathan warned him in a deadly even tone. "Go do what you must to see to the Sanctuary defenses. Ella will join you when she can."

Jaczon snarled, "Boy, get out of my way."

Talek stood his ground.

"She is the High Socra. No one threatens her."

Power flashed through the hallway, knocking Jaczon down as he tried to push past the men.

Talek calmly stated. "Our job is to make sure she completes whatever task she deems priority."

Jaczon sat on the floor, his face puce with anger as he glared. His wife knelt at his side.

"Jaczon, go prepare. I'll go see what I can do to assist the girl and Petroj." She brushed back his disheveled hair, but could do little to soothe his ego. "Maybe she can reclaim what is lost."

He knew the Sanctuary had accepted the strangers. The players in the game were changing. Jaczon didn't like change. "Watch her."

The Socra hurried down the hallway after Ella.

FOURTEEN

The Chancellor's patience thinned as the dirigible fleet journeyed toward its target. He paced the width of the command deck behind the hapless pilot. Rumors swirled through the ranks of the Chancellor's instability.

Each of the dirigibles held a member of the Chancellor's council. The sole purpose was to achieve the destruction of the Sanctuary. Their deaths meant nothing. The Chancellor knew the majority of the Drakkon were there. How convenient of them to assist in their own destruction. He remembered the feeble fortress from his long ago childhood. A spark of energy caught his attention. His key – it was at the Sanctuary. He damned the Tmavě Jeden for stealing the Key.

"Tell the fleet to increase speed," the Chancellor snarled at the dirigible's captain.

The captain followed the command without a murmur. The dirigible structure groaned and creaked as it was pushed beyond its capacity.

Ella slowly approached a plain door. The man, Petroj, opened it to reveal a heavily shielded room. A plain, metallic-looking sarcophagus sat in the middle of the room, its lid askew. A hooded figure sat on the lid, his legs hung listlessly over the side. Nothing about the figure gave the impression of health. Ella approached the middle of the room slowly. The moment she entered the room, the figure oriented itself toward her as a lodestone pointed towards a magnetic pole. The effect was alarming.

"Who are you?" Petroj demanded.

Ella looked between the man in front of her and the form on the sarcophagus.

"I'm here to claim something lost to me a long time ago." Her gaze settled on the middle of the room as she took a step closer.

Petroj blocked her from approaching the sarcophagus.

"What could you have lost that is here?"

"My heritage, my father, everything – nothing." Ella stepped around him, absently. "Things have yet to be determined."

The woman made very little sense. Petroj couldn't let her near the husk of a man who sat in the center of the room. The man's very presence outside his module left them all vulnerable. Petroj put his hands on Ella's shoulders to stop her forward movement. "You can't go near this man. He's dangerous."

"Apparently, so am I." Ella quickly shrugged her shoulders and freed herself from his grasp. "You need to stop getting in my way. We'll figure each other out soon enough."

She reached the cloaked form and pushed the cowl back. Ella stumbled back several steps. The emaciated face of her father stared back at her.

"Daddy?" She didn't recognize the voice that came out of her mouth.

Daddy? Petroj was floored. He knew that Ethias had been out in the Otherverse, come back, but a family? The Socra came to stand by Petroj's side.

"Amazing, isn't it?"

"A daughter? He had a daughter?" Petroj looked at his mother in horror. "The bond with the Chancellor hasn't been severed!" Petroj lunged forward as he watched time slow down to infinitesimal increments.

A caricature of a welcoming smile graced Ethias' face. Alarms sounded in Ella's head, but she dismissed them. This was her father. He would never hurt her. She knew he loved her. She was his little dragon. Ethias bent forward, his arms extended in the act of an embrace. Ella mirrored the gesture, too caught up in the reunion to notice the death in her father's eyes. But instead of an embrace, Ethias wrapped his hands around Ella's throat. His thumbs pressed against her windpipe with crushing force.

She choked out her protests. "This is not how it was supposed to be!" she howled in her head. Her eyelids fell as the world dimmed. She heard shouts in the background. "I'm not ready to die!"

With a desperate surge of energy, Ella forced her fists up between the arms that had cared so tenderly for her as a child. With a powerful outward shrug, she shoved herself free from her father's grasp. Ella stumbled back as she sucked oxygen into her deprived lungs.

Hands grabbed her arms, stopping her flight. Ella recognized Nathan. She didn't have time to notice much more before she was shoved into the Socra's arms. A cool metal cup was pushed into her hands. The thundering of her heart calmed down enough for her to hear the struggle behind her. She watched Talek, Nathan, and the other man subduing her father. Petroj injected Ethias with a syringe that had been lying on a nearby table. Within moments, her father sagged into unconsciousness.

"That is my son, Petroj." The Socra murmured in her ear. "He has been instrumental in protecting our people from the

Anakarei." She stroked Ella's hair in a comforting motion. "If he had any idea this would have happened…"

The impact of what had just happened sank in. Tears welled in Ella's eyes. She wasn't sure if they were anger, fear, sadness, or all of the above. "How could he have known?"

The praxitrol provided the Chancellor with a front row seat to the drama. He smirked as the woman walked into the chamber that held his Key. Bracing himself at the observation rail, the Chancellor anticipated a touching reunion. After all, all reunions should be very hands on. The Chancellor continued to study the woman through his pet's eyes. Under the control of the praxitrol, he knew that the victim retained a portion of themselves, a powerless observer to the puppet theatre of their lives. Trapped, Ethias was screaming hysterically in his own mind to stop. The panic was sweet music.

He watched with satisfaction as the woman's eyes fell shut as Ethias strangled his own progeny. The sight was arousing. Satisfied, he shifted his focus to his other tools scattered around – NO!

His focus snapped back as he watched the woman break his pet's hold. He sent power crashing through the connection, too little too late. The men in the room wrestled his brother into the stasis box. Once more dormant, the last thing he felt from his pet was tears of gratitude at the failure of his actions.

The Chancellor splintered the railing with his fists. Nobody on the bridge moved outside his or her proscribed duties. A predator was in the room. Any untoward movement would end them all.

Ella handed the cup back to the Socra.

"What happened?" she croaked, her hand rubbing gently against the already darkening flesh around her throat. "Why'd he attack me?"

Petroj looked at the woman in front of him.

"The Chancellor's influence is greater than I thought. I didn't think he would be able to exert control from the capitol."

Absently, Ella corrected him. "The Chancellor isn't in the capitol. He is on his way here." She circled the container that held her father's body. "He'll be here soon."

"CRAZCK!" Petroj looked at his mother in horror. "Why didn't you say something?"

"Your father is working on the logistics," The Socra calmly stated. "We need to take care of this first." She gestured to Ella. "Explain to Ella the effects of praxitrol and how you've found a way to combat it."

Talek shot at look at Petroj. "You can counteract the effects of praxitrol? Since when?"

Petroj grimaced as he shook his head. "I can't counteract it. I can only change its focus." He placed a hand on the lid. "I don't know if I can help Ethias."

"I can." Ella said softly. "I can break its hold forever."

The Socra and Petroj looked at Ella with disbelief.

"That's impossible…"

"I've had more resources than you." Ella looked around the room, seeing the packs Nathan and Talek had dropped by the door she walked over and started pulling bundles from her pack. "The Chancellor sent assassins to our world. We captured one, and he survived the process."

"The process?" The Socra asked.

"Yes, the process." Ella allowed herself to rest against Talek. Gently Ella pulled her beloved quartz statuette out of the bag, unwrapping the cherished relic from her childhood.

The normally opalescent surface was incandescent, nearly blinding her.

"Where did you get that?" The Socra gasped as the statuette glowed.

Puzzled by her reaction, Ella looked at the Socra. "My father gave this to me when I was a little girl. It must be tapping automatically into the ley line energy here."

"The Drakkon is one of the most powerful artifacts lost to time." The Socra slowly walked toward Ella, stopping a foot away. "It is said all Drakkon are born from it."

"Born from it?" Ella looked at the glowing statuette in her hand. "I don't understand." She turned her head away from the Socra as she racked her brain. "I understood this artifact was not listed in the Script, therefore, you shouldn't know about it."

"Ah, there is an oral component to our history that is passed down to the highest ranking Socra on Drakkonon. Since Mellanei is gone, I am she." She reached her hand out to stroke the Drakkon, but stopped short of touching it. "We had to have a way to be able to identify what was lost if it ever resurfaced."

Ella closed her eyes as she sorted through her memories looking for references. The Socra looked at Talek in askance.

"She carries all the ancestral knowledge," Talek murmured to the Socra. He paused for a beat. "All of it. At the Temple, the ancestors gave her what she didn't have from her father."

"No one person can handle that amount of knowledge. She'll go insane."

Talek put a cautioning hand on the Socra's arm. "Ella's mind is unlike any other."

"Her ability to organize the information is unexpected and needed," Nathan said. "She is more than Drakkon. She is of Earth as well. She can access and organize the histories."

"The High Socra was never meant to hold all the knowledge. The Grand Council was meant to help bear that burden."

"The council has been gone for generations." Talek stated. "We will have it again, but right now she is the most valuable tool we have."

Ella drew in something between a gasp and a breath as she came back into the now.

"I have so much to learn about this world and culture. The oral history was a clever way to remember the lost objects in case they fell into the wrong hands."

"We have much to discuss, you and I." the Socra said to Ella. "I think you have many things to share."

"First things first." Ella placed the Drakkon on the table with the syringes. She unwrapped the other bundles, taking out the ingredients. She mixed the formula in a bowl.

"You found a way to break the control of the praxitrol?" Petroj asked.

"Yes," Ella confirmed. "You said you'd found a way to change the focus. What did you mean?"

"Our scientists were never able to gain enough of a sample. One day the Chancellor let something slip when he was speaking to me." Petroj looked at all the compounds with interest. Some he recognized, some he didn't. "It made me think that it was dependent on the blood of the Drakkon. I had to experiment a little. But with time, I was able to make the hunters loyal to me."

Ella looked at the man in front of her. "There are others?"

"Yes, but the praxitrol they use is based on my blood. Will you be able to help them?"

Talek answered for Ella. "Yes. The principles are the same, but we'll have to account for the change of the donor blood."

Ella held out a syringe. "We'll need a sample of my father's blood so we can get started." She looked at the sarcophagus. "Then I need to assess the damage done to him."

"No!" Talek stood in front of her as Petroj went to obtain the sample. "He tried to kill you."

"He didn't try to kill me." Ella corrected him, "The Chancellor did. Remember, somewhere in there is my father."

Ella took a deep breath and exhaled then walked to the module. "Since he is already tranquilized, the process may be easier."

Ella passed the Drakkon over the liquid in the bowl. A blinding flash filled the room. Negative images overlay everyone's vision. The liquid in the bowl now danced with energy. With great care, she filled the syringe and took a deep breath. Everything hinged on this moment. She would either save or kill her father. God help her, she prayed this saved him.

Not wasting any more time, Ella leaned over the edge and plunged the needle straight into Ethias's jugular. She barely had time to empty the syringe before he reared up roaring, his arms flailing. The last thing Ella felt was her father's fist crashing into the side of her head.

The Chancellor roared his denial as he felt his connection completely severed with his key.

"This is not happening!"

He ripped a bolted table from the floor, sending it crashing through the outer wall, creating a hull breach. Crews rushed to the scene only to turn around and leave. No one would face the Chancellor in a rage. High altitude winds ripped at his clothes, sucking unsecured items out of the ship. The severed link throbbed with the excruciating exposure of raw nerves.

The stink of the sewer followed Davist back to the Wyvern's hidden entrance. He could barely stand the stink of himself. He pounded on the door and waited impatiently for entrance. Behind him claws scrabbled against the sewer bricks. He shone his light back along the passage. Bright eyes glittered back at him.

Finally the door opened. "Gah! Man, your stink could kill every Anakarei agent in the bar." Davist flipped Pacol an obscene gesture. Pacol returned it with interest. "Get upstairs before you spoil the food." Pacol held his shirt over his face in an effort to stave off the stench. "What happened to you? Did you fall in a cesspit?"

Davist ignored Pacol. As far as he was concerned, everything could wait until he had cleaned the muck off himself. He had no idea what was crawling on him, but he didn't want to conduct an inventory.

Mistress Smyzac met him at the top of the stairs with a gunny sack.

"Strip! Put your clothes in the bag."

The older woman's scrutiny was uncomfortable.

"Quickly boy! Those clothes are going to start walking away with you in them!"

He didn't need to be reminded how filthy he was. He stripped, giving the full sack to Mistress Smyzac. Hot footing it into the bathroom, Davist all but sobbed in relief as the hot water started to peel the layers of muck off his body. He heard the bathroom door open and Pacol walked in carrying a bundle of clothing.

"Mistress Smyzac is scary."

Pacol laughed at his friend in sympathy. Over the last several days, he had caught the sharp edge of the woman's tongue. She hadn't been wrong in her rebukes.

"That she is." He set clean clothes down on the bench in the bathing room. "What did you find?"

Davist scrubbed himself industriously.

"It's not good. The Chancellor mobilized for the Sanctuary. He took the majority of the dirigible fleet, leaving a basic guard on the Complex."

"The Sanctuary? Are you sure?" Pacol sank down on a bench that lined the wall opposite the shower. "I have no way to warn them."

"Frankly, I think that's the least of our worries." Davist reached for a towel to wrap around his hips.

"What do you mean?"

"Orders were left for the under council to round up anyone suspected of being Drakkon or sympathizers."

"And do what with them?"

"That's the question." Davist looked his friend and leader straight in the eye. "I couldn't get any information on the plans after that. As I hit the sewers, I was already hearing of disappearances."

"Well, crazck."

"Pacol! Watch your mouth!" Mistress Smyzac's rebuke had both men jumping. "If sympathizers are being rousted, we have to organize."

Davist grabbed the clothes on the bench, diving back into the shower stall. The woman was proving to be unstoppable when she was interested in anything.

"Mistress Smyzac, can you please let me get dressed?"

"I don't know why you're bothered, boy." She laughed at his discomfort.

Silence seemed to be the best offense. Davist dressed with his ears burning a dull red that matched his cheeks. Davist stepped out of the stall and saw that the others hadn't moved from the room.

"We've got to do something for the city. A balance has always existed in the city between the believers and the others." The old woman joined Pacol on the bench as she spoke. "The Chancellor has upset that balance." She gave the men a shrewd look. "I have a few contacts in the military command which haven't been tainted by the Chancellor. I'm calling them in for a meeting."

The men looked at the old woman with horror and respect. They knew Mistress Smyzac was connected, but to have military contacts at the Complex was unthinkable.

"How high up are your contacts?" Davist asked.

"They have enough influence to make a difference, but not enough to draw attention." Mistress Smyzac smiled. "They'll be here in a few hours."

"You can't arrange things without talking to me first." Pacol sputtered. "I'm running this operation."

The soft little old lady demeanor changed, hardened. In its place, a sharp woman who would do anything to protect her family looked at Pacol. "This is my establishment. You are here by my pleasure. You can leave any time you'd like." Power emanated from her, revealing her to be a socra. "We have a city to preserve. It's no good to us in ruins. We work to save everyone."

Pacol sat up straighter; the stinging reprimand cut his soul. "You're right. The Chancellor is out to see his end game, consequences be damned." He looked at his second. "We'll be ready to meet with your contacts."

Mistress Smyzac reached up, patting both men on their cheeks.

"There you go. That wasn't so bad." Then she walked out the door.

Pacol let out a breath he hadn't known he was holding, "Gods help anyone who crosses that woman."

Ella woke up with a throbbing head. "What happened?" A soft cool cloth gently swabbed her forehead.

"Your cure had some unintended consequences." Petroj's voice came from her left.

The room spun as she turned her head in that direction. Firm hands stopped her from turning her head anymore. Talek's face filled her field of vision. "Don't move. You have a concussion. We've sent for a healer."

"Consequences? Is my father okay?" Ella feared the worse had happened. "Tell me, is he alive."

Talek filled her on Ethias's condition. Moments after she had administered the formula her father had had a seizure. His body flailed uncontrollably, and they had to move him onto a pallet on the floor to find a way to keep him from hurting himself. "He has been dormant for the last little while. I can't tell if he is unconscious or worse. But he is alive."

Relief and worry warred in Ella's already throbbing head.

"How long have I been out?"

Ella didn't bother to move even her eyes as Nathan entered the conversation.

"You've only been out about fifteen minutes."

Ella raised her hands to clasp Talek's wrist.

"Nobody else was hurt?"

Talek smoothed her hair. "Just bumps and bruises. Only you took a wallop." He kissed her gently. "I wished you hadn't."

Ella savored the moment despite the pain.

"Trust me, me neither."

The door to the chamber opened, and a flurry of feet entered the room. A woman moved into Ella's field of vision.

"Well, you've certainly gone and done it."

"Behte," the Socra chided. "Please do what you can do. She needs to be up as soon as possible."

Behte waved a dismissive hand at the Socra as she looked at her patient. "Always in a hurry, never time to heal properly." Behte rubbed her hands briskly together then held them several inches over Ella's body.

The warm, soothing flow of healing energy startled Ella, as the woman slowly brought her hands up her body. The warmth intensified over her numerous bruises and scrapes, leaving a slight tingling. When Behte reached her head, the heat intensified to be almost unbearable. But just as the feeling was becoming vastly uncomfortable, Behte raised her hands. She clapped them together, shook them from the wrists.

"There, you should be able to sit up."

With assistance from the healer, Ella sat up. She expected the hand that assisted her to be hot. Instead, it was cool to the touch. Nothing hurt, a slight tingle, no pain.

"Thank you."

Behte waved off her gratitude.

"Is there anyone else I need to attend too?"

"Not at the moment." The Socra escorted her to the door. "We'll need you and the other healers rested and ready."

"Yes, we've seen the preparations." She gave the Socra a swift and firm embrace. "We'll be ready." She turned and left the chamber.

Ella looked at the face that had aged significantly from the image she'd had in her mind from her childhood. A part of her was angry at the time lost, the rest was grateful she'd found him again. "I'm going to have to assess the damage done to him."

Nathan and Talek both protested, but the Socra raised her hand.

"Ella, please explain what you mean."

"This drug renders the victim helpless and can do serious damage to the brain itself." She moved over to sit by her father, placing her hands on his temples. She didn't give anyone in the room a chance to protest.

Ella found herself in a moldering, miserable mess of jumbled memories. Shredded pieces of her father's life lay strewn across the ground. Ella didn't look too closely. She wasn't ready to see herself in any of the damaged memories. Carefully picking her way across the boggy ground she looked for any spark of life. She didn't know if she was looking for the father of her youth or the stranger of the now.

Noises that she couldn't identify surrounded her. Broken bits of machinery littered the mindscape. The body of his motorcycle lay twisted against the rotting trunk of a tree. Other elements she didn't recognize, but they all had significance to her father. She felt immersed in the middle of a

Dali painting. She wouldn't have been surprised to see a melting clock or two.

This was her father's mind. Ella cleared her own ego and concentrated on finding him. Following her instinct, she found herself in front of a cave. Debris littered the opening. A dank odor wafted from the entrance. Ella couldn't imagine anyone being there, yet her intuition told her otherwise.

"Daddy?" Ella called. "It's Ella."

The only answer Ella received was a scuffle in the dark of the cave. Gathering her resolve, she stepped into the dark wishing she had a light. A stray memory from her first experience of mind walking, when Nathan was talking her through how to manage the flow of information from the mind lock floated across her mind. You control the environment. Build what you must to control the tumult.

"Okay, Nathan, you're on!" she murmured. "I need a light to see through the dark and guide the lost." A light appeared at her shoulder just behind her head, bathing the area ahead of her in a revealing glow. She gasped at the filthy cot and ragged blanket lying against the far wall of the cave. A skeletal figure cowered against the wall. She approached him slowly, her hands showing.

"Daddy?"

The figure flinched at her voice, drawing into a tighter ball against the wall. Ella noticed the walls. Scribbled over and over, on every possible surface, were the words–I am Ethias. I am not lost. I will be found.

Ella choked back a sob. She knew what she had to do.

She drew herself to her full height and called out, "Ethias Hixson!"

The figure didn't move.

She pulled on all the ancestral power she possessed, filling her voice with power and love. “Ethias Hixson! You are not lost! You have been found!”

An eye, full of despair, peered out from under a shank of filthy hair. Ethias lowered the arm that shielded his face, revealing a visage ravaged by deprivation. Ella fell to her knees, the weight of her sorrow at seeing her once vibrant father so decimated.

Ella held out her hands as she reiterated, “Ethias Hixson, you have been found. It’s time to go home. Take my hands.”

He stared at the hands proffered by his daughter. “You can’t be here. I’ve finally died.” Ethias croaked, his voice destroyed from years of screaming. “He said the only way I’d ever be free is if I died.”

“No, Daddy,” Ella choked back tears of rage mixed with grief. “The Chancellor lied. You will be free again.” She reached up and gently stroked his face. “You raised a smart little dragon. I found a way to break his hold.”

Ethias stared at the woman standing in front of him. He was so afraid it was another trick of his brother. “How could you have broken the hold? Only the ancestors know the cure.”

She closed her eyes as she felt the surge of the collective power of their ancestors rush forward to embrace their lost child. Her blue-green eyes glowed with love and power. She reached down, grabbing her father’s shoulders. She embraced him, not allowing his fear or shame to deter her. The ancestors swirled around them both.

Ethias sobbed as he clutched his daughter. With the fear of a man whose hope had been crushed, he asked again, “I’m not dead?”

Ella confirmed his ‘alive’ status with a watery laugh. “Your body and mind are a little worse for wear. But you are alive." She pushed back from his tight hold slightly. "Are you ready to rejoin the real world?"

"Yes, let us leave here." He attempted to gain his feet. His spirit was as weak as his body. "You're going to have to help me."

"Daddy, I've done things and seen things that have seriously stretched my understanding of the cosmos. Helping you return to the world will be a cakewalk."

He stared at his daughter. "You really are fearless."

"Nope," Ella denied, as she and her father walked out of the cave. "I'm just highly adaptable. Somehow, I think that's a hereditary thing."

He stared in horror as he saw his broken life strewn across a ravaged mindscape. "So much is lost."

"The structure is there. We just have to do a lot of cleanup." She nudged her father. "I wonder if the Drakkon have any good therapists."

When Ethias was startled into laughter, the sky changed color to a soft periwinkle at the introduction of the happier emotion.

"Would you look at that?"

Not waiting for him to think about the process, Ella brought them back to reality.

A high keening erupted from Ethias as he and Ella emerged from the mind journey.

"Shh! Daddy. You're okay." She brushed his hair back from his forehead. "Welcome back."

The Socra called for the healer to return to the room, as she knelt at Ella's side. "Your journey was successful."

Ella watched her father closely. "Yes, but it'll take him awhile to recover."

With the return of the healer, two bundles of energy came close on her heels. "Petroj! Jaczon needs you!" Alexi and Natov's voices tumbled over each other. "There are dirigibles!"

Petroj bit back a curse as he grabbed the boys by the scruff of their necks.

"How would you know that? I know that you both were told to stay inside."

Neither of the boys said a word.

Petroj gave them both a shake. "Stay here. I have to get to my father."

He sent an apologetic look to his mother and ran for the door.

"I guess that means the Chancellor is here," Ella said to no one in particular.

The Socra waved Ella out of the room.

"Go, I'll care for your father."

Ella ran down the corridors, letting instincts guide her. Nathan and Talek followed closely. The passages filled with people running to fulfill assigned tasks as others moved toward evacuation points that would protect them from the oncoming barrage. Boxes of supplies lined the walls. They dodged running messengers as they found the large room where Petroj and Jaczon were issuing orders. She pushed her way to the front of the room and watched quietly as the Drakkon took defensive positions. As a break in the planning occurred, she cleared her throat.

"You!" Jaczon snarled. "What do you want?"

“I can feel the love, I really can.” Ella stared at the man who was clearly in military mode. “You need my help.”

“Tell me, mistress.” Jaczon gestured to the dirigibles floating in the distance outside the window. “Do you have some sort of magic that will make all those enemies go away?”

Ella pondered the man in front of her. She had seen his son and wife in action. The Sanctuary wouldn’t have let him in if he wasn’t of pure intent. She used air quotes, “I have no ‘magical solution’ to the enemies that are about to assault us.” She quickly held up her hand to forestall any continuing barrage. “That doesn’t mean I can’t help.”

“Jaczon,” Petroj interrupted. “Do not discount her contributions. She broke the Chancellor’s hold on Ethias.”

Jaczon shook his head in disbelief. “Our best and brightest couldn’t. Some girl from another world fixed the problem in an afternoon?”

“He is free of the taint and drug. His recovery will take time, but he will recover.” Petroj waved his hand to the large room carved into the side of the plateau with a large opening facing the east. “We need an edge that the Chancellor cannot anticipate.”

His eyes narrowed as he contemplated the woman in front of him. “Is it true you are Ethias’s daughter?”

“Yes, but don’t let that bother you. You should also know that makes me the Chancellor’s niece.”

Jaczon and Petroj froze. “What did you just say?” Petroj hissed.

“That cursed individual is a traitor to his own kind.” Ella felt the rage amplified by the indignation of the Ancestors. “He betrayed everything he was because he coveted an inheritance he had no right too.”

“Explain.” Jaczon barked.

“Simply put, Ethias and the Chancellor were brothers, born of the bloodline of the High Socra,” Ella calmly explained. “The order of birth has never held sway in the selection of the High Socra. The Ancestors and the Sanctuary choose.” A lump of sorrow filled Ella’s throat. “For several generations, the oldest child had held the office. The Chancellor assumed he would follow the pattern, but this time was different. Ethias went to the Sanctuary with his parents for a celebration. His brother stayed home. A miracle occurred. He was embraced by the Ancestors and by the Sanctuary barrier, leaving no doubt about succession.”

Petroj looked at his father. “How old is Ethias?”

“His bloodline held a longevity that was mythic throughout our race. Nobody knows.” Jaczon thought hard about the history he knew. “The Anakarei didn’t come into power until three hundred years ago.” Jaczon looked at Ella. “Your father slipped through the Node a hundred years into their occupation when it became evident they were trying to destroy all things Drakkon.”

“The Chancellor tried to destroy his family. Only my father survived.” Ella grimaced. “For his hubris, the Chancellor’s name was wiped from the history of the Drakkon. On my world, we call that aberrant thinking. He’d have been locked up.”

Talek picked up the history. “The Anakarei showed up shortly after the attack on the family.” Jaczon contemplated Ella. “So, what does this mean for us? You show up to be our savior?”

Ella clenched her jaw. She understood the man’s animosity. She was swooping in to ‘save the day,’ something she had her own doubts about.

"Do you know me enough to trust me?" Ella gave Jaczon a nasty look. "No, but you need the knowledge I have. You have a world in crisis. I can help eliminate a part of the problem. The rest you'll have to sort out."

"Alright, not a savior then." Jaczon gave a gruff snort. "I don't like your attitude."

"You should be used to that, Father." Petroj interjected.

"He's your father?" Ella looked at the equally stoic man. "How does your mother deal with the two of you?" She held up her hand. "No, don't answer that. I really don't want to know."

"You said you are not from this world, yet you have an understanding that not even our wisest leaders have. The Sanctuary embraced you as a long lost child." Jaczon stood toe to toe with Ella. "Who are you?" he asked.

Like so many times in the past twenty-four hour period, Ella felt the embrace of the Sanctuary and the Ancestors. Clarity filled her. She understood Jaczon's question. "I am your High Socra, chosen to bring forth the Times of Strife and Miracles and the peace that will follow."

She leaned forward and laid her head on Jaczon's, embracing him. "I'll do my best to take care of the Chancellor. I'll need you to take care of the rest." The words and energy flowed between the two.

Jaczon's arms remained stiffly at his side, as the initial shock of her embrace lessened. She stepped back, and his face was a mixture of embarrassment and wonder.

Ella focused on airships surrounding the mesa the sanctuary was built on. "The Sanctuary barrier can hold the dirigibles off for a time?"

"We need a plan. What do you propose?" Jaczon asked, still unsure of Ella.

A detailed map of the Sanctuary appeared in her head, complete with the entrance to the plateau's surface. Ella's smile evoked fear in the hearts of everyone who saw it.

"I'm going to give him a chance to wipe me out personally."

Ella let the men shout and argue about the stupidity of the plan she had just announced. The only non-participant was Talek. Talek knew she wasn't intending to commit suicide.

"Aside from making yourself a target, what is the real plan?" he asked. As she leaned against his side, Talek slid his arm around her shoulders supporting her.

"We have to draw him out of the dirigible fleet. He is the drive behind this attack. I'm sure he has key personnel drugged to fulfill his bidding." Talek continued to listen. "If I can neutralize him, I might be able to break the bonds simultaneously. I'm thinking that would cause enough chaos to let Jaczon and his crew to get themselves a dirigible fleet."

By this time, the arguments had faded and the men were paying attention.

"Go big or go home?" Nathan said in a dry tone.

The corners of Ella's mouth kicked up in wry amusement. "In for a penny, in for a pound, Nathan." She let the levity drain from her face. "We don't have much time. I've got to get up to the top. Talek, I need you to be ready with the sedative. We'll lure him with the Drakkon. He is still after what he considers his birthright."

Alexi entered the room, walking directly to Petroj carefully carrying a basket. "Petroj, the Socra says you're to give this to the lady."

"You can give it to her yourself." Petroj gestured Ella over. "Ella, I'd like you to meet Alexi."

Alexi gave a courtly bow to Ella, and she responded with a bow of her head, “Nice to meet you Alexi. You have something for me?”

“Your father told the Socra you’d need this soon.” He handed her the basket.

She uncovered the wrappings to reveal the Drakkon. The statuette gave a glowing pulse at her presence. “Thank you, Alexi. Please return to the Socra.”

“Yes, ma’am.” Alexi ran from the room.

“I’m surprised that boy didn’t come barreling in on full speed,” Jaczon muttered.

Ella arched an eyebrow his direction.

Petroj laughed.

“He and his brother are full of energy. My mother will have them well in hand. They may prove useful in your father’s recovery.”

The energy emanating from the statuette comforted Ella as she swaddled it again in its protective wrappings.

“What more needs to be done in preparations?” Ella asked Jaczon.

“We just have to get our volunteers for the dirigible assault.”

She recalled her own first flight.

“I’m assuming everyone has more flight experience than I do?” Talek and Nathan both stifled their laughter. Jaczon had no idea what was so amusing.

“We’ve always had a group with advance flight skills,” he said. “They’ll be ready.”

Ella continued to glare at her guardians. “Maybe when all of this is done, I can take some flying lessons from them. My landings aren’t so good.”

Before Jaczon and Petroj could respond, Talek interjected, “I’ll teach you what you need to know.” Her lowered his forehead to touch hers and whispered, “When all this is done, we’ll figure everything else out.” He gripped her shoulders. “I need you to be alive. Don’t do anything that will get you killed.”

“I noticed you didn’t say safe,” Ella whispered back.

“You’re facing one of the most ruthless foes the Drakkon have ever known. He is one of our own.” His grip tightened painfully. “There is nothing safe about this.” He kissed her forehead. “I need you alive.”

“I’ll need you on the plateau with me.”

“I wouldn’t be any other place.”

FIFTEEN

Petroj was loath to interrupt the couple's intimate moment. A runner had brought back information that all the defenses were in place.

"We need to get you in position." Ella stepped back slighting from Talek's embrace.

"Do you have any idea how you'll get The Chancellor's attention?" Petroj asked.

"I'll just be my charming self," she quipped. "I can feel him on the psychic plane that all Drakkon share. I know that he can feel me, but he can't pinpoint me because of the Sanctuary barrier." She rubbed her hand along Talek's. "Once I'm on the plateau, the barrier will recede to cover everything but the surface. I'll be hard to miss."

Jaczon had to trust that Ella could do what she said and that her guardians would protect her. He turned his attention back to the preparations.

The Chancellor seethed with rage, the edges that defined his human form shimmered and buckled. He could feel the presence of his brother's brat and an artifact he'd thought lost to him. She was just an obstacle to be broken and turned to his purposes, just like her father. He deserved to rule the Drakkon. The Socri were weak. Drakkonon wasn't enough. The Otherverse was his to rule.

The Chancellor stormed into his quarters, needing a place to plan. He growled a terrible sound. "That creature controls the Drakkon. That's how she severed my link with my key." The pallid human cracked and ashy bronze struggled to emerge as his rage erupted. The artifact was crucial in taking complete control of the Drakkon.

He stalked into the command deck.

"Captain, I want you to start the offensive."

"Sir! We have no way to penetrate the barrier," the commander countered.

"Are you questioning me?" the Chancellor whispered as he moved to stand in front of the man. Without a second thought, the Chancellor whipped out a knife and slit the man's throat. He looked at the second in command. "Do you have any questions about my orders?"

"No, sir!" The now Captain snapped a salute as he started barking out orders. Nobody on the deck hesitated. The pooling blood around the former captain's body was a stark reminder of the Chancellor's absolute rule.

Ethias's brother left the command deck after conveying his orders to the rest of the fleet with the dead captain's body in full view. The sound of armaments launching made him happy. Men in the narrow corridors scrambled to make way.

Ella felt the barrier shudder under the initial bombardment. The shock made her collapse against the passageway wall.

"They've started!" she gasped. Her connection with the barrier made each salvo personal. "We've got to get up top right now!"

The trio started running. Ella took the lead with Talek and Nathan hot on her heels. After traversing a maze of ever climbing passageways, they reached the exit to the plateau. Ella carefully pushed the door out. The hot outside air rushed into the cool of the tunnels. The glare of the light blinded her. Ella faced Talek and Nathan.

"You both are going to have to wait here."

"We need to be on the surface with you," Talek protested.

Ella could feel how close the Chancellor's presence was on the Drakkon psychic plain.

"He needs to think I'm alone. It will make him cocky, prone to mistakes." She gave Talek and Nathan a smile that promised retribution. "In the Chancellor's eyes, I'm just a puny, interfering female."

"You can't do this alone." Nathan looked at the woman who was one of the most precious things to his race. "I'm not alone." Ella grew serious, "I have you both and the Ancestors." She shrugged. "Plus, I have a black belt in karate."

"Great, a karate dragon." Nathan pulled Ella into a tight hug. "I won't say good luck. I'm going to say stay alive." He gave her a shake. "We need you alive."

Talek stepped closer. "I need you alive."

"I'll do my best." Ella knew the odds were against her. "I've got my arsenal of Drakkon knowledge, my own experience, and the support of the Ancestors. Somehow, that should give me an edge."

Ella stepped out into the bright light. She felt the barrier retreat behind her. The door was perfectly camouflaged in a cluster of boulders. A step to the left took her out of its sight. There, in the shadow of the boulders, she quickly shed her clothes. She'd meet her enemy in Drakkon form.

The Chancellor stood at the hull breach, preventing the repair crew from finishing. The rupture wasn't fatal to the ships integrity. His perch in the ship gave him the perfect view of rocky surface of the plateau was devoid of plant life. His goal was to obtain the Drakkon and then destroy the Sanctuary. Mid-plan, a flash of color caught his eye, blue-green with a glint of gold around the neck – the female.

"No!" The Chancellor roared. He flung off his cloak as he leapt through the hull breach. He rocketed toward his prey on the plateau. Wind tore at him as he transformed, the tatters of his clothes floating to the ground like ashes in the wind. In his Drakkon form, the beat of his enormous wings displaced the air around the dirigible, causing it to destabilize.

"Petroj! Where did that Drakkon come from?" Jaczon yelled at his son.

"May all the gods help Ella." Petroj watched the sky in horror. "She did it. It's the Chancellor."

Jaczon barked into the com unit to the units spread throughout the Sanctuary. "Do not engage the rogue Drakkon!" Units rushed to their stations. "I repeat do not engage! We are to defend against the dirigibles only!"

Jaczon stared at his son. "I hope she can do what she says."

Petroj kept an eye on the sky and prayed for the first time in a very long time.

A warning itch between Ella's shoulders was the only warning of the aerial attack. Her wings snapped open as she skipped and glided from the Drakkon that bulleted down from the sky. The Chancellor's Drakkon form was enormous.

Tattered wings and blotchy, dull scales reflected the Chancellor's decayed soul. His rage fueled his approach. All Ella could do was evade the attack. She could hear her sensei yelling at her, 'Immobilize your attacker and run!' She didn't have a choice on the running part. She was in the fight of her life.

The ground shook from his impact on the ground. A cloud of dust plumed, obscuring her view. She wasn't going to stick around on the ground vulnerable. Giving a few powerful wing beats, Ella launched straight up for the sky. She was counting on physics being relatively the same on both worlds. The mass of the larger Drakkon would make it more difficult for it to gain altitude.

She flew straight for the sun hoping to blind the Chancellor for a few precious moments. "Think Ella! Think Dammit! What do you have to use as a weapon in this form." Ella searched frantically through the vast catalogue of her mind. None of the information was helpful. She couldn't keep her focus divided. The glimmer of the barrier niggled something in the vast vault of information. She was one of the few Drakkon that could handle raw ley line energy. To do this she would have to land.

Abruptly changing direction, she flew straight back down the same path she had ascended. The Chancellor barely saw her coming. Extending her talons, she raked them along his underbelly. The bellow of pain was satisfying.

Pain ripped through the Chancellor as he saw his prey changed direction. He barely had the time to move out of her way to avoid a collision. At the speeds they were moving, any collision would have proven to be fatal. He intended to survive this confrontation. Tucking his wings along his back, the Chancellor allowed his superior weight to gain on his target.

Then a flash of light blinded him, causing him to deploy his wings in a braking maneuver. The Chancellor glided for a few precious moments as he cleared his vision, only to see the creature had already landed in the middle of the plateau. She waited for him as if she were to serve him tea. He'd make her scream for mercy and then drink her blood.

Ella intellectually understood that this moment of conflict would manifest as she watched the great beast that was her uncle prowl around her, his tail whipping back and forth. The talons at the ends of his hands and feet left great gashes on the ground. She called on everything in her to keep a visage of calm. Beneath the surface, she scrambled for the energy that powered the Sanctuary. She had to leave plenty to keep the oasis safe while giving herself the edge. She felt the Drakkon statuette humming along with the ley energy.

Ella almost didn't see the Chancellor's tail whip in for a strike. She leapt up, hissing with pain as the barb on his tail connected with her own leaving a long gash. Determined, she decided she was going to get some answers.

"So, uncle, we meet."

"You are nothing, little girl." The Chancellor roared his denial of their familial relationship. "You are the unfortunate byproduct of an experiment. One I shall terminate."

"Is that any way to speak to your family?" Ella taunted the Drakkon in front of her as she gathered the power to her. "Family is sacred. Precious. I don't have a lot. So I rejoice when I find lost members of my own."

"I HAVE NO FAMILY!" the Chancellor thundered. His Drakkon voice bugled across the space that separated them. Ella felt the hate, resentment, and sickness that dwelt inside the creature in front of her.

"Well that's a funny thing." Ella continued to push at the emotional button the Chancellor had provided. "You killed your parents, tried and failed to kill your brother." Ella gave the equivalent of a shrug in her Drakkon shape. "And now I'm here. You just can't get rid of us." Her voice developed a menacing quality. "Sometimes family has to take care of its mistakes." She pulled on memories of her family. Ella rose to her full height with her wings extended, "Erren Hixson, with the permission of the family you turned your back on and tried to destroy, I name you kin-traitor and bring you to justice!"

A burst of raw ley energy burst from Ella, hitting The Chancellor square in the head. The Drakkon flew up in the air, falling to the ground with an impressive impact. Ella loped on all fours to where her uncle lay. Talek and Nathan ran to her side.

"No stay back!" She shouted at them, "I have to make sure he is out." She looked at the Drakkon that lay sprawled on the ground. She circled the motionless form with caution. All her senses were jangling a warning she couldn't interpret. "Toss me a shirt." She called to the men. Talek wadded up a long tunic, hurling it towards her.

Ella drew her humanity around her, as she pulled the tunic over her head. The pendant swayed under the fabric as she approached the head of the downed Drakkon. Without warning, a foreleg lashed out knocking her toward the gapping maw of the Chancellor. Ella tucked and rolled avoiding the snapping teeth. The rocks on the ground dug into her thinly covered flesh.

The energy bolt had weakened the Chancellor considerably. She knew the initial downing had been too easy. However, Drakkon versus human, the odds were on his side. Ella jumped to the side as she heard the passing whistle of that damn tail of his.

She was going to have force the Chancellor back into human form. Reaching for the ley energy again, she wound up like a major league pitcher and let loose. The Chancellor had so kindly provided his head as target. He reared back. Ella's bolt caught him in the throat. She flung bolt after bolt of energy. The Chancellor collapsed, stunned by the repeated energy bolts to the head.

This time Ella didn't hesitate. She delivered a round-house kick to The Chancellor's space just behind the eye ridge. She felt the bone crack, her foot stung from the force of the impact. The Chancellor's eyes widened, before blanking and collapsing on the ground. She stood there breathing heavily, her body racked with pain, crackling with unused energy. A rock formation on the opposite side of the field of battle shattered as Ella discharge the excess power.

She started to sob "I killed a man." She shuddered with the horror of what she had done. "How could I have done that?"

Talek reached his mate first. "You didn't kill him." He tenderly cupped her face and forced her to look at him. "You didn't kill him!"

"What would you call what I did?"

"Ella, he still breathes," Nathan gently said.

Confused, Ella gaped at her companions. "What?"

"He breathes." Talek gently turned her head. "He's not dead." He shook his head. "I don't know if you did him a kindness or a disservice."

Nathan approached the downed Drakkon. "We need to force him to change." He looked at Ella. "Do you think you can make that happen?"

Ella was still grappling with the reality that she hadn't killed her uncle. "Yes, give me a minute. I have to think about this." Her system was still buzzing from the aftermath of the energy. With the Chancellor unconscious, she was going to have to trigger the transformation using the ley energy. She really didn't want to play with any more ley lines today.

She laid her hands on the Chancellor's head. She simply concentrated on pulling the human form out of the Drakkon. A brilliant flash of light and an average looking, naked, middle-aged man lay sprawled on the rocky ground in front of her.

The Sanctuary barrier held against the dirigible barrage as the battle raged on the plateau. Without warning, the Sanctuary barrier grew opaque, expanding beyond its normal boundaries. The dirigibles were now inside the barrier. No more weapons fire. No movement on the ships.

"All teams, board the dirigibles! Go, Go, Go!" Jaczon shouted into the com.

Drakkon carrying human shaped counterparts flew up to the ships. They boarded the ships, meeting no resistance. Each team checked in with Jaczon in the command center. The message was the same. All crewmembers were unconscious.

Jaczon looked at his son and marveled. "We have a dirigible fleet." He laughed. "I don't know what that girl did, but I'm impressed."

Petroj didn't wait to see what else his father had to say, he ran for the door. He nearly mowed down his mother in the process.

"Go! See to the girl and her guardians!" the Socra ordered her son.

Petroj continued on his way. He met up with the trio, supporting a naked man between them. Ella limped behind them.

"Let's put him in the chamber where Ethias was, and we'll put him in the containment module." Petroj motioned for the men to follow him.

Ella whimpered. Now that the adrenaline was wearing off, every bruise and injury started to manifest in the most painful way. Ella wanted to sleep for a month. She lagged behind the group as her exhaustion set in.

When Talek glanced back to see where his mate was, she was gone.

“Petroj, I need you to help Nathan. Ella’s gone.” He retraced their steps. “I need to find her.”

They waved him on. Talek ran back the way they’d come. A few minutes passed, and he found Ella slumped against the passageway wall. The dim light made her pallor all the more alarming. He eased down to the floor at her side and quickly did a physical inventory. Talek started cursing when he found the gash along her back that ended above her knee. The deep tissue bruises were already manifesting in that particular red purple that said they would hurt viciously.

“Come on, bright one! Open your eyes for me.” Talek just needed to make sure she could hear him. Ella groaned, curling into his embrace. He lifted her into his arms and staggered to his feet. He had to get her to a healer.

“Talek?” Ella whispered.

“I’m here.”

Her voice was a mere thread of sound. “I don’t feel so well.”

“No, I would imagine you don’t.” He tried not to jostle her as he hurried down the passageway. “Just rest. I’ll get you to a healer.”

The Socra met him in the passageway with Behte. “What is wrong with you people? I said rest.” The healer muttered.

“Behte, she did what she had to do,” the Socra defended the pair.

“Let’s bring her to the chambers we had prepared for you both.” Behte briskly led the way.

Pacol never dealt well with authority. Being in the middle of the Complex, the facility that stood for everything he loathed made him edgy. The troops were sparse, but they were busily bringing in the supposed ‘sympathizers’ of the Drakkon.

Based on the people he saw coming in, he could tell the ones left in charge were pulling for numbers not accuracy.

The uniform he wore chafed, too tight around the neck and too short at the wrists.

"How much farther do we have to go?" he whispered to the man he followed.

"Shut it!" hissed Lieutenant Tenzer.

Pacol let the disrespect slide. If it had been one of his own men, Pacol's boot would have been shoved so far up his backside; the man would have been crazcking leather for a week. The tunnels became danker with each passage they crossed. Just as Pacol was about to burst with irritation, the lieutenant came to a door covered in rust.

The lieutenant gave a syncopated rat-ta-tap-tap. A double tap came back. He followed it by a triple tap. The door swung open revealing a huge storage room, its whereabouts having been lost in the complicated maze of the Complex. A muted roar of conversation, punctuated by children playing, filled the space.

Pacol turned to Tenzer in amazement. "Nobody knows about this place?"

"I've looked on the plans for the facility," Tenzer nodded and said, "it's not listed on any schematics."

"Excellent." Pacol saw the communal living situation. "You're smuggling all the people down here?"

Tenzer gestured for Pacol to follow him. He was led to an office. Three other men in uniforms leapt to their feet. "At ease men. Pacol, this is Corpsmen Alco, Kelvet, and Velmee. Gentlemen, this is Pacol." The other men stiffened at the name. Pacol's name was on the most wanted list of the Anakarei.

“Good to meet you all.” Pacol wasn’t about to let past history interfere with the current crisis. “Tell me the situation. More importantly, is there any other way in or out of this place?”

Tenzer sketched a mock salute. “I hear you’ve been travelling the sewers lately. We’ve got our own entrance.”

Pacol received the news with relief. “That’s good. Do you have totals on the daily arrests?”

“Since that happens to be my detail, I have the count.” Tenzer paused, clenching his jaw. “I couldn’t stand by and let this happen to innocents.” He looked at Pacol. “I don’t care if a person is Drakkon or not. If they aren’t breaking laws, they don’t deserve to be treated like animals.”

Pacol clapped the lieutenant on the shoulder. “You’re not the only one who feels this way. We are here for the same reason. Who do we have here? What resources do we have among the civilians?”

Kelvet raised his hand.

“Man, we don’t have time to stand on protocol here. Speak up.”

“Mostly they’ve been working class folk.” Kelvet looked at his superior. “They are grateful to have a safe place, but are restless and want something to keep them occupied.”

“We’re keeping the children on a regimented schedule of classes and games,” Alco chimed in. “My wife works in the complex, she saw what was happening. We were the first down here. She’s been organizing them.”

“How many more do we have to support you?” Pacol asked Tenzer. “Do we need to get any of my men here to help you?”

Tenzer looked relieved at the offer of help. "At this moment, we're good. I don't want to risk exposure by bringing anyone new into the barracks."

"That you do. Let's talk logistics."

The men mapped out the current needs. The shift change claxon rang. Tenzer jumped. "We need to go now. Getting you out will be easier with the shift change."

"You need anything, contact us at the Wyvern," Pacol suggested. "Let's set up a regular check-in. That way if anything goes wrong, we'll know about it."

Tenzer nodded his agreement. "We'll discuss it tomorrow night at the Wyvern. Come, we have to go."

The Wyvern taproom was business as usual, its normal mid-day mix of uniform and civilian, nothing out of the ordinary. Pacol had a twitch he couldn't shake. The feeling had yet to fail him when it came to trouble. He watched the crowd carefully, nothing. Hour after hour went by. Suddenly, a uniformed patron grabbed his head. He let out a guttural howl and collapsed. Three more went down after him. Outside the Wyvern window, a handful of random men and women exhibit the same behavior. The majority were in uniform.

Pacol ran to assist the fallen. They were in a catatonic state, barely breathing.

"Call the medics," Pacol called to the bartender, as he rallied other customers to help him move the affected patrons to a quieter part of the tavern. He pointed to a young man. "You, there!" The young man looked spooked, ready to run. "I need you, come here."

"I don't know anything."

"All I need you to do is watch these poor souls while I look outside." Pacol moved toward the door. "I'll be right back."

Fortune smiled on the Wyvern, nobody had collapsed in front of the establishment. He could see other small crowds. Pacol assumed they were other victims. As soon as he came back in, the young man ran.

"I ain't getting sick!"

Pacol rolled his eyes. Mistress Smyzac came out from the back. "The emergency services are overwhelmed. Take them upstairs. We'll care for them."

"You know what they are." Pacol blocked the old woman. He wasn't about to see her harmed.

"Yes," she acknowledged. "The tide has changed. The heavy chains of the praxitrol have been broken. Let's get them upstairs."

He allowed the old woman to bring the collapsed patrons upstairs. Pacol only hoped that they were doing the right thing.

Ella woke up with a start. The adrenaline burn and pain she expected never manifested. She firmly put a check in the plus column. Ella saw she was in a small chamber with soft lighting. A soft snore emanated from close beside her. Turning her head towards the sound, she saw Talek, sleeping on his side next to her. His breath tickling her ear, she allowed herself to revel in the moment. Her arm involuntarily twitched.

Talek's eyes popped open. He saw her watching him.

"Hello."

"Hi."

He propped himself up on his elbow. "How are you feeling?"

"Surprisingly, okay." Ella wiggled her toes and then started to stretch experimentally, still no pain. "How long have I been out?"

“Two days.” Talek said. “You had some help with that.”

“Help?”

“Never annoy a healer.” Talek grinned. “Behte made sure you got the rest she felt you needed.”

“Oh.” Ella had to recover from the yawn that interrupted her thought process. “I suppose that is some wise advice. How are things?”

Talek sat up, helping Ella into a sitting position. He handed her a robe. “The dirigible fleet is parked on the plateau being readied for an assault on the city. We have a battalion of prisoners. Some of whom are praxitrol victims. The rest are soldiers, following orders. We’ll have to sort them out. See where their loyalties lay.”

Ella nodded. “What about my father. How is he doing?”

“He is well.” Talek pulled Ella to her feet and guided her to a table set with simple meal. “He sat with you while you were asleep.”

“Really?” Her heart warmed at the news.

“He’s stronger every day.” Talek ran a comforting hand down her arm. “You’ll be able to make up for lost time soon.”

“The Chancellor?”

“Contained in one of Petroj’s cocoons.” He turned his chair to face her. “Interesting thing, whatever you did to him. He has reverted to a child.”

“A child?” Puzzled, Ella looked at Talek, “What do you mean?”

“He gained consciousness before we contained him. He recognized his brother, but not as an adult.” Talek shook his head in bemusement. “I don’t know if this is permanent, but he’s reverted back to his childhood. Decades have been either stripped or repressed from his memory.”

“How’d you get him into the containment unit?”

“Behte recognized the problem, she shepherded him as a child-keeper would, settled him down as if he were taking a nap.”

“Does Behte think the condition will be permanent?”

Talek rubbed Ella’s shoulders. “Behte couldn’t say. I’ve asked for additional security to monitor his progress.”

Ella took a bite out of a roll from the table. She needed to think about this. The man had caused so much misery, but she didn’t want to be his end.

A knock saved Ella from responding. Talek answered the door. The ever-efficient healer bustled into the room with the Socra.

“Ah good, you’re awake!” The model of efficiency, Behte examined Ella and gave her a clean bill of health. “Quit putting yourself in dangerous situations.”

Ella meekly bowed her head. “Yes, ma’am. I’ll do my best.” She knew better than to cross the healer.

The healer left the room, leaving the Socra with Talek and Ella.

“I understand we have a dirigible fleet.” Ella said.

“Jaczon has grand plans of knocking the Anakarei out of their comfortable seat of power.” The Socra shook her head.

“Do we really have the means to mount a full insurrection?” Ella asked.

“Jaczon has been preparing for this move for a very long time,” the Socra said. “Your presence only adds fuel to the fire. You are now an icon to the Drakkon cause.”

"I just wanted to learn about my heritage, and, if I were lucky, find my father." Ella shook her head. "I'm not a political pawn."

The Socra laid a sympathetic hand on her shoulder. "You have lost so much due to your uncle's machinations. Had your father been at your side, you would have come to age knowing your heritage and your responsibilities."

"I know that I have responsibilities, but I also know that I don't have sole responsibility. There is a council of Drakkon to help with all of this. Where are they?"

Talek knew Ella was frightened. "

I explained to you on Earth, the council has been destroyed."

"Are you sure?" Ella grasped at any straw she could think of. "They just didn't go into hiding?"

"Ella," the Socra said sharply. "You know the histories. You know they were hunted down, slaughtered by the non-Drakkon of this world."

"So, what are we going to do?" Ella flung out. "Do to them what they've done to us, rule with impunity, discriminating against those who are not Drakkon? What about those who have been sympathetic and helpful?" Ella started to get annoyed. "No, if we are going to free the capitol and free this world. We are going to do it for everyone. Not for the Drakkon specifically."

"It is what it is," the Socra repeated the generational line. "You can't change history."

Ella stared at the older woman. "That's crap, and you know it." Ella got up, looked around the room. "Talek, where are my clothes?"

Closing her eyes, she caused the barrier to become opaque and impassible. The thrum of approval of the Sanctuary filled her. “The dirigibles won’t be going anywhere until I have a conversation with your mate.”

The Socra looked at the young woman who was the High Socra. “You are a resourceful being.”

Ella wasn’t sure what to make of the Socra’s reaction.

“Okay, you’ve confused me.”

“My mate has played the long game of politics for so many years, sacrificing so much for the good of the Drakkon, he forgets that what he has been doing is for the good of everyone.” The Socra went to the door, asked the person standing there to hand her a package. “I think you’ll find these will fit you. I think you’ll like them.”

She placed a bundle of clothes in Ella’s hands. The fabric was sumptuous. Jeweled tones embroidered with luxurious metallic threads. She picked up the different pieces-a tunic, pants and a loose jacket. She found herself stroking the opulent fabric unconsciously. “These are beautiful. Thank you.”

“You’ll make a better point dressed as a High Socra…” The Socra stood in the doorway before she exited the chamber. “We are in the Time of Strife and Miracles. It is time for us to see things differently. You’ll bring us that different perspective.”

“Wow, that woman can certainly make an exit.” Ella stared after the Socra.

Talek interrupted her. “She’s right. You are so much more than you know. Traditions are important, but sometimes they can’t withstand the test of time. You’ll show us the new world, the new Otherverse we live in.” He softly kissed her on the lips then playfully tousled her hair. “Get dressed. We have a civil war to stop.”

“Get out. I’ll deal with you later.”

Talek laughed as he left the room.

The command center hadn't changed much from when Ella had arrived. The bustle, if anything, had increased. Ella stood at the door dressed in the clothes of her station. She tapped into the energy of the Sanctuary, reveling in its power. She waited patiently, allowing her personal energy to draw everyone's attention.

The noise abated voice by voice, shuffle by shuffle. Not even a rustle of clothing disturbed the silence Ella's presence demanded.

"Jaczon, a word," she said.

Jaczon saw Ella standing in the doorway. "Not now. Be a good girl and run along."

Not a soul stirred in the room as a struggle for power played before their very eyes.

"I don't believe you understood me." Ella enunciated every word carefully. "A word. Now!"

Used to obedience to his every command, Ella's disobedience irked him. Giving some final orders regarding the deployment of the dirigible fleet, Jaczon finally gave his full attention to Ella. Her high ceremonial garb startled him.

"What are you playing at, girl?" he growled as he stalked to her.

"I'm not playing at anything." Ella kept her voice level. Talek and Nathan stepped into view, flanking her. "I'm here to tell you to stand down. The dirigibles won't be going anywhere until I say so."

"You have no authority here. You are an off-worlder who just happens to be acceptable to the Sanctuary." Jaczon crowded her, towering above her in an attempt to get her to back down.

Energy crackled around Ella. "You'll want to take a step back, Jaczon."

"Or what?" He crowded her some more. Jaczon found himself flying across the room as a bolt of energy flew from Ella's hands. The other occupants scrambled out of the flight path. He hit the wall with a thud, his breath forced out of him on impact.

Ella moved into the chamber without challenge. Heads bowed deferentially as she passed. She came to a stop a few feet from Jaczon's gasping form. "I'll repeat the request again. Jaczon, a word."

Jaczon looked at the woman who stood above him with a mixture of anger, humiliation, and respect. "Where would you like to converse?"

"Let's take a walk."

Jaczon ignored the proffered hand. He wasn't ready to accept anything from her. He followed her out of the command center. They walked through various corridors until they reached the room where they'd held the first meeting. The octagonal chamber stood empty.

"Ah, Tennei," Ella greeted the Socra. "Excellent. We are going to take a little trip. I need everyone to hold hands." Everyone but Jaczon complied. Giving an impatient sigh, the Socra grabbed one hand, Ella grabbed the other. Ella tapped into the Sanctuary power with practiced ease.

The room whirled, Jaczon closed his eyes. He felt his stomach drop. Opening his eyes, he found himself in a room that was five times the size of the chamber in the Sanctuary. The layout was similar, octagonal in shape. The biggest difference was the transparent dome that allowed light to flood the room.

"Now, we can talk." Ella walked out onto the ledge where she had taken her first flight. She sat, gesturing everyone to follow. "We have a problem."

Jaczon's anger evaporated as he realized he was in the lost Temple of Drakkonon. "Why have you brought me here?" He started to rise to his feet. Ella made a gesture with her hand. He found himself seated. "We have to strike while the government is in disarray."

"We won't be doing anything without a plan. The plan will not include any form of payback." Ella looked at everyone in the small circle. "Enough damage was done by a lone, rogue Drakkon. Think of how terrified the population would be if the Drakkon took over without any kind of consideration. The average citizen is guiltless."

Jaczon refused to meet her gaze. He wanted to cling to his anger and aggression. "They would take away our rights, our dignity. I should know. I worked in the belly of the beast for years."

"Yes and your view point is distorted." Ella understood Jaczon's rage. "I'm not saying you aren't entitled to your anger. You just can't let it color your actions from here on out."

"I don't understand you." Jaczon stared at the woman in front of him. "How can you be so peace loving? Look what the Chancellor did to your family! To you!"

Sadness slipped through her calm demeanor. "You don't think I'm not angry? I lost my childhood. I'm saddled with a destiny and responsibility I never wanted. I have to learn on the fly and pray I'm making the right decisions." Ella leaned forward. "I can't afford to get angry. I can hurt people if I get angry."

The flight across the room at the Sanctuary came to Jaczon's mind. He still ached from slamming into the wall.

"I need people who understand the politics and the traditions I never have known." Ella took a deep breath, held it for a count, and then released it. "The Grand Council of the Drakkon has been gone for generations. I need that wisdom. So I need to build a new council."

Ella pointed at Jaczon. "You understand the politics of the Anakarei. I'm going to need that information to help build the new government." She switched her gaze to the Socra. "I only have the knowledge in my head with no application of the Drakkon ways. I need you to help me." She gestured to Talek and Nathan, "These two have already been named guardians."

"You can't just name the council," the Socra sputtered, "There are protocols."

"Protocols that are hundreds of years out of sync with the current affairs," Ella continued. "With the Drakkon scattered throughout the Otherverse and the Temple reopened, things are changing." Ella got to her feet and gestured at the Temple. "I keep being told that this is the time of Strife and Miracles. Well, I'm demanding the miracle of change from everyone here. Put aside your prejudices and help me build something we can be proud of."

Jaczon rose to his own feet. "And if we don't?"

"I won't hesitate to do what is necessary for the greater good." Ella replied with stark intent.

"I will join." Jaczon held out his hand, palm down, Talek placed his hand on Jaczon's and Nathan followed suit. The Socra rose to her feet, placing her hand in the circle. Power filled the room as Ella's hand rested on top.

The rebirth of the grand council filled everyone with hope.

A powerful wave of node energy washed over the group. Their combined strength kept them on their feet. A crash of thunder sounded as thirteen portals opened around the perimeter of the Temple grounds. The building sang a welcome note as the gathering of the lost Drakkon began.

ABOUT THE AUTHOR

Born on a dark and stormy night on the other side of the world from Richmond, VA, Leila Gaskin began a life full of imaginative wanderings. Inspired by her journey, Leila takes inspiration from the places she has lived. She is the author of several short stories ranging from horror, speculative fiction, and science fiction. Hot Flashes is her debut novel.

With her dog as her co-pilot and the cat as the navigator, Leila explores her world and tells her stories.

Connect with Me Online:

Website: http://www.leila-gaskin.com

Twitter: @leilagaskin

Facebook: https://www.facebook.com/LeilaGaskin

www.ingramcontent.com/pod-product-compliance
Lightning Source LLC
LaVergne TN
LVHW020533100826
845148LV00010B/1444

* 9 7 8 0 6 1 5 8 7 1 8 5 1 *